Catch You Later

To Mary
Enjoy!

Boris

Catch You Later

Boris Erlank

Khanya Publishing

California

2015

First published in the USA in 2015 by Khanya Publishing,

khanyapublishing@gmail.com

ISBN 978-0-9963330-0-9

eBook ISBN 978-0-996330-1-6

To my wife, Philippa

Acknowledgements

I owe a great debt of gratitude to my writing group: Claire Burdett and Ben Sonstein spent many, many hours discussing the emergent characters and giving me invaluable input. As the novel took shape, Lizzie Bradbury and Melissa van Hoosen joined the group. They provided fresh perspectives and motivation. Through an extreme stroke of luck I subsequently met my editor, the very talented Deborah Hooper, who provided the honest criticism and tidying-up, which my writing needed.

I also wish to acknowledge the unwavering support of my family. Their "you can do it" attitude throughout the writing process was a constant source of motivation. My wife, Philippa, read many drafts and engaged in plot and character discussions. She provided me with the time and space to pursue this venture alongside my day-job and spent many hours proof reading. My children, Lara and Richard, who live in South Africa, kept me in touch with the thinking of Generation X, and spurred me on whenever I visited with them. My brother, Olaf, and his wife, Daleen, were gracious hosts during my many visits to Cape Town. I stayed in their home in the heart of Constantia; this allowed me to research background and detail for the novel. Most importantly I would like to thank my mother, Irmela, who instilled in me a love for reading and literature from a very young age. She followed the development of *Catch You Later* with great interest. Through her great passion for theatre she helped me visualize and improve the action in certain parts of the book.

I would like to recognize the great work, which Ms. Judy Underwood's Writing Salon does in the San Francisco Bay Area. A couple of courses with the salon gave me the confidence that *I could do this*.

Lastly, this book acknowledges the tireless work of the thousands of volunteers and underpaid staffers engaged in the struggle to fight HIV/AIDS. They are a true inspiration.

Chapter 1: Danielle

Cape Town, November 1997

Chris heaved himself out of the pool and stretched out on a towel in the sun. Nala, his golden retriever, opened one eye but did not budge from her spot in the shade. Her tail swished to chase away a fly. Chris savored the warmth seeping up from the flagstones.

A shadow fell over him and he heard his father say, "Enough sun, Chris."

"Ah, Dad. Just a minute to dry off."

His father motioned with one hand in the direction of the shade under the oaks and asked, "What are your plans for the afternoon?"

With a sigh, Chris got up and moved to a lounger. "Nothing much, just hanging around," he said.

"Have you done all your homework? I thought you still had exams."

"It's Friday, Dad. I only have one Math test left; I'll look at my notes on Sunday."

"Honestly, I don't know why we pay that school so much money if they don't stretch you a little. Can't they give you extra Algebra or something? Next year, when you're in Grade Seven, you won't be able to just coast along."

Chris shrugged and, looking away, was relieved to see his mother coming up the steps from the tennis court. She carried her garden clippers and an armful of roses. Her blonde hair shone in the sunlight and was held back by a pair of sunglasses perched on top of her head.

She said, "Chris got an A plus for his Art exam, did he tell you?"

"Well done."

Chris soaked up his father's approval, which felt as warm as the day itself.

"But if you want to be an architect, you have to do well in Math as well as Art."

Chris turned away and scratched Nala's neck. She licked his fingers.

Dr. du Toit turned to his wife. "Danielle, darling, I keep telling Chris to get in the shade and you're out gardening at the hottest time of day."

"Oh, Jacques, stop worrying. It's a glorious day. I just wanted some flowers to brighten up the studio for my little ballerinas."

She flicked a hair from her husband's shoulder, stepped back, and surveyed him. "You look very smart; you should wear golf shirts to the hospital more often."

"It's only because the air conditioning can't keep up."

"Will we see you for dinner?"

He looked at his watch. "I hope so; I have a new patient – he'll likely need a triple bypass. Then I give a lecture at five and, after that, I have my rounds." He paused, shrugged. "It all depends on Mrs. Stern – her body keeps threatening to reject the new heart."

"Poor old dear; give her my best wishes … and this." She handed him a rose. "We'll go on ahead to Marco's and save you some pizza."

"Thanks." He jingled his car keys and turned to Chris. "I've got tickets for the Newlands cricket game tomorrow. Want to come?"

"That would be awesome, Dad!"

Jacques gave his wife a kiss. "Please remember to turn on the house alarm when you leave for the restaurant."

"Yes, dear." She waved as he got into his Audi. "Don't break any hearts!"

Chris rolled his eyes. "Mom, that's such a lame joke."

"Yes, but it's *our* joke." She stuck a thumb in her ear and waved at her son with her fingers spread wide.

He was grateful that none of his friends were there to see her. Mothers could be such an embarrassment.

At the kitchen door, she turned. "If you get bored, come down to the studio. I could do with help painting the set for next week's performance."

The studio was a converted barn. Chris stepped inside and was filled with the usual sense of anticipation – here one could still cling to remnants of make-believe and fantasy. He liked the airy space with its gleaming floors and light shafts made visible by puffs of powder. On one side of the room, a group of girls was warming up in front of large mirrors; the opposite side had draped windows that gave a shrouded view of lush foliage and the Constantiaberg Mountains.

The set for the year-end performance consisted of a couple of fake boulders and a wooden bridge (borrowed from the local nursery), three plywood trees and, the centerpiece, a two-meter high "castle". Chris mixed shades of gray paint and set to work. He painted the outline of a turret with a balcony and a stone arch for the main gate. When he closed his eyes he could see the castle, tall and strong, a refuge against storms and soldiers alike.

"You're really good at this."

Chris looked up and blushed. One of the ballerinas had come over.

"I'm Julie," she said, sitting down on a boulder. "Julie Noble."

"Yes, I know," he stammered.

She tilted her head in a questioning gesture.

"I asked my mom." *Ah jeez, he could have kicked himself. That made it look like he was interested in her.* "I mean, we were just talking about the performance and she sort of told me who everybody is."

"I see." She took a sip from a little Liquifruit carton and held it out to him. "You want some?"

He put down his paintbrush and reached for the carton. The touch of her hand was soft and unexpectedly cool. He nearly dropped the juice, and then was mortified by the rude sucking noise he made with the straw. Julie smiled and Chris racked his brains for something witty and intelligent to say.

"You're the princess, aren't you?"

She was about to answer when Danielle interrupted. "Julie, dear, please go with Mrs. Andrews and try on your costume."

Mrs. Andrews approached them, her arms full of costumes. With her black frizzy hair and smiling face poking out from the layers of colorful fabric, she looked like some huge alien flower.

"We've got a helper for you," Danielle told Chris. "This is Mrs. Andrews' son, Desmond."

They shook hands. The boy was a little taller than Chris, and had wisps of hair on his upper lip – something Chris instantly envied and admired. Desmond had the same dark olive skin as his mother. He had also inherited her hair, but in his case it was cut short and kept flat with copious quantities of gel.

"Are you sure this is not too much trouble, Mrs. du Toit?" said Mrs. Andrews. "Desmond could just wait in the car while I fit the costumes. I just couldn't leave him alone at home, you know, with all the gangs and unpleasantness in our neighborhood ..."

"Of course, I understand. And I'm glad you brought him. Believe me, it's a blessing to have another pair of hands to help with these sets. Desmond, do you like to paint?"

Desmond nodded and, after a short discussion, was given the task of painting trees.

The rehearsal resumed, but Chris found himself being distracted by his new helper, who was far more interested in the dancing than the painting. Desmond kept up a whispered commentary: *"Oh, Lordy, Fatty's going to fall." "That one dances like a drunk baboon."* Chris had often watched the girls dance but never with such a wickedly critical eye. He had to suppress his laughter.

Danielle was working with a group of her youngest students. The nine girls tiptoed towards her, formed a semi-circle, and went through a routine of repeated bows and stretches to symbolize the awakening of flowers.

"Heads up and smile! Smile, Stephanie. You're a happy flower!"

"The twins are cute but the others don't look like flowers to me," Desmond whispered. *"They're more like weeds."* The chuckles provoked by this witticism earned both boys a reproachful glance from Danielle.

4

After fifteen minutes of rehearsal, Danielle called a halt. "Right, girls, that's coming on fine. Time for the other dance: St. George and the dragon. Let's see if we can get it right." She clapped her hands. "Places, everyone!"

On the count of three, she started the tape. "The townsfolk" danced around in fear and confusion, waiting for St. George to rescue the princess. "The dragon", a rather plump girl, minced about like a circus elephant on its hind legs. Desmond commented that she could not scare a mouse. Despite this, the townsfolk screeched and scattered, oblivious of their carefully choreographed moves. A dark-haired child, awkwardly wielding a plastic sword, portrayed "St. George". Every time she accidentally touched the dragon there were tears and howls of protest.

"The princess is pretty," Desmond said and Chris spun around from his painting.

"OK, girls." Danielle rewound the tape. "I know this is not easy, but I'm sure you can do it. Let's try it once more. Everybody to their places! "

The music started and the townsfolk approached from stage right. Julie skipped past holding a straw hat, picking imaginary flowers and blowing kisses – one of them directly towards Chris.

"She likes you," Desmond teased and Chris felt the heat rise in his cheeks.

Heavy drumbeats signaled the arrival of the dragon, who once again came prancing in with little butterfly motions of the hands.

"Stop!" Danielle cried and turned off the music. Chris could see that her neck was beginning to show tell-tale red blotches. His mother rarely got angry with him but he remembered the time he had kicked a soccer ball through the picture window in the lounge. Her neck then had been the color of a crab.

"Melissa, please remember you are a fearsome dragon. Listen to the music! Stretch out your arms. Move them slowly, like this." She demonstrated, then rewound the tape, suppressing a sigh.

Desmond chuckled. "This lot are hopeless."

Again the sword prodded the dragon's stomach, again Melissa howled in protest. The other girls laughed and so did Chris and Desmond. Danielle turned on them. "It's easy to sit there and make comments! I bet you wouldn't find it so funny if you had to do it."

Chris, who rarely heard his mother raise her voice, was instantly shamed into silence. Desmond, however, had grown up in an environment where raised voices were the norm. He was totally unfazed and said, "Would you like us to try? I'm sure we could fight better than that."

Chris looked with alarm at the skin indicator going from pink to red. He was convinced that his mother was going to lose her temper at such cheekiness. But then he realized that the dark-skinned boy with the big brown eyes was entirely sincere. His mother must have come to the same conclusion.

"All right, then, the boys want to show us how to fight."

"I bags be St. George," Desmond said as he picked up the sword. "You can be the dragon."

"Oh yeah, great!" Chris said sarcastically. "This stupid dragon has nothing going for it, no fiery breath, no teeth, not even claws! How am I supposed to fight?"

"Just pretend!"

"Hang on, I have an idea." Chris dashed into the garden. He returned with a small spade and fork, as well as a piece of green shade cloth. He draped his improvised cloak over his arms and shoulders.

"Not bad," Desmond said.

Danielle started the music and the dragon came lumbering across the stage. Chris visualized himself as Darth Vader. He would show this upstart Desmond /St. George. He pulled a grotesque face, raised his arms menacingly, and made loud hissing noises. Desmond, who had been pretending to survey the countryside, did a smart turn on the ball of his foot and struck a pose that reminded Chris of the pictures in his book on Greek mythology. Slowly the two circled each other. As the music rose, sword and claws clashed in a frenzy.

Out of the corner of his eye, Chris could see that his mother was about to intervene in the fight. He pulled back and the two boys resumed circling each other. They were in the grip of the music and the battle, yet still managed to execute Danielle's choreography.

The music reached its climax and, with melodramatic gurgling, the dragon succumbed. St. George placed a foot on the chest of the slain beast and raised his sword. Then, as the music changed, Desmond took the hand of the princess and guided the townsfolk off to dance.

The group had not yet rehearsed their curtain calls, but once the dance was over, Desmond reached out to help Chris to his feet, motioned for the girls to line up left and right, and led them in a deep bow. Mrs. Andrews beamed and stepped forward to hug Desmond till he drew away in embarrassment.

Chris saw his mother's expression of pride and admiration. He felt his throat go tight and his chest swelled as if his heart would burst from its cage. The feeling surpassed even the glory of being crowned Victor Ludorum at his school's athletics competition.

Then, as if things couldn't get any better, Julie asked if he could help her unclip her necklace. The clasp was entangled in her soft brown curls. As his hands brushed against her neck, his fingers trembled and he was relieved when he managed to unhook the necklace. When she turned to thank him, the light caught in her dark green eyes, Chris was transfixed.

From that moment onwards, he lived for the dance classes.

##

The family's Friday pizza dinner at Marco's was usually a relaxed affair. Tonight was different. Chris's father was late, which put him at a disadvantage. Therefore, when Danielle tackled the subject of Chris's dancing head on, her husband was caught off guard.

"What do you mean? Chris is going to take up dancing? Surely not!"

"Why not?"

"Oh, come on, Danielle. You know why not. I don't want people to think my son is a sissy."

"So this is about you and what people will think of you. Is that the problem?"

"You're twisting my words ..."

Chris was thankful when the waiter arrived and his parents had to pause.

They ate in silence until Danielle resumed the conversation. "Jacques, Chris is one of the tallest boys in his class and the best at sport.

No one is going to think he is a sissy. Besides, even if they did, you of all people understand that overcoming adversity builds character."

"Yes, but I also know that life tends to put enough obstacles in one's way without one having to deliberately go and look for more. I've always been supportive of your dancing, but I really have to draw a line here. Our son ... it's such a girly thing to do."

"Tell that to Baryshnikov!" retorted Danielle.

"I would, if he hadn't died of AIDS."

"That's Nureyev."

"Don't split hairs; you know what I mean, and besides ..."

"*Please stop*," Chris whispered urgently. "*People are looking at us.*"

His mother closed her eyes and took a deep breath. "You're right." To her husband she said, "We can discuss this later."

When Chris came down to the kitchen the next morning, his father was humming a tune and preparing breakfast in bed for his wife. Sometimes Chris believed his mother had supernatural powers. During the night, she must have woven her web of midnight magical mystery. A compromise had been reached: Chris was allowed to take up dancing as long as he also learned martial arts.

Desmond and Chris soon found out that dancing was hard work, but they stuck at it, and made good progress. After lessons, Desmond stayed around. He was awed by Chris's world: pool, tennis court, a tree house and a batting cage for cricket practice. And when they tired of outdoor activities, there was the Aladdin's cave that was Chris's playroom. It was filled with everything from a PC with computer games to books, dinosaurs, CD player, Scalextric racing cars, chemistry sets and even a proper telescope. Desmond quickly figured out that this could be used to spy on the gardener and the neighbors.

Over the summer, he became a regular visitor at the du Toit home and Chris's best friend.

##

Two years later, November 1999

Chris leaned forward in the passenger seat. Although he trusted his mother's driving, it was his habit to help watch out for obstacles whenever they drove to Desmond's house. The narrow streets in Grassy Park were littered with obstructions: abandoned cars, children on bicycles, roaming dogs, and teenagers loitering or smoking in surly groups.

He glanced towards the driver's seat. "Mom, you know Dad doesn't like it if you drive with the windows down; it's not safe, especially here in the Cape Flats."

In response, Desmond, from the back seat, said, "*Agh,* Chris man, you worry too much. It's OK here in the daytime. My ma says the gangsters sleep all day long, anyway. It's only at night that one has to be careful."

Danielle suppressed a sigh, closed the window, and turned on the air conditioning.

"It's good to be careful," she said, "but you have to find the balance. Do you remember what the minister said in church last Sunday?"

Chris shook his head. It was bad enough having to *go* to church; his mother couldn't seriously expect him to actually listen.

"He said you can't run away and hide from the task God has set out for you. If I were too scared to drive into the Cape Flats, then Desmond and his sisters would not be able to come to dancing."

"Dad says God looks after those who look after themselves."

"Yes, well, your father tends to have his own peculiar interpretation of the Bible."

Chris decided to drop it. He looked around and noted that there was little grass to be found in "Grassy Park". The name must have been a euphemistic statement of hope when the apartheid-era city planners of

9

Cape Town laid out the tight grid-pattern streets of this dusty "mixed-race" suburb.

They passed row upon row of small single-family homes with chicken-wire fences, the sun pounding down on low tin roofs. The squat houses were all of a uniform design and Chris was quietly outraged that the architects could have been so lazy. He was convinced that he could have done a much better job. The homeowners had tried to give their homes individuality by lashing out with paint. A bright pink house with blue window frames stood next to a yellow one, which in turn had a battleship-gray neighbour with a purple front door.

Even though the houses, set against the backdrop of Table Mountain in the distance, had a quaintly picturesque quality, Chris knew from Desmond's stories that behind this pretty façade lurked a culture of crime and gangsterism.

The more he looked, the more Chris noticed signs of deprivation and hopelessness around him. The odd cracked windowpane had been replaced with cardboard, while half-hearted attempts to plant shrubs, or even maize, were no match for the southeast wind that regularly blasted through the Cape Flats. Wind-shredded remains of discarded plastic shopping bags clung listlessly to shrubs and fences; a painfully thin dog lay under a dusty bush. Chris thought it had the furtive, permanently fearful look of an animal bewildered by random acts of violence from the people it tried to please. He thought of Nala, who preferred liver to chicken and, despite his father's protestations, slept at the foot of his bed. He would never admit it to his father, but he agreed that Nala was spoilt.

The mangy dog watched the Range Rover's slow progress. A group of pre-schoolers, playing unsupervised amongst the litter on the sandy shoulder of the road, waved at them. Danielle smiled and waved back.

"Watch out, Mom!" Chris shouted and his mother slammed on the brakes.

A soccer ball rolled into the road and was immediately followed by two laughing boys in their teens. They seemed completely unperturbed by the approaching vehicle.

"Hey, that's my cousin Eric," Desmond said from the back seat. He pushed the button to lower the window. As they inched past he leaned out and shouted, "Eric, you guys are being bloody stupid; why don't you check where you kick the ball, man?"

"*Gaan naai*, Desmond!" came the rude reply.

"Screw you, too!"

"You think you're a whitey just because you sit in a fancy car. Watch out, we'll get you, you *moffie* faggot!"

The boys scooped up their ball and, with an unmistakable middle finger gesture in the direction of the car, hurried back to their game.

Chris noticed that his mother had tightened her grip on the steering wheel.

"What was that all about?" he asked Desmond. "It didn't sound much like the Afrikaans we learn at school. What's a *moffie*?"

"My sister says it's a man who *naais* other men rather than women …"

Danielle cut in, "It's not a nice word, it's very derogatory, and I don't want to hear you use it."

She half-turned to Desmond. "They weren't serious about hurting you, were they?"

Desmond laughed with all the bravado of a fifteen-year-old. "Don't worry; Eric's just a windbag. I'm not scared of him."

They drove on in silence until they reached a neat-looking house painted lime green. Danielle parked the Range Rover. As they got out, Desmond's mother, who had been hanging out washing on the line next to the house, put down the plastic basket and bustled to the gate.

"I'm so pleased you're finally here. I can't stand the suspense anymore. Tell me! Tell me how the auditions went!" She beseeched Desmond with her eyes, then looked at Chris.

Desmond maintained a poker face, shrugged his shoulders, and said, "Well, you know, it's hard to tell …"

"Come on, don't do this! You'll give me palpitations." She fanned herself with a corner of her apron.

"We did it, both of us!" Desmond shone with pride and excitement. "We're going to be dancing in *Oliver* at the Opera House - in front of thousands and thousands of people. We're going to be famous!"

"That is *fantastic*!" Desmond's mother smothered him with a hug. "I'm so proud of you. It's hard to believe - my son to dance in a real musical!"

"Ma, you're killing me. I can't breathe."

Mrs. Andrews let go of Desmond and bestowed a similar Mother Earth embrace on Chris, "Oh, I'm so *heppy*. Congratulations, Chris! Congratulations, this makes me so *heppy*." She turned to Danielle and took both her hands. "Mrs. du Toit, I don't know how to thank you. Dancing will be Desmond's ticket out of this place. I cannot thank you enough. "

"You're right to be proud of Desmond, Mrs. Andrews." Danielle looked at the boys. "They deserve this opportunity. But we mustn't get ahead of ourselves; there's still a long road to be traveled. Professional dancing is a tough business."

But Mrs. Andrews was in no mood to entertain even the slightest doubt. "You're the best teacher he could have," she declared, hands clasped, a glance skyward. "With the Lord by his side, and your help, Desmond can do anything. He'll go right to the top! I know it. I know it for a fact. Do you have time for a cool drink? We must celebrate. Please, you must come in."

She turned towards the house, still talking, although half to herself now: *"I still can't believe it. Wait till I tell my sister. She's going to be so jealous."*

Mrs. Andrews led them up the polished steps to the front door. "Please excuse the mess, I was just about to get started on the vacuuming. The girls are just no help at all. You know what it's like with teenagers. I wonder where they are? They should be here to greet you. Desmond, you can tell them the good news. Where are they?"

She let rip with a piercing, "Rachel, Maria!"

Josie Andrews' voice had been trained in the church choir to carry far and wide. Both Chris and his mother instinctively put their hands to their ears.

Chris had noticed on previous occasions that Desmond was oblivious to this high-decibel form of communication. It seemed that he and his sisters had acquired the art of letting their mother's voice bypass their auditory senses. Hence, when Josie and her small entourage walked into the living room, Rachel and Maria were supine in front of the TV.

The wall opposite the TV was dominated by an oil painting depicting a charging bull elephant. It hung above a display cabinet filled with china. The walls were painted a bright yellow and the room was crammed with maroon velvet furniture. Crocheted doilies covered every available surface: armrests, coffee tables, even the music center's oversized speakers.

When the girls saw Danielle they got up to greet the visitors and were soon joining in the excitement with hugs and congratulations.

"Now, please, you must sit. Girls, clear that couch. Why do you always have your magazines all over the place? Come, make some space for our guests," Josie ordered before she disappeared into the kitchen.

Desmond and Chris launched into a blow-by-blow account of the auditions.

"There must have been nearly a thousand kids."

"Come on, Desmond, it was more like two hundred," Chris corrected.

"OK, say five hundred. We waited and waited for hours. Then they made us all dance in large groups. The main selector was this stern lady with gray hair tied back. She didn't smile once ..."

"There was a guy with a clipboard. We were halfway through our routine when he just said, 'Next'. We were convinced that the whole group had flunked out."

Josie reappeared from the kitchen with a tray loaded with glasses, a jug of juice, and a plate of cookies.

"I'm sorry that I didn't have time to bake anything fresh. You know how it is; the kids are in and out of here like a swarm of locusts. When my cookies come out of the oven they don't even get a chance to cool down before they are all eaten."

She put down the tray and the boys attacked the cookies.

"Chris, your manners," his mother reprimanded.

"Sorry, Mom." Chris passed the plate to Rachel.

Rachel turned to him. "Maybe I should get your autograph before you get too rich and famous. Do you want to sign my T-shirt?" she teased, pushing out her budding breasts towards Chris.

"Rachel! What's wrong with you?!" her mother scolded.

Chris blushed and Desmond laughed until he started to choke on his cookie.

The boys asked to be excused and Desmond led the way to his bedroom. Carefully, he shut the door. "I've got something to show you, but my mother mustn't see." He dug about under his bed and retrieved a shopping bag. With a flourish, he pulled out a pair of running shoes. "Nike Airs, just like yours, and brand new. I haven't even worn them once."

"Why are you hiding them from your mother?"

"*Agh, man*, she always asks a million questions about where I get the money."

"I thought you earned it with your weekend job at the supermarket."

"Yes, exactly; it's just that sometimes I also do a few favors for a friend of my cousin – my mother doesn't like that."

"What sort of favors?"

" Just … favors; deliveries, that sort of thing."

"Desmond, you told me the other day that your cousin is a drug dea …"

"*Shhhh*, man. Why do you bring that up now? You sound just like my mother." He turned his back and said over his shoulder, "Honestly, I don't think I can tell you anything anymore."

Chris felt hurt. "I can keep my mouth shut. You know that. Like the time when you got caught …"

"Just leave it." Desmond stroked the shoes as though they were a pair of kittens. "Anyway, I just wanted you to see them. Cool, eh?"

Chris nodded.

When they went back to the living room, Danielle looked at her watch. "We need to be on our way; do you think I could quickly use your phone? I would like to catch Chris's father and tell him the news before he goes to the hospital."

"Of course; Rachel, go show Mrs. du Toit where the telephone is in my bedroom."

Danielle asked Chris, "Do you want to tell Dad?"

"No, it's all right, Mom. You tell him." Chris reached for the last cookie.

Danielle shut the door, sat on the edge of the bed, and looked around the small bedroom. The curtains were a plain fabric, but expertly sewn. The wardrobe, dark wood, ball-and-claw-foot design, matched the bed- frame and dresser table. The edges of an oval mirror looked frayed. Here, too, there was an abundance of doilies.

She let her hand glide over the quilt and found herself transported back to the small guest room in her in-laws' home - the same cramped austerity. She thought back to how naïve she had been, trying to make a good impression on Jacques's parents when she and Jacques were dating. He had always been reluctant to go back to the gloomy farmhouse with its even gloomier occupants. After dinner, old Mr. du Toit used to read from the Bible; then Danielle and Jacques were each shown to their separate rooms and two Alsatians were let in from the yard to patrol the corridor. Jacques, of course, had slipped in through her window. After all these years, she still found herself blushing at the thought of their sex, all the more delicious because it was illicit and … silent.

The thought of Jacques brought her back to the present. She dialed and her husband picked up after the second ring.

"Du Toit." She pictured him at his desk in the spacious office upstairs at home; the cherry wood shelves filled with medical books and journals; sports trophies and medals carelessly placed amongst the books wherever there was space. He would no doubt keep his eyes on the computer screen or whatever papers he was reading whilst talking to her.

"Hi, darling, it's me."

"Danielle, I was just thinking about you. How did the auditions go?"

"They both made it! Can you believe it? I'm so proud."

"Congratulations! I know this is something that you really wanted. Is Chris excited?"

Danielle sensed the accusation in the choice of his words: "…something that *you* really wanted". She knew that he was hoping this "phase"' would come to a natural end. He wanted Chris to follow in his footsteps and excel at rugby, cricket, tennis, golf; have him add to the endless collection of trophies that proved the alpha male status of the du Toits. She let it pass.

"Oh, yes. They are both very excited, though they certainly haven't registered just how many hours of rehearsal and hard work lie ahead of them. Right now, they're bathing in visions of fame and success."

"Hope they don't get too carried away."

She decided to change the subject, "You sound busy; what are you up to?"

"Just finishing some notes for my lecture tomorrow and looking over something that Harry Noble dropped off."

"Oh?"

"One of his prototype ideas. Anyway, I'm glad you caught me. I'll be leaving for the hospital in ten minutes."

"Will you meet us at Marco's? I promised Chris we would go out to celebrate tonight."

In the background, she could hear the family's golden retriever barking.

"What's up with Nala? Why don't you just put her outside?"

"Believe me, I tried. But she was even worse outside – kept running up and down the fence line. There must be a skunk or something out in the street."

"Silly dog. You can let her out when you leave, we won't be much longer. In any case, Mercy should be there soon so she can deal with Nala. If you have any shirts that you want ironed, just put them on the bed for Mercy."

"OK, will do. Drive carefully. I've got to run."

"Bye, Jacques ... love you." But the phone had already gone dead.

They had left Grassy Park and turned on to the highway when the car phone rang. Chris answered the call. His father had had the phone installed in case Danielle broke down somewhere and needed help. Chris thought it was the coolest thing ever but he knew that his mother did not share his enthusiasm. She saw it as yet another manifestation of the

16

security mania that was sweeping the country and making everyone paranoid. She rarely touched the phone.

"Chris, how are you, how did the auditions go?"

"Hello, Aunt ... I mean, hello, Wendy; Desmond and I both made it."

Wendy van Houten was one of his mother's best friends and someone whom Chris really liked. She always spoke to him as though he were an adult – maybe because she had no children of her own. On his thirteenth birthday, right in front of his father, she'd said, "Now, look, when you call me 'Aunt' you make me feel like a dinosaur. I don't care that your father thinks you must address all adults as 'Aunt' or 'Uncle', you are now a teenager and I want you to just call me 'Wendy'."

"Congratulations! Well done, I bet your mother is very, very proud. Is she there with you? Put her on speaker-phone."

The two friends chatted and Chris didn't pay too much attention. It was all about an AIDS charity. He knew that Wendy was involved with numerous charities and his mother was one of her most stalwart supporters. Twice already the dance group had provided entertainment at fundraising events. His ears pricked up, however, when he heard Wendy begin to talk about a building project.

"I've found the perfect site for our orphanage – it's an old farmhouse in Hout Bay, very close to the squatter community. It will need to be completely gutted and expanded, but I think we might even add an AIDS clinic, do awareness training and ..."

"Whoa, Wendy! How're we going to pay for all this?"

"We'll just have to redouble our fundraising efforts. By the way, what do you think of the name 'Khanya' for the AIDS center, it's the Xhosa word for 'enlightenment'."

"Sounds good to me."

Wendy finally rang off as the white Range Rover wound its way up the familiar streets of Constantia. It felt cooler here, where only dappled light found its way through a canopy of trees. The ancient oaks stood guard along the roads and softened the severity of high security walls.

They turned into a quiet cul-de-sac and Danielle slowed the vehicle in front of a wrought-iron gate with a brass number "5". She pressed a remote-control and the gates swung inwards without a sound, allowing her to steer the car up the brick driveway past the tennis court. She swerved around the fountain and parked near the front door. The house was built in a neo-Georgian style, double story, with slate-tiled roof and sash windows placed symmetrically on either side of the covered entrance. White window frames and moldings offset the pale cream walls.

As they got out Danielle said, "The roses look tired; remind me to get Jonas to cut out the dead ones. This heat is really getting to be too much for the garden. Look at that fountain – will you do me a favor and top it up later?"

She fished around in her handbag for the keys and unlocked the door. Chris followed her into the bright and airy entrance hall … where they both stopped suddenly, rooted to the spot in horror by the sight that greeted them. A thick blood trail meandered from the foot of the stairs across the marble floor, all the way towards the kitchen door. There it ended under the bullet-ridden body of their golden retriever.

"Nala!" Chris cried and rushed towards the dog. Gently he touched her legs, which felt cold and stiff. Her golden fur was caked and encrusted with an oozing liquid the colour of mulberry jam.

"She's dead, Mom! She's dead!" He tried to keep the rising fear out of his voice as he knelt down and cradled Nala's head in his hands.

They heard a muffled noise from the kitchen, followed by the clatter of breaking crockery.

"Mercy!" Danielle shouted. "Oh, my God! Mercy!" She rushed past Chris down the passage to the kitchen where she found the housekeeper on the kitchen floor, wide-eyed with fear, struggling to free herself. Mercy's hands had been tied behind her back with nylon rope. Her feet were also bound and her mouth covered with masking tape. She was breathing noisily and perspiration had soaked the edges of the pink cloth *doek* she wore on her head. Mercy had managed to prop her ample frame into a sitting position and was ramming her shoulder against a leg of the kitchen table in the hope of propelling a knife or other useful object on to the floor. A shattered coffee mug testified to at least partial success.

"Mercy, what happened? Are you hurt?" Danielle rushed towards her, pulled the masking tape off her mouth, and started to undo the nylon rope around her wrists.

Mercy drew in deep gulps of air like someone whose head had been held under water.

"Madam, they shot Nala! I was sure they were going to shoot me, too." She started to shake all over as the shock set in.

"Who shot Nala?"

"Two gangster *skollies*. They were hanging around outside when the taxi dropped me off. I thought they were just looking for work, but when I got out my key to unlock the gate, they grabbed me from behind, round my neck, like this." She rolled back her eyes and squeezed her own neck till she gagged and coughed.

"Yes, yes, and then? What did they ..."

A crashing noise could be heard from upstairs. It sounded like a TV set, or a computer, had been dropped. The two women froze.

"Dad?" Chris called from the hallway. "Dad, are you OK?" His voice cracked a little and sounded eerie in the quiet house.

Chris laid Nala's head on the floor, slowly got up, and walked to the bottom of the stairs. He paused. "Dad?" Tentatively, Chris took the first stair and waited. There was no further sound. *Oh God, no! Please let Dad be OK, please, please, please, dear Lord.* His steps were silent on the thick white carpet of the stairs. He was filled with dread but compelled to move forward. His father needed him.

Mercy whispered, *"Doctor left half an hour ago, he not home."* She grabbed Danielle's arm, "The *skollies* are still upstairs!"

Danielle leapt up and raced down the passage. "Chris, get back here!"

As she burst into the hallway, she instantly took in the surreal sight of a hooded figure at the top of the staircase. He was pointing a gun at Chris, who was halfway up the stairs, motionless, staring at the intruder. The gunman was startled by Danielle's appearance. He swung the gun from one to the other. At that moment, the security alarm went off – Mercy had managed to reach the panic button near the back door. The piercing noise completely unsettled the gunman. Despite the hoody, Danielle could see the panic in his young face. She did not break her stride, and the athleticism of a lifetime propelled her across the marbled hallway to the foot of the stairs. The first shot missed her narrowly and shattered the glass in the front door; the second shot hit her in the shoulder. And yet, like a wounded lioness, she kept going up the stairs; as she lunged past her horrified son, a third shot exploded and hit her in the chest. She reared up between Chris and the gunman, appeared to hover in mid-air, then slowly crumpled. Chris reached out instinctively and managed to break her fall as the gunman turned and fled along the upstairs passage to make his escape through one of the bedroom windows and across the garage roof.

When the Armed Response Guards arrived, six minutes later, they were met by Mercy, crying like a wounded animal - deep guttural sobs interspersed with high-pitched wailing. Chris was only dimly aware of their arrival. He cradled the lifeless body of his mother. Not a sound from Danielle, no single word of farewell. She had died instantly.

In deep concentration, he watched blood seep into the thick white carpet and was reminded of some long forgotten fairytale where the princess spilled a drop of blood in the snow, and the world was never the same again.

##

The next week was a nightmarish blur. His father spent time with the police or holed up in his study. Chris and Mercy were left to deal with the endless stream of well-meaning friends and acquaintances that dropped off food "for the two bachelors". By the third day, Chris was ready to scream at the sight of another concerned-looking matron peering at him over a tinfoil-covered lasagne dish. So he followed his father's example, locked himself in his room, and left Mercy to deal with the overflowing freezer.

After the funeral, a crowd of more than a hundred gathered at the du Toit home. There were people everywhere: in the lounge, the kitchen, and the family room. They even spilled out on to the patio. Chris found that if he kept his eyes downcast, and stayed in motion, he could avoid conversation. As he moved around, the groups would part in front of him. He tried to ignore the expressions of concern and pity, the whispers: 'What's to become of the boy?' 'Agh, shame.'

Occasionally someone would touch his arm, try to say a few words. He only had to give them a wan smile, a nod, and keep going. He wanted this day to end but he also dreaded its ending. Once everybody had gone home, they would take off their black clothes and get on with their lives. What would he and his father do?

He noticed that Mercy was at a complete loss. Under normal circumstances, when there was any form of entertainment in the du Toit home, she and Danielle were a finely tuned team. Now there were caterers in black silently swarming through her domain and she did not know whether to give them instruction or wait for them to instruct her. So she stood, in a white apron, clasping and unclasping her hands.

Chris came to a standstill behind a pillar. He observed his father at the far end of the lounge, shaking hands and accepting condolences. Right in front of Chris, two women sat on a couch with their backs to him. He didn't know them, so assumed they were staff from the hospital. He could not help but overhear their conversation.

"... did you see them, father and son, both so controlled, not a tear?"

"As for the maid, I thought she was going to throw herself into the grave on top of the coffin. Honestly, what a spectacle..."

"He's handsome, isn't he? Not an ounce of fat."

"And look at this place, he must be loaded."

"Every single woman in Cape Town will want to drive the sadness out of those eyes. Mark my words, our famous heart surgeon will be remarried in less than a year."

"Well, I would agree with you, except he comes with baggage. Taking on a teenager..."

"That's no problem – why do you think God gave us boarding schools?"

They laughed and a wave of nausea swept over Chris.

He leaned against the coolness of the pillar and had the strangest sensation. Time stood still and everything around him faded into a blur. His heart was racing and he felt icy cold. In the middle of the blurriness there was one spot of surreal clarity: his father; his father laughing and joking with a woman whose face Chris could not see; his father waving and then fading away into the blurriness. For that instant, Chris felt what it was like to be completely alone in the world, an orphan. That would be his lot, he knew. An unbearable loneliness broke out like a demon inside the pit of his soul. He couldn't breathe, the walls closed in, he felt hot; he pushed himself away and made for the outline of the patio door, which seemed to be a mile away. On his way, he passed Wendy.

"Are you OK, Chris? You look awfully pale."

He nodded, charged through the door, and on across the lawn. It felt as though a *dementor* had swooped down on him, sucking out all hope and any last shreds of happiness. Darkness enveloped him, despite the glow of the afternoon sun. He couldn't breathe, so he ripped off his jacket and tie, threw them on the ground, and ran down the slope to the studio.

An hour later, as the sun set and the funeral guests started to leave, Chris was oblivious to the furtive, knowing glances the guests exchanged as they passed the studio with its blaring music. He was pouring sweat, lost in the music, seeking relief in the world of dance.

When everyone had left, and the caterers had finished clearing up, his father came to look for him. Dr. du Toit stood in the darkness for a while before turning on the light. Chris was aware of his father watching, waiting, and still he gyrated, leaping through the air, clinging to the pain in his limbs and his heaving lungs; clinging to the pain that told him he was still alive. Eventually the doctor walked over to the music system and turned it down.

"What did you do that for?" Chris stopped, panting hard.

"It's late. You should come inside now."

"When I dance, it's like she's right here. I can hear her, almost see her..."

His father said nothing. Absentmindedly, he stroked dust off the music system. Eventually he said, "Chris, would you like me to make an appointment with a psychologist?"

"A shrink? Why, you think I'm crazy just because I say I can hear Mom when I dance?"

"No, of course not, that's totally natural. I was just thinking some grief counselling ..."

Chris walked right up to his father. "I'm fine! You hear me, I'm perfectly fine! Why don't *you* go and see a psychologist?" He reached passed his father, turned the music back up, and resumed dancing. His father watched him for a few minutes, then turned away and pulled the door shut behind him.

Chapter 2: Desmond

More than eight years later, March 2008, Monday

Chris carved a straight line through the water, executed a perfect tumble turn, and started on his eighty-ninth lap. He felt the water's familiar embrace but today its soothing magic failed to wash away his frustrations. *Pompous prick*, he thought, did another turn, and shot off with too much kick. The kick was intended for Harold P. Fagan and all the other smug, self-satisfied stuffed shirts who wouldn't give a recent graduate a chance.

The guy in the next lane was catching up. Chris increased his pace to stay ahead.

Harold Fagan had flipped through Chris's portfolio and described his work as "naïve". "The only things people with money are building now are shopping centres or casinos," he'd said. "Don't get me wrong, I like what you're doing, it's very idealistic. But it isn't commercial. Maybe you can come back and see us when you've had some real experience in the real world."

He became aware that someone was trying to attract his attention and stopped at the deep end of the pool.

"Hi, Chris, how's it going?"

Chris took off his goggles. "Desmond, what's up, what brings you here?"

"Just chilling; I knew you'd be here. Thought I might come and see what you're up to. Spend some time with my buddy, you know."

"I'm touched," Chris said. "Dare I ask what it is you want?"

"What d'you mean - 'what do I want?' Can't a guy come down and see his buddy without there being the immediate assumption that he wants something? Maybe I just want to see your sweet face, maybe I've come to tell you that you've won the lottery."

With one fluid motion, Chris heaved himself out of the pool and picked up his towel. "Desmond, if you're looking for a loan, forget it. I can't even remember what a decent wad of money smells like."

"What a little ray of sunshine you are." In the mock tone of a spinsterish schoolteacher, Desmond continued, "It does not become you to be so negative. Cynicism and worry will make you old before your time..." He stopped his sermon to massage the skin under his eyes, eradicating even the slightest hint of any wrinkle that might show itself on his perfect dark skin.

"Dare I ask how the job interview went?"

Chris gave a thumbs-down. "Fagan said something along the lines of: 'I'm afraid there's little demand for such pseudo-modernistic environmental architecture. We only build shopping centers.'"

"They don't deserve you. It's a blessing they turned you down. You wouldn't want to work for people that cannot appreciate genius." With a shrug and an expansive gesture of his left hand, Desmond dismissed the architectural fraternity.

Verdict delivered, he took a step back and appraised Chris in the critical manner of a horse-trainer considering the merits of a stud stallion. "At least you seem to be in good physical shape. That's just as well, because I have a proposition for you. Far from looking to get money from you, as you so hurtfully intimated, I, your good friend and buddy, have gone to considerable trouble to find you here and to offer you an opportunity to actually *make* some money." He stretched out his arms as though he were conducting an orchestra. "How do you like that?"

"I'm listening."

"Can we get a cup of coffee somewhere?"

"Sure, I'll get changed and meet you upstairs. You can order me a pineapple juice."

Desmond found a table in the Health Line juice bar where low-carb everything was on display and the trendy chair cut into his back. The club's hi-tech image of aluminum, steel, and exposed air-conditioning ducts was toned down here with shades of aquamarine and a dash of pink.

In the weights area in front of the bar, he watched a personal trainer showing a woman how to do stomach exercises. The man looked bored, and Desmond was tempted to walk across and tell him off. *Don't just go through the motions, man. Give this lady some special attention; she's paid for it.* If there was one thing Desmond found hard to excuse, it was lack of passion.

He turned his attention to a phalanx of stationary cycles. Most of the riders were peddling furiously, not getting anywhere. *Story of my life,* Desmond thought. However, not everyone was taking it quite so seriously. A couple of chatterboxes in trendy leotards were cycling at a much more leisurely pace, making sure that their perspiration did not reach a level where it might impair their make-up or get in the way of their gossiping. Finally, at the end of the row, a girl was reading a novel as she cycled, her legs moving mechanically. Desmond was reminded of a masticating cow.

Ten minutes later, Desmond watched as Chris walked from the changing rooms past the weights area and exercise bicycles. Even in faded jeans and T-shirt, he caused the chatterboxes to stop talking and watch him go by. The bookworm stole a furtive glance, no doubt fusing the fantasy hero of her novel with the lithe specimen in front of her. Desmond noticed the expression of longing that crossed her face.

"It's not fair," Desmond said as Chris folded himself into a chair. "I have to bust my gut to stay in shape, and to get the odd date, whilst it all just comes naturally to you."

"What do you mean, 'it all comes naturally to me'?" Chris was still preoccupied with the morning's rejection and the feeling that *nothing* was coming to him, natural or otherwise.

"Didn't you see the looks those girls gave you? Not to mention some of the guys! All positively lecherous. I bet any one of them would hop into the sack with you, if you so much as crooked your little finger." He nodded towards the stationary bikes. "See that girl reading a book? Now, if you really wanted to do a good deed and make someone's fantasies come true …"

"Stop the drivel. What's this - Psychology 101? Let's try and make poor old Chris feel better? You might as well can it and get to the point."

"Jeez, you can't let a few bum job interviews get you down like this. Bloody hell, I've stopped counting the number of unsuccessful auditions I've been to. It's just as well you decided not to be a professional dancer. Sometimes life sucks."

Chris drank his juice and did not respond.

"In all the time I've known you, you've been Mr. Golden Boy: popular, good at sport, lots of pocket money, artistic. You've got it all, man; born with a silver spoon in your mouth. So, OK, the last few months have been a bit rough, but don't you think you're blowing it out of proportion? You're not exactly homeless, on the streets."

Chris went pale and stared into space past his friend. When he spoke his voice was devoid of any emotion. "There have been quite a few days when I've felt I've had a pretty raw deal."

Desmond could have kicked himself for his insensitivity. He'd been so intent on getting Chris to snap out of his self-pity that he had momentarily forgotten about Danielle's murder.

"Hey, I'm sorry, man. That was a dumb thing to say. I always seem to switch my brain off at the wrong times." Quickly, he tried to change the subject. "How's your father these days?"

"He's got his patients, so I suppose he's fine. I caught a snippet in the paper the other day about him treating the Minister of Police. Old J.J. Mulazi needed something like a triple bypass."

"I saw that, too. It wasn't a 'snippet', it was front-page news." Desmond gestured with his right hand to emphasize an imaginary banner headline: "*Minister J.J. Mulazi back in office thanks to the dedicated nursing staff at Groote Schuur Hospital and the skills of Dr. Jacques du Toit.* I meant, when did you last actually speak to him?"

" Not so long ago," Chris said, studying his fingernails. "He came to my graduation, of course, and he called me a couple of weeks ago. I shouldn't complain, he's still paying for my flat and giving me an allowance till I can find a job. But talking to him is as awkward as ever." After a pause, he added, "I don't think he ever really got over her."

And neither did you, Desmond thought, but kept this to himself. He took a sip of his cappuccino. "Do you remember St. George and the dragon? Don't you miss it sometimes – as a career, I mean? You were pretty good at modern dance, you know."

"I was never in your league."

Chris motioned for the waitress to bring him another juice and then looked directly at his friend. "So, let me guess, you want me to dance?"

"You're psychic! How did you know? Fact is, the Toreros have a fantastic gig lined up and we need you."

"Oh yeah? The last time I performed with the Toreros I got arrested. Have you forgotten that?"

"Come on, Chris. Your old man bailed you out within an hour and you got let off with a warning. You must admit, it was pretty funny."

"Tell that to my father! It was not funny at the time when the drug squad came in and raided the Railway Hotel during our show. You remember, that Aussie pothead, Bruce, set me up by hiding his stash of *dagga* weed in my tog bag."

"His logic was faultless. He knew your father would bail you out, whilst he would probably have had to do time in jail or even be deported back to Australia."

"He set me up!"

"Are you ever going to forgive and forget? He apologized and you should move on. You really have a problem letting go, you know. Maybe you should see a shrink."

Chris leaned across the table and punched him on the shoulder.

"I suppose Bruce is still with the Toreros?" he asked.

Desmond nodded. "And he still surfs all day and screws all night. There is a never-ending supply of girls who adore a 'professional' surfer. No point in being jealous."

"I'm not jealous. I just don't trust the guy."

"Look, it's just a one-night gig, and it's well paid."

"I don't know, I haven't danced in ages. It'll take me a while to come up to speed."

"You're a quick study and the group isn't doing anything too taxing; just need to entertain a bunch of rich ladies from the southern suburbs."

"Hang on a minute, what exactly *is* this gig? You know my rules – I'm not into the stripping scene."

"God, you're such a prude, wouldn't hurt you to loosen up a bit. This is for a good cause. The Khanya AIDS Foundation is holding a charity event – gala show at Groot Constantia winery; very highbrow invitation-only event for folks who can pay a thousand bucks for a glass of champagne and a canapé. We're to provide the entertainment."

"The Toreros at a classy venue like Groot Constantia?" Chris laughed. "No offense, Desmond, but that sounds nuts."

"I cannot for the life of me understand why you should be surprised. We are simply being appreciated and moving up in life." Desmond laughed when he saw the disbelief on Chris's face. "You know I've been volunteering at the Khanya center," he went on. " I got chatting with Wendy van Houten about the gala – remember how she got your mother and the dance group roped in when they were planning to build a center? Anyway, Wendy agreed it would be really neat to do something different, spice things up for the audience …"

"Yes, but the Toreros? I mean ..."

Desmond picked up his cup with his pinky pointing straight into the air. He imitated a women's voice: "Darling, just because the audience wear hats, and keep a stiff upper lip, doesn't mean they don't enjoy a bit of titillation." He paused. "We'll keep it tame and tasteful. Don't look so worried."

He drained the last of his cappuccino and added slyly, "Guess who else is now working full-time at Khanya?"

Chris shrugged his shoulders.

"Julie – Julie Noble."

"Our Julie?"

"The very same; the subject of all your adolescent fantasies."

Chris was surprised. Julie, the princess who had broken his thirteen-year old heart. Throughout the first year of his and Desmond's dancing, Julie's presence in class had been his biggest motivator to keep going. His mood for the week regularly hinged on whether she had talked to him, smiled at him, snubbed him ...

When it came to the year-end concert, he had summoned up all his courage and asked her to be his girlfriend. That's when he found out that she and her family were relocating to Johannesburg.

Chris felt a cramp in the region of his heart as he relived those long-ago feelings of intense frustration and helplessness. Johannesburg! It might as well have been the moon. How was he ever going to see her again? He had been furious with his mother, with Julie, with everybody; why had nobody told him? He could still feel the embarrassment of Julie shrugging her shoulders and shaking her head when he asked whether she wanted to go steady with him.

Desmond laughed. "What are you thinking? Your ears are turning red. Is that a sign of blood going to all your extremities?"

This time he anticipated Chris's punch and managed to avoid it. The cappuccino cup went clattering to the ground. Sheepishly, Chris picked it up.

"OK," he said, "enough of this. What do you need me for?"

Desmond suddenly turned serious. "I have to go down to Hermanus to see Rachel; she's not doing so well. My ma is staying with her, but she just isn't able to cope."

"I'm really sorry to hear that. I thought her AIDS was under control."

"*Ja well*, she got pneumonia. As my ma would say, 'It is what it is.' Anyway, since I've set up this whole gig, I don't want to leave everyone in the lurch – you'd do me a great favor if you could fill in for me. Will you?"

Chris knew how close Desmond was to his sister and how much the AIDS foundation meant to the whole family. He said, "Sure, I'll do it."

"Promise?" Desmond's tone deliberately evoked memories of when they had played together as kids. "Cross your heart and hope to die?"

"Promise; but no guarantees as to the quality of my dancing."

Desmond raised his empty cup. "They'll just have to give the old broads lots of champagne. Incidentally, since that police raid we don't perform at the Railway Hotel anymore. We've moved up in the world to De Waterkant Club. Come see our act there tomorrow night, that way you can pick up on the routines."

Chris nodded.

"Wendy and Julie will also be there to see the show – you could join them."

"When is the actual event?"

"Saturday."

"Saturday! Are you crazy? That's five days from now!"

"You promised." Desmond grinned mischievously.

"You tricked me, you cunning bastard." Chris actually smiled for the first time in days. Dancing had helped him through many a tough patch before; if nothing else, it could be a diversion.

"OK, I'll see you tomorrow night, then. I want to make damn sure that Wendy knows they must provide plenty of champagne; the only way we'll get away with this is if the audience is stone drunk."

Chapter 3: Julie

Khanya AIDS Foundation, Hout Bay near Cape Town, Tuesday

Julie cherished the quiet hour before dawn when she had the office to herself. She cradled a mug of steaming tea and studied her to-do list. With the AIDS gala only four days away, it was going to be a busy day: meet with the caterers, florist and wine merchant; contact the choir; write Wendy's speech - and view the Toreros' performance. She put a question mark next to this last item and sighed.

A rooster crowed and the smell of wood fires drifted across the street from the Mandela Park squatter camp. From the far end of the building came the clanging of pots and pans – preparations for breakfast were under way.

The most urgent item on the list was the introduction for the event program. Julie was about to switch on her computer and get to work when she looked up and saw a child standing in the doorway. The girl was in her pajamas, barefoot, clutching a toy rabbit that had been cuddled hairless. The child's dark face was barely visible in the dim light but Julie could see that she was sucking her thumb.

Julie put down her mug. "You're up early, Nikiwe."

The girl came around the table and clambered on Julie's lap.

"Did you have trouble sleeping?"

A quiet whisper: "*I had dreams.*"

Julie lifted the child's face to look into the far-away brown eyes. "Same dreams as before?"

Nikiwe nodded. "I dream of my mommy and daddy. It make me sad."

Julie hugged her, "It's OK to be sad, Nikiwe. But you should know that your mommy and daddy are watching over you, that's why you see them in your dreams."

"Do *you* have dreams?"

"Not every night, but sometimes I dream of my daddy – especially when I have a problem and I don't know what to do.   When I wake up, I also feel sad, because I would love to hug him, but it's a good thing that at least I can talk to him in my dreams."

Julie rocked the child for a while, then retrieved a blanket from the filing cabinet and settled Nikiwe in an armchair that was much too big for the cramped office. "You stay here with me and catch up on your sleep, OK?" Nikiwe touched the golden crucifix that Julie wore on a chain around her neck as though it were a good-luck charm. She nodded and closed her eyes.

The Khanya AIDS Foundation was based in an old farmhouse, built in the Cape Dutch style with exposed wooden beams and walls thick enough to withstand an army. The early occupants would have had a view of vineyards reaching up to where the side of the valley was covered in *fynbos*, proteas, and pine trees. Now, when Julie looked out of the window, she saw a dusty soccer pitch and, across a busy road, a squatter camp. This sprawling settlement provided Khanya with its raison d'être: a bastion in the fight against HIV and a refuge for AIDS orphans.

Julie had just booted up her laptop when her cell phone rang. She frowned when she saw that it was her stepfather. Since marrying Julie's mother, Matt Baxter had taken over as managing director of Noble Enterprises. She pictured him in the spacious office in Johannesburg, seated at the very same desk her father had once occupied.

"Julie, hope I'm not dragging you out of bed."

"Far from it. What's up?"

"It's your mother ..."

Julie tightened her grip on the phone. "Why, what's wrong? Is she ill?"

"No, no, no, nothing like that. It's just ... she's up and left. She didn't say a word, didn't leave a note, nothing." The words came tumbling out. "You know we've been frightfully busy – both Greg and I are working till all hours on this deal with the Malaysians – so I've probably been a little neglectful, but I thought she'd understand ... "

Julie suppressed a sigh, "Tell me about it - Greg and I have hardly spoken to each other in the last two weeks. Do you know where Mother is? Have you tried her cell phone?"

"She's turned it off but we have ascertained that she took a flight to Cape Town yesterday afternoon. I'm ninety-nine percent sure that she's at the Constantia house ... "

"What makes you think that?"

"She didn't pack much, so she had to go where she's got clothes and make-up and, well ... that's where she goes when she's ... depressed."

He didn't need to elaborate. They both knew what he meant.

"Anyway, I phoned the house last night and this morning; it just goes through to answering machine." He paused. "Julie, I hate to impose, but could you pop around there and see if she's OK? I could send someone from the Cape Town office, but I thought ... "

"Of course – I really don't think we want to get any of the staff involved. I'll call you as soon as I've spoken to her."

##

Bridget Noble-Baxter stood framed by the columns of the verandah. A friend had once described the house's style as "bombastic" but Bridget preferred to think that it had a *Gone-with-the-Wind* quality; all it needed was Clark Gable.

The loneliness of the empty house had driven her outside. She closed her eyes, feeling the morning chill through her dressing gown, inhaling the luscious cocktail of summer scents: jasmine, sweet pea, wisteria, a hint of roses. Bridget tried to clear her mind, let the garden work its soothing magic.

Six marble steps curved down to the lawn, which stretched to a fountain set against a row of Greek conifers. Beyond the trees, the Constantiaberg Mountains reflected the first light of day: a dark palette of greens, copper and rust. She marveled at the way light played tricks on the eyes. On hot days, the mountains were a distant blue mass. But now, at dawn, they appeared close by: ravines and ridges were shown in clear relief, tantalizingly close. She thought about going for a hike, the way she used to, years ago. Maybe she could persuade Julie to come with her.

Above the mountains, the indigo of the night sky was yielding to a brighter blue. The underbellies of a few stray clouds reflected a rich pink that would have looked surreal or kitsch if anyone had tried to paint it. Birds chattered in the trees; a wild guinea fowl and her young scurried across the grass. On either side of the immaculate lawn, rambling bushes and flowerbeds conveyed the carefully crafted wilderness of an English country garden. She resolved to thank the gardener for his efforts during her absence.

The phone rang, startling her out of her reverie. She turned away reluctantly from the garden and went back into the house. As she walked into the family room, she tried not to look at the half-empty bottle of gin on the coffee table. Had she really drunk that much last night?

The answering machine had already kicked in with its annoyingly cheerful message. Then her daughter's voice, anything but cheerful:

"Mother, please pick up. I know you are there..."

Bridget quickened her step and bumped her leg against the table. *Damn, that's going to leave a bruise.* It flashed through her mind that bruising easily was just another of the sad realities of reaching middle age, along with night sweats, insomnia, and many other small indignities. She reflected that the perky adage "Fifty is the new thirty-nine" really didn't cut it, not when her body was constantly reminding her that it was indeed fifty years old.

"... I have a million-and-one things to do for the gala today and ..."

Bridget reached the phone and her "Hello, Julie darling," sounded dry and cracked. She hadn't spoken to anyone since the taxi-driver had dropped her at the house yesterday.

"Mother! What are you doing in Cape Town? Matt's worried sick about you. He called and said you'd just taken off. How could you do that to him?"

Bridget tried to control her voice. "I was going to call you a little later; was hoping that we might get together for tea or lunch. The flight down from Johannesburg was awful and the house is so ... so empty."

"What did you expect? You didn't tell anyone you were coming. The staff haven't been there to air the place or stock up the kitchen. You really gave us all quite a fright. I'd better call Matt and tell him you're OK."

"Aren't you the least bit interested in why I felt it necessary to leave Johannesburg?"

"Mother, I really would prefer not to get involved in any of your squabbles with Matt."

Bridget slumped into a chair, steeled herself for an attempt to get Julie to see her perspective. "He's become so irritable over the last few months," she began. " I've tried to talk to him but he shuts me out. He's constantly involved with work and ..."

"What do you expect?" Julie cut in. "The man runs a major company – *our* company. That's what's paying for your travels, the clothes, the apartment in London, and all the other things ..."

"Julie, is that what you think of me? That all I'm interested in is the money?" Anger gave her strength. "Surely you know me better than that. Your father and I started with nothing ... nothing! I don't give a hoot about the money, I have enough to last me two lifetimes. You may find it hard to believe, but I actually love Matt, I want to spend time with him."

"I'm sorry, Mother. It's just that *everyone* seems so busy."

"Well, that's the point. I'm tired of doing nothing – if Matt is going to spend his life at work, then I want to get back into the action at Noble Enterprises. But they continually freeze me out. I am convinced that Greg is behind it. He is stoking Matt up against me and ..."

"You never miss an opportunity to have a go at Greg, do you?"

"Darling, you're not there. You don't see what's going on ..."

"Mother, we've been over this. I really don't want to fight or to upset you. Matt and I were just worried about you and wanted to make sure that you were OK."

Bridget waited. When Julie continued, her tone had changed. "Tell you what, I'll let Matt know that you will stay in Cape Town for a while. I have a ridiculously hectic schedule today, but ..."

"Do you need any help? Is there anything I ...?"

"No, no; it's all under control. I'll call Eunice and Josiah so that they can come and get the house set up for you. Josiah can drive you to the hairdresser. You know that'll make you feel better."

Bridget lifted a hand to her temple and closed her eyes.

Julie continued, "I was planning to come through to Groot Constantia to go over final details for the catering. Since I'll be in the area, I could stop by and we could have lunch together. Would you like that?"

"Yes, darling, that would be nice. Thank you. I shall look forward to seeing you."

"Bye, Mother." The phone went dead.

For a long while Bridget stared at the receiver, then slowly replaced it. She looked out of the window and involuntarily rubbed the spot where she had bumped her leg. The rich colors of dawn had yielded to the bland brightness of day. She was grateful that Julie was taking charge, though she resented being treated like an indulged child. She was perfectly capable of getting the staff to sort out the house, of taking the Mercedes out of the garage, and driving herself wherever she wanted to go. Yet it was nice to feel that someone cared, even though it was in that exasperated heaven-help-me kind of way that Julie seemed to have perfected when doing things for her mother.

She addressed her image in the mirror above the fireplace: "Bridget, my girl, you'd better take charge of your life. No one else is going to do it for you."

She picked up the half-empty gin bottle and dropped it into a wastebasket on her way upstairs. What was it Matt always said that really annoyed her? *"Go put on your face and face the day."*

"Julie, you're a saint. I don't know what I would do without you." Matt was effusive in his thanks. "I think it is a great idea for your mother to spend some time in Cape Town. Please do me a favor and spoil her a bit. Take her shopping or out on the wine route. Just put it on my tab. You girls should have some fun."

Julie did not have the heart to tell him that it was exactly this "here-is-some-money-go-have-fun" attitude that was driving her mother crazy.

"I'm not making any promises. We have the AIDS gala coming up this weekend so things are pretty hectic, but I'll see what I can do to keep Mother amused."

"Thanks, Julie, I do appreciate it." He paused. "If your mother decides to stay into next week, then I might have to ask you a big favor."

"What favor is that?"

"Next week we have a very important visit from our new business partners in Malaysia. I may need you to jump in and act as hostess – at least for one dinner. You know what these people are like; they will feel slighted if they don't meet the Noble family."

"Let's talk later in the week. By then I'll have a better grip on the gala. But yes, if Mother isn't up to it, I wouldn't leave you in the lurch."

"Thanks, Julie. It's such a relief that you really understand how the business world works – you're going to be a perfect executive's wife one day."

She had to smile. Normally she would bristle at such a patronizing remark, but, coming from Matt, she knew that it was intended as a compliment.

"Talking of which," Julie went on, "you might mention to Greg that I'm beginning to forget what his voice sounds like. As far as I remember, he promised to come to Cape Town to attend the gala – I suppose there is very little chance of that actually happening?"

"I'll tell him. Although, if you came up next week, you two lovebirds would have a chance to catch up then. Don't worry about booking any flights, I'll send the jet. Talk to you later."

##

As the Khanya canter gradually came to life around her, Julie pushed the conversation with Matt from her mind. Nikiwe had woken and gone in search of breakfast and now the old farmhouse was full of the noise of children beginning their day – the clatter of footsteps in the corridors, the rise and fall of chatter, the sound of a Xhosa TV soapy coming from the day room. Julie was just about to make a second attempt to start working when the center's administrative assistant, Prudence Khumalo, came in, full of her usual gossip and good cheer. Julie was never quite sure how seriously she should take Prudence's stories, and today's was no exception. With wide eyes and dramatic gestures, Prudence recounted a gunfight she had witnessed the previous night between two warring taxi groups. She demonstrated how she'd crouched on the ground to dodge flying bullets. "… And then there was this man who lay on top of me to protect me; very, very handsome." She laughed. "But when the fight was over, he stayed there, trying his luck. I slapped him from here to yesterday."

Prudence took her customary fifteen minutes to freshen her make-up and fingernail polish – all the while chatting incessantly. Julie pointedly looked at her watch from time to time, and eventually Prudence started to shuffle through the chaos of files and unpaid invoices on her desk and Julie could finally concentrate on writing the program introduction:

Myths and misinformation surround the spread of HIV AIDS in South Africa. There are those who still believe that it is a "gay" disease, whereas in reality it is the women and children of South Africa who bear the brunt. The widespread belief that sex with a virgin can cure the disease places young girls at particular risk.

The HSRC (Human Sciences Research Council) has established that 11 percent of South Africa's 42 million people are infected with the virus and, in certain communities, the infection rate is as high as 25 percent. Over the next decade, the country will have to deal with an explosion in the number of AIDS orphans. Already the traditional extended family structures are creaking under the load. It is simply not sustainable for a widow, living on a state pension, to support up to ten orphaned grandchildren. And yet that is the lot of an ever-increasing number of seniors in our country.

The Khanya AIDS Foundation is committed to educating and enlightening, and to finding innovative ways to house and help the most vulnerable in our society: the AIDS orphans. We welcome ...

Julie's train of thought was interrupted by a discussion between Prudence and Hendrik Joubert, a volunteer who took care of maintenance at the center. Hendrik was a small, wiry man with a big heart and a broad Afrikaans accent. It was impossible to tell his age: somewhere in his sixties, Julie guessed. His face had the quality of tanned leather and his hair was gray; yet he could scurry up a ladder or heave roof tiles like a young buck. Hendrik had lost his wife to cancer. He'd sold his farm to pay for the medical expenses and, after she'd died, had been at a complete loss until his church group put him in touch with the Khanya center. A lifetime of wrestling a living from a family farm had made him the ultimate handyman – he could fix everything from blocked drains to baby cots. At Khanya, the conventional wisdom was, "If Hendrik can't fix it, it's unfixable."

"But Hendrik," Prudence said, "how are we supposed to pay for those wooden beams? Can't you somehow patch them up?"

"Man, you know I wouldn't ask for the money if it weren't necessary. I'm telling you, those beams are *vrot,* rotten. They either have woodworm in them, or they got wet or something, but the whole roof structure of the dormitory is beginning to sag. Someone could get hurt."

"But that's part of the new block – that building is only five years old. It's impossible ..."

"I'm telling you those *bleddy* beams are beginning to look like my auntie Adele's bow legs. I can try and put in a support, but it's not going to last and ..."

The conversation was interrupted by footsteps thundering down the corridor towards the office. The cook, Mama Mercy, burst into the room. With hands on hips, she planted herself in the doorway, blocking out the meager rations of light that came in from the corridor. Julie was surprised to see a frown on Mama Mercy's usually smiling face. An energetic and cheerful woman, and an excellent organizer of her band of kitchen volunteers, Mercy knew little about nutritional theory, but she knew exactly how to fill up a growing teenager with bread and stew, whilst stretching the precious meat ration to provide broth for the elderly.

Now, as she stood in the doorway addressing Prudence, Mama Mercy's voice evoked centuries of injustice. "The butcher man, he says you have not paid him. He cannot send us any more meat. How am I going to feed all these people without meat? Tell me that, Prudence! Why you not pay the butcher man?"

Prudence was defensive. "The butcher will get paid next month. We have the money on fixed deposit and it will come free next month. He should not be on his high horse, anyway. He sells us all the meat that nobody else wants."

Mama Mercy switched to her native Xhosa and her vocal torrent reverberated round the small room. Julie could only understand fragments.

Prudence got out of her chair. "Mama, please! The children will hear you."

"Are you saying I use bad meat for cooking?"

"No, Mama, no! I would never say such a thing about your cooking. You are the best cook in all of Hout Bay. I only meant the butcher is not giving us his very best meat and he is a rich man – he can afford to wait a little for his money."

"You tell him that," Mercy said, her finger an inch away from Prudence's chest. "And if I don't get my meat delivery, you can stand up in the dining room and tell thirty people why there is no lunch!"

She swung around on her heels and steamed off towards the kitchen.

Prudence made a dismissive gesture. "*Attattattattat*. She woke up on the wrong side of the bed; such a storm in a coffee mug."

Julie decided that she was not going to get any work done in the office. She gathered papers and her laptop into a briefcase.

"Where are you off to?" Prudence asked.

"Going to meet with the printers, check up on the tent, the entertainers, the caterers, and … a few other things."

"Good luck. As you can gather, money is as short as ever, so we need this event to be a success."

"I know; no pressure, then."

Hendrik held the door open for her and muttered, "Doesn't look like I'm going to achieve anything here today. I'll come with you and unlock the gates so you can get your car out."

"Thanks, Hendrik, that's sweet of you." Julie was amused to see the old man blush a little at her thanks.

They walked down the corridor with its hotchpotch of brightly painted murals, which attested to the enthusiasm, if not the artistic ability, of numerous volunteers. As they passed the day room, Julie briefly glanced in. A number of African women occupied the sparsely furnished room where they were watching a re-run of a Xhosa language sitcom. Half a dozen toddlers played on the floor.

Hendrik followed her glance to a woman who sat away from the others. He said, "Thabo's mother really hasn't been looking well these last few days. She comes down from her shack every day with Thabo and the baby, but she'll need hospice care soon."

Despite the summer weather, the woman was wrapped in a blanket. A baby lay on a rug near her and with one big toe she gently tapped the baby's stomach as if to reassure herself that it was there.

Hendrik whispered, "*She is now too weak to lift her baby. Thabo looks after the baby, feeds it, and changes the nappies. She just sits there and looks at the baby. Man, it can tear your heart apart. Thank God they have this place to come to. At least it gives Thabo a break. I don't know what will happen to him and the baby once she dies.*"

"We'll find space for them here."

"I worry about Thabo. He doesn't play with the other boys and he hardly ever speaks."

"Hendrik, you cannot take all the world's problems on your shoulders. Maybe Grace is just going through a bad patch. Maybe she'll get better. Let's not give up hope yet." But there was little conviction in her voice.

They moved on and nearly collided with four young African boys chasing each other down the corridor. Hendrik nabbed one of them by the shoulder. "Hey, Danny, what's going on? You know you kids aren't supposed to run around inside."

"Sorry, *Oom* Hendrik, we were just playing."

"Why don't you rather play outside? It's such a nice day."

"There are *tokeloshes* and other bad spirits outside. They will catch us and cut us up for *muti,* to be sold to the medicine man."

"What nonsense! Who tells you such silly stories? I promise you there are no *tokeloshes.*"

"Samuel says there are *tokeloshes* and they come up from the river. He says if we go near the old stables by the river, then the *tokeloshes* will pick up our smell and come and get us at night."

"Samuel is a fool." He turned to Julie. "How that man ever became a security guard is beyond me. He is more likely to shoot himself in the foot than catch any burglars."

"Now, now, Hendrik. Don't look a gift horse in the mouth. We are very grateful for the donation of security services from Noble Enterprises."

"*Humph*, I don't think we need any security guards. Particularly not a stupid *bleddy* dimwit like Samuel who fills the kids' heads with nonsense about *tokeloshes.*"

"Come," he said to the boys, "you can play in the garden. I fixed the slide yesterday. Where is Thabo, why are you not playing with him?"

One of the boys said, "Thabo never plays, he never even talks." With big rolling eyes he went on: "Maybe a *tokeloshe* got his tongue."

"Get out of here," Hendrik commanded with mock anger and the boys ran off, laughing, to join their friends on the climbing frame.

Hendrik shook his head. "Honestly, these kids have enough worries without Samuel stirring up more fears. I need to talk to him."

They went outside and Hendrik disappeared down the dusty track towards the padlocked gate whilst Julie crossed a patch of grass and weeds to where her Golf was parked under a tree. She locked her briefcase in the boot and walked around to the driver's side. She caught the heavy scent of blue gum, which told her that it was going to be a hot day. She'd have to find somewhere suitable for lunch with her mother, maybe at a winery …

The sound of crashing tree branches stopped her in her tracks. Bewildered, she looked up, and a shower of leaves, twigs, and pollen rained down and blinded her. She was dimly aware of a dark figure leaping from the tree and grasping her wrists, dragging her towards the nearby bushes. A montage of images, gleaned from newspaper reports of rape, stabbings, and murders, flashed through her mind.

Julie screamed as she tripped over an exposed root and hit the ground hard. Her assailant let go and she struggled on hands and knees to crawl away. Then, as she looked up, she froze in terror. A young boy, his dark face expressionless, hovered above her. A jagged, fist-sized rock was held menacingly above his head, ready to strike. Sheer fright constricted her throat and she shut her eyes, waiting for the blow. *How can this be? Where have we gone so wrong? Dear God, why?*

She felt a stirring of air as the rock sailed inches past her head and hit the ground behind her with a thud.

When she opened her eyes, she saw that Hendrik was standing next to her car. The old man was breathing hard - he had evidently sprinted over when he saw what was happening. As she watched, he bent down and picked up a three-foot- long viper by its tail. The rock had pulverized the snake's head.

"*Morsdood,* dead!" Hendrik pronounced. "I wonder what stirred this one up; they normally stay down by the river and away from people. You're very lucky that Thabo was around. Must have seen it from his perch up in the tree. Could have been very nasty for you."

Julie staggered to her feet, wiped her hands, and inspected her grazed knees. She breathed deeply and fought to gain control over her runaway emotions. She turned to thank the boy who had come to her rescue, but Thabo had disappeared.

"Let's get the sister to put some antiseptic on that knee. Then you'll be as good as new." Hendrik offered her his free left arm.

Julie looked at the snake in his right hand and shuddered. "Thanks, Hendrik, I think I can manage. You'd better get rid of that beasty before Mama Mercy or the kids see it. I'll catch you later."

Chapter 4: The Toreros

Tuesday evening

Tuesday nights are notoriously slow at clubs and bars in Cape Town, but this Tuesday was different for one particular club in the trendy Waterfront district. It was the monthly "Ladies' Hunt at De Waterkant" - an opportunity to seriously let one's hair down. By nine p.m., the mainly female crowd had the barmen sweating.

Julie watched a group of women whom she guessed to be in their thirties. By day, they were probably soccer moms and members of book clubs, but tonight their revealing dresses and loud voices signaled the desire for a good time. They were well into their third round of cocktails, laughing riotously at each other's jokes, and flirting like mad with one of the barmen. Julie assumed he'd been brought in for his blond surfer looks as much as for his bar-tending abilities.

"Hey, Stuart," one of the women called across the length of the bar, "we're starting a new game. Every time you keep us waiting for a drink longer than three minutes, you have to take off a piece of clothing." She and her friends shrieked with laughter as Stuart spilled the cocktail he was working on.

Desmond and Julie had found a table with a prime view of the stage. The club occupied part of a converted warehouse and exuded post-modern industrial chic: an abundance of stainless steel and funky bold color accents. Looking up into the dark void, Julie could make out crisscrossing steel girders carrying stage lights and loudspeakers. The walls were painted burnt ochre; in places, the plaster had been stripped away to expose hundred-year-old brickwork. For Julie, the venue evoked a sense of hellfire and brimstone. With some alarm she noted massive speakers, which, to her, added to the underworld atmosphere. In front of the stage was a dance floor, around which patrons sat at small tables arranged in three semi-circular tiers. On the highest tier, furthest from the stage, was the sweeping bar with stainless-steel counter, glass shelves, and mirrors. It held a decadent array of bottles, lurid colored glasses, and silver shakers.

Two women in high heels and low cleavages sauntered down the row of tables. Martinis in hand, immaculately made up, they exuded nonchalance. Stopping at Desmond and Julie's table, they casually folded their frames into the two empty chairs.

"Excuse me," Julie said, "those seats are taken. We're expecting friends to join us."

The women turned in unison and looked at her in feigned surprise. Julie clenched her teeth and felt her chin jut forward. She wasn't invisible, dammit.

"Oh, sorry, I didn't see you," the brunette said. She tossed her long hair, flashed Desmond a broad smile, and ensured that he got a full view of her cleavage as she got up. Her blonde friend brushed past Desmond, leaned down, and whispered theatrically, *"Come and join us if you get bored."*

Julie held up her hands like claws and growled at their retreating backs. "God, what have I let myself in for? I don't know that I can stand a whole evening surrounded by bitches on heat and gays on the prowl." She quickly added, "No offense."

Desmond laughed. "Spare a thought for those of us who are on stage and the objects of all that lust and desire. It's a tough job, but someone's got to do it."

Julie looked at her watch. "Wendy's late."

"The privilege of the rich."

Julie shrugged.

"How did she get to be so loaded? I've never heard mention of a Mr. van Houten."

"According to my mother, Erik van Houten was quite a bit older than Wendy and her family did not approve of him. But Wendy's always been headstrong; she was madly in love so she married him anyway and settled on his tobacco farm in Zimbabwe. He did OK with tobacco but then, despite Wendy's objections, he branched into weapons manufacture. That's how he became seriously wealthy."

Desmond said, "Probably supplied South Africa during the sanction years."

"I don't know the details. Anyway, he died of a heart attack about ten years ago and, in Wendy's own words, she's set herself the task of using the van Houten fortune to atone for the manner in which it was acquired."

"She doesn't have any kids, does she?"

They were both startled by Wendy's voice. "Who doesn't have kids?"

"Oh, just talking about an old friend," Desmond said quickly, leaping to his feet to pull out a chair for Wendy. She gave him a peck on the cheek, and greeted Julie with a hug.

"I'm so excited to finally see where you work. What a vibe!" Wendy glanced around. "Who would have thought you could create an orange and mauve décor and get away with it!"

As Wendy engaged Desmond in animated discussion about the venue and its patrons, Julie sat back and watched the two of them. People who first met this bustling, kindly woman were apt to underestimate her. She was a very astute businesswoman and intent on maximizing the social returns on her charitable investment. The Khanya center was one of her most treasured projects. Julie had always admired Wendy's sense of poise and presence. The golden brown hair had been expertly styled and now, as she turned her gaze on Julie, her green eyes smoldered as mischievously as they had twenty years ago when she had bewitched Erik van Houten.

"Penny for your thoughts?"

"Nothing. I was just thinking that you look well."

Wendy acknowledged the comment with a nod. "So, are you excited? Do you think we're doing the right thing?"

Julie hesitated and then had to raise her voice to be heard above the noise. "I'll reserve judgment till I see Desmond and his Toreros go through their routine. I'm still very concerned about how a group of male strippers will go down with our audience at the AIDS benefit ..."

"Exotic dancers, please!" Desmond interjected with mock indignation.

Julie said, "It *is* very risqué."

"That's exactly the point," Wendy said. "There's no fun without risk. I'm convinced they'll be a hit; we might just have a riot on our hands." She winked at Desmond when she saw Julie's shocked expression and continued, "You know, people think women over forty should pursue demure interests such as art and classical music. I promise you, under their make-up, five-hundred-rand hair-dos, and extra-lift bras, they are still very, very interested in a bit of ... fun."

"How would you know what women over forty think?" Desmond asked.

"Oh, you're such a smooth pretender." She touched his shoulder. "But thank you for the compliment." Her voice softened. "I can't believe that you'll be missing the gala; especially since you hatched this whole plan and worked so hard to get the Toreros lined up for us."

"It's a bummer, but it's just one of those things ..."

"Julie tells me you've found a substitute. Will he be dancing tonight?"

"No, tonight he'll just observe. He should be here any minute; in fact, you know him. He's Chris du Toit, the heart surgeon's son."

"Chris?! Of course I know Chris. I see his father from time to time, but I haven't seen Chris in years. His mother was a very dear friend of mine."

Julie leaned forward. "We had already moved to Johannesburg when Danielle du Toit ... died. I remember my mother being very upset and refusing to speak about it. Did they ever catch the intruder?"

"No, it was a most frustrating business. Appears that nothing much was stolen. Danielle obviously caught them by surprise. They never arrested anybody. The police eventually just wrote it off as another robbery gone wrong."

For a few moments she was absorbed in her own thoughts, then shook her head. "Let's talk about something else. How was your day? Did you make progress with the caterers?"

"Before you launch into that," Desmond said, "can I get you a drink?"

"I'd love a gin and tonic."

Ten minutes later Desmond, closely followed by Chris, made his way back. Julie watched as they picked their way through the rowdy crowd with the drinks held aloft. Every time Chris had to squeeze past someone he flashed an apologetic smile. That same smile - it tugged at something deep inside her. *Funny how a person's smile doesn't change*, she thought. It was like those old photographs. She had thought the image would have yellowed and faded beyond definition. Yet, Chris smiled, and there it was, in bright Technicolor, her thirteen-year-old self, leaning forward to accept his shy, awkward kiss. She touched her lips.

"Look what I found." Desmond motioned with his head whilst putting down the drinks.

"Chris, my boy, how wonderful to see you!" Wendy beamed and enfolded Chris's hand in hers. He bent down to kiss her cheek and give her a hug.

"It's good to see you, too."

Julie noticed that something had changed in all these years – Chris had a strong five o'clock shadow.

"And of course you remember Julie, " Desmond said.

He looked up and she could see the hesitation in his eyes, the frozen smile.

She reached across the table to shake his hand.

##

Chris searched her face for the impish smile that had tormented him in his dreams so many years ago. Her face betrayed little emotion but the chin was pushed forward in the defiant manner that used to intoxicate and infuriate him.

He shook her hand and observed a pink flush in her cheeks. It made him remember an incident during dance class when one of the other ballerinas had repeatedly tugged at Julie's ponytail. Suddenly, with no warning other than a reddish flushing of her cheeks, Julie had grabbed a broomstick and would have beaten the other girl over the head if Danielle had not intervened. A pink flush was definitely not a good sign.

He lowered himself into the chair next to Julie; an awkward silence descended. Was it his imagination or did she actually shift away? Then, luckily, a band appeared on stage and distracted them. The music combined jazz with an African beat and soon had many of the crowd on their feet.

Julie appeared to be fascinated by her drink and oblivious to the glances that Chris stole in her direction. The drumbeats intensified and Wendy got to her feet. "Hey, what's up with you lot? Come on, dance!" she commanded and pulled Desmond out of his seat to join a few other couples jostling between the tables.

"What's up with those two?" she shouted in Desmond's ear. "You're not going to leave me with them, are you? They look like they're going to be about as much fun as a priest in a brothel."

"Who knows, a priest in a brothel could be very entertaining."

Ten minutes later, when they returned to the table, Wendy was out of breath and aglow from the exertion. "That was great fun! You two should try it."

Desmond looked hard at Chris and made little encouraging motions with his hands. Chris turned to Julie, who appeared to be absorbed by someone or something behind the bar. He cleared his throat but she did not seem to hear him.

The embarrassed silence that followed was broken by Desmond saying that he had to go backstage, and suggesting that Chris come with him to say hello to the others. Before they were even out of earshot, he was remonstrating with his friend: "What on earth is up with you?!"

"I'm sorry, I thought she might have forgiven and forgotten by now. But clearly she hasn't. I suppose she just hates my guts."

"But you haven't seen her in years."

"That's not strictly true. Did you know that she came down from Johannesburg for her final honors year at Cape Town University?"

"Yeah. So?"

"Well, I didn't know that. No one told me. So we had this … incident, a chance encounter. It went all wrong."

"But I thought she was the object of all your dreams and desires, the girl you nearly wanked yourself blind over."

"Don't be crude." Chris was angry. "That was ages ago; I was what, thirteen, fourteen?"

"So what happened for her to hate your guts?"

"It was just one of those stupid, stupid things. Me and the guys were having drinks at Forries after a soccer match. I guess we were pretty plastered. Then, just our luck, a couple of first-year student debutantes came in to sell flowers for charity. I mean, what moron sends innocent little debutantes to Forries to sell flowers? Anyway, one of them comes to our table and Hughie was kind of rude to her. You know what an asshole Hughie can be when he's drunk."

"I can just picture it; I've never been crazy about your soccer pals." He paused. "For one thing, they have muscles in all the wrong places."

Chris stopped. They were in a dim corridor leading down the side of the building. "What do you mean?"

"Nothing, just a joke. They have muscles where other people have brains. Anyway, what did Hughie do?"

"He says to her, 'I'll buy your flowers if you give me a match.' She's all confused and says something about smoking not being allowed. So Hughie carries on, 'No, I have a different match in mind, my prick and your throat – a match made in heaven,' or something to that effect. He then cans himself laughing at his own stupid joke."

"And I suppose you were all swept up by this witticism and joined in the laughter?" Desmond's voice was dripping with disapproval.

"You don't have to rub it in. We were drunk, so yes, we all laughed. Shame, man, this poor girl with her basket of tulips just about burst into tears."

"That wasn't Julie, though, was it?"

"Oh no, Julie was chaperone for the debutantes that evening: the fool who brought them there. She had overheard us, so she comes over with the sweetest smile on her face and starts to come on to Hughie. 'You're such a stud! Really hot stuff.' Hughie sits there grinning like an idiot as she picks up two mugs of beer and empties them: one in his lap and one over his head. He never saw it coming."

"I remember that she always had quite a temper."

"We were laughing, and only when she turned and looked straight at me did I recognize her. I was shocked."

"Was that the end of it, then?"

"No. A couple of days later I happened to spot her on campus, so I went over to apologize."

"And?"

"Let's just say she's not one to forgive and forget very easily." He mimicked Julie's voice: " 'A real man stands up and acts when it matters; there's no point in being sorry when it's too late.' I was stunned. Before I could say anything, she just turned and walked away."

##

The Toreros greeted Chris like a long-lost friend. The cramped dressing room exuded the disheveled, testosterone-laden air of a sports locker room. Clothes were strewn everywhere and the pungent smell of deodorant and hair gel hung in the room like a limp life-form.

Farm-boy Riaan was nearest the door, "Hey, *my boetie,* how goes it? Guys, look what the cat dragged in." He grinned broadly and gave Chris a crushing handshake. James Buthelezi and Bruce McKay greeted him with raised fists, knuckles touching. Chris noticed a couple of empty Castle lager cans. Bruce had a full one in his hand; he'd always joked that his mother's milk had been 90 percent beer and that his body needed no other sustenance.

Chris did his best to forget his past history with the Australian. "Bruce, my man, how's the surfing?"

"Crap for me, but great for beginners – I had two chicks there today – a blonde and a brunette, both stacked." He gestured with his hands.

James laughed. "What did you teach them, surfing or riding?"

"Let's just say they're coming to see the show tonight and then I have to give them remedial lessons."

The banter continued and Chris enjoyed catching up. The Toreros, including Desmond, were a group of six, and about as diverse a bunch of guys as one could possibly find. Bull Khumalo, a mountain of man, sat on a stool in the corner, trying to take up as little space as possible. Cedric, the nominal leader of the group, was the only one who seemed concerned about the actual performance. He had started to peer anxiously at the wall clock. "Guys, guys! We only have sixteen minutes. James, get that gorgeous behind of yours into your tights." Chris noticed that the group still had the habit of ignoring Cedric. He sighed. They could be much better if only they would listen to him, because as well as being the leader he was also a gifted choreographer.

One of the group said, "Hey, I have an idea – why don't we get Chris up on stage? He can do it!"

"*Ja man,* nothing like throwing a dog in the deep end to make him swim."

"Come on, don't be a wuss; we're doing the same old bullfight number. If you screw up, we'll just pretend the bull gored you and drag you off stage. It'll be a laugh!"

"There's some good talent out there. If you come on stage with us, you might even get a piece of ass to take home tonight."

They all laughed and after a few more minutes Chris made his escape and let them get on with their preparations and make-up. Desmond briefly grabbed his arm as he was leaving he room. "Julie and Wendy are my people. You wouldn't believe what they are doing in the fight against HIV. I want you to be nice to them, d'you hear me?"

"Yes, boss!" Chris gave a mock salute and returned to the women determined to try harder.

A little later, when the band took a break, he had Wendy enthralled with stories of his backpacking travels through Asia and Europe. Even Julie seemed to be drawn into the spell of his storytelling. Then the conversation turned to the AIDS center and he was gratified to find that Wendy was interested in his professional opinion as an architect.

"Chris, you have to come out and visit the center. We'd love to expand the place but we haven't progressed past drawing up a few sketchy plans. Old Hendrik is a sweet handyman, but all his designs end up looking like farm barns."

"Can't say I have much experience with designing orphanages."

Wendy brushed his protestations aside.

"Karma, Chris, Karma. What you give is what you get. It'll do you good to get your mind off yourself."

"Funny, that's exactly what Desmond said to me earlier today." With a half-smile, he added, "Are you sure this isn't a set-up?"

Before Wendy could answer, Julie interjected, "It might come as a surprise to you, but people actually have more important things to do than to set you up."

He did not know how to respond because he was not sure whether she was serious or joking. She turned to Wendy and continued, "I'm sure Chris has a bunch of other things to keep him occupied and you know that Greg has offered to help us find an architect."

OK, she's not joking. Chris felt his anger rising, *Whatever happened to the girl I knew? This Julie has an unbelievable knack of getting under one's skin.*

Deliberately ignoring Julie, he turned to Wendy, and gave her his most engaging smile. "I'd be very happy to help; I just wanted you to know that I don't have much experience. And I've got nothing else on this week, except, of course, my dance rehearsals every morning. Shall I come around one afternoon?"

Wendy touched his arm. "Oh, that would be wonderful!"

Pointedly, she said to Julie, "I know that we could find us any old architect to draw up plans, but we need more than that to prove that the concept can work."

"What do you mean; what concept?" Chris asked.

"AIDS is destroying traditional family structures," Wendy replied. "I'm not just thinking of a few alterations at Khanya. I want us to create a prototype living space for a totally new type of family unit – something like a kibbutz, where a couple of care-givers can provide a family atmosphere for a dozen children. It's going to require an architect with extraordinary empathy and ingenuity. It's an opportunity to make a very real difference in the life of thousands. "

It was on the tip of Chris's tongue to make some self-deprecating retort but then he realized that Wendy was totally sincere. A passion had crept into her voice that completely dispelled her previous homey tone. He could picture her in the role of formidable boardroom director. Chris was intrigued, but before he could quiz her more, the band started to play.

Wendy insisted that Julie and Chris go and dance and soon they were gyrating with the rest of the crowd. Her movements were unique - an effortless blend of the rhythms of Africa with the poise of a ballerina. She kept her distance and never once made eye contact with Chris. He thought that she had perfected the art of maintaining an invisible shield around her. The dance floor was crowded but no one crossed the moat into Julie's space – she was untouchable in her castle made for one.

He wished he knew what she was thinking, but failing that he could at least watch her.

Chris's teenage fantasies of women had been shaped by an eclectic mix of the repressed sexuality of the swoon-if-you-see-an-ankle Victorian novel combined with furtive *Hustler* images. Looking at Julie's soft brown curls and flawless skin now, however, he was reminded of a Jane Austen heroine.

She was wearing a sleeveless green dress: a timeless classic that would have been as appropriate for the opera as it was for a club. Lights and laser beams bounced off a myriad silk threads, and it seemed to Chris that Julie was a light source, radiating rather than reflecting. She had pushed her hair behind her ears, but one unruly strand kept breaking loose, falling across her left eye.

The music changed to a slow song. He took a step towards her and tucked the unruly coil of hair behind her ear. Her skin felt smoother than anything he had ever touched before. He let his hand trace the outline of her ear – a dainty, perfectly formed ear with a peculiar golden earring.

"I like your earrings, very unusual."

"I inherited them from my grandmother – they are Celtic, supposed to bring one good luck."

"Do they work?"

He was about to take her in his arms for the dance when she said, "I need fresh air."

Out on the balcony, a number of people stood in groups or alone, most of them smoking. Julie moved to the far end, rested her elbows on the railing, and looked down on the city lights and the harbor beyond. A breeze had come up; it played with the tips of her hair.

"Julie ..." he hesitated, hoping she would turn to face him, but she didn't. "I know I upset you. That incident at Forries, it was stupid and I'm sorry…what else can I say?"

She didn't say anything for a while, and he was beginning to wonder whether he had simply thought the words, not actually spoken out loud. When she finally spoke, she still didn't turn, but rather addressed the breeze.

"You think I'm upset about that?"

He had to lean in right behind her to hear her voice and her perfume surrounded him: a hint of citrus and something that made him think of sea-spray. He found himself fighting an overwhelming urge to take her in his arms.

"That infantile little episode was just annoying, boorish, and rude; it didn't really upset me."

"It didn't?"

She rounded on him and for the first time that evening looked straight into his eyes.

"Why didn't you write?"

"What?"

"When I moved to Johannesburg, why didn't you write?"

"Julie, I was, what ... thirteen years old? Thirteen-year olds don't write."

"You were the first boy I ever kissed; I was in love with you ..." She turned away to hide her emotion.

"Julie, I ..."

"I was lonely and miserable in Johannesburg. I didn't have any friends." He could hear the reproach in her voice. "Every day I waited for the post, hoping, dreaming ..." She looked at him and he could see her struggling to maintain her composure. But the hurt, buried for so long, could not be repressed any longer. Her tears seemed to collect the light from a million stars, falling down her cheeks like strands of purest silver.

"Julie, I am so sorry ..."

He pulled her towards him, feeling the dampness of her tears against his chest. He was aware of a strange sensation – it was as if those strands of silver had penetrated his chest and wrapped themselves around his heart, giving it a cosmic jolt. He felt more alive than he had ever felt before – on a plane of consciousness that he hadn't even known existed. He stroked her hair and let her cry.

"I clearly remember that evening at the year-end concert when I first found out that you were leaving. The performance had been great and we were all having cool drinks and sandwiches. Do you remember?"

She nodded.

"Your parents were there and they brought that intern ... what was his name? ... Greg. I wanted to punch him every time he looked at you; I hated the way he was possessive about you and condescending to everyone else. But of course he was all grown up already, drinking wine, and we were just kids."

She sniffed. "Greg's been good to me. He's always there when I need him."

He ignored the accusation in her tone.

"You know what I did that evening, when you left?"

She shook her head and the silky feel of her hair against his chest radiated to his spine.

"I smoked *dagga* for the first and only time in my life."

She looked at him then, a faint smile curving the edges of her mouth, "You didn't, did you? You were only thirteen!"

He nodded. "Desmond gave it to me; said it would make me feel better. We went up to my tree-house, he rolled the *sols* like an expert, and we smoked."

"And *did* it make you feel better?"

"I coughed my lungs out and I've never felt so ill in my life. It was a miserable experience for which I still haven't forgiven Desmond. God knows what was in that weed."

She laughed and it was as though suddenly his old friend had reappeared.

"I got your shirt all wet; I don't usually bawl my eyes out like that. Sorry."

He took her hands in his. "Why didn't you contact me when you came back to Cape Town last year?"

"Oh, that was a whole a different story. I'd planned to look you up – not just you," she added quickly, "also Desmond and my old girlfriends from dancing. But then I'd barely arrived before I found out that you were engaged ..."

She broke off and her eyes widened. She seemed to be looking at something right behind Chris. He swung around and saw the silhouette of a man with a camera phone brazenly taking pictures of them both.

"Hey, what are you doing? Stop that!" Chris protested.

The man inhaled deeply on his cigarette, which briefly illuminated his face as he slid the cell phone into the pocket of his white jacket. When he spoke, his voice was asthmatic. "Sorry, didn't mean to upset you. It was just such a perfect picture: two lovers against the backdrop of the city lights." He took another drag from his cigarette, held it between thumb and forefinger before flicking it across the railing. The cigarette missed Julie by inches. The man turned and headed towards the dance floor.

Chris was incensed. "Hey! Wait!"

Julie held him back. "Just let it be."

"Do you know this guy?"

"No... but ..."

"But what?"

"I have a feeling I've seen him before. I think he might be stalking me."

"Julie, that's even more reason to go after him! You should tell the police."

"Tell them what? They'll laugh at me. They're not interested unless you actually have a knife sticking out of your ribs."

He looked at her, desperate to hold her, protect her.

She said, "I've told Greg. He's going to get someone from the company's security group to look into it. They're very well connected. I'm sure it's nothing, though, probably just my imagination." She smoothed her skirt and tried to give him a reassuring smile.

Greg, always Greg, Greg, Greg, Chris thought. Before he could say anymore, however, Wendy came to find them. The show was about to start.

# #

A deep husky voice boomed from the darkness above: "And now, ladies, the moment you've all been waiting for … (*dramatic drum roll*) … South Africa's answer to the Chippendales, only bigger, bolder, beefier … *(loud applause, cheering, whistling, and catcalls)* … Please welcome, the Toreros!"

White smoke billowed across the stage and poured down on to the dance floor where the excitement was palpable amongst the cheering, packed crowd tottering on their high heels. Multicolored laser lights darted through the smoke. Music erupted from the speakers and mingled with the primeval screeching of more than a hundred women. Julie pressed her fingers into her ears. Five Toreros, up to their knees in a white cloud, exploded into action. Desmond was in the middle. They wore billowing buccaneer shirts, brass-studded black pants, and embroidered boleros. Each had a big red bullfighter's cloak that was used to great effect in swirling, coordinated movements as they went through an energetic routine.

Julie glanced sideways at Chris. He was concentrating hard, his body moving to the rhythm of the music as he followed the dancers intently. She could see the damp patch of her tears on his shirt; still feel where his hand had touched her forehead, her ear. She felt confused.

The dance was interrupted when a gleaming black Harley Davidson rolled on to the stage, the roar of its engine overpowering the music. The rider parked and got off slowly, menacingly. He was the biggest African that Julie had ever seen, dressed only in black leather pants, sunglasses, and a helmet with curvaceous horns that would have looked very silly on a lesser man. Julie winced when she saw the light reflecting off his one-inch diameter nipple rings.

The voice came over the speakers again: "Ladies, please welcome 'The Bull'. We need two volunteers to help our brave Toreros prepare for the fight." Hysterical pushing and shoving ensued and Julie saw a couple of bouncers edge in between the stage and the crowd. Three of the dancers had disappeared backstage and the remaining two picked volunteers from the baying hoard in front of the stage. Egged on by the crowd, the volunteers helped the dancers take off their shirts. They proceeded to rub oil over the torsos of two fighters whilst "The Bull" stomped around hissing, snorting, and cracking his fingers in readiness for the battle.

"This is so corny," Julie said to Wendy, and yet she couldn't help but feel excited by the wrestling match that was now underway between the oiled and bare-chested men. She noticed that Wendy was watching the fight intently, her lips slightly parted. She shrieked when one of the Toreros was lifted into the air by The Bull and tossed over his shoulder.

Julie leaned towards Chris. "Will you be doing that?"

"No, that's Riaan; he was a gymnastics champion. I'd break my bones if I attempted those falls."

The Bull was eventually subdued, draped over the Harley, and driven off stage by the triumphant Toreros.

All six dancers participated in the next number: a Zulu warrior dance led by James Buthelezi. Julie had to concede that they certainly looked the part, with authentic leopard-skin headdresses, body paint, and loincloths. Chris explained that James came from a clan with strong connections to the Zulu royal family. He was proud of his heritage and demanded that the others practice the dance steps until they were perfect. The crowd got caught up in the rhythm; many kicked off their shoes and tried to emulate the rhythmic frenzy of the dancers.

For the next number, Bruce appeared alone.

"He looks like David Beckham," Wendy shouted across the table.

Chris said, "He's hopeless at soccer, but an excellent surfer."

Bruce picked a volunteer from the audience to tango with him. Julie recognized the volunteer; it was the brunette that had tried to sit at their table.

Bruce had the obligatory rose in his mouth and swept her from one side of the stage to the other. He certainly could dance: there was a feline quality to the way he played with his prey. But the brunette decided to play her own game. When he swooped her towards him, she reached out and ripped Bruce's shirt off his body. He took it in his stride; it was all part of the act and what the monthly regulars expected.

"Now she has to take off a piece of clothing," Chris shouted. "That's the rule."

"What sort of a dumb rule is that?"

The brunette played her part with aplomb; she slipped her dress off her shoulders and stepped out in black bra and panties. The crowd loved it. "Off!" they yelled. "Off, off, take it all off!" The brunette fumbled with Bruce's pants, throwing them aside to leave him stripped down to his tanga. They continued with their dance and, after more urging, the girl whipped off her bra and flung it into the crowd.

Julie could not help but wonder how she would feel the next day when she was sober and had to contend with the photos eagerly being snapped by her blonde friend.

Wendy was not easily shocked but, when Julie glanced at her, she could see that her friend was taken aback. She leaned towards her. "Are you sure this is what we want? We can probably still find *some* other type of entertainment ..."

Before Wendy could answer, Chris reassured them. "Don't worry, it won't go this far. The guys actually do know how to control things, depending on the audience. If it gets too hot, they simply cut it short."

As if on cue, the stage curtain dropped.

##

It was near midnight. After the show, the Toreros had all stopped by to chat with Wendy, Chris, and Julie. Desmond and Cedric settled down to talk about the program for the AIDS gala. The other Toreros were in high demand and were soon dragged off by groups of club patrons. Julie spotted Bull, having his photo taken with a girl sitting on each knee and a third on his shoulders. James and Riaan had joined a large group where cocktails and laughter flowed freely. With a jolt, she realized that the man who she suspected had been following her was on the periphery of that group. He looked like something that had dropped out of an Armani catalog – lean build, dark-blue shirt, flashy watch. His dark skin was a stark contrast to the white suit and made it difficult to distinguish his features. She felt his gaze as he looked directly at her, his face expressionless.

Julie tugged at Chris's sleeve and drew his attention to the man. Chris immediately got up to confront him but the boozy crowd hampered his progress across the club. He was only halfway there when Julie saw Mr. Armani turn and head for a passage at the back of the club. Chris followed.

Wendy, Desmond, and Cedric had not noticed anything. Julie looked around nervously, unable to pay attention to the conversation. On the dance floor she saw Bruce, fully entangled in the tentacles of the brunette. When Julie looked over her shoulder again, she was shocked to see the man in the white suit approaching her from a completely different direction. He must have circled the building; there was no sign of Chris.

Was this man some crazy admirer, was he going to ask her to dance? Julie recognized her predicament: if she refused to dance, it could be perceived as racist. The man might create a scene. Her imagination ran wild. With so many drunken people around, it could be explosive. Yet she had no intention of dancing with a man who had been stalking her.

Acting impulsively, she leapt up and made for the dance floor. Going over to Bruce and his partner, she tapped the brunette on the shoulder. "Excuse me, may I cut in?"

The girl fluttered her eyelashes indignantly. She was about to protest when Bruce said, "It's OK bunny, run along." With a sardonic smile he added, "This lady pays for my services, so she gets preferential treatment." The brunette gave Julie a withering glare and turned on her heels. Bruce blew a kiss in her direction and took Julie in his arms.

"To what do I owe this pleasure?"

"I just felt like dancing," Julie lied. "Sorry if I spoiled things for you. She seemed ready to lay you right here and now."

Bruce laughed. "Not to worry, plenty of those minnows in the sea. I like to fish for the real thing." With that, he guided her across the dance floor and propelled her through a number of steps that she did not know she was capable of. When the music slowed, Bruce pulled her close to him. She looked over his shoulder but couldn't see any sign of the white suit. She began to relax. It was probably just her imagination; too much time spent watching movies.

She was startled when Bruce kissed her neck and gently blew against her earlobe. It was ticklish and made her laugh.

"It's good to see you laugh." He grinned mischievously. "What's with you and Chris? I didn't know he had finally found himself a decent girlfriend."

"Me and Chris?" She shook her head. "We knew each other as kids. But that's a long time ago. There's nothing between us. Whatever gave you that idea?"

"For starters, the way you study him all the time. But the dead give-away is the manner in which he's looking at me right now. If looks could kill ..."

"There's nothing between us," Julie said emphatically.

"Well, in that case ..." He literally swept her off her feet and gave her a passionate, lingering kiss.

Julie was completely speechless with shock. When Bruce put her back on her feet, she was just in time to see Chris glowering at her from the back of the club. His jaw was set and his face pale. He turned and walked out.

Next to her, Bruce laughed out loud. "I told you there was something going on between the two of you."

##

Chapter 5: Khanya

Wednesday afternoon

Chris turned off the main road and drove down the dirt track towards the Khanya center. The old farmhouse with its deep verandah looked welcoming. He slowed to a crawl as he passed a group of barefoot children playing soccer on a dusty pitch that bordered the track. Some of them waved and pointed to a hand-painted "Visitor Parking" sign that dangled from a blue gum tree. He parked his BMW, an eighteenth birthday gift from his father, next to a tired-looking Golf. He and his vehicle were quickly surrounded by an admiring, chattering group of African kids.

"Nice car, *meestar*. Take me for a ride."

"No, me, me!" the others chorused.

"Do you play soccer? Come play with us, please."

"No, I want to ride in the BM."

"One day, I'm going to get one of these," one of the boys said, patting the car, "and a *beeeg* house for all my children." He stretched his arms wide.

"You don't even have a girlfriend," his friend teased. "How can you have children?"

"Hokai!" Chris smiled, lifting his palms. "Slow down. You guys seriously scare me when you talk about girlfriends and children. How old are you, anyway, twelve?"

"Me, I will be thirteen next month."

"What's your name?"

"Danny."

Chris introduced himself and shook hands with the boy, who seemed to be the leader of the group.

"You've got plenty of time, Danny, trust me. Can you tell me where I will find Miss Wendy?"

"Meez Wendy, she's not here, but I can take you to *Meez* Julie."

"OK." Chris tried to hide his unease. After last night, he did not know what to expect. For a while he'd thought they had a real connection, but then she'd sent him on a wild goose chase after a mythical stalker and thrown herself at Bruce the moment his back was turned. He remembered that, even when he was thirteen, he had never quite known how to approach her, and that feeling was back with him now.

He picked up his rucksack, locked the car, and motioned for the children to lead the way. They formed a small procession, with Chris towering above the others like an idol on a litter. The children were full of cheer and open, innocent questions, which Chris answered as best he could. "Why you here?" "What you do?" "Where do you live?" "How much does that nice belt cost?"

Near the kitchen, they encountered Mama Mercy who was heaving two garbage bags out to the bins. She squinted against the sun to look at the little group.

"Mama Mercy, this *meestar* is here for ..."

She stopped, her eyes growing wide, and dropped the bags. "Chris! My Chris!"

"Mercy!?"

His mind went into overdrive. What was Mercy doing here? She had stopped working for the du Toits when Chris went off to university; since then, he'd only seen her when she came to the house at Christmas to bring home-baked cookies – although she had also attended his graduation. He remembered her telling him then that Wendy had found her a job at an orphanage. The details were fuzzy, though, because he had not really paid much attention; he'd been focused on his friends, their families, and the graduation.

Mercy's hands flew up to cover her mouth. Chris knew that gesture so well. She was embarrassed about the gap between her front teeth and had always covered her mouth when she laughed. Then she did another thing that Chris remembered – she started to dance a little jig, slapping her thighs, her round face gleaming with pure joy. As he watched her, still feeling dumbstruck, it seemed to Chris that she looked just the same as she had when he was a schoolboy. The only indication that she had got older was the gray hair protruding from under her colorful *doek*.

"You've come! You've come to visit Mercy, just like you promised!" She rushed forward and clasped his hands in hers as if to seek reassurance that it was really him. Her grip was not as strong as he remembered but those hands still brought with them the unmistakable smell of Sunlight dishwashing liquid. For a moment, he was transported back to the kitchen at home with Mercy bustling about, cleaning or baking.

Chris was aware that the children had grown quiet, and were watching the two of them with curiosity. He felt that they could see right through him; at any moment they would expose the deceit and tell Mercy that he was here to see Wendy and Julie, not her at all.

"This is my boy." She looked at a couple of the older children. "The one I've been telling you about – he is strong, he is smart, and he gone to university. You must grow up like him!"

"He's not your boy, "Danny said, laughing. "He's white!"

"*Ow.* What do you know? You have much to learn." She reached out and clutched Danny against her bosom. He resisted with the self-consciousness of a twelve-year-old. "You are my child, too, are you not? I am your mama." She gave him a hefty pat on the back, and then shooed all the children back to their soccer match.

She was still shaking her head as she bent down to retrieve the garbage bags.

"Please, let me." Chris picked up the bags and followed her down the track, past the soccer field, to the garbage cans near the main road. All the way she chattered, telling Chris about the orphanage, the cooking, and the children – their likes and dislikes, their squabbles and their pain.

He felt a pang of jealousy. His Mercy, the woman whose life had revolved entirely around him, had found another purpose.

As if sensing his thoughts, Mama Mercy looked directly at him. "They really need me," she said. There was both defiance and pleading in her voice.

Chris felt guilty. He'd noticed an unfamiliar heaviness in the way she walked. He'd always thought of her as ageless, a permanent beacon. But now he could see the swollen ankles, the slight limp, the wrinkles as well as the gray hair. Mercy, after all, was not indestructible.

"These children are very lucky to have you. I am glad." He paused. "I'm sorry that I did not come to visit earlier. I've been busy."

She shrugged it off, which made Chris feel even guiltier. They walked on in silence, Chris's conscience screaming louder with every step. Finally, he stopped.

"Mercy, I can't lie. I didn't really come to see you; I came to see Wendy and Julie. I didn't even know that this was the place where you work now."

A broad smile lit up Mercy's face and this time she did not try to hide the gap in her teeth. "I taught you well; you are an honest child." She paused. "You are here, are you not? When your head does not know where to go, your feet will show you the way." She looked at him for a long time as he stood, garbage bags in hand, in the afternoon sun. Pollen from the blue gums drifted down and created the illusion of a golden shower all around him.

"If your mother could see you now ..." Her eyes filled with tears. "She would be so proud." Mercy looked up into the sky. "I'm sure she's watching." For a while, she was lost in her own thoughts. Tears rolled down her face. "I wish ... every day I wish I could have taken that bullet instead of her."

He put the bags down, found a tissue in his pocket, and handed it to her.

"You mustn't talk like that, Mercy. Look at what you're doing here; these children need you." He waited for her to compose herself. "I also think about it every day. In my dreams, I see the shooting over and over again. I hear the gun and I see Mom, her blood ... and when I wake up, I keep thinking: *What could I have done? How could I have stopped that man?*" His voice was bitter.

"The anger; it is still inside you." It was a statement, not a question. She didn't need to say anymore. Chris knew exactly what she was referring to – the night of his mother's funeral. He blushed at the memory of his behavior.

She asked, "Have you been to church yet?"

He shook his head.

"Chris, a man who does not make peace with God cannot be at peace with himself." She dried her eyes. "Maybe one day you and I can go together."

He nodded, but with little conviction. Mercy had said "maybe"; he could agree to that.

As they walked slowly back to the farmhouse, Mercy enquired, "So, you are here to visit our Miss Julie; you like her?"

"It's not what you think, Mercy. I'm here to see Miss Wendy. It's business."

"I see," she said, but from the tone of her voice, and the coy sideways glance, he knew that she chose to read more into the visit. Mercy was an open book to Chris. The desire to match-make ran in her Xhosa blood as strong as the need for oxygen.

"Our Miss Julie make us so proud," Mercy went on. "She be so clever, also gone to university. "

"I know." Chris reflected on how shocked Mercy would be if she knew about his one and only encounter with Julie at university.

"She could do anything, go anywhere. But no, she choose to come here. She finds money for us. All the time she works, talks to people, shows them Khanya center. I bring tea; and the people, they give us the money for the medicine, clothes and ... for meat." She paused to let this sink in, and then concluded in a solemn voice, "Miss Julie, she be an angel."

"A real-live angel?" Chris raised his eyebrow.

When he was in his teens, he had worked hard to try and shake Mercy's literal interpretation of the Bible. She had grown up in a time and place where people believed in *tokeloshes* and ancestral spirits. Chris, with the wisdom of a sixteen-year-old, had condemned "the Church's cynical exploitation of African culture" which encouraged belief in angels, resurrection, the fires of hell, and heavenly harps. The "discussions" he and Mercy had about religion and the Church had always ended the same way: Mercy proclaiming that "The Lord's ways are mysterious," and Chris storming from the room in frustration.

But Mercy was not going to get drawn into an argument now. She just shook her head. "Naughty boy," she said mildly.

By now, they had reached Julie's office. As she knocked, Mercy turned and looked Chris in the eye. "You be nice to her - there aren't many angels around." Then she placed her hand on his arm and said, "You must stay for tea. I will bake your favorite scones."

He tried to protest, but she wouldn't have any of it. He watched her as she headed towards the kitchen, humming a tune that stirred more old memories - happy memories.

##

Julie was on the phone and motioned for Chris to sit down.

"Look," her knuckles showed white as her grip tightened on the phone, "we agreed on Pongracz. I'm not backing off that and serving some cheap plonk ..."

She paused, listening, and then interrupted, "I don't care what the wine guide says. Our sponsors are expecting Pongracz, and that's what they're going to get...

"No, I don't want to taste it. Mr. Johnson, I appreciate your suggestion, but my answer is no. Please make sure we have the champagne we ordered. I will be at Groot Constantia in an hour and we can discuss where you set up the champagne bar. Good-bye."

She put the receiver down with more force than necessary and pressed her middle fingers against her temples. "God, I'm surrounded by imbeciles. How difficult can it be to deliver twenty crates of champagne? That man has called me at least six times this week. And the florist is carrying on as though this were a highcsociety wedding. *Urggghh!*"

She turned to Chris. "Sorry, I just needed to vent. I'm afraid Wendy's been delayed. She tried to get hold of you, but none of us had your number."

"We can always do it some other time." Chris rose from his seat.

"No, no, you've come all this way. Wendy asked that I give you a tour of the place and that you meet with her in the village later – at the Mainstream coffee shop. Do you know it?"

"Yeah."

There was a pause. Julie appeared to be searching for something on her desk. Chris wondered how best to address the subject of the previous evening; he wanted to pick up from where she had leaned against him, where he had rediscovered the laughing girl with the dimples who had been his childhood love.

They spoke simultaneously:

"About last night ..."

"Look, I'm ..."

"What did you want to ..."

"Sorry, you first."

Julie said, "I'm sorry I made such a spectacle of myself last night. It's been real hectic; I was just tired. I mean, really, to get emotional about what happened so long ago." She gave a little laugh.

"I've thought a lot about it. You had every right to be angry ..."

"Please, just forget it. We were kids; it's long past."

65

She got up, all businesslike, and handed him a brochure. "Let's start with this – it gives an overview of what we do at Khanya."

Chris hid his disappointment. He said, "That guy, the one who is stalking you ..."

Again, she gave a dry little laugh. "I was probably just being neurotic. Things look so different in the light of day." She put on a bright smile. "Greg always says I have an over-active imagination. Let's just forget about it – please."

She looked her watch. "I'll give you a quick rundown, then I have a call scheduled with a reporter from the *Cape*. After that, I have to scoot across to Groot Constantia – sorry to be so rushed."

He followed her down the corridor, touching and admiring the original sash windows and the wooden paneling. The beveled windowpanes were so heavily leaded that the afternoon sun sprayed rainbow colors across the floor. Their footsteps echoed in unison and he inhaled the smell of wood polish.

"How did dance rehearsal go this morning?" she asked.

"So-so; it's a bit like riding a bike, you get back into it fairly quickly. The only snag is that Cedric has changed the choreography in places. That threw me initially."

"Please tell me there won't be any full-on stripping like Bruce did last night. I'll absolutely die of embarrassment."

"Don't worry. We'll stick to dancing."

"I still can't believe that Wendy is OK with this. A bit of music, or a quiz, would have been just fine. I get a knot in my stomach just thinking about it."

Before Chris could answer, she opened the door to the dormitory wing. There were four rooms, each with six double bunk beds, twelve gray steel lockers, and a number of tables with assorted schoolbooks strewn across them. Chris noted the cheap construction: low ceilings, whitewashed walls, painted concrete floors.

He said, "I assume this gets pretty hot in summer."

"You bet, and freezing cold in winter." Defensively, she added, "They did the best they could with the funds available."

Everything was spotlessly clean. A couple of floor mats and thin curtains brightened the rooms. The children had stuck pictures and posters

66

from magazines up on the walls near their beds. Chris noticed that they favored pictures of cars, Hollywood celebrities, and sports stars. There were also a few random pictures of vacationing families, beaches, and wedding scenes, which had been torn from magazines.

Julie gave him an overview of the daily routine at the center as she led him out on to the covered verandah with its long wooden tables and benches.

"In summer, we spend our time outdoors. The children love it when they can eat out here, do their homework, draw or play. They really get on like one big family. In the winter, when they do homework in their dormitories, we seem to lose that family spirit. That's what gave Wendy the idea that we should build cottages and emulate a more natural family setting – back to the kitchen table being the heart of the house with a caring 'parent' to supervise meals and homework."

"How many children do you envisage per 'family'?" Chris asked.

"Ideally, no more than eight; but that's where the design has to be flexible. The reality is that we can't keep up with the demand for care-givers and will likely need to have up to twelve kids per cottage."

"Would they be separated the way they are now in their dormitories?"

"No. The whole point is to make it a proper family where older kids can help look after the younger ones, everyone chips in ..."

"And the girls hog the bathroom," Chris quipped.

"Excuse me! Many men I know spend ages preening themselves."

Chris looked at her. "What sort of men do you hang out with?" She was about to get all puffed up when he added, "That was a rhetorical question; just joking."

"Not funny." She looked directly at him. "Why did you leave in such a hurry last night?" she said suddenly.

The question caught him off guard. He looked past her at a clump of trees and the mountains beyond. Eventually he said, "It was late and I'd had a long day."

He knew that it was a lame answer and it seemed to him that a shutter went down in her eyes. She was suddenly in a hurry again and looked at her watch.

"Oh, jeez," she said. "I've got to call that reporter. Look, sorry, I have to run. Just … just browse around. Do whatever it is architects do. We can use all the land down to the river. Wendy will tell you more."

"Take it easy when you drive up to Constantia," he called after her, as she headed back to the office. "There were a lot of motorbikes racing up the valley when I was driving here. No point in getting yourself into an accident."

Left alone, he stepped down into the garden, past a climbing frame, towards the river. The property was so overgrown with grass, weeds, and trees that he could not actually see the river from the house. But he could see the pine-covered land beyond, rising up towards a craggy ridge.

As Chris wandered among the pines and blue gums, he pictured cottages set amongst these trees. He sat on a log and started to sketch the old farmhouse. It was a gracious building, with a bell-shaped Cape Dutch gable and six shuttered windows. He thought it would be good to try and repeat some of the design elements in the cottages. By contrast, the dormitory addition was a flat-roofed eyesore with small windows; a ten-year-old could have come up with a more aesthetic plan.

Next, Chris started on some ideas for a Khanya family cottage: a large open-plan living area incorporating a kitchen, a bedroom for the boys, and one for the girls, plus a separate room for the care-giver. For a cottagey feel, he added a fireplace. Even as he drew, he knew that what he had in mind was much too big and expensive. He was about to start on a smaller version, when he sensed that someone was watching him.

Chris looked around but saw no one. He shrugged it off and returned to his work. Thus far, his brief had been minimal but he thought he might have a more meaningful discussion with Wendy if he could put a few ideas on paper. His second sketch was a scaled-down version of the first, but, as he studied it, it became increasingly clear how tricky this assignment was going to be. Under normal conditions, a family of ten or twelve people would occupy a very significant home with multiple recreational spaces, bathrooms, etc. *How to create …*

This time, he knew he was not imagining it. He spun around and nearly fell off his perch when he saw a slender boy standing less than three feet behind him, intently studying the drawings.

"Hey, you gave me a shock," Chris muttered, gradually recovering his composure. "Do you always sneak up on people like this?"

No answer. He guessed the African boy to be in his early teens. He was at that lanky stage where children look more like marionettes than like real people. In the case of this boy, the impression was further accentuated by tennis shoes without laces, a shirt that was too small, and shorts that were too big; a piece of rope did duty as a belt. However, although he might have looked slightly comical from a distance, close to, the boy's face commanded immediate respect, with high cheekbones and eyes slanting upwards and outwards. Chris was reminded of photographs he had seen of young Masai warriors.

"I'm Chris."

The boy looked at him, his face inscrutable. Chris wondered whether he was deaf. The eyes moved from the sketchpad to Chris's face and back.

"What is your name?"

No answer. Chris shrugged and resumed his work. Wordlessly, the boy settled down on the log next to him.

After several minutes of silence the boy said, "Thabo. My name is Thabo."

"Pleased to meet you, Thabo."

"Why are you drawing houses?"

"I'm working on designs for cottages to be built here."

Thabo's quizzical expression compelled Chris to explain. "The people here think it would be nice if you and the other kids could live in smaller groups, like families, rather than all together in one big house, "

"I don't live here," Thabo said indignantly.

"Oh, I'm sorry; I had assumed you did. What brings you here, then?"

"My mother, she is sick, so she comes here, with the baby. But she is going to get better."

"I'm sure she will." Chris deliberated on the ethics of giving hope to a boy whose mother more than likely had AIDS. Was it best to be honest? He'd often thought that that people who advocated total honesty were emotionally lazy and brutal. Maybe he should not have said anything; losing a mother wasn't something to be trivialized. He forced himself to stop this train of thought and resumed his work.

Thabo appeared to lose interest. He broke a branch off the tree, stripped it, and drew patterns in the sand at his feet. After a while, Chris noticed that Thabo was in fact drawing house plans. He got down on his haunches and looked at what the boy had done.

"What's this?"

"Fireplace - in the middle, keeps everyone warm."

"And this ...?"

Thabo explained his plans. Chris listened carefully, then took out a second sketchbook from his rucksack and handed it to the boy with a spare pencil. Thabo started to draw.

Chris got up and walked amongst the trees to measure the size of the clearing with his strides. Next, he got out his cell phone and took pictures of the vacant land. He became aware that Thabo had stopped sketching and was watching him.

"What?"

"Your phone – it can take pictures?"

"Yes, see." He showed the boy what he had taken. For the first time, Thabo's face expressed emotion. He stroked the screen of the phone.

"My mother has a cell phone," he said quietly. "She only uses him once a month to call our people in the Transkei. That phone, he cannot do pictures."

Chris had a sudden thought. "I think I may have a spare phone like this one in my car. When I go down into Hout Bay later, I will see if I can get a new SIM card. If it works, would you like to have it?"

Now Thabo's face was a palate awash with emotions: disbelief, joy, fear of being disappointed. He broke into a grin and nodded his head vigorously.

They picked up their sketchpads and worked in companionable silence for the next twenty minutes, then compared notes and discussed the merits of their respective plans.

##

Julie concluded her call with the *Cape Times* reporter and decided to take a short cut through the kitchen on her way out. She was late for her next meeting but the delicious aroma of fresh-baked scones stopped her in her tracks. Then she saw Mama Mercy, a frozen statue at the kitchen sink, a plate and drying cloth in her hand, staring out of the window. Julie touched the older woman's shoulder.

"Mama Mercy, are you OK?"

She followed Mama Mercy's gaze to where Chris and Thabo sat, side by side. They appeared to be pouring over a sketchpad. Thabo tapped on the paper, as if to emphasize a point. Chris seemed to be listening intently.

Mama Mercy steadied herself on the edge of the sink and sighed. "That boy is hurting deep inside."

"I don't know. Thabo looks more content and happy to me than he has for quite some time."

Mercy turned to face her. "I'm talking about Chris," she said, and Julie heard a note of reproach in her voice.

"Look at him," she continued. "You are woman; a woman must see when a man is hurting."

Then she sighed, picked up two tea mugs and a plateful of scones, and made her way outside. She hadn't offered Julie a scone. In Mama Mercy's view, even angels needed the occasional rap over the knuckles to ensure that they kept their eyes open enough to see what was important.

##

A gnarled oak provided a sea of shade for the courtyard at the Mainstream coffee shop. Chris nursed his cappuccino and reviewed his sketches.

A tinkling doorbell made him look up and for one heart-stopping moment he thought his mother had stepped into the coffee shop. But of course it wasn't his mother, it was Wendy, wearing her sunglasses perched on top of her head exactly the way Chris's mother used to wear hers. Blowing a kiss to the manager, and stopping to greet various people as she passed, Wendy made her way towards the courtyard. Chris watched her. As she stepped into the light, he was reminded of women he'd seen on obscenely large yachts on the French Riviera: navy top, white cotton pants, a matching tailored jacket, professional-grade make-up. And yet she was one of the most down-to-earth people he knew.

"Sorry for being late." She sat down and placed her order. "Today's been crazy. My financial manager suspected corruption at one of our charities; very unpleasant." She gave Chris an account of the financial controls she'd put in place for every charity that was supported by the van Houten trust.

Chris said, "I bet the charities hate that."

"You'd be surprised. Often they have volunteers doing the books; they're trying their best and actually welcome help. Today was a case in point: we sat for three hours with the treasurer of this charity and came to the conclusion that he was completely out of his depth. I'm getting someone to coach him and I'm hugely relieved that it was not deliberate wrongdoing; helps to maintain one's faith in humanity."

The waiter brought Wendy's tea and a pastry, and she changed the subject to Chris's visit.

"So ... did you get a chance to look around the center? What do you think?"

For the next twenty minutes, Chris walked her through some of the sketches. Wendy asked questions and elaborated on her vision. She liked the idea of dotting the houses amongst the trees but kept coming back to the challenge of creating generic designs for replication elsewhere.

"We have to recognize that here at Khanya we have an exceptionally pretty setting. Elsewhere, one is likely to get less desirable land, often dry and flat, maybe next to a railway line. The cottages must have a village feel. We must avoid the feeling you get in the old townships with their matchbox houses."

"I know exactly what you mean. Maybe we could place them around a common central area. If the cottages were connected ... like this ... it would provide a completely sealed, safe area for small kids to play. That way, one person could supervise a lot of them."

"That's a great idea. And if there were some sort of communal seating area, the older kids could hang out there in the evenings."

Chris embellished his sketch, bringing the concept to life with a few lines.

"You're good!"

After the weeks of rejection, those words meant more to him than Wendy could ever have guessed.

He said, "And, do you know, I have found myself an apprentice. A young boy at the orphanage: Thabo. He's only about thirteen but he really seems to have a gift for drawing."

"Thabo? I thought that was the child they were all worried about because he doesn't play with the other children and doesn't talk to anyone."

"I don't know about that. It wouldn't surprise me, though; he's probably way ahead of the others in his interests. Have a look at this." He showed her some of the boy's sketches.

"Thabo made me realize that we'll never build anything affordable if we insist on the notion of rooms with separate functions. The rural huts of Africa simply contain one large communal room where people cook, eat, socialize and, at night-time, roll out their sleeping mats and go to bed. I'm looking to adapt this by designing one large common-purpose room, but providing a loft area for sleeping. "

"That certainly would get us away from those soulless dormitories. What it would mean is that when the little ones go to bed up in the loft they don't have to feel alone; the older kids could sit right beneath them at the kitchen table doing homework. I like it."

They discussed the matter for another ten minutes and agreed that Chris would prepare proper plans.

"How was Julie when you saw her?" Wendy asked.

"Seemed OK, though rather rushed and a little stressed. She was chewing out the wine merchant."

Wendy sighed. "That's our Julie, always the perfectionist. She's my godchild, you know. I love her to bits, but I do wish she would loosen up at times."

"I don't think she's at all enamored with the idea of the Toreros dancing at the gala."

Wendy leaned back in her chair. "That's an understatement. I must say, there were moments last night where I was also a little concerned, but," she raised her hands for dramatic effect, "where would we be if we never took any risks?"

There was something Chris wanted to know. He searched for a tactful way to broach the subject. "Julie mentioned Greg last night – Greg Louw. We got interrupted. What's the story between those two?"

"You know that Matt Baxter is Julie's stepfather and the managing director of Noble Enterprises?"

Chris nodded.

"Greg is Matt's right-hand man; he practically runs Noble Enterprises. He also happens to be Matt's nephew. I'm sure that partially explains his meteoric rise, but I'm told he is a very competent business executive."

"I see … but that does not explain his relationship with Julie."

"When Julie's father died, Greg sort of filled the void. He became Julie's big brother and mentor, the person she turned to for advice. I have at times been a little concerned that he is too domineering. Somewhere along the line, I think Greg has just assumed that he will marry Julie one day."

"And is Julie just going along with this? It doesn't sound like the independent-minded Julie I remember."

Wendy shrugged. "She had a tough time after her father's death, and Greg was there for her."

She flicked a few crumbs off the table and watched as a squirrel darted to pick them up. "I know Bridget is very concerned about the age gap. That's why she encouraged Julie to come to Cape Town, to get some perspective before rushing into marriage."

"Where is Greg?"

"He's in Johannesburg at the head office, but they see each other quite regularly. He has the company jet at his disposal and Matt actively encourages the relationship. Matt thinks of Greg as the son he never had and, much to Bridget's annoyance, is forever inventing excuses why Julie should come up to Johannesburg or Greg down here. They aren't formally engaged but, like I said, Greg Louw considers Julie to be his territory."

She nibbled at her pastry and wiped her hands on the napkin. Chris noticed how perfectly her nails had been painted – nothing garish, a pale red that matched her lipstick.

"I'm afraid the Khanya center has become a convenient hideaway for Julie, a halfway mark between university and the real world," she continued. "I think it would be good for her to spend some time overseas, do something else. But I'm just the godmother, I can't tell her anything."

Wendy motioned for the waiter to bring her fresh tea. She looked directly at Chris. "What about you, anyone special in your life?"

"No, I'm currently focused on finding a job." He hoped to kill off this train of conversation.

Wendy, however, was not to be dissuaded. "I'm surprised. I thought I heard somewhere that you had quite a reputation with the girls."

He shifted in his chair. "I don't know what you've heard, but I broke up with a girl just around the time of my finals. The situation was … difficult, and I didn't need that kind of stress and theatrics in my life."

"Why don't you tell me about it? At times, Cape Town can be such a village - I've heard various accounts, but I would like to hear your side of the story with Sandra Richter. That is who you are talking about, isn't it? Was she your girlfriend – or your fiancée'?"

Wendy sipped her tea, looking straight at him over the rim of the cup. "I know her mother, and from all accounts Sandra was devastated when you broke up."

In the short silence that followed, Chris noticed lipstick on her cup and for some reason it annoyed him, made him wonder if there was something hiding behind the mask of perfect make-up. He was tired of the Sandra affair, tired of his friends' stupid jokes, and tired of justifying his actions. He was tempted to simply get up and walk away. But then Wendy had always treated him with respect and she reminded him of his mother. If he couldn't trust her, whom could he trust?

As he began to speak, he let his mind go back to a winter's night six months earlier: his birthday. His friends had taken him on a pub-crawl and, fearing his father's disapproval at least as much as the police, he had abandoned his car and taken a taxi back to his apartment.

He teetered past the security desk to the elevators.

"Good evening, Mister Chris," the guard said. "Happy birthday!"

"Good evening …" Chris squinted to read the nametag, but it would not come into focus. He studied the toothy grin, the uniform that in some places was nearly as shiny as the shoes. The guard's only weapon was a two-way radio, the size of a brick.

"How … how d'ya know it's my birthday?"

"I'm not supposed to say, but there is a special surprise waiting for you upstairs." The guard winked and displayed even more tobacco-stained teeth.

Chris wished the fog would clear. His eyes felt as dry and scratchy as his throat, and his head hurt. He was already regretting the last few down-downs and desperately needed to pee. The guard guided him to the elevator.

When he finally managed to unlock his apartment door, his senses were overwhelmed by the thick perfume of lavender and incense. Burning candles covered every available surface of his austere bachelor flat. Some inner recesses of his alcohol-drenched brain noticed that there were even candles on his draughtsman's table, right next to a project he'd been working on. He was too drunk to react.

"Bloody hell, who's died?"

"Surprise!" A blonde girl, barefoot, in tight black pants and a satiny green top, rose from the couch. "You're very late," she reproached him, pouting. "Nearly missed your own birthday party."

Chris was stunned. He swayed on his feet, desperately trying to place the face. She came towards him, took his hands. Her eyes were a deep green, the same color as her top. Eyes like that, not to mention the beautiful breasts inches away from his chest ... surely he would have remembered if he'd met her before? Finally he said, "Do I know you? How ... how'd ya get in?"

"You ask too many questions." She pulled him down on to the couch. Her hands felt soft and cool as she stroked his arms, kissed his neck, and ran her hands through his hair. She wore an expensive perfume and her hair reflected the glow of the candlelight. Out of the corner of his eye, Chris noticed a packet of condoms peering out of her purse, which sat next to a pair of champagne glasses on the coffee table. This girl's a pro, he thought, and wondered which of his friends had laid on a hooker for his birthday.

When Chris finally fell silent, Wendy asked quietly, "So, what happened next?"

Chris sighed. "Of course, it turns out she was not a hooker at all, but rather a Social Sciences student with a serious crush on me. In fact, she'd been stalking me, watching all my swimming competitions and soccer matches. She found out where I lived and it was easy enough to sweet-talk the security guard into letting her into my apartment.

"I don't deny that I felt flattered – I felt a bit like a pop star, having a girl break into my room, throwing herself at me." He cast down his eyes.

"Anyway, I agreed to see her again and we went on a couple of dates. Next thing, about a month later, I get a rare call from my father. Sandra's old man, Bob Richter, had cornered him at the golf club and told him that we were secretly engaged and going to get married as soon as I graduated. Bob Richter wanted to discuss how the two dads could work together to provide a 'suitable' house for the young love birds: 'Nothing too elaborate, but Sandra does need a stable for her horse, you know.'"

Wendy shook her head. "I can just imagine what your father, the ultimate self-made man, had to say to that. I guess he was also upset to hear from someone else that his only son was 'engaged'." She made quotation marks in the air with her fingers.

"He was mainly condescending," Chris replied. "I distinctly remember him saying that I should 'keep my penis in my pants and concentrate on getting a degree'. Anyway, next day Sandra is on campus flashing around the biggest damn diamond engagement ring you've ever seen. Her mother had lent it to her until I could 'buy an appropriate one'. " He looked at her. "I'm telling you, Wendy, that whole family is bonkers, stark raving mad. The parents have indulged Sandra for so long that she cannot tell reality from fantasy anymore. What she wants, she gets. "

Wendy nodded. "I can well believe it. I was actually invited to her sweet sixteen party, for which the Richters had hired the ballroom at the Mount Nelson. It was quite a spectacle. Most of us there agreed that 'sweet sixteens' are amongst the American exports we can well do without."

"My friends thought the whole situation was hilarious. I was the laughing stock of the entire campus. I tried, in the most gentle way possible, to break up with her. She became completely hysterical. Next day, her father came by my place. Guess what he wanted?"

"What?"

"He started out pleasant enough. Said he had a little proposition for me. He would give me a house and a job at a ridiculous salary in his property development company if I married his daughter after graduation."

"What did you say?"

"I said nothing – I was speechless; so he offered to up the salary even further. Eventually, I said I'd think about it, just to get rid of him."

"I'm not surprised. Bob Richter has dealt with local councils and regional authorities for years. He's used to paying whatever it takes to get what he wants. That's how he made his fortune."

"That evening I sat down and thought about his proposition. The more I thought about it, the angrier I got. Eventually, I wrote him a letter in which I firmly rejected his offer and probably said more about his skills as a parent, and as a pimp, than I should have."

"Ah, not a very good idea. I hate to tell you, but this might explain why you are having trouble finding a job. Bob Richter is very influential in the building industry."

Chris scratched his chin. "I hadn't thought about that. You really think he has that kind of clout?"

"Afraid so. Anyway, what happened next?"

"They told the entire world what a complete bastard I was before Sandra went on an extended trip to Europe with her mother. She's a nice girl, but completely screwed up. I do sometimes wonder whether I could have helped her if ..."

Wendy's cell phone rang and gave them both a start. She flipped it open. "Hi ... yes, yes ... no, I have no idea where Desmond might be. What's the problem? I see. Chris is here with me, maybe he can help; just a minute."

She covered the phone. "It's Julie. They've got the workmen there to construct the stage but it's much smaller than planned. She needs to know whether it can work for the Toreros." She looked at her watch. "The work crew is getting ready to knock off, so she needs to know whether to call them back for tomorrow or whether you guys can live with it as is."

"Tell her I'll be there in ten minutes."

"He'll be there in fifteen minutes," Wendy said into the phone. "Yep, sure it will be all right. The guys will simply have to improvise ... Bye."

Chris got up. "Can you do me favor? I still have Sandra's old cell phone. I promised it to Thabo. Could you give it to him when you go up to Khanya? I don't want to disappoint him."

"Sure, but don't you have to give it back to Sandra?"

"Believe me, I tried," he said with a rueful smile, "and she told me exactly where to shove it."

He handed her a sleek camera-phone and hurried to his car.

##

Chapter 6: "Handyman"

Wednesday evening

Bridget Noble-Baxter sat on the verandah of the Camps Bay Hotel and sipped a gin and tonic. She felt pleased with herself. It had been a good day, strengthening her belief that she had done the right thing to leave Johannesburg and come down to Cape Town. Lunch with Julie had been better than expected; Julie had even consulted her mother on a number of issues relating to the gala. They had reviewed a speech (which needed shortening); had discussed the florist who wanted to do blatant advertising; and worked through the protocol for dealing with dignitaries. In a small way, it made Bridget feel that she still had what it took to be an executive.

After lunch, she had spent a most agreeable afternoon shopping, buying, among other things, a cream outfit to wear to the gala. She then decided to give the chauffeur the rest of the day off, and, on the spur of the moment, had driven herself to the Camps Bay Hotel to meet an old lawyer friend for cocktails.

Bridget loved the ambience of the hotel: waiters in starched uniforms, white wicker chairs on a deck well above the crowd, sweeping views of palms and the beach beyond. Even at six o'clock, the sun was still strong and Bridget was pleased for the excuse to keep her sunglasses on – her friend had been suitably complimentary about her appearance.

"Bridget, if you want to get back in the saddle at Noble Enterprises, there's nothing stopping you from marching in and taking charge. You and Julie, between you, have the majority shareholding."

"I know; so much has changed, though. The company has grown, there are lots of new faces. And then there are so many new product lines; and everything is being done with computers ... "

"There you go, doubting yourself again." He wagged his finger. "The Bridget I know climbs in first and asks questions later."

"You're right. If I think back to when we started ..." She shook her head and gazed over the ocean. "We were so naïve, but we did it, we learned fast. I just really need to figure out how to find that balance – to have the excitement of the business, but also time to spend with Matt. There are still so many places I want to see. Have you ever been to the Okavango Delta?"

They chatted about their favorite travel destinations and watched as, one by one, the sun worshippers packed up their things, the beach volleyball groups took down their nets, and mothers admonished their kids about sandy feet in the car.

Bridget noticed a striking-looking couple at a table near them. With a subtle gesture, she pointed them out to her friend. The woman had bleached hair and pale, almost translucent skin. She wore a black cocktail dress and high heels. Her partner was the exact opposite: dark skin and a white suit. Even from a distance, Bridget could tell that his silk shirt was not off the peg.

"*Ebony and Ivory*," the lawyer commented. "The new South Africa."

The man in the white suit leaned back and held up his cell phone to take a photo of his companion. She smiled broadly and Bridget marveled at the brightness of her red lipstick. Then, without warning, the man swiveled in his chair and took a photo of Bridget and her companion. Bridget looked away quickly – she imagined that his action implied he thought she had been rude to stare at him and his girlfriend, and she agreed that it might certainly seem that way.

After her friend had escorted her to her car, Bridget decided to take the scenic route home. She was in no hurry and, after the heat of the day, decided it would be nice to drive along the ocean. The road had been hewn into the mountainside, with a steep drop to the crashing waves below. The sun was low over the sea now; its reflection bathed the cliff face on her left in warm shades of brown and orange. In some places, gnarled trees grew out of crevices in the side of the mountain. As she drove, she marveled at the tenacity of nature, the way those trees survived, battered by wind, with little soil, and with what moisture they had coming mainly from the fog. Bridget lowered the car window and slowed down to inhale deeply and listen to the sounds of the ocean. A fishing trawler, heavily laden, made slow progress along the coast, a squabbling flock of seagulls in its wake. They could be heard even above the noise of Atlantic Ocean breakers crashing against the shoreline.

She glanced in the rear-view mirror and was startled to notice a vehicle right on her tail: a large black SUV with tinted windows.

"Oh, get a life," she said out loud. It was infuriating that commuters used this single-lane scenic route. They had, of course, seen it all a thousand times before and just wanted to get home fast. She moved as close to the rock face as she could, just in case the vehicle behind was foolish enough to overtake on this winding road. Other than that, she tried to ignore the SUV and focus on the road ahead and the splendid scenery.

Bridget passed a lay-by where a car had pulled off the road and a pair of lovers sat on a low wall. The man had his arm protectively around the woman's shoulder. They held champagne glasses and gazed at a flock of birds silhouetted against the sun. Bridget tapped the horn of her car and waved. The couple raised their glasses, acknowledging her greeting. She wondered whether she could possibly persuade Matt to join her for a few days. It would do him good to unwind; why shouldn't they too spend time toasting the sunset with a bottle of champagne?

The SUV driver honked his horn; it was not merely a tap, but a howl of impatience.

It was no use – the spell of the fading light, the lovers, and the ocean was broken.

"Well, if it's speed you want ..." Bridget gripped the steering wheel and put her foot down on the gas pedal. The plentiful horses under the hood jumped into action; the road curved sharply, and the rock face on her left was dangerously close, but Bridget was determined to shake off the pesky SUV. She felt the thrill of her vehicle's power and road handling as the Mercedes raced along the steadily climbing road. As she approached a blind corner, she prayed silently that there would not be any cyclists on this narrow stretch.

When Bridget stole a glance in the rear-view mirror, she was surprised and irritated to see that the SUV had stayed right on her tail. Her annoyance gave way to anxiety as her mind flashed to various newspaper reports of road-rage incidents. In one particularly gruesome incident, a woman had been beaten to death with a hockey stick. *Where was her cell phone?* She was now glancing in the mirror repeatedly to try and get a look at the driver. *What sort of a person was doing this? Was he or she alone?* But the tinted windows made these hard questions to answer - she could not even see if there was a passenger in the car.

The road opened up into a long, straight stretch, and the SUV pulled out to overtake.

"Maniac!" Bridget took her foot off the gas pedal and squeezed as close to the rock face as she could to let the SUV pass. She glanced over to look at the driver, but could see nothing. The car appeared like some driverless automaton - a predatory hulk of metal.

Then suddenly the SUV swerved and hit the side of the Mercedes. A violent shudder ran through the vehicle and Bridget fought for control as her car veered on to the dirt shoulder, kicked up dust, and threatened to plow into the wall of rock. She was numb with shock and fright, her entire being focused on a single imperative: *keep the steering wheel straight.* The shiny skin of the Mercedes came within inches of the solid rock. As if in slow motion, Bridget observed the dry branches of scraggly trees hungrily reaching out to inflict damage. She wrestled the car back on to the road.

There was no time to recover. With a thud, the SUV hit her again. The jolt was so strong that Bridget nearly let go of the steering wheel. Pain shot up her leg as the driver's door got battered. *Why was this happening? Why, why, why?* She felt nauseous; out of the corner of her eye, she could see the menacing black hulk right next to her, coming at her for the third time. Bridget had the presence of mind to slam on the brakes with full force. She ignored the pain in her leg and just kept the foot on the brake – hard. Her body strained against the seat belt and she heard the tires screech like a demented animal. The Mercedes swerved and its left tires hit the dirt shoulder again; then there was a sickening crunch as rock connected with the car's silver sheath and tore into it. The hungry branches got their way, gleefully scratching the side of the car and ripping off the mirror as though it were a doll's head. Bridget fought with all her strength and managed to stop the car in a cloud of dust and dirt. When she looked up, the SUV was speeding away round a corner.

She was aware of her own labored breathing, the pain of the seat belt across her chest. Some part of her brain registered that she could not remain where she was – any car coming round the bend behind her was likely to pile into the back of the Mercedes. The engine was still running. In a trance, she inched the damaged car forward a few hundred meters to a deserted picnic spot, where she pulled off the road.

Numb with shock and disbelief, she looked at her hands. They appeared to be welded to the steering wheel and she surveyed them dispassionately, as if they were foreign objects. She noticed the brown spots on the once-immaculate skin. *When had her hands lost their youth?* she wondered. After a minute - or was it ten? She'd lost track of time - Bridget made a conscious effort to unclasp her hands from the steering wheel.

##

While Bridget was having cocktails in Camps Bay, Chris was driving up the hill towards the Groot Constantia winery. Vineyards stretched as far as the eye could see on either side of the road. There were magnificent rose bushes at the end of every row of vines and their scent hung in the air.

Even though he had been to the estate many times before, the architect in Chris still derived quiet satisfaction from the sight of the winery's manor house. It was classic Cape Dutch – simple, gracious, beautifully proportioned. He knew from previous visits that the walls of the building were a foot thick and all the wood was solid teak – imported from Indonesia in the heyday of Dutch colonial rule.

He parked his car and glanced at the view. A southeasterly wind had swept the air clean and the early-evening sun, like some giant Midas, spread a veneer of golden warmth over the Cape Flats. He could see all the way to the Hottentots Holland mountains in the east: due south was the Indian Ocean, where the breaking waves looked like white lace on a gray skirt.

Chris walked past the slave bell to the function hall, a converted wine cellar behind the manor. It was cool inside due to the thick stonewalls, clay tile floors, and shuttered windows. His eyes took a moment to adjust to the dimly lit room with its cavernous cathedral ceiling. He nearly bumped into one of the round tables that had already been set up by the catering company. A number of oak vats had been retained on one side of the hall and the unmistakable aroma of fermenting wine filled the air. At the far end of the cellar, he spotted Julie, standing on a makeshift stage. He thought that she looked small and vulnerable, surrounded as she was by a gang of burly workmen.

Chris was gratified to see the relief on Julie's face when he joined her. She introduced him to the foreman and said, "I'm not sure that this is going to work. What do you think?"

Chris paced the width of the stage and peered into the distant darkness of the cellar. "It's a great venue but people at those far tables are going to have a hard time seeing the stage. Is there any particular reason why the stage is at this end?"

The foreman held out a dog-eared roll of paper for his inspection. "That's the way it was laid out on the plan," he said, sounding defensive.

"What about the electrics? Where will you get power for the stage lights and sound system from?"

"They don't have heavy current here, so we've got to use a generator. We can put the power wherever you want it."

Chris spread the plan on the windowsill and took out a pencil. He turned to Julie. "The size of the stage is not the main problem. Even though it's a bit small, we could make do. But I'm worried that people at the back won't be able to see. Now, if the hall is only going to be half full ... "

"It's sold out," she interjected. "We have people on a waiting list. Ideally, we'd try and squeeze in a few more tables."

"Great," Chris muttered. "Well, in that case, I suggest we bring the stage into the middle of the cellar." Quickly, he sketched his ideas. "It will give you a bit of extra space for more tables and give everyone pretty good visibility."

"How will the Toreros access the stage?" Julie asked.

"Through the audience. We've done that before, it works well. Just need to clear a path here," he indicated on the plan, "and build a ramp for Bull to come in on his bike."

The foreman was incredulous. "Someone's going to ride through the audience and on to this stage on a motorbike?"

"Yeah. Didn't anyone tell you?"

"Cool, but the stage was not designed for that sort of weight. We'd better stick a few extra supports under it."

Chris spent the next twenty minutes discussing the details of the revised layout with the foreman and his team. He designated the exact location for the light and sound controls, for the stage lights, and where the mobile generator was to be parked.

The foreman looked at his watch. "OK, boss. We've got the plan. Me and the boys will be back tomorrow. We've got another job lined up in the morning, but we'll come and shift this lot in the afternoon."

Despite the gloomy light, Chris noted the hint of panic that stole across Julie's face. He turned to the foreman. "We'd really like to see the stage moved tonight – any chance of making that happen? I've got a crate of beers in the back of my car. We could break those out as soon as you're done."

The foreman looked unconvinced. "It's been a long day, man. The boys are tired."

Chris glanced at Julie. "The man's got a point. Do you think we can sweeten it with a hundred rand overtime for each of the guys?"

"Yes, of course; that should be fine. We really appreciate all you're doing for us." She smiled at the foreman.

"OK, then," he said, and walked over to his crew. They were evidently satisfied with the deal and set about dismantling and moving the stage.

Julie blew out a deep breath, touched Chris's arm. "Thank you," she said. "That was close. I don't think I would have slept a wink tonight if the stage hadn't been set up."

Her touch was light and cool and he was disappointed when she drew her hand away. He allowed himself a brief fantasy moment, picturing Julie tossing and turning amidst her crumpled sheets. How he wished he could be there, comfort her, help her relax ...

"You just happen to have a whole load of beers in your car?" she whispered. *"How come? I'm beginning to wonder about the way you earn your living."*

"I thought you had that all figured out," Chris quipped. "When I'm not selling booze from my mobile *shebeen* I sell my body to sex-starved women."

Julie's expression told him that she was considering whether there might be some truth in this.

"God, woman! Don't you have any sense of humor? I don't have a crate of beer in my car; I don't even have a single *dumpie* or can."

"Then what ... ?"

"You're going to race down to the bottle store and get us a crate of beer whilst I help the guys with the stage. Do you have enough money?" He took out his wallet.

"Yes, yes. Don't worry; I've got my credit card."

Just as well, Chris thought, looking wistfully into his very lean wallet.

"I'll be back in about twenty minutes."

It was dark by the time Chris and Julie watched the workmen drive off in their dilapidated truck. The vehicle looked as tipsy as its occupants. It tilted to the left, one headlight pointed at a crazy angle towards the stars, and gray fumes spluttered from the exhaust. Three of the men were squeezed into the cab and two squatted on the open flatbed.

They cheerily waved their beer bottles as the truck trundled off into the darkness.

Chris shut the solid double doors and watched as Julie locked them. Aware that she would be gone in a few minutes, he plucked up his courage. "I'm starving," he said. "Do you want to go and find something to eat?"

In the dark, Chris could not make out her expression. She hesitated. "I'm pretty tired, I thought I might just … "

"I'm not asking you to go party, or on a date. I'm just suggesting we grab a pizza or pasta or something. You've got to eat."

"OK, then. You're right – I am actually quite hungry. Where do you want to go?" She fished her car keys out of her handbag.

"Marco's does a great pizza. Let's go in my car, we can pick yours up on the way back."

A fog had crept up the valley, obscuring the buildings and distant city lights behind shifting shrouds of deep gray. There was no one about, and no sound other than the crunching of their footsteps on gravel as they made their way through the darkness to Chris's car. Julie shivered and Chris wanted to put his arm around her shoulders, but he was scared that she might misinterpret the gesture.

He rummaged through the trunk of his car to find a sweater. She accepted it gratefully. "The boot of your car is a real Mary Poppins' bag," she said, laughing.

"Please don't equate me with Mary Poppins in front of any of my friends. They'd never let me live it down. I prefer to think it's a product of my Boy Scout training."

She looked at him without comprehension.

"You know: '*Be prepared*'."

Ten minutes later, Chris was ushering Julie into the familiar surroundings of Marco's. The restaurant was full, and Marco, as usual, was multi-tasking: directing the pizza chefs, pouring wine, and finding time to talk to his customers. His forehead glistened with perspiration and every once in a while he twirled the edges of his impressive moustache with his fingers.

"Christopher, my friend! Where have you been? It has been too long." He clasped Chris's hand and shook it. "Why did you not call? I would have kept the special table for you."

Chris was grateful for the warm welcome and before he could even introduce Julie, Marco turned his full charm on her. He welcomed her effusively and kissed her hand.

"Never mind, for such a *bambolina*, and, of course for Chris, I always have a special table."

They ordered a carafe of house red and agreed to share a Four Seasons pizza.

Julie looked around the room, taking in the straw-covered Chianti bottles, the plastic grapes, the yellowed postcards. "You're obviously a regular here," she said. "It's cozy. Is this part of the standard seduction routine?" Her face was inscrutable and he suspected that the question was asked only half-jokingly.

"No, I used to come here with my parents. It was a bit of a ritual for us. We would come here for dinner most Friday nights. See those postcards decorating the counter? I swear they've all been there for the last fifteen years."

Julie looked a bit wistful. "We rarely went out as a family. My parents were building up their own business ..." She looked away, lost in memories. Again, Chris wondered what had happened to his impish childhood friend. Where was she in this contained and reserved woman? But he was convinced that the Julie he remembered hadn't really gone away - she just needed liberating, and he wanted to be the one to do it.

He said, "I have to qualify that, most Fridays it was just me and my mother. My father would invariably be held up at the hospital and arrive as we were finishing our meal. Marco was funny. He always gave my father a hard time, threatening to run off with my mother if he left her waiting again."

At the counter, Marco was handing pizza dough to two young girls. "Did you ever do that as a kid?" Chris asked.

"Do what?"

"I used to make all kinds of things out of pizza dough: alligators, hippos, birds. Marco baked them in the pizza oven for me."

For a while they watched the two little girls, as, faces furrowed with concentration, they worked their dough. The girls wore matching tartan dresses and red ribbons in their hair. The younger girl had smudges of flour on her dress, her ribbon was coming undone, and a few strands of blonde hair fell over her face. She blew them away and watched as her older sister created an elaborate heart shape from braided rolls of pizza dough.

"Do you wish you'd had a brother or a sister?" Chris asked.

She looked at him, puzzled, contemplating the question. "I'm not sure. It's one of those things you can't do anything about, so it's pointless to dwell on it."

"That's a very existential view. If we only ever dwelled on things that we could 'do something about', life would be pretty narrow, don't you think? Great philosophers have spent endless time thinking about the universe, the stars, and man's purpose here on earth. Not much anyone can do about it, but it's still intriguing. Think of how much wonderful poetry has been written by people who were in love, with no hope of their love being returned. You might say that's pointless, but I don't think so."

Julie took her time to reply. She played with a strand of her hair, and looked at the two little girls, appearing to think about what he'd said. He liked this about her, and it struck him how different she was from Sandra, who'd barely let him finish a sentence.

Eventually, she turned to him. "I think you misunderstand me on purpose. What I meant is that I never consciously missed a sibling when I was a child. For as long as I can remember, I felt like an equal partner in our family. When my father died ..." she paused. "I suppose I really could have used a brother or sister then."

Her eyes filled with tears which reflected the candlelight. Chris did not trust himself to say anything but instead reached across the table and took her hand. For a while, neither of them said anything. Then Julie asked, "What about you?"

"Well, I had Desmond. He came pretty close to being a brother; in fact, he often came here to dinner with us." Chris wanted to lighten the mood. "One good thing about my father usually being late was that Desmond, my mother, and I could talk about dancing as much as we liked."

"Why didn't you take it up as a profession? Wendy told me that both you and Desmond were pretty amazing dancers when you were in your teens. "

The pizza arrived. It tasted every bit as good as Chris remembered.

They ate in silence for a while, until, glancing up, Chris noticed that Julie had a strand of cheese on her chin. He leaned across the table and wiped it off. "Glad to see you're enjoying it."

"Are you telling me that I'm eating like a pig? I must say, this was a good idea. I didn't realize how hungry I was." She smiled. "What? What are you looking at? More cheese on my face?" She wiped her face with a napkin.

"No, it's just ..."

"What?"

"I like to see the dimples when you smile. It reminds me of ... it brings back lots of memories."

He lifted another slice of pizza on to her plate, grateful that she did not probe for specific details of his memories, or, more precisely, the confused and rapturous fantasies of a fourteen-year-old.

They sipped their wine and watched in silence as one of Marco's assistants took the children's dough creations out of the oven and placed them on red paper plates. The two little girls rushed to the counter and picked them up. The older girl proudly held the baked heart aloft and presented it to her mother with a flourish. The younger sister, three steps behind, was upset to find that her sister had pre-empted her and Chris anticipated a flood of tears. Instead, the child stood quite still, then turned and veered towards their table. She approached shyly, her face a picture of concentration, and lifted the paper plate, with its lump of pizza dough, towards Julie.

Julie leaned forward. "What a pretty heart. Did you make that all by yourself?"

The girl smiled and thrust the plate at her.

"For me? Oh, that's so sweet of you." As the girl moved forward, however, the plate tilted precariously. Chris saw Julie reach out but, before she could accept the plate, the "heart" slid off, fell to the floor, and broke into two pieces. The little face looked utterly bewildered, then slowly crumpled. The girl's eyes filled with tears.

"Don't cry, sweetie." Julie knelt down, carefully picked up the pieces, then lifted the girl on to her lap.

"Come, I'm sure we can fix it. Chris, see if you can go find us some tomato sauce."

The girl wiped her tears and watched intently as Julie scraped melted cheese off her pizza and used it to stick the two heart pieces back together. Chris observed them from the counter. He was suddenly reminded of a time when he had fallen off his bicycle and his mother had cleaned and bandaged the scrape on his knee. He could see his mother's face in his mind, clearer than he had seen it for a long time. With bitterness, he thought that many of his good childhood memories lay buried under the ever-present memories of *that day* – the day that turned into the longest night. He felt the familiar black wave of anger. He closed his eyes and steadied himself against the counter. *Breathe ... breathe ...*

Back at the table, Julie and the little girl each dipped a finger in tomato sauce and spread the gooey substance over the entire heart. The crack became all but invisible. They licked their fingers in unison.

"There, good as new!" The child gave Julie a hug and happily rejoined her family.

A short while later, Chris felt a draft as the door opened and Marco came out from behind the counter to meet the latest guest.

"Dr. Jacques!" Marco exclaimed. "This is such a pleasant surprise!"

Chris spun around in his seat and watched, dumbfounded, as Marco clasped the newcomer's hands in his. Then he heard the familiar sound of his father's voice.

"Hello, Marco, good to see you. Looks like winter is coming early."

Chris felt a panic that he knew was irrational. But he was just beginning to reconnect with Julie and was petrified that an interrogating parent would spook her.

"We should probably go," he said.

She looked at him in surprise and choked on her last bite of pizza.

It was too late, anyway. Julie had now seen his father herself.

"You naughty man," Marco was saying, waving an admonishing finger. "You are late again. Some things never change." He took a surprised-looking Dr. Jacques du Toit by the arm and led him firmly towards Chris and Julie's table.

"Chris, why do you not tell me that your papa is coming to join you?"

"Hi, Dad." He stood up and shook his father's hand. Marco brought another chair and excused himself to attend to another group of guests.

Dr. du Toit looked from one to the other. He ran his hand through his hair and made no move to take off his coat or to sit down. Quietly, he said, "This is rather awkward; Marco just assumed ..."

"We were about to ..." Chris began, but Julie quickly interjected, "About to have coffee. Please do join us." She smiled and held out her hand, "I'm Julie Noble, you probably won't remember me but I used to take dancing lessons with your wife many years ago."

He shook her hand and both men sat down.

"Please, call me Jacques."

"We were just talking about you," Julie said, and Chris struggled to hide his surprise.

"Were you really?"

"Chris was telling me about the great times he had coming here with you, his mother, and Desmond."

"Ah, yes. Marco's has always been an important place for our family."

Chris started to worry that Julie would go on and say something about his father regularly being late. "You and Julie have something in common, Dad," he chimed in quickly.

"What's that?" Jacques asked.

"She fixes broken hearts, just like you."

"Are you in the medical field, then?"

Julie laughed and showed him the doughy, sauce-covered blob.

They ordered coffees – no wine for the doctor since he was on call - and Marco insisted that he would surprise Dr. Jacques with a special dish.

"So, you are Harry and Bridget Noble's daughter," Jacques said. "I knew your father well. How is your mother?"

Julie gave a non-committal answer. Chris could not help but feel a rising irritation as his father continued to quiz Julie about her school, her studies, and her work.

"Dad, you sound like the Spanish Inquisition ..."

Both Julie and his father looked at him in surprise.

"I'm just interested," the doctor said.

"And I really don't mind in the least," Julie added. Chris shrugged, feeling left out and resentful as the two of them resumed a conversation about AIDS prevention. He allowed his mind to wander.

He snapped back to attention, however, when Julie asked spontaneously, "Can I persuade you to come to the AIDS gala?"

As Chris rolled his eyes at her behind his father's back, Jacques hesitated. "It's not really my kind of ..." he began.

"Oh, come on. It'll be fun. And you can see Chris dancing."

"Chris is dancing?" Jacques looked at his son. "You didn't tell me you were back into dancing. I thought you were looking for a proper job."

"I was ... I mean, I am." Chris cursed himself for being so defensive. "This is just a one-off gig to help Desmond out. I only got roped in a couple of days ago."

His father said he would consult his diary and let them know.

Just then, Julie's cell phone rang. She looked at the screen. "It's my mother. I don't mean to be rude, but I think I should take this."

"Go right ahead, we're used to it," Chris said with a sideway glance at his father. Dr. du Toit ignored him and smiled at Julie, nodding his head in understanding.

"Hello, Mother."

"What? Hold on ... Slow down, Mother ... Are you sure? Yes, yes ... OK, I'll be right over. No ... no, don't worry. It's OK. I'll be there in ten minutes, just wait for me."

Chris felt a growing sense of foreboding.

"It's my mother. She's been in some sort of accident. She insists that someone tried to run her off the road."

"That sounds bizarre," Chris said. "Were they trying to hijack her car?"

"No, no. It really doesn't make sense but she thinks they just wanted to scare her. Look, I'm sorry, but I'd better go across and see her. She's at home."

"I'll take you," Chris said.

"I can get a taxi, really."

"Don't be silly. I'll take you." Chris reached for his jacket and gestured for Marco to bring the bill.

"Sorry, Dad. Hope you don't mind."

"Of course not. Go now. I'll take care of the bill."

Chris and Julie hurried out into the darkness.

The restaurant was busy and it was twenty minutes before Marco had a chance to stop by and see how Dr. Jacques was getting on with his meal. He found the special Veal *Limone* untouched and his guest lost in thought, staring into the night outside the window.

Marco touched the doctor's arm. "Is everything OK?"

Jacques seemed to surface from a far-away place. He turned to face him. "Do you remember when I first used to come here with Danielle?"

"But of course. You were amongst my very first customers."

"I was still an intern; we could barely afford to share a pizza. You always gave us each a free glass of wine."

"Ha, that was from my marketing budget. Your *bella donna*, she was very good for my business. Other people came in just to be near her. She had … how do you say? She had an aura, a positive spirit that attracted other people."

"I proposed to her right over there, at the small table next to the fireplace."

"I remember. God gave you a beautiful, beautiful wife. Her smile could light up a dark winter's day." Marco pulled out the chair which Julie had vacated and motioned for a waiter to bring two glasses; he proceeded to fill these from the carafe that Chris and Julie had left.

The two men drank quietly. "We were so happy." Jacques' voice was flat when he added, "God might have given me a beautiful wife, but he took her away so soon, without warning. It would have been less painful if I'd never known her."

"You don't mean that," Marco reprimanded gently. "Many people never know one day of the happiness that you had in your hands for a number of years." After a pause he continued, "You also have a wonderful, wonderful son. Nobody has taken him away from you."

"I shouldn't be drinking." Jacques looked at his pager. "I might get a call ..."

"Always the same with you: work, work, work. Do you really think the hospital will grind to a halt if you turn that thing off for one evening?"

The two men looked at each other. Marco was afraid he had overstepped the mark.

Eventually, Jacques reached for the carafe and refilled their glasses. "You're right. Every man has the right to get drunk once in a while." Then he asked very quietly, "Do you know what day it is today?"

Marco shook his head.

"Today is my twenty-fifth wedding anniversary."

They lifted their glasses in a mute salute. Marco pretended not to see the moisture in the other man's eyes. He pulled out a large handkerchief and blew his nose noisily.

##

Chris barely had time to take in the imposing façade of the Noble mansion as Julie hurried up the front steps. His brief impression was of a White House imitation. Julie unlocked the door and Chris heard the buzz of an alarm system starting its countdown. She flipped open a panel with an array of flashing green lights and muttered, "Seven-oh-oh-seven" as she pressed the keypad. The buzzing stopped.

Chris followed her down a wide passage. He got a brief glimpse of the formal lounge with over-sized leather furniture and striking oil paintings. Then they passed the dining room with its huge table and enormous crystal chandelier. Chris found such a vast, dimly lit, and silent house rather creepy. It felt like an empty luxury hotel. Their feet made no sound on the thick carpet.

They found Bridget in the family room, propped up on a sofa. She had one leg raised on a cushion with a drying cloth wrapped around it. *Clearly this is where people actually live,* Chris thought as he took in the warm colors, the TV, and framed family photographs.

"Mother, what happened? Are you OK?" Julie rushed to her mother's side, took the older woman's hands, and sat on the edge of the sofa.

Bridget put on a smile. "I'm all in one piece, I checked; no broken bones, mainly bruises. But it was scary, very, very scary; I still can't understand it. He tried to ram me off the road."

"Where did this happen?"

"On the coastal road; I came back from Camps Bay via the long route – I just wanted to enjoy the sunset ..." Chris noted the tremor in her voice.

"And after this ... this incident, you drove here all by yourself? You should have called me immediately, or the police, or someone."

"I ... I didn't know what to think. I just wanted to get home." For the first time, she seemed to notice Chris in the doorway. "Oh, I'm so sorry to have dragged you away ..." She struggled to sit up, patted back her hair, and extended a hand. Julie introduced them.

"You are Danielle and Jacques' boy; I remember you. What was that show you all danced in together?" She pressed her fingers against her temples, "*Arggh*, my memory; yes, I remember: St. George and the dragon. You were so cute. You look just like your father."

Chris got a whiff of gin and noticed the half-empty glass next to her. "But you have your mother's smile. She was a dear, dear friend of mine. Julie, why didn't you tell me ..."?

"Mother, not now." Julie picked up a small plastic bottle from the coffee table and read the label. "Vicodin? Where did you get these? How many have you taken?"

"Only one; they help me sleep. My doctor prescribed them." Bridget snatched away the bottle and put it into her handbag, doing up the zip with a gesture of defiance.

Chris saw Julie hold her breath as the bottle disappeared from sight; she appeared conflicted as to whether she should tackle the drug issue now or later. He was grateful when she let it drop, deciding instead to focus on the road incident.

"How come you were driving, anyway? You know you're not supposed to. Where was the driver? " Chris wondered what she meant. Then he noticed Julie's look of disapproval as Bridget drained her glass of gin.

"Be a darling, Chris, and pour me another. There's a bottle in the kitchen."

He was not even out of the room before they started to argue. When he came back, he heard Julie say, "This is a mess. I don't know if we should call the police now, or leave it till morning." She was twisting a strand of hair around her finger. "We don't know if this was random or you were targeted deliberately; I'm going to call Greg, he'll know what to do."

Bridget closed her eyes and lay back. "Do what you like."

Julie remained seated, undecided.

Chris handed Bridget the glass. "I'm so sorry that you had such an awful experience. Did you get a look at the person trying to run you off the road?"

She shook her head. "The sun was low and it was one of those SUVs with tinted windows."

"Why don't you tell us everything that you *do* remember?"

She struggled into a more upright position and Chris propped a cushion behind her back. He pulled up a chair and listened carefully as Bridget described the whole sequence of events, starting from the time she gave the chauffeur the rest of the day off and met with her lawyer friend at the Camps Bay Hotel. When Julie tried to interrupt, he gently stopped her, wanting to hear Bridget's full story, right up to the point where she reached the picnic spot to regain her composure before driving home.

"I don't suppose you got to see the license plate?"

She shook her head, looking at him like a schoolgirl who wants to be forgiven for not knowing the answer to a homework question.

"I'm pretty sure that it was a Pajero, though." She seemed eager to redeem herself. "In fact, I *know* it was a Pajero; it was very similar to the one Matt has back home, except this one was black."

"The Pajero will have sustained some damage: paint scratches that match your car." He turned to Julie. "That could be very useful information for the police. Do you want to call them?"

97

"I'm going to call Greg first and see what he says." As Julie got up the drying cloth slipped off Bridget's leg and Julie gasped at the sight of blood.

Chris tried to pre-empt any panic. "I'm sure it's not as bad as it looks," he said. "Show me where I can find a first-aid kit; I'll clean up the wound whilst you go and make your phone call."

A few minutes later, he had assembled a bowl of hot water, towels, antiseptic, and a first- aid kit. He spread the towels under Bridget's leg and proceeded to carefully wash away the dry, crusted blood.

"You're going to have some spectacular bruises here. I can see a number of scratches but fortunately there's only one fairly deep gash."

Bridget sipped her gin and watched him.

"You are your father's son. Did you also study medicine?"

"Oh no, I'm an architect." He smiled at her apologetically. "Would you rather we go find a proper doctor?"

"No, no, you're doing a great job. I'm impressed. Where did you learn?"

Chris shrugged. "Don't really know. I suppose I've seen a fair number of sports injuries; as a kid, I sometimes went to the hospital with my dad and hung around the ER waiting for him. I remember, one evening, there'd been a gang fight. Eight drunken men came in waving their guns, demanding that their injured friends be treated first. Three of them were badly hurt. One had a screwdriver sticking out of his back."

"Why on Earth did your father have you watch that?" Bridget shuddered.

"I think he was hoping that I would follow in his footsteps. But there was no chance of that. I remember when they pulled out that screwdriver, all I could think was: *A blood fountain, gross!* I don't know how the hospital staff put up with it."

Chris poured antiseptic on a piece of cotton wool. "Hold tight, this is going to sting." He had expected her to flinch, or even cry out, but was impressed that she just kept still, watching him intently as he cleaned the wound and started to bandage it.

From next door, he could hear Julie say, "Greg, I know her license has been suspended and she shouldn't be driving, but I still think the police

… Yes, she'd had a drink at the Camps Bay Hotel and she's had a couple more since coming home … But surely we can explain to the police …"

Chris concentrated on the wound and pretended not to have heard. Bridget seemed quite unconcerned, though. She said, "I know what Greg is going to say."

"What?" Chris looked up and noticed her mouth drawn in resigned bitterness.

"He's going to say that I was drunk and crashed the car. And that I am now making up this whole story; that it's all a figment of my imagination and that I am being a drama queen."

"Why would he do that?" Chris was puzzled. He himself had not doubted her account of the incident.

As if on cue, from next door, he heard Julie say, "No, I'm sure she isn't making it up."

Chris felt Bridget's muscles tense. She looked at him and mouthed, *"Told you so."* Then she said, "I won't bore you with the ins and outs of company politics at Noble Enterprises. Let's just say that Greg and I rarely see eye to eye."

Julie was saying, "I don't see what the press has to do with it … I know she is the chairman of the company. That's even more reason to get to the bottom of this. Maybe it is a disgruntled employee, maybe … Yes, darling, miss you too. OK, will let you know. Tell me if you find out anything."

Julie did not look happy when she came back into the family room and inspected the bandaged leg, "How bad is it?"

"It's a nasty gash but I think I managed to clean most of it," Chris replied.

"You're marvelous," Bridget said. "If I end up with a little scar, it will always remind me of you." He wasn't sure if she was teasing.

Julie seemed troubled. "Greg thinks it would be better not to drag the police into this." She looked at her watch. "Especially since it is now about five hours since the actual incident. They'll want to breathalyze you; the press is going to pick up on the story, and nothing much good is going to come out of it."

Chris was surprised that Bridget just shrugged her shoulders in acceptance. "Really?" he said. "Someone has just tried to run your mother off the road. Were it not for her quick thinking, it could have been a far more serious accident. And yet you are OK with just letting it be; not even reporting it to the police?"

"Chris, please. You have to accept that Greg is looking at the big picture here. He has to consider the impact of bad press …"

"But it doesn't make sense. Never mind what Greg says, what do you think?"

"I agree with Greg that the security resources of Noble Enterprises can do a better job in protecting my mother than the police can – it's most likely a disgruntled employee. Greg will assign her a new driver and launch a quiet, behind-the-scenes investigation."

Chris was aware of Bridget's intent gaze. She was watching the exchange between them like someone who had placed a bet on a boxing fight. Chris wondered what he would do if it were *his* mother. He certainly wouldn't leave it as Julie proposed to. He'd lock his mother up and place a twenty-man security contingent and armored vehicles around the place. But then, he realized that he was probably a little paranoid when it came to protecting mothers.

"What are you smiling at?" Bridget asked.

"I was just trying to visualize how my mother might have reacted if anyone tried to keep her under lock and key. I couldn't even get her to lock her car door when driving through Grassy Park." He turned to Julie. "OK, it's really none of my business - I'm sure you will all figure out the best course of action." He looked at his watch. "Do you need me for anything else? Otherwise I'd best be off."

Bridget seemed genuinely sorry to see Chris go, though by now the Vicodin was kicking in and she looked ready to sleep. Julie walked him to the door. The moon had risen and the night was quiet except for the swishing sounds of a sprinkler system. The perfume of jasmine and roses enveloped them as they stood between the high pillars of the front porch. He sensed her hesitation and conflict. Quietly, she asked, "Do you think she might have just made up the whole story?"

"Is that what Greg thinks?"

She nodded.

"I obviously don't know your mother well at all. But if she made up that story, then she is the best damn actress I've ever come across."

She touched his arm and looked him in the eyes. "I don't want you to be mad at me."

He studied her face for a long time, trying to understand his own emotions. "I'm not mad at you; I just wish I understood you better."

He kissed her forehead and walked into the night.

##

Chapter 7: Sand and Sea

Thursday morning

Chris felt great after an early-morning swim and a two-kilometer jog from the Health Line Club to Desmond and Cedric's apartment in Sea Point. The doors of the apartment block reflected a serene expanse of ocean and palm trees under a halo of early dawn.

He pressed the button for Apartment 402 a second time – longer, more insistent. The front door buzzed and a disembodied voice emanated from the intercom: *"Keep your knickers on!"*

"And a very good morning to you, too, Cedric." Chris ignored the elevator, sprinted up the stairs, and entered the apartment without knocking. He'd seen it many times before, but the spectacular sea view, and the uncluttered, clean lines of the apartment, never failed to fill him with pleasure and admiration. Gleaming wooden floors served as a backdrop for two exquisite rugs. The furniture was sparse: a couple of modern leather sofas, a stainless-steel lamp with a fluted lampshade, a sleek dining table, and a dramatically lit bronze sculpture in the corner. One wall was dominated by a moody Vietnamese painting of two young peasants with bare chests working in a yellow field. The dark background of the painting suggested an approaching storm.

Chris crossed the room and opened the balcony doors to let the sound and smell of the ocean wash over him. He inhaled deeply and gazed over the palms to where the first rays of the sun bounced off the sea and paved a golden path across the water. He felt happier than he had in months, excited at what the day might bring. Despite interruptions, the evening with Julie had been … promising.

"D'you mind?" Cedric, wrapped in a luxurious black dressing-gown, came in from the bedroom and closed the door to the balcony. "It's drafty in here and I don't want to catch a cold."

"You must be joking. It doesn't get better than this." Chris watched Cedric as he walked to the fridge. "You look like you really could do with a bit of sunshine. After three years in Africa, it's about time you got rid of that English pallor and got a proper tan."

"I have no intention of ending up a wrinkled hag," Cedric answered tartly. "Would you like orange juice?"

Chris accepted a glass of juice. "What's Desmond up to? He was supposed to be ready and waiting."

"God knows; trying to make himself presentable, I presume."

"I can hear you," Desmond shouted from the bedroom. "Be there in a minute."

Cedric unfurled a yoga mat and let his dressing-gown slide to the floor. He sighed. "Desmond's always late. I've given up ..." He inhaled deeply and started stretching, folding his body like a pair of scissors to touch his forehead against his outstretched legs.

Chris couldn't help but feel that Cedric was showing off. But then again, Cedric was a choreographer and dancer; he was supposed to be supple ... and to show off.

Finally, Desmond emerged from the bedroom dressed in his running gear. "Sorry to keep you. I've been packing so I can be ready to head straight out to Hermanus and see my sister later this morning. Ready?"

Gulping down his juice, Chris followed him out, trying to tread lightly so as not to disturb Cedric, who by now had adopted a lotus position and appeared to have drifted off into his own universe. But as they reached the door Cedric intoned, "Go forth and be productive ... *ommmmm* ... but do not be late for dance rehearsal ... *ommmm* ... ten o'clock sharp."

Desmond shut the door with more force than necessary. "Drama queen! It gets a bit tiring to live with someone who *literally* believes that 'all the world's a stage'."

On Beach Road, the morning commute was in full swing: cars, buses, taxis, and motorcycles wound their way towards central Cape Town. Desmond was nearly flattened by a group of chattering girls in their gray and white school uniforms.

"Like a bloody herd of rhinos," Desmond muttered.

"Be nice. Besides, you weren't watching where you were going – better wake up, buddy."

At the traffic lights, a newspaper seller wove his way amongst the cars. His broad smile could mislead people into thinking that there might actually be something cheerful in the paper. As Chris and Desmond jogged across the street, he waved the paper at them and shouted, "Hey my boss, have a break, have a Kit-Kat, read the paper. Fresh news, *freeeeshhh* news! Two dead in home robbery gone wrong! *Tiiimes*, get it here!"

Chris looked at him and, for an instant, thought the man resembled the dark hooded figure of his nightmares. The headline hit him with a jolt. Even now, over eight years later, it was as though a vat of caustic memories was being poured over him. The dark feelings threatened to engulf him.

Desmond nudged him as the lights turned orange and Chris resolved to buy the paper on his way back. Who knows? The killer was out there, and maybe he was using the same modus operandi.

They reached the broad promenade that wound its way for miles along the Atlantic coast   Here the sound of seagulls and lapping waves was louder than the traffic noises and they settled into a rhythmic stride.

"What's with Cedric?" Chris asked. "He seems a little tetchy this morning."

"The Queen Mother has announced that she's coming for a visit at Christmas-time. Wants to get away from the English winter and see her darling son."

"So? I thought he gets on well with her."

"Who wouldn't? I mean, she lets us stay in this apartment rent-free and she sends Cedric 'a little something' every month." He paused. "A couple of hundred pounds goes a long way."

"I still don't see a problem," Chris said.

"His mother has long resigned herself to the fact that there will be no pitter-patter of little grandchildren in her house. But she really has her heart set on seeing Cedric's name in lights as a big-shot choreographer or stage producer." He paused. "Cedric, the silly ass, has told her that he's staging a major production."

Chris groaned. "Why did he do a dumb thing like that?"

"Money," Desmond panted, as they overtook a lone female runner, plugged into her iPod, a Labrador running beside her. "Hey, slow down a bit … Anyway, Cedric saw a pair of sculptures that he fell in love with. You know how he gets when he 'absolutely has to have something'. So he spun his mother a bullshit story about a new stage production, and she sent him the money. "

"And is the sculptor handsome?"

Desmond looked at him. "Sometimes you're a real bitch, do you know that?"

"I suppose that comes from hanging out too much with the likes of you and Cedric," said Chris, laughing. "So what's Cedric going to do?"

"I don't know, rob a bank? I'm so tired of being short of money – all this constant bickering about rands and cents." He paused. "Cedric's probably going to lean on the Toreros to 'be in rehearsal' and pretend to be in the early stages of putting some serious show together. Might need a few extras. How about ...?"

"Don't even think about it!" Chris picked up the pace. "It's bad enough that my father knows I'm dancing this weekend."

Desmond was surprised by this information and Chris told him about the chance meeting the previous evening. As he told the story, he suddenly stopped in his tracks. "Damn, how could I have forgotten?" He banged his fist on the guardrail, causing two seagulls to take flight.

Desmond bent forward, trying to catch his breath. "What... what have you forgotten?"

"Yesterday was my folks' wedding anniversary." He did a mental calculation. "I think it might even have been their twenty-fifth. That's why my father was at Marco's."

"You should call him."

"Maybe."

Chris set off again, but now they jogged in silence. It was a perfect morning. The sun was reflected in a myriad of crazy patterns by the glass façades of the apartment buildings on 'millionaire's mile'. The promenade was filling up with joggers of all ages and sizes. They were joined by moms with pushchairs and jaunty pensioners out for a walk before their morning bagel and coffee at Giovanni's. Desmond and Chris passed a play-park where a number of African nannies had congregated with their charges. No doubt the madams were having a lie-in or a soak in a bubble bath before facing the day. Two of the nannies wore the typical uniform: pink smocks and matching *doeke* to cover their hair. Chris's mind wandered to Mercy. It had been such a surprise to see her at the orphanage and he still felt embarrassed that he'd never made the effort to visit her.

He noticed that one of the nannies was keeping watch over a small boy on a slide and he remembered how Mercy had tried her hardest to fill the void left by Danielle. She'd shown her love the only way she knew: by feeding him, fussing and clucking, ironing his shirts, and polishing his sports trophies. He smiled as he remembered the colorful blue dress and Sunday-best white hat she had worn to his graduation ceremony. No parent could have beamed with more pride than Mercy. Sometime after the ceremony, he'd noticed that Mercy had disappeared. He'd found her sitting on a secluded bench, in tears. He'd put his arm around her shoulders and let her cry as he listened to a bird tweeting in the tree above them. Mercy had turned her tearstained face to Chris and said, "If only your mother could be here today. At least it is a comfort to know that she is with the Lord Jesus and the angels ..."

A baby in the play-park started to cry. He caught a fragment of the nanny singing a lullaby: *"Tula, tu, tula tu, tula baba; tula tu, tula tu, tula sama."*

Chris quickened his pace, unaware that Desmond was falling behind. *Mercy and her Lord Jesus*; the memories came tumbling into his mind and with them a darkness that he hadn't felt so intensely in a long time. His chest tightened and yet he kept picking up speed.

The night of his mother's funeral - that was the first time the demons had descended upon him - and he had danced to keep them at bay. As long as he kept moving, the protective dome of his mother's aura had surrounded him. He remembered the argument with his father that night in the studio, and that afterwards Jacques had turned and left him, left him alone with those dark clouds, the hatred, the thoughts of revenge that were so horrible he could not believe that they came from within him. It was as if he had been invaded by something that wanted to devour his soul.

He had no idea how long he'd carried on dancing after his father had left, but eventually Mercy had come down to the studio. It must have been past midnight. She'd watched him for a while, then quietly walked on to the dance floor so that he could no longer ignore her.

"Speak to me, Chris. I know you're hurting."

"You ... know ... nothing!" he panted in a voice that he could not recognize. Then he stopped dancing abruptly, pointed a finger accusingly at her. "Why? Why did this have to happen? Tell me that!" His anger had been overwhelming, frightening. He knew he was out of control but he did not care.

"Chris, it is not up to us to ask why. We do not understand it now, but the Lord has a plan for each of us. Your mother is with our Lord Jesus now ..."

Chris raged. He wanted to lash out and hurt. Panting and sweating from hours of dancing, he'd screamed at her: "Where ... where was the fucking Lord Jesus when this scumbag, this piece of garbage, broke into our house and shot my mother? Where? Was he asleep at the wheel or what? He should have been there! One little bolt of lightning and he could have vaporized that piece of shit!" Despite the pain there was a sensual, adult pleasure in the use of expletives. The crude words, infused with hatred, rolled off his tongue. "Fucking piece of shit!" he re-iterated, knowing that Mercy disapproved of swear words even more than his parents – his mother...

"Chris, you must not carry this hatred in your heart; it will eat you from the inside out, the way a fruit fly ..."

"If ever I catch that murderer, I will ... I will put a knife in his eyes, I will smash his brains in with a hammer." A part of him stood beside him and watched this lunatic with amazement. "I will cut off his fingers one by one – I will hear him scream for mercy and I will laugh in his face!"

"The Lord will deal with him on Judgment Day."

"I've told you ... Jesus fucking Christ is nowhere to be found when you need him!"

Mercy's face was something to behold. She had never, in fourteen years, laid a hand on him, but in that moment Chris was convinced that she was going to slap him good and hard. He wanted it, expected it. But it did not happen. Instead, Mercy drew herself to her full height, reached out and pulled him into a tight embrace. Initially he struggled, but she only tightened her grip and started to sway from one foot to the other. Softly, she sang the ancient African lullaby: "Tula tu, tula tu, tula baba; tula tu, tula tu, tula sama."

Chris had finally broken down and cried; cried for the loss of his mother, the loss of his family, and the loss of any hope of joy in his life, ever. He'd cried until he felt like the mop that his father had wanted to throw away but that Mercy insisted on using to wash the marble floors in the hallway: frazzled, wrung out, wet, and limp. His only consolation was that the dark demons had been dispelled. That night, he'd fallen into a deep, dreamless sleep.

He felt the warmth and the light and allowed the memories to fade away and his running to slow. It was good to smell the ocean, to watch the seagulls. Desmond caught up and flopped down on the grass next to the pathway. "What ... what the hell got into you?" He was struggling to breathe.

"Nothing. It was nothing. Seems to me like you're out of shape."

Desmond groaned and looked at his watch. "I need to be getting back."

"OK, let's just do a detour past that building site on Milner Road."

"You're not going to make me traipse through a bloody building site again, are you?"

"We won't stop. I just want to see how they're getting on. They should be pouring concrete for the fourth-floor deck today."

They veered away from the ocean, crossed Beach Road, and headed up a side street. Ahead of them, in the distance, was a massive construction site where the Green Point Stadium, a designated site for the FIFA World Cup, was taking shape. Chris felt the acute frustration of not yet being employed as an architect.

Coming into Milner Road, they were confronted by a billboard proclaiming: "*Stadium View – 26 luxury apartments and penthouses. Magnificent sea and mountain views, private elevators. Another prestigious development by Richter Construction.*"

Despite the early hour, the site was bursting with activity. Churning concrete-mixers were lined up at the gates, making Chris think of giant dinosaurs digesting their food. Near the end of the block, he stopped and tugged at a panel of the six-foot-high fence. It swung sideways and he motioned for Desmond to follow him.

Desmond rolled his eyes. "Come on, man. We have no business being here. You'll just get us into trouble."

"Don't worry - just a quick look. I come here often and many of the guys know me." Chris was keen to explain the intricacies of the building operation going on in front of them to his friend, but Desmond was uncomfortable, and kept edging back towards the gap in the fence. "Yes, yes. We've seen it now. C'mon, let's go ..."

So intent was Chris on the concrete pouring, however, that he didn't hear Desmond. Something about the operation did not feel right to him. The normal rhythm that pulsed through a building site seemed disturbed. He watched as the concrete-mixers emptied themselves into a crane scoop the size of a VW Beetle. The crane cables appeared to tremble like over-tightened guitar strings as the scoop raced up to the fourth floor and disgorged the doughy concrete over a steel mesh. The crane operator was in such a hurry that the scoop smeared an unsightly trail of gray sludge across the scaffolding. Chris was reminded of snotty-nosed kids at the swimming pool – one of his pet hates.

He held up his hand to shield his eyes. "That's weird. What the hell do they think they're doing?"

"What d'you mean?"

But Chris had stalked off towards the concrete-mixer, where he approached a tall man who, unlike most of the overall-clad workers, was dressed in khaki pants and a jacket.

"Are you the foreman here?"

The man nodded slowly, eyeing Chris up and down.

"I think you may have a situation up there," Chris said.

The foreman's eyes followed the direction of Chris's outstretched arm. It took him a minute to collect his wits. Then he turned to Chris, his expression dark. "What are you playing at? This is a hard-hat area. Piss off!"

"Hey, I'm just trying to help. The guys up there are cutting corners. Someone's going to get hurt. You should stop the pour."

"Are you mad? Not on your fucking life. Get out of here before I have you thrown out!"

One of his colleagues approached. He held a large wrench in his hand. "Is there a problem, Joe?" he asked.

"This joker wants us to stop the pour."

Chris kept his voice level. "Look, you guys don't have nearly enough supports for the amount of concrete you're pouring. That whole damn floor could collapse."

"What the fuck do you know?!" The foreman came right up to Chris now and poked a finger under his nose. "I've been doing this since before you were even in nappies ..."

A number of workers within earshot stopped working and inched closer.

Desmond had stayed a few feet behind Chris. "Come on, man, just leave it," he urged.

"Yeah," the man with the wrench said. "Listen to your friend and mind your own *bleddy* business." Contemptuously, he looked them up and down, from the Nike running vests to the training shoes. "Why don't you boys go play with your Lego blocks?"

Chris fought to keep his voice calm. "You're cutting one corner too many here. I'm sure you've all got bonuses riding on meeting schedule, but you'll really be screwed if you end up with an accident and the building inspector shuts down operations."

"Jeez, sonny. Are you threatening to call in the inspector?" The foreman's expression grew more menacing. "You're seriously screwing with the wrong guys ..."

They were interrupted by the arrival of a large BMW. It bumped its way over the uneven ground and came to a halt a few yards away from the knot of men that had formed around Chris, Desmond and the foreman. The driver leapt out. With his sunglasses, Schwarzenegger shoulders and ill-fitting jacket, he looked like a caricature of a Chicago mobster. He opened the rear door of the car for his boss: a bald man who grunted as he stepped out of the vehicle and made his way over to the group. "What the hell is going on, Joe?" he said to the foreman. "We're spending a bloody fortune on overtime to work through the nights and you all stand around here to *ginnegaap* and have a nice chat!" With heavy sarcasm, he added, "If I had known, I could have brought some nice tea and *koeksisters*."

"Morning, *Meneer* Richter." Chris noticed that the foreman had lost his threatening demeanor and clearly did not want to antagonize the boss. "We're on track with the pour for the fourth floor; just got a little situation here with this busybody ..."

"You!" Richter had recognized Chris and his face had turned dark red with anger. A vein pulsed across his bald scalp as if a small snake was embedded in his skull. "You have a bloody nerve, coming here on to *my* site," he spat. "You're trespassing ...What *bleddy* cheek to come here ..."

Chris said, "Mr. Richter, I don't want to cause any trouble, but you have a serious safety situation here. That fourth floor ..." He pointed.

"It doesn't have enough supports. The whole lot could collapse, you could have an accident …"

Richter strode to within inches of Chris and hissed, "Get off my site!" He glared as the younger man stood his ground. "Get off my site before *you* have an accident."

Chris felt his own anger rise at the man's unreasonable reaction. He was aware of a vein pulsating in his neck and his jaw was clamped so tight it hurt. He looked hard at Richter for a full ten seconds. Finally, he held up his hands in surrender. "Fine! On your head be it." He turned and strode to the main gate with Desmond following closely.

"Don't you dare set foot on my site again," Richter shouted after him, "or you'll be sorry!"

Desmond breathed out audibly as they reached the road. "That was close! Why do you have to go around picking fights with people?"

"I don't pick fights with people! That scumbag is driving his crew so hard they're going to have a serious accident. What am I supposed to do? Just stand by?"

"Chris, you can't solve world hunger by yourself. Just give it a rest."

They walked in silence. Chris wondered who the site architect was and, more importantly, *where* he – or she - was. How could they not be there? If Chris were in charge of a building site, he'd be there, night and day, watching impatiently as his ideas became reality. He found such apparent indifference incomprehensible.

Desmond interrupted his thoughts. "So, was that your prospective father-in-law? The one who tried to buy you for his little girl?"

"Yeah, that was Sandra's old man."

"Phew. Lucky break. Must say, I'm relieved that you had the good sense to get out of that relationship. He's nasty!"

His opinion expressed, Desmond changed the subject. He wanted to know if Chris would mind taking over his spot as soccer coach for the kids at the Khanya center that afternoon.

Chris shrugged. "Sure, no problem. I was planning to go back and look at the site again, in any case." He paused. "Give my regards to your mother and to Rachel. I'm sure it will cheer them both up to see you." Chris thought of the young girl who had playfully thrust her chest at him, daring him to autograph her T-shirt, on that day when they had found out about the auditions and his mother had been murdered. And now Rachel was wasting away with AIDS, Sandra was somewhere in a psychiatric clinic in Europe, and Old Man Richter was mad as hell. The day had started full of promise but was rapidly going downhill. He headed to the Health Line Club, hoping that a hot shower would wash away the muck and let the day re-start.

##

After dance rehearsals, Chris picked up a sandwich and drove to the Khanya center. Mama Mercy leaned out of the kitchen window and shouted a greeting as he passed, prompting Chris to stop and chat. He established that the kids were busy with homework but would be very pleased to play soccer in an hour's time.

He settled on his favorite log and began to sketch. Ten minutes later, he had the familiar sensation of someone watching him. Without turning he said, "Hello, Thabo. How are you today?"

Thabo sat down next to him.

"Miss Wendy was very impressed with your house plans," Chris said.

"Yes, she told me."

They sat in silence, with Chris working and Thabo watching. The boy took out his cell phone and stroked it as though it were a pet hamster.

"Thank you," he said quietly.

Chris nodded. "I need to go look at the land down by the river. Want to come?"

The property was at least three acres in size, with the area closest to the river fenced off. A dirt road led from the main road, past the farmhouse, to a gate in the fence. They approached the gate, where a security guard sat on an upturned plastic crate, smoking a cigarette. Chris noticed that the six-foot-high fence was brand-new and made of wire mesh, with barbed wire along the top. It seemed excessive for keeping children away from the river.

"Good afternoon, *tate*," he said respectfully to the old guard. "May we go down and look at the river?"

"Nobody must go there; is not safe. Children can fall in the river and there are snakes in the grass."

112

"It's OK, the boy is with me. We'll be fine. Miss Wendy said we can come down and look around."

The guard scratched his head and, after some more assurances from Chris, unlocked the gate with a muttered warning: "Stay away from the old barn, is not safe."

Once the other side, Chris paced out sections and made notes, while Thabo found himself a long stick and scanned the grass for signs of snakes. The guard watched from a distance. After five minutes, he settled back on his crate with a cigarette and a worn copy of *Drum* magazine.

Chris led the way towards the coolness of a clump of blue gums near the river. There, amongst the trees, they came upon an old barn. Chris was intrigued. The building appeared to be abandoned and in need of some repair but, like the main house, it exuded sturdiness. He immediately started to think about incorporating it into his plans. The two of them circled the barn in search of an opening, but the windows were firmly shuttered and every door was padlocked. Chris resolved to speak to Wendy about the barn and to explore the possibilities at a later stage.

Chris and Thabo carried on along the dirt road, which led to a short pier where weeping willows fringed the banks of what was really no more than a stream. It was quiet except for the twittering of birds and the croaking of a frog. A mother duck was guiding her ducklings to the shallows.

They sat on the edge of the pier and Thabo let his bare feet dangle in the water. He said, "I often come here." In response to Chris's questioning look, he added, "To think."

"I thought no one was supposed to come here."

Thabo shrugged. "There is a place to slip under the fence. Old Samuel is a fool; he thinks he can scare people away with his stupid *tokoloshe* stories, but it doesn't work with me."

Chris savored the tranquility and the sun on his back. He remembered hiking trips with Desmond in the Boland Mountains where he had swum in rock pools with water so clear and cold that it simultaneously took one's breath away and bestowed an almost superhuman vigor. He wondered if Julie enjoyed hiking and let his mind wander to images of Julie bathing in a rock pool …

His thoughts were interrupted by the sound of a vehicle coming down the dirt track towards the barn. It was a white panel van with no markings. The driver backed up against the barn door and his passenger, a young man with spiky red hair and a freckled face, jumped out to unlock the door and open the back of the van.

Chris decided that this might be a good opportunity to get a look inside the barn. He motioned for Thabo to follow him, but the boy had disappeared.

Chris approached the driver and extended his hand. "Hi, I'm Chris du Toit. I'm an architect working for the Khanya AIDS Foundation." It hit him that this was the first time he had ever said it out loud: "I'm an architect." It felt good. He had to stop himself from repeating the words.

The driver looked startled and ignored the outstretched hand.

"What brings you guys here?" Chris asked. "I thought this barn was not in use."

The driver was about to answer when the red-haired man joined them. "We work for Noble Enterprises, " he said. "You might have heard of the company?"

Chris nodded.

"We are growing fast and we have a storage constraint. The Khanya center is allowing us to use the barn for storage on a temporary basis."

The driver seemed to have found his voice and added, "Noble supports this place a lot. One hand washes the other – know what I mean?" He smiled.

"D'you mind if I look around inside?"

Chris noticed an anxious flicker on the driver's face. He was a large African man with a round face and an open expression. He pushed his cap to the back of his head, scratched his chin, and looked at the redhead. Close up, Chris saw that the man's boyish hairstyle was deceptive and that he was probably in his forties. "Today we're on a bit of a tight schedule," he said. "Can we maybe push it out to next time? We come by quite regularly."

Chris looked at his watch. "Oh, jeez. I'm late for soccer practice, anyway. See you next time."

As he walked away, Chris stole a glimpse into the back of the van and was surprised to see that it contained only one solitary crate, the size of a large suitcase. By the time he reached the gate, Thabo had reappeared, like a shadow that had gone walk-about and attached itself to its owner again. The guard stood to attention and saluted as they passed.

For the first time in weeks, Julie felt as though she was finally getting on top of things. The gala was now largely out of her hands; all she could do was pray that everything would come together – and that the weather would be kind. *Dear God, please keep the southeast wind at bay*, she prayed silently. She had just sent another press release and now even her emails were up to date. She stretched her arms, wriggled her fingers, and longed for a massage to loosen her neck muscles. That made her think of Greg. She looked at her watch: four p.m. He would no doubt be in meetings and would not appreciate being interrupted by a phone call. The massage would have to wait till her next trip to Johannesburg.

She closed her laptop and walked down the hall to the day room day room. Despite the sparse furnishings, Julie liked the room. The high ceilings, wooden floors, and pale walls kept the room cool in summer. There were a dozen women in the room – a mix of patients and volunteers. Five of the women sat around a table chatting and crocheting. Julie spoke to them and admired the half-finished baby booties and jackets. Three toddlers sat on a mat in a playpen and, in the TV corner, a group of young children watched a cartoon show. Julie walked to where Thabo's mother, Grace, lay curled up on a sofa with her eyes shut; her baby was next to her in a pushchair.

One of the volunteers whispered, *"Isn't she adorable? She's got her mother's beautiful eyes."*

The baby kicked her legs and reached for the sky. When Julie picked her up, the child's puckered lips broke into a smile; she touched Julie's face.

"Thank God Grace came for her meds during her pregnancy. At least this little one is HIV-free," said the volunteer.

Julie nuzzled her nose in the child's neck and made soft blowing noises. The baby squealed with delight and pulled at her hair. The mother woke and drew herself up into a seated position.

"Hello, Grace. How are you today?"

Grace said, "A bit better, thank you. Has my baby been crying?"

"Oh no, I was just playing with her."

Julie looked at Grace's soulful brown eyes and high cheekbones. It struck her that Grace must have been a very beautiful woman before the disease ravaged her. Now her arms were painfully thin, the once full lips dry and cracked, her dark skin damp with perspiration.

"Can I get you anything … maybe some tea, water?"

"Water, please," Grace attempted a smile.

"I'll just go and change the baby, then I'll bring you some water. Julie left the room, carrying the child on her hip like an African woman, and returned five minutes later with a mug of water. Grace drank slowly and watched as Julie sat down on the couch and bounced the baby on her lap. The child smiled and made happy noises.

One of the girls who had been sitting on the floor watching TV slid over to the sofa and squeezed herself in next to Julie.

"Hello, Kholeka. Can I see your teeth?"

Kholeka grinned, showing two missing front teeth.

"You're such a big girl now. You're already getting your grown-up teeth."

The girl put her thumb in her mouth, curled up into ball, and snuggled up close to Julie. She watched as Julie continued to play with the baby.

She said, "I don't want to be a big girl; I want to be a baby."

"But why?"

"Everybody loves babies."

Julie hugged the girl with her free arm.

They were distracted by voices and shouting from the garden. Grace stretched up to look out of the window and seemed surprised by what she saw. "Thabo is playing soccer. Who's that man?"

Julie followed her gaze. "That's Chris. He's helping out today because Desmond had to go and visit his sister."

To Julie, the soccer practice appeared to be a free-for-all, until she saw Chris get everybody organized. He took on the role of goalkeeper, and one-by-one the children dribbled the ball towards the goal and tried to kick it past him. There were peals of laughter as balls flew anywhere and everywhere. One boy managed to trip and fall over his own feet. Julie watched as Chris stopped them, demonstrated, coached, showed them how to slow down, focus.

Five minutes later, Danny managed to get the ball past Chris to score the first goal. He shrieked "*La duuuuuuma*", pulled the front of his T-shirt over his face, and circled the goalposts with his arms spread wide. There was much high-fiving and congratulation.

"Little show-off," the volunteer said, but she was smiling.

A couple of minutes later, Thabo managed to blast the ball past Chris's head into the goal. He stood quite still and then, as the others rushed over to slap his back and high-five him, a grin spread across his face.

Grace lifted her hand to her mouth. The light caught her eyes and she appeared more animated than Julie had seen her for a long time.

"He's a good boy, my Thabo," she said.

"He's a wonderful boy", Julie echoed as she watched Chris, his hair tousled, wipe the perspiration off his forehead and walk over to shake Thabo's hand.

Chris joined the children on the verandah where Mercy served apple juice and cookies. He couldn't help but notice that the juice had been severely diluted. It brought a lump to his throat when he saw how disciplined the children were in helping themselves to cookies. There was no shoving or grabbing, everybody took just one. When Mercy nodded her head, they first offered a second cookie to "Coach Chris" before each helping themselves to a second one.

Julie came out to join them and Chris hung back whilst the children crowded round to tell her who had scored, who had nearly scored, and what a great time they'd had.

"I know, I know," she laughed. "I watched you from the day room."

"You did?" Chris asked.

Julie ignored the questions and addressed Thabo: "Your mother enjoyed seeing you play. I think she's ready to go home now. Can you go help her?"

"Yes, Miss Julie." Thabo was almost at the door, when he stopped and turned round. "Thank you, Coach Chris," he said.

The other children dispersed, leaving Chris and Julie alone.

"What's the story with that old barn near the river?" Chris asked. "Can I get a key to have a look around?"

"Now?" Julie looked puzzled. "Why? It's just an empty old barn."

"Well, it looks pretty sturdy and I was wondering if there is some way to incorporate it. Thabo and I were down there earlier and a couple of guys from Noble Enterprises showed up to store stuff."

"Oh yes, they're upgrading a warehouse and asked if they could store some overflow in the barn. It shouldn't be a problem for you to have a look around, though. We have the keys in the office."

A couple of minutes later, Chris and Julie were walking down the dirt road to the gate. Samuel actually smiled when he saw Julie and immediately opened the gate for them. They continued to the barn and Julie produced a bunch of keys.

"That's odd," she said. "These padlocks weren't here before. They're all new." Indeed, Julie's keys turned quite easily in the original door locks, but that was of no use since strong shiny new clasps and padlocks had been fixed to the doors.

"Well," Chris said, "it's not really surprising, given how isolated this place is. They obviously wanted to make sure that no one would break in."

Julie frowned. "Yes, but they could have let us know."

"It's no big deal. Maybe they spoke to Wendy or someone else at the center."

"Sorry about that, I'll talk to Greg when I see him up in Johannesburg on Sunday. He'll have a word with the operations manager and I'm sure we can get you access next week." She turned and headed towards the river. Chris followed.

He asked, "You're going up to Jo'burg?"

"Oh, didn't I tell you? My stepfather asked me to come up and play hostess for some overseas clients he has to entertain."

"I see. You certainly have a wide and varied group of people making demands on your time."

They reached the river. The mother duck and her young were still there. Julie veered left, following the narrow bridle path that wound its way along the riverbank. The earth was dark and moist, like chocolate cake. Two riders, one behind the other, were approaching from the opposite direction, and Julie and Chris had to step off the narrow path and press themselves against a rambling hedge to let them pass. The front rider tipped her hat and thanked them. Then she recognized Julie and stopped for a few pleasantries. The horse pranced restlessly and Chris stepped up, held the bridle, and patted the horse's flank. The animal settled immediately.

"It's gorgeous down at the beach," the rider said. "No wind at all; we've decided to buy some meat and have a *braai*. Do you and ... your boyfriend want to come?" Chris felt the heat of her gaze.

She flashed him a smile. "You've got a great touch ... with horses."

"Thanks, Monica," Julie said, a bit shortly. "Maybe some other time."

"OK then. Have fun, you two."

When they were alone again, Julie turned to face Chris. "What do you mean, 'I have a wide and varied group of people making demands on my time'?"

"It's none of my business." Chris shrugged and led the way along a narrow portion of the path.

"That's a fine cop-out. Of course it's none of your business, but I'm still interested in why you would say that."

"When you're not running around for the Khanya AIDS Foundation, you're doing things for your mother. And it seems as though you're pretty much at the beck and call of your stepfather and ... and what's this guy's name? Greg."

"So? I like to do things for other people. Especially people I care about. Is that so unusual?"

"No." Chris paused. "But what about you? Where are *you* headed? What is it *you* want to do?" He looked over his shoulder to try and read her expression. She had a frown on her face.

"Have you been talking to Wendy? You sound an awful lot like her. Why does everyone always have to be headed somewhere? What if I am exactly where I want to be and where I should be?"

They had reached the point where the river ended - in a lagoon, teeming with birdlife. A heron watched them pass. It was low tide and the lagoon was separated from the sea by a sandbank. Only a trickle of water found its way along a narrow gash in the sandbank, across the beach, and into the ocean.

Chris stopped to admire Hout Bay's spectacular natural harbor, where boats entered and left the sheltered bay through a natural passage between two massive peaks. Ancient seafarers had prayed with relief when they found this calm haven, with its sweet water, along the stormy and forbidding coast of Africa. Steep cliffs reflected the ochre and lilac glow of the late-afternoon sun, and out in the bay windsurfers moved about this magnificent amphitheater in a graceful dance.

"Last one to touch the waves is a rotten banana," Julie teased, kicking off her sandals and running towards the sea.

Chris whipped off his shoes and charged after her. She reached the water just before him, but when her feet touched the icy waves she shrieked and turned. He caught her in his arms then. It seemed the most natural thing to do. The breeze played with her hair and the glow of the sun illuminated her eyes. Her irises were a curious mixture of green and gray and the light danced in her pupils. He felt an overwhelming urge to just hold her, to have this moment etched in his brain: the smell of the sea, the warmth of the sun on his shoulders, and her playful, laughing face so close to his.

"I won!" She beamed and backed away half a step.

They walked along the water line, where cheeky waves played catch with their feet. Chris watched as Julie danced away from the foam crowns. Something swelled inside him: pride that he was able to make her happy, a desire to protect her.

"That rider assumed I was your boyfriend; you didn't correct her. Why?"

"Oh, don't flatter yourself. It just seemed like too much bother. Besides, I don't really care what people think of me."

"You don't? It wouldn't bother you if she told all her friends that you ... that you ..."

"Sleep around? Is that what you wanted to say?"

He could not interpret her expression. It seemed half-mocking, half-serious. She continued, "It would bother me if people I care about, or whose opinion I value, thought badly of me. The rest ..." She shrugged her shoulders. "I believe people generally spend too much time worrying about what others might think." She looked him in the eyes. "It's very narcissistic to think you're always the subject of other people's attention."

Chris could not figure out how his question had been turned against him. He sensed a rebuke, however, and dropped the subject.

By now, they had reached the western end of the beach with its quaint harbor, curio shops, and fish market. Seagulls were feasting on the remains of the day. Spontaneously, they decided to have a picnic supper on the beach and bought a bottle of wine, a baguette, and a tub of smoked *snoek* fish paté.

The sun set and a breeze rose from the sea. Chris guided Julie to a sheltered hollow behind a sand dune. They sat close together and wriggled their feet into the sand to where the warmth of the day was hoarded a few inches under the surface. It felt like the captured warmth of a bed on a Sunday morning. Chris poured wine into two cups and Julie spread paté on the baguette. It was very quiet; the seagulls had settled for the night and the dune barrier muffled the sounds of the ocean. He lay back against the warmth of the sand and saw a bright star appear in the east.

"Sirius, the evening star. It always makes me think of the Little Prince and his rose; do you know that story?"

"Vaguely." Julie sipped her wine. "Remind me what it's about."

"A French pilot crashes his plane in the desert and meets this young boy, a prince from a tiny planet. His most precious possession is a single rose; it's the most wonderful thing in the world to him. When he comes to Earth, and sees fields of roses, he is heartbroken, because it makes him feel that his rose is not special."

"Why does Sirius make you think of the prince and his rose?"

"When Sirius appears in the early-night sky, it is quite singular: a solitary, sparkling jewel on a bed of velvet. Half an hour later, there are hundreds and thousands of stars and you think, *oh well, it's just one star amongst billions – nothing special about it.*"

"That's a very sad way of looking at things."

Chris tried to read her expression in the fading light.

"Think about it," she went on. "You're saying that because there are billions of people in the world, no single individual matters. If I remember correctly, the whole point of the story was that the Little Prince goes back and still finds that his rose is the best, most special rose in the world."

"Do you really think that every single individual on this Earth matters?"

Julie looked at him, shocked. "You don't?"

"That's not what I said," he answered defensively. "But when fifty people get blown up by a bomb in Iraq, or tens of thousands die in a tsunami in Indonesia, I think the human mind cannot grasp that they are all individuals. It is too overwhelming to think that each of their families felt what I felt when ..." He did not finish the thought.

She squeezed his arm. "I suppose that's part of why I do what I do. Try to at least help a little where I can."

They ate in silence and listened to the sounds of the night. Birds rustled in the reeds and a lonely cricket struck up a persistent chirp. From afar, there was the sound of music and laughter spilling out of a beach bar. Then suddenly Julie grabbed Chris's arm and pointed to the silhouette of an animal outlined against the night sky.

"Is that a jackal?" she whispered.

"Nah, it's a dog. Here, boy, come," Chris called, clicking his fingers.

The dog approached cautiously. It was a fully-grown Alsatian with dark markings along his back.

"He looks kind of wild." Julie started to get up.

"Don't; never show fear."

"Come, boy." He held out a piece of bread for the dog.

The dog took the bread and Chris stroked his back and neck. He could feel the tags on the dog's collar but could not read them in the dark.

"People really shouldn't let their dogs roam free on the beach," Julie said.

"He's friendly, and in beautiful condition – aren't you, boy?" Chris continued to stroke the dog. "Obviously not a stray; probably just an independent-minded dog taking himself on his evening walk."

"You like dogs." It was a statement rather than a question.

Chris nodded.

They sat in the dark and talked, the dog sitting companionably alongside them. They talked about their likes and dislikes, their shared experiences at university, their friends and interests. Chris could no longer make out Julie's features, but, because he could not see her, his other senses were in overdrive. He was conscious of her hand on his arm when she wanted to emphasize a point, of her leg brushing against his when she shifted her weight, and of the perfume which he had first noticed when they had danced at the club. Her voice reminded him of classical music and he loved the sound of her laughter. There was a radiance about her that he could hear and feel without seeing.

They had much in common – both were single children and had lost a parent at a young age. "I miss my dad," Julie said. "But I don't often speak about him anymore. That makes me feel guilty." She turned towards Chris and sighed. "You can't go around talking about the dead all the time, can you?"

"No, you can't. We're all expected to move on with our lives. But I know what you mean." After a brief silence, he asked, "What happened with your dad?"

"He suffered a massive heart attack – he was forty-five years old. No warning, fit as can be." Again, they both sat quietly for a while. "No one really expects to die at forty-five; my parents' company was in an expansion phase and heavily leveraged. It was a mess. My mother automatically became chairman – she did what she could, but ..." Julie stopped, apparently hesitant to dredge up dark memories. "Noble Enterprises does highly specialized medical work. They make artificial joints, heart-lung machines, even vaccines. My father was very inventive, an absolute genius with exotic materials, alloys, and biochemistry ..." She sighed. "But he probably could have used the help of a good accountant."

"Soon after my father's death, Matt Baxter approached my mother and proposed a merger of his company with Noble. It was a good fit. He had the business skills, finance, and capacity to exploit the many patents that my father had registered. My mother is actually the chairman but Matt, and Greg, run the merged company."

She paused and Chris waited in silence.

"Matt's been good to us. I was truly happy for my mother when she married him. And as it is, he's done a tremendous job with the company. He has expanded the market and is exporting a lot – mainly to the Middle East and Asia."

The dog had snuggled up close for warmth and lay pressed against their knees. Julie tentatively stroked his back. Chris refilled their wine cups.

"Why are you and your father so tense with each other?" Julie asked.

"Are we?"

"Yes, you are. We only spent ten minutes with him at Marco's, but it was clear that you were uncomfortable – both of you."

"I didn't know it was so obvious." He thought about her question and found it hard to articulate his thoughts. *When had it started?* He could remember a time when he and his father had had an open, "normal" relationship – when they had laughed together or played tennis. His father had always been busy at work but he used to find time for Chris. He remembered the electric train set he had had when he was about eight or nine; they had spent hours playing with it together. The memory made him ache with loss and he was grateful for the darkness.

"After Mom's death, my father basically escaped to the hospital. Initially, I was farmed out after school to various friends' houses, but I couldn't stand it. They all treated me with that 'Oh, you poor, poor dear' attitude, as though I were something fragile. The only place I felt at home was with Desmond's family. His mother went through one almighty crying fit and then said it was time to dry our tears and do what Danielle would have wanted us to do. She found us a new dancing teacher and I ended up spending most of my time at Desmond's house. If it had been left to my father, I think my dancing would have stopped immediately. I resented that – dancing made me feel close to my mother. It kept the memory alive. When I danced, it was as though I could hear her, guiding me, telling me to concentrate, slow down ..."

As he spoke, part of Chris felt like chiding himself for being so pathetic – carrying on about his loss. But he was also astonished how strong his need to talk was; he had never expressed these feelings to anyone.

"About a year after Mom died, my father got himself a girlfriend. I hated it when she was around, making cow eyes at him. I felt miserable and jealous and upset that he was forgetting my mother. On top of it, I felt guilty that I was begrudging him a bit of happiness. I suppose I was a real shit to live with. Every time he spoke to me, I'd snap or grunt, and eventually he made less and less effort to communicate. In the end, the girlfriend stopped coming to our house; I guess they met at her place.

"Anyway, it was coming up to the second Christmas after my mother's death. I was dreading it. Mercy had tried valiantly to maintain the Christmas traditions. She'd baked mince pies and cookies and put a wreath on the door. She played Christmas carols on the radio and even got me to help her decorate a tree. On Christmas Eve, before she went to celebrate with her own people from the church, she'd laid the table for my father and me and had the full Christmas dinner ready in the warming drawer. I was beginning to think that maybe it wouldn't be too bad, so I wrapped a few gifts for my father, and waited." He paused.

"So, what happened?"

"He pitched up – eventually - with her. They'd had a few drinks and she was even more cow-eyed than usual, pawing him all over, laughing at every stupid joke he made. I was ready to puke, but I set another place at the table and served the Christmas meal. After dinner, we sat by the Christmas tree to unwrap presents. After a while, my father went off into the garage and came back with my present – a puppy: a miniature version of Nala."

Chris kept stroking the dog at his feet. The feeling of the animal's fur seemed to bring his memories alive in the minutest detail. "My dad, he was so pleased with himself – beaming from ear to ear as he brought in that puppy." Again he paused. "And I ... I just wanted to hurt him. I wanted him to feel the loneliness and the pain that I felt. So I lashed out." He sighed. "I instigated one almighty row. I told him he was a completely insensitive ass to think that one could just buy a new puppy to replace the one that was killed. And then I said that I supposed the next step would be for him to marry Old Cow-eyes and give me a new mommy, and that then we could forget all about Mom, and Nala, and live happily ever after."

"*You* said *that?*" Julie whispered.

"That ... and a lot more. My father got very angry in a cold, unemotional sort of way - really scary. He was furious. In very precise tones, he told me that he had had enough of indulging my spoilt-brat behavior. He also told me that my continuing with dancing was obsessive, that I needed to grow up and realize that it was pointless to live the dream of a dead woman."

Julie leaned her head against his shoulder and squeezed his hand. She said nothing and waited.

"I stopped serious dancing the very next day and concentrated on sport – but only sports that my father had never played. If I wasn't going to fulfill my mother's dreams, then I certainly was not going to fulfill his."

"What happened to the puppy?"

"It got taken back to the breeders the day after Christmas without another word being said. It was so stupid – I would have loved to have kept it." After a moment, he added, in a barely audible whisper, "*I also would have loved to have kept dancing.*"

"We never spoke about that incident. The girlfriend disappeared soon after, and my father made a point of never bringing any female guests home with him again. I feel bad about that, that I screwed his chances of another relationship. Now I'm out of the house, I reckon he just sits there by himself."

"There's no doubt that you behaved like an adolescent brat, but I don't think you have to beat yourself up over your father's chances with the ladies. He is still very, very eligible, believe me."

"How come you're such an expert on men?" he chuckled, thankful to her for breaking the somber mood.

They sat in silence and the touch of Julie's body pulsed through him. The wind died down and the mountains that formed the Hout Bay valley were silhouetted against the pale glow of the moon. The dog appeared to have appointed himself as their guardian and had settled at the top of the dune, a few meters away. Eventually, Chris started to point out constellations to Julie: Orion's Belt and the Southern Cross.

"Everybody knows those two. Why don't you show me something I haven't seen before?" Her voice flowed like a rich dessert wine, intoxicating him. Unable to resist any longer, Chris lay on his back and pulled her down on top of him. He caressed her hair and started to massage her neck.

"I've been dreaming of a neck massage all day," she murmured, as she relaxed under the touch of his hands.

Alone in our private universe, Chris thought. His hands worked their way down from her shoulders, exploring her back all the way down to the curve of her hips. He shifted position and let his lips touch her ears, her neck, her throat. When he undid the top buttons of her blouse she did not protest.

He stopped to pull off his T-shirt and put it under Julie's head so that her hair would be protected from the sand. He continued to undo her blouse; his mouth explored further and he could feel the erectness of her nipples. He kissed her, gently at first. Her perfume was all around him now. Julie's hands were running through his hair, pressing down on his shoulders. Despite his best intentions to take this slowly, to savor the build-up, he was soon overwhelmed by waves of passion and found himself kissing her hard. Julie responded, arching her back and pushing up against him; he wished she would never stop running her hands over his bare back and shoulders.

"You'll have to keep me warm," she whispered with a teasing smile, as she stretched her arms above her head and let him take off her bra. Bathed in moonlight, her breasts reminded him of the statues he had seen on his travels through Italy. Except these breasts were warm and responsive to the touch of his lips, his tongue.

"Julie," he breathed. "My Venus."

Suddenly the dog growled and started to bark.

"Shit!" Chris whispered. *"Someone's coming."*

They waited, motionless. The dog continued to bark. Julie sat up and fumbled to put on her bra and blouse whilst Chris retrieved his T-shirt.

The dog became very agitated, ran back and forth, urged them to follow.

"Shhh," Chris hissed. *"What is your case?"* He pulled Julie up.

"Talk about bad timing," he grumbled.

Without a word, Julie leaned up and planted a kiss on his cheek. Chris chose to interpret it as a promise of future opportunity and was somewhat mollified.

They followed the dog over the crest of the dune towards the lagoon. At the river-mouth, where the sandbank separated the lagoon from the sea, there was a commotion. As they got nearer, Chris could make out two shadowy figures. They were struggling to pull a rubber dinghy across the sandbank from the lagoon into the ocean. The dog stood close by, barking.

"Voetsek, piss off, *voetsek!"* one of the men kept saying to the dog, whilst heaving and pulling the rubber dinghy. He lashed out with a kick. This only served to agitate the dog more.

"Is there a problem?" Chris asked. He couldn't make out the features of the two men. They were dressed in dark clothes with baseball caps pulled low over their eyes.

"Just get your stupid mutt away from us," the taller man said aggressively.

"He's not ours; don't know where the owner is." Chris snapped his fingers, "Here, dog, come here, sit!"

The dog obeyed and stopped barking.

In a more conciliatory tone, the man thanked him and explained that they had been out fishing, misjudged the time, and got off course in the dark. With Chris's help, they pulled the dinghy across the sandbank. He was astonished at its weight and thought to himself that they must have had a really good catch.

"Get in," Chris said, and gave them a final shove into the waves. The men lowered the outboard motor and headed off towards the harbor.

He walked back to Julie, put an arm and around her shoulder, and bent down to kiss her. "Now, where were we?"

Gently, she pushed him away. "Chris, this is going way too fast - we weren't going to go any further, anyway – certainly not without a condom."

Chris fished in his pockets and silently held out a small square packet in the palm of his hands.

He could not make out her features in the dim light, but Julie's voice had lost its quality of golden wine. She sounded like a lawyer when she said, "You mean, you had this all planned out? Do you just assume that any female will say yes whenever you ask?"

"That's unfair. I always carry a condom with me – AIDS prevention one-o-one."

"I can't help but feel that it degrades women when men think they can have sex at the drop of a hat."

"You're being completely unreasonable. I would have thought that you, who deals with AIDS all day, would appreciate it if people were prepared. What do you expect?" His voice had an edge of anger to it now. "I suppose your ideal relationship is a long-distance one with a phantom fiancé? No physical touch necessary!"

"My relationship with Greg is none of your business," she hissed. "I just prefer it when sex is part of a mutually agreed relationship – not just some guy thinking he's going to get lucky tonight."

"We'd all love to live in a perfect world. Where do you think all the unwanted pregnancies and AIDS cases come from? I think the only responsible thing to do is to *always* carry a condom with you."

128

"You're such a Boy Scout," she spat. "Be prepared, *tweet, tweet, tweet.*" She spun around and headed up the path back towards the Khanya center.

"Wait," Chris shouted. "You shouldn't walk along there by yourself."

"Why?" she shot back. "Because there might be someone *else* lurking that wants to have sex with me?"

"C'mon, Julie, don't be like that!" Chris shouted after her, but she did not break her stride. He sighed in exasperation and turned his ire towards the dog. "You've caused quite enough trouble for one evening. Why don't you just bugger off home? Shoo! *Voetsek!*" The dog looked at him with his head cocked to one side and a hurt expression on his face.

"Oh great! Now you're also going to try and make me feel bad. What is it with everybody? It's not even full moon."

Despite his irritation, Chris followed Julie at a jog to make sure she got back to Khanya safely. He was just in time to see her drive off in her Golf.

For a long time, Chris stood in the moonlight next to his car. The whole evening played itself out in his mind like a video. Every once in a while he stopped – paused - looked at a scene again. *Damn, where did it go so wrong?* He felt hurt and confused by Julie's reaction. Maybe the interruption had given her time to think: think about her relationship with Greg. Yet she'd seemed eager; surely the relationship with Greg couldn't be that strong? He had a chance.

"Damn fishermen!" Chris shouted into the night. The smell of the blue gums hung about him like an olfactory fog. He sniffed and again rewound the videotape in his brain. *Weird*, he thought. *That rubber dinghy was damn heavy; but I didn't smell any fish.*

##

Chapter 8: Bull

Dress rehearsal, Friday morning

A north wind had sprung up overnight. Clouds raced and tumbled across the sky like a flock of sheep herded by an invisible hand. The wind roared through the oak trees and ripped at the leaves to bring about an early autumn. The branches bent and strained but held on to their leaves. Summer still had some fight left in it.

Inside the wine cellar at Groot Constantia, it was cool. The aroma of coffee and croissants mingled with that of wine-stained oak barrels.

Chris sat at a table near the middle of the hall and sipped his coffee. Next to him, Bull read a book and mechanically devoured one croissant after another. Neither of them paid much attention to the stage, where Cedric was going through an intricate choreographic routine with James and Riaan.

Chris took out his cell phone and scanned for messages.

"Stop doing that; it's irritating." Bull didn't even glance up from his book.

"What? I was just checking for ..."

"You've checked it three times in the last five minutes. If you want to speak to her, call her."

Chris quickly put the phone away and tried to change the subject. He took the heavy book from Bull's hands. "Let me see what you're studying – Human Physiology? Why on Earth ... I had no idea you were interested in medical matters."

Bull shrugged his shoulders. "I want to get a wife."

Chris could not hide his astonishment. "You're joking, right?" He looked at his friend's impassive face. "I mean, you are what ... thirty-two years old? Surely you don't need a book to tell you about ... you know. I mean ... there are easier ways to learn about women."

Bull snorted. "I can't keep messing around with boxing and dancing and hoping for a breakthrough. I need a job; to get a job, I need a qualification. So, I'm studying to be a fitness instructor." He tapped the book. "This is hard to read."

Chris put down the book. "But, Bull, if you're in love, and you have each other, what does it matter whether you have a job or not? Marriage can be a partnership where you build something together." He paused and added, "My mother supported my father whilst he did his specialization."

"I must have a job to pay for *lobola* – at least ten cows, maybe even a bull for a nice girl"

"I see. So, who's the lucky lady? When are we going to meet her?"

Bull's expression, as he looked down at Chris, seemed to say, *Don't you know anything? Can I be bothered to explain this to you?* The silence dragged on and Chris turned his attention to the stage.

Eventually, Bull relented. Slowly, in the tone of a primary-school teacher, he explained how it was. "When I have the job, I will go back to my village and the headman will pick a wife for me. But first I must have the money to pay for her."

"Seriously? In this day and age?"

Bull shrugged. "It is the way of my people. You only value that which you pay for. No one would respect a woman if her family just gave her away for free." He made a dismissive gesture as though he were tossing *mielie* pips to chickens.

Cedric, shouting from the stage, interrupted with his usual sarcasm. "If it is not too much trouble, can I get you gentlemen up here with us, please?"

Half an hour later, Cedric was venting his frustration. "Guys, guys, what's going on? Why did that costume change take so long? We had a full minute of dead time on stage!"

James said, "The dressing room is miles away and these bloody tables are an obstacle course."

"I could do a few summersaults or cartwheels to fill the gap," Riaan commented. He then executed two perfect backward flips and walked across the stage on his hands. Chris smiled. Riaan, with his shock of blond hair and permanently cheerful disposition, reminded him of a wind-up doll; a flexible perpetual motion Ken, perhaps.

"Thank you … thank you." Cedric rolled his eyes. "I'll think of something else." He looked at his watch. "Where the hell is Bruce? Has anyone heard from him?"

Of course they hadn't. They'd all been on stage together for the last forty minutes. Cedric inhaled deeply, and reached over his head to stretch out his neck muscles. Then he said, "Well, let's do it again. Riaan, you're in the middle, James on your right, Chris on your left. I want to see some serious cowboy swagger."

He raised his arms theatrically. "Music!" he cried, and the three dancers - in full cowboy-dress with lassos - started their routine.

Before they had done more than a few steps, however, Cedric was shouting again. "Lights!" he yelled to the back of the hall. "Where are my lights?"

An invisible hand responded and the stage was bathed in red, white, and blue. Psychedelic stars rotated on the dancers as they went through a high-energy routine, stomping their cowboy boots. The music rose and a chorus of *"Yeahs"* erupted from the speakers as the dancers, one by one, ripped off their shirts. When it was Chris's turn, the Velcro fasteners on his shirt did not perform as expected and the fabric tore. Riaan took one look at his flabbergasted expression and collapsed laughing.

"Wardrobe malfunction," James yelled, and joined in Riaan's uproarious laughter. Even Bruce smiled.

"Come on, guys! This kind of thing might happen tomorrow and, if it does, you will just have to carry on." Cedric was beginning to get irritated.

Riaan mimicked Cedric's British accent: "Stiff upper lip - the show must go on." He gave way to further fits of laughter. Cedric glared at him but even he couldn't suppress a grin.

Eventually, the three on stage regained their composure and the routine continued. Their specially modified jeans came off easily enough, leaving them in the Stetson, jockeys, and boots garb of New York's famous *Naked Cowboy*. Riaan picked up a guitar whilst the other two herded imaginary cattle, swinging their lassos through the air.

James held up his hands. The music stopped.

"What now?" Cedric asked impatiently.

"How the hell are we going to snare members of the audience with all these fancy table decorations and glasses about? Stuff's going to get broken, surely? This is not like the nightclub."

"*Hmm,* good point. We'll have to get a couple of volunteers to come and stand left and right of the stage at the beginning of the dance." Cedric made a note on his pad. "Riaan, stand there on the left for a minute and pretend to be a damsel in distress. Then we can work through how James can lasso you and get you up on stage."

Riaan leapt off the stage, took off his Stetson and used it to coyly cover his chest. He lifted one elbow to his forehead and simpered in a high-pitched voice, "Help me, help me, I'm a damsel in distress."

"Stop it!" Cedric' voice rose an octave and he wiped the perspiration off his forehead. "This is not a melodrama! I want to see precision and professionalism."

He clapped his hands. "Music! Only the last two minutes."

Chris and James scrambled to find the right place in the routine and swung their lassos through the air. As the music reached a climax, James threw the lasso over Riaan's head. Because of the Stetson, the noose did not drop down to Riaan's chest as intended, but rather settled around his neck. With gurgling theatrics, Riaan pretended he was chocking. He tugged hard on the rope; James lost his footing and crashed off the small stage on to the nearest table. The sound of splintering wood and glass filled the hall as James disappeared in a heap of white cloth, flowers, and broken glass.

A hushed silence fell.

"Are you OK, James?" Riaan looked ashen.

No answer.

Cautiously, Riaan approached his motionless friend.

"*O vok,* shit! He's ... he's lights-out or something."

Slowly, James opened one eye. "Your white ass is dead meat." He lunged up from the debris but Riaan was too fast for him. Relief swept over the others and they laughed as James pursued Riaan around the hall.

"Stop it," Cedric shouted in the end, gasping for breath between fits of laughter. "Just stop it! Guys, we really have to get serious now – the show is tomorrow." With a groan, he sat down on the nearest chair.

Bull, who had continued to sit impassively at his table near the stage while James and Riaan chased round the hall, slowly rose, and, as Riaan ran past, he grabbed him by the arm. Wincing from Bull's vice-like grip, Riaan found himself unceremoniously dumped on the edge of the stage. Bull then turned around and uttered just one word: "James!" He motioned for James to get back on stage, which he did, smartly.

This was the moment Bruce chose to make his entrance. He kept his sunglasses on and even in the dim light of the hall it looked to Chris as though the Australian might have spent the night under a bridge – he was unshaven, his hair was disheveled, and his shirt was seriously crumpled, even by Bruce's standards.

"Oh, thank you for joining us," Cedric oozed. "May I ask what it is that detained his lordship?"

Bruce grinned. "You wouldn't appreciate it. Let's just say a nice young piece of ass couldn't get enough of me."

"You were supposed to have been here an hour ago. This is a dress rehearsal!" Cedric's voice rose. He reeled back and screwed up his nose when Bruce passed him. "God, have you had beer for breakfast, or what?"

"Don't shout, mate, my head hurts."

While they had been arguing, Bull had silently approached the two men. Now he stood, arms folded, blocking Bruce's path. "Go! We don't want you here," he said.

Bruce took off his sunglasses and let out a nervous chuckle. "C'mon, Bull, don't make a big case out of this. You know I'll pull it off in the end."

The other man stared directly at him, not speaking, until Bruce averted his eyes. "OK, look, I'm sorry!" he muttered. "Is that what you want to hear? I'm sorry."

"*Ubuntu!* Do you know what that means?"

Bruce looked at the others for help but realized that he was on his own. His mouth pulled into a churlish expression as he shook his head.

"It means we are in this together – brothers. If one screws up, we … will … all … go … down." Bull punctuated each word with a poke of his large index finger against the surfer's chest, keeping his fierce gaze on him until finally Bruce lowered his eyes and shrugged his shoulders in defeated submission.

Bull turned to address the whole group on stage. Quietly, deliberately, he said, "What is this to you guys? Just a joke? A bit of fun? Well, let me tell you, I expected more. There are African groups making it big all over: Sun City, Green Point Stadium - even overseas, like London. I thought we finally had a shot at something big. And you all are assing around. This has gotta be done right."

He paused. Chris was amazed. Bull was a usually such a quiet, contained man. He had never heard him make such a long speech before.

Now, the big man lifted his fist and looked at his watch. "You have thirty seconds to decide to get serious. If not, I'm out of here." He put his book and water bottle in his tog bag and stood, waiting, ready to go.

There was a stunned silence. Then everybody spoke at once, all desperate to persuade Bull that they were indeed serious.

By eleven o'clock, when Wendy arrived, the Toreros were finally going through their routines with energy and precision. She watched as Chris, Riaan, and James went through a perfectly synchronized dance set to jazz music.

"That was great," Wendy said to Cedric, applauding. "By the way, I'm going to need some background on the Toreros so that I can introduce them." Wendy fished a Mont Blanc pen out of her handbag and flipped open a leather-bound notebook. "What can you tell me?"

"Well, other than Desmond, Riaan is the only one who is a trained ballet dancer. He comes from a small farming community and used to compete at national level in gymnastics. He's a choreographer's dream: with his gymnastics background, you can make him do almost anything."

"What about James?"

"Fashion addict, always dressed to kill. James fancies himself an entrepreneur. He's got a Business Science degree and has started a venture leasing out ice-cream vans."

Wendy laughed. "Seriously? I somehow don't see James selling ice cream."

"Oh, he doesn't get his hands dirty, that's why he leases out the vans. I'm not sure the business is making any money, but of course that's not really a problem."

"Why?"

"His father is Mangope Buthelezi, the head of Indabo Investments – they're royalty amongst the new elite. I mean, come on, James went to Bishops - that's where he and Chris became buddies; they were both on the school's first soccer team."

"How did he become part of the Toreros?"

"His family is from Zululand. You know how bad AIDS is up there. I think James must have lost two, if not three, of his cousins to AIDS. He wanted to get involved with an AIDS cause. Chris introduced him to Desmond, who was volunteering at Khanya, and Desmond persuaded him to join the Toreros. He's just a natural at anything physical: soccer, boxing, dancing ... sex."

Wendy raised an eyebrow and followed Cedric's gaze to where James was stretching near the stage. His skin, the color of dark chocolate, glistened and he displayed perfect white teeth as he laughed at one of Riaan's jokes.

Wendy scribbled a note. "So tell me about Bull."

"Bull Khumalo. His real name is Sandile, but everyone calls him Bull. He hails from the Transkei. He has one of those 'I-grew-up- in- a-matchbox' sob-story backgrounds."

"You'll make me cry, if you put it like that."

"No, seriously, I just can't fathom how people like him do it. He never knew his parents and was brought up by a grandmother on some godforsaken patch of land in the middle of nowhere. Virtually no formal schooling and having to herd cattle from the time he could walk. At sixteen, he went to work in the mines in Johannesburg."

"Have you ever been in a gold mine?" Wendy asked.

"No."

"You should go sometime – one mile underground, narrow, oppressive tunnels, damp, hot ... and the noise! And then there's the feeling that billions of tons of rock are just waiting to crush you. I take my hat off to anyone who works in that environment."

"He did it for years," Cedric said. "It allowed him to follow his real passion – boxing! Bull was quite the champion boxer amongst all those mineworkers. A couple of years ago, he was discovered by a boxing scout and persuaded to go professional."

"How's that worked out for him?"

"So-so; couple of small wins. But there's no money coming in. He finds supplementary work where he can and is busting his gut to get a breakthrough ..."

Just then, Julie rushed into the hall and interrupted them. "Wendy!" she exclaimed. "There you are! I've been trying to call, but your cell is on voicemail."

"Sorry, I turned it off when I watched the guys rehearsing. What's up?"

"I've just had a call from the office of the Minister of Health. She – the minister - has decided to grace us with her presence tomorrow."

Bull, James, and the others crowded around. Chris hung back at the outer edge of the circle.

"Old Dr. Beetroot?" James asked incredulously. "Why would she want to come to an AIDS event?" He imitated the minister's voice: "Beetroot juice and ginger extract is all you need to protect yourself against AIDS."

"Didn't she decline our invitation weeks ago?" Wendy asked.

"She didn't actually decline. The ministry simply did not bother to respond to our invitation. When we followed up, we were told very bluntly that 'The minister is very busy.'" Julie looked at the group and raised her hands for emphasis. "But it looks as if there has been a change of heart – maybe her colleagues have persuaded her that this would be a great opportunity for her to repair her image – show some support for an organization that is fighting AIDS."

"Well," Wendy said, "that's great news, then; any small impact we can make on the Minister of Health and her attitude to AIDS ..."

"That's exactly where the problem is, though; her aides are deeply concerned that someone could ridicule or offend her. They want assurances from us that she will be treated with full respect and," she looked around the hall, "then there's the logistics of it all! She's got a bunch of bodyguards and she wants four of her aides to attend – where are we going to put them all?" Her face was flushed when she added, "And - to top it all - now suddenly the SABC is all keen to send a crew ..."

"The SABC ...?" Bull asked, awe in his voice. "We'll be on national TV?"

"More than likely they'll just focus on the minister."

They all chattered excitedly and Chris noticed that Julie appeared to relax somewhat as she too recognized that, on balance, this was a very positive development. Eventually, she said, "Seriously, where are we going to put her?" How do we work her into the formal proceedings? I mean, the programs have been printed ..."

"I have an idea," Cedric chimed in excitedly. "James here does an excellent praise-singer routine ..."

"Ah, no!" James groaned. "You know I hate doing that whole groveling bit."

"But you're so good at it," Cedric answered. "And you look stunning in that Zulu dress-up ..."

"It's a brilliant idea," Wendy said. "We can wait for the other guests to be seated and then you can lead her in with the full praise-singer bit, chanting her virtues and accomplishments. That way, we make a big fuss of her, she doesn't have to say anything, and we don't have to alter the program."

"But she's got no accomplish ..."

"Then praise her ancestors."

It took a few more minutes of unabashed soaping up by the group before James agreed.

Julie looked at her watch. "Shoot, I have to run; I'm meeting with the chief protocol officer of the ministry at one and then I'm supposed to see the producer from the SABC ..."

Chris, who had remained in the background up until now, said, "Would you like me to go with you?"

"Why? Do you think I'm incompetent? Or do you have hitherto undisclosed experience in ministerial protocol and TV production?"

"Hitherto!" Riaan mimicked and laughed. "What sort of a word is that?"

His interjection allowed Chris to hide his embarrassment and annoyance. "Just trying to be helpful," he muttered, avoiding Wendy's eyes, which were darting between him and Julie. Nothing seemed to escape her attention. Now she turned to Julie. "I think it would be a good idea if someone goes with you. You should never go into a negotiation alone – at a minimum, you need someone else there to take notes."

"I'll go," Cedric offered. "I've worked with TV producers in the past. They're easy to deal with." He made a dismissive gesture. "You just have to suck up to their preposterous egos. I'm not a boffin on ministerial protocol, but, " he paused for effect, "I once saw the Queen live and in person. That must count for something."

It was agreed that Cedric would accompany Julie. They were barely out of earshot when James said, "There goes a man with a simple philosophy in life."

"What do you mean?" Chris asked.

"Cedric believes any and everything in life can be had through sucking up."

"What else do you expect from a *rooinek* Brit?" Riaan chipped in.

"I don't know about you all, but I'm peckish," Wendy said. "I'd like to treat you gentlemen to lunch."

This idea met with general approval. The Toreros went off to change while Wendy spread out a seating plan and set her mind to figuring out where to put the Minister of Health and her entourage.

##

Initially, the hostess at the Winery Restaurant told them they would have to wait half an hour for a table but she rapidly crumbled under the charm offensive of the five men.

"I'm used to getting my way in restaurants, but you guys are pros," Wendy joked. "I could get used to this." Every head in the restaurant turned to watch her and the troupe of men make their way to a table with a view over the vineyards.

Chris joined Wendy in ordering almond crusted trout; the others settled for ostrich steak or roast springbok. When Bruce tried to order wine, however, Bull intervened. "No wine, we still have a lot of work to do this afternoon."

They relived the morning's rehearsal and James pointed out that the stakes had now been seriously upped. Chris was astounded to observe, for a second time that day, how excited and talkative Bull seemed. He kept saying, "This is our chance, man. National TV; this is it!"

Wendy talked them through the proceedings for the next day and gave them a rundown of the dignitaries and well-known people who would be there: Cape Town's mayoress, several TV stars, the vice-chancellor of the university, members of the ANCs women's league, the wives of a couple of famous golfers, and the chief superintendents of both the Groote Schuur Hospital and the Red Cross Children's Hospital.

"Pretty impressive," James said. "Sounds like it will be mainly women."

Wendy shrugged her shoulders. "The battle against AIDS seems to have become mainly a women's issue. Don't the women of Africa always have to bear the burden when the going gets tough? The only thing that seems to rouse the men is charity golf events."

"The men of Africa are warriors," James answered. "They respond to the call for battle. If they think AIDS is just a matter of tending to the sick, they will leave it to the women. But if they can be made to see it as a war, then they will respond."

"I hadn't thought of it in those terms. Maybe we should find some time to brainstorm after this event. I'd love to find a way to get more men involved in this battle. "

Chris was halfway through his trout when Wendy asked him, quietly, "So, what's up with you and Julie?"

His first impulse was to dismiss the question the way he usually dismissed any probing into his private life. But when he looked up at Wendy, he could see that there was no guile in her question, only genuine interest and concern. He was struck by the thought that this was probably how a mother, *his* mother, would have talked to her son. He looked around, but the others were paying no attention. Bruce was taking bets that he would get the waitress' phone number before coffee was served and James was egging him on.

Chris shrugged. "I don't know if *anything* is going on between me and Julie. She's very ... complicated. One minute, I think we're moving in the right direction, the next she acts like the Ice Queen." He looked out at the dappled green light that filtered through the vines. A hummingbird hovered at the edge of the fountain, its beak pecking at the water whilst its wings gyrated so fast that they were almost invisible. "Maybe I'm chasing a ghost, trying to recapture what I felt when I first met her."

"Chris, you may have to cut her a little slack here. You know, I've chaired and organized God knows how many charity events. For Julie, this is the first time that she has the reins, and we know that she's a perfectionist. So of course she's tense. If you want my advice ..."

Chris nodded his assent.

"Give her a call and offer to help her tomorrow morning. The day of the gala is always a very stressful time. You can really show your support just by being there, helping with the unexpected things that always crop up."

"Do you think …?"

A well-groomed woman, more or less Wendy's age, interrupted them.

"Hi, Wendy; I don't want to be rude, but seeing you here with these gentlemen ... well, me and the bridge girls ..," she pointed to a group of three women at a nearby table, who all gave little waves and smiled, "we're just dying of curiosity about the gala tomorrow."

Wendy introduced the Toreros to her friend, who insisted that she did not want to interrupt and did not want to sit down, but then proceeded to interrupt anyway. Chris felt the smile on his face become frozen and wished the woman would make up her mind – stay and join in the conversation, or go. His mind wandered to Wendy's suggestion. *Should he call Julie? What if she gave him another serious brush off?* Then he heard Wendy's friend say, "…and is it true that there will be a bachelor auction?"

Wendy made a great attempt at the Mona Lisa's inscrutable smile. "You and the girls will have to contain your curiosity until tomorrow, won't you?"

After the woman had eventually returned to her friends, where she could be seen leaning excitedly across the table and talking animatedly, Chris turned to Wendy and asked suspiciously, "What's this about a bachelor auction?"

"Yeah," said James. "I must say, man, I'm surprised that you're prepared to go along with it. I thought it wasn't your sort of thing." He looked at the growing alarm on Chris's face. "Desmond didn't tell you?" It was a statement rather than a question.

Bruce grinned gleefully, while Riaan said, "Oh dear, oh dear. He knows nothing about the auction. Maybe we should've just left it as a surprise for tomorrow."

"That would be cruel," Wendy interjected.

"Cruel is good," Bruce answered.

Chris groaned, looked desperately at Wendy. "Tell me it's not true," he pleaded. "To me, that's just the tackiest ..."

But she brushed his protestations aside. "You're over-reacting. It's just a fun way to raise a little more money. Besides, we will hold a ballot for the audience to choose only one of you to be auctioned off. There's only a small chance that you'd be the one."

Chris wasn't convinced. "And suppose I am 'the one', what is it I am supposed to do?"

"Just spend an evening with the person who bids the highest price, go to dinner..."

"They own you for the night, my mate," Bruce interrupted. "You never know who you might end up with. You could end up being a sex slave to ... old Dr. Beetroot herself!"

"Rubbish!" Wendy said. "It's just harmless fun, and of course we'll pay for the dinner."

Chris felt a cold anger. *Desmond had a nasty habit of being economical with the truth*, he reflected, remembering the days when Desmond had even deceived his own mother by pretending to earn money as a supermarket packer, when in fact he was drug delivery boy for his cousin. Chris had always protected his friend's secrets and he hated being deceived in this manner. *It was about time that Desmond learned that his deceit had consequences*, Chris told himself. *He could damn well come back and do his own dancing.*

Rising from the table, Chris pushed back his chair and excused himself. He was conscious of the silence behind him as he strode out on to the patio with his cell phone drawn like a gun, Desmond in its sights. But Desmond's cell went to voicemail and when he tried his mother, Josie's phone just rang and rang. Chris was perplexed. In all the years that he had known the Andrews family, Josie had never been without her cell phone - it was the lifeline of her business. His anger gave way to concern - something was wrong.

He walked through the vineyards to collect his thoughts and returned as the group was getting ready to leave.

"You OK?" Bull asked.

Chris nodded. "I'm still mad at Desmond; I'd love to just walk away and let him stew. But that would not be fair on you guys – or the AIDS cause."

Bull put his big arm around Chris's shoulder, then turned to Bruce. "You see, this is *ubuntu*. My man Chris here, he gets it."

##

Chapter 9: The Gala

Saturday morning

Julie was alone at Groot Constantia. She stroked the silky drapery of the white tent, big enough to seat two hundred people. Flags fluttered and flapped like tethered birds from the three poles that supported the structure. The tent looked like a cruise liner on an expansive sea of grass. Then, as she stood there, the sky darkened and the oak trees groaned as the southeaster threatened to free the billowing tent from its anchor hooks.

Desperately, Julie hung on to one of the tie ropes that had come loose; her hair lashed across her face and her hands were sweaty, but she did not dare let go. Suddenly, an immense gust rampaged through the trees and lifted the tent into the air with Julie still clinging to one of the wildly snaking ropes. In wonderment, she looked down as the wind carried her over the countryside below, then over suburbs with tiny gardens, over highways teaming with Dinky cars. She flew on and on above the scrappy clouds, occasionally glimpsing vineyards, mountains, forests, and streams.

The wind dropped her in a wheat field, in a place that felt familiar. She recognized it from a Grade Five school camp. The teacher had taken them on a farm visit to learn where food came from. All around her, golden wheat had stretched waist-high to the horizon. She remembered that she had asked her teacher how it was possible that there were hungry people in the world when there was "so uncountable gazillion much" wheat for bread.

She turned and was horrified to be confronted by a massive tornado; it grew by the minute and came hurtling towards her. Julie stood mesmerized; she tried to scream but her throat closed up. As she watched, helpless, the swirling cone wreaked havoc all around her. It tumble-dried the devastated remains of a farmyard: roof sheeting, a tractor tire, hay bales, chickens, cackling wildly; even a donkey was suspended against the dark-blue sky. Julie's heart pounded. She turned to run but there was no shelter anywhere. Frantically, she looked around for some means of escape. As the tornado bore down on her, she crouched, covered her head, and listened to its roar.

With her eyes tightly shut, she sensed a change. A warm, protective shield appeared to have sprung up around her. The elements crashed against it but could not breach its enveloping barrier. Thwarted, the twister turned tail and disappeared like a beaten animal. She felt herself held by a pair of strong arms, then a whole body wrapped around

144

her, a deep calm emanating from it. She heard the last whimpers of the disappearing storm; a bird started to chirp. She relaxed.

##

For a while, Julie lay very still, lingering in that hazy zone between sleep and waking. All night, the southeaster had rattled at her sash windows and caused the oak tree outside to creak. She clung to the fading dream ... *Just a little longer; I want to see his face – let me see his face.* Her arms were tightly wrapped across her chest, clutching her shoulders. She stretched her legs like a cat after its midday nap and felt the caress of cotton sheets stretched over her waist, her thighs. Then a whole Hallelujah chorus joined the single chirping bird and there was no denying that, behind her tightly shut eyelids, dawn was marching across the windowsill. And still she hung on - wishing and wanting to see the ending of her dream.

Chris is coming to pick me up, she thought. Chris! Why did he make her feel so unsure of herself? After the brush-off she'd given him the previous day, she had been surprised when he'd called and offered to help her with all the last minute preparations.

The gala, it's today!

Her eyes flew open to take in the familiar pale-peach walls, her Chagall print with its flying donkeys. She shoved the sheets aside, walked to the window, and opened the curtains. With an expert yank, Julie shoved the paint-encrusted sash open. She inhaled deeply and savored the cool tightening of her skin as the air wove its way through her nightdress. The view of the mountain from her third-floor apartment window was partially obscured by an oak tree – the source of all the chirping. Traffic sounds drifted up from the street and mingled with the smell of coffee from the bakery on the ground floor. It was a glorious morning – not a breath of wind. "Thank you, God, thank you!" she said and turned towards the shower.

##

Chris circled the block to make sure he was at the correct address and then found parking right outside Julie's apartment building. He took it as an omen – it was going to be a good day. He felt his spirits rise, although at the back of his mind anxiety about Desmond, and his family – who he still had not managed to get in touch with – continued to niggle. But he tried to put these worries to one side – he was determined to enjoy the day. This part of town, close to the university, was very up and coming. Shiny new developments, their ground floors sporting boutiques, juice bars, and restaurants, surrounded him on all sides. Julie's block, however, was

145

different from its neighbors, a pale-cream, three-storied building with old-fashioned sash windows. The smell of freshly baked bread lured him to make a quick detour through the bakery before pressing the buzzer for Julie's apartment.

"You're very punctual," she greeted him. "Have you had breakfast? I've just put on some coffee. Do come in. My head's already spinning with all the things we need to do today…"

Was she babbling to hide nervousness? She looked lovely in a floral print dress, her hair pulled into a ponytail, and her face slightly flushed with excitement.

He said, "I'd love some coffee … and I brought us some croissants. Lucky you, living right above the most amazing bakery."

She led him into the open-plan living area and he had a chance to look around the room whilst she busied herself laying out breakfast things on the counter. He was disappointed that the furnishings gave away so little about the occupant. A rental company might have provided the cream sofas and plain oak furniture. There was no TV and the only personal items were a pile of books on the coffee table and a mohair blanket on one of the sofas. He pictured Julie in the evenings, curled up under the blanket, and reading … what? Probably Jane Austen?

As if probing his mind, Julie said, "I don't get enough time to read. The Khanya center keeps me so busy that I also haven't yet had a chance to do anything to this place."

"I love the attention to detail in these older places. Those are really solid picture rails you have there. First chance I get, I'm going to introduce picture rails into the places I design."

She looked up at the picture rails as if seeing them for the first time and shrugged. "I really don't want to get weighed down by … stuff."

He was about to ask whether that meant she was planning to move abroad, but decided not to. He didn't want to repeat the mistake of appearing to prescribe what she should do with her life.

They started on their breakfast of yoghurt with granola, croissants, and coffee. Chris noticed that Julie had little appetite, and appeared preoccupied with her long to-do list, which she went through as they ate. She was in the process of explaining the security arrangements, when she stopped mid-sentence, gasped, and pointed. Chris spun around to see a spider running up the wall above the kitchen sink.

"*Aggh*, I hate spiders! Do you think it's poisonous?"

He watched the spider. It was flat-bodied but of impressive size - he guessed it to be two inches across. It had come to a halt on top of one of the picture rails and appeared to be watching them.

"I'm sure it's pretty harmless."

She shuddered. "Can you ... can you get rid of it for me?"

Chris took a broom from the closet and gently swept along the picture rail, hoping to coax the spider on to the bristles of the broom, but it kept evading him. He felt a tug as the broom caught on something. Pushing hard, he dislodged a small object.

"Watch out!" Julie cried.

This was the moment the spider chose to clamber on to the broom and start a rapid descent down the handle towards Chris's hand. Up close, it really was quite an impressive specimen, but Chris kept his cool, crossed the room to the open window, and shook the broom until the spider was dislodged.

"I thought you were going to whack it," Julie said faintly, uncoiling herself from the protective position she had adopted, hands over head.

"No, you must never do that; they can easily get away and hide in corners. And if ever you do manage to whack one, it leaves a nasty smear on the wall; much better to let it climb on to the broom and chuck it out of the window."

Chris picked up the object that had fallen from the picture rail and examined it. It looked like a microphone. He gave it to Julie, who appeared completely puzzled by the small shiny object.

"Why would someone bug your apartment?"

She looked at him blankly, then her expression changed. "I know, the landlord told me that the previous tenant was a single mum with a toddler. Apparently, she was totally neurotic about keeping an eye on the nanny whilst she was at work. She had all manner of video cameras and stuff installed. This must be something they forgot to take out."

Chris was not convinced. He wanted to search for any other surveillance devices but Julie was suddenly all businesslike.

"My God, look at the time; we've got to get going." She grabbed her keys, punched a code into the alarm system, and led him down the stairs.

##

The couple sitting at a bistro table outside the coffee shop certainly attracted the occasional second look. Even in post-apartheid South Africa, where inter-racial couples were more and more common, they were a striking pair. She had platinum-blonde hair and protected her milky skin with a broad brimmed hat. He was dark-skinned, dressed in smart chinos and a silk shirt, absorbed in the morning paper. She sipped her espresso, smoked a menthol cigarette, and casually observed the passers-by.

"Here they come," she said under her breath and picked up her cell phone.

Julie and Chris emerged from the main entrance of the apartment block, and drove away in his BMW.

The man folded his newspaper. "Did you get them?"

She showed him the pictures on her phone.

"Hmm? Not great."

"Well, what do you expect, the way they rushed past? I couldn't exactly jump up and say 'Hey, wait, I want to take your picture.'"

"Keep your voice down." He looked over his shoulder. "The boss will want to get a better picture of the guy; we'll have to try again later." After a few moments of silent contemplation, he turned to his companion and smirked. "Looks like our boy spent the night. Bet they fucked like fish all night long."

"Don't be crude. He didn't spend the night."

"How do you know?"

"The clothes; if he'd come here last night, he wouldn't be wearing shorts and a T-shirt; he'd be in jeans or evening clothes."

"Maybe he brought a change of clothes."

Her bright-red lips curled into a smile. "Only one way to find out." She stubbed out her cigarette, picked up her bag, and fished out a small set of tools that might have been mistaken for a bunch of keys. A few minutes later, they both casually strode towards the entrance of the apartment building.

At Groot Constantia, Chris and Julie found the estate manager engaged in a furious argument with one of the caterers.

"Look at the treads your *bleddy* truck has made on the lawn! And you went through those rose bushes!"

"Sorry, man; it's just one little rose bush and the grass will recover when you water it."

"Why do you even bring that thing across the lawn?"

"It's our mobile kitchen; we must have it right by the hall. Otherwise we cannot get hot food to the people."

"Well, you were supposed to park it at the back of the hall. Who's in charge here, anyway?"

Chris watched as Julie stepped into the mediator role. She got the caterers to move their truck and appeased the estate manager by soliciting his advice on how they could avoid any further damage. They went through the vehicle access and parking plan and, in response to Julie's charm and calm demeanor, the estate manager summonsed two of his crew to help with traffic management.

Volunteers started to arrive and the normally sedate wine estate began to buzz with activity. Soon Julie and Chris were as busy as Chicago air-traffic controllers at Thanksgiving: directing people to set up a welcome booth, to lay out goody bags and information leaflets, to decorate tables and put up signs to direct the crowd. Chris managed to intercept and redirect a truckload of Portaloos just as they were about to be offloaded near the main entrance. He spun around at the sound of growling dogs. The Minister of Health's security staff had arrived. Chris took them to the hall, where the sniffer dogs, trained to locate bombs, were bewildered by the smell of wine. They howled, milled in circles, and got in the way of the caterers.

The sundial on the lawn inched towards eleven o'clock and the refreshment station for volunteers saw a steady throng of people. The smell of coffee mingled with delicious aromas from the caterers' field kitchen. Chris, atop a ladder, fixing a large red AIDS ribbon above the entrance to the hall, suddenly felt hungry. The lawn below him resembled a beehive and Julie, clipboard in hand, was at the center of it all. She had found her groove and was calmly directing the swirl.

"I never realized how much planning and effort is required to pull off an event like this," he said to the woman who was making a pretense of holding the ladder below him. He looked over at Julie with renewed admiration. She must have felt his gaze, because she turned and gave a wave before bringing her attention back to the wine merchant. She made him open his coolers and seemed satisfied that he had indeed brought the right champagne. Chris chuckled as he remembered his first encounter with Julie at the Khanya center, when she'd been busy chewing out this same wine merchant.

"Hey, Chris! Can you come in here and have a look, man? Some asshole has moved my console." Chris followed the ranting lighting technician and they spent the next twenty minutes assessing various options and helping the technician test the stage lights.

Wham! Suddenly, the wine cellar was plunged into darkness. The diesel generator made a whining sound and stuttered to a halt. Within seconds, the chef could be heard cursing that his pastries would be ruined.

A quick bit of trouble-shooting ascertained that the generator had not been sized to cope with both the caterers' ovens and the stage lights. This time it was Chris who found himself in the mediator role – working out a roster to allocate electricity once the generator had been started up again.

It was near noon when he finally caught up with Julie, who was perusing her lists at a table in the big white tent. She had taken off her shoes. He handed her a small carton of juice.

"You remembered, my favorite: lychee juice." She smiled. "Want some?"

He shook his head, but sat down next to her.

"I won't laugh if you make a rude noise with the straw." She looked around her, with something like relief on her face. "I'm so grateful that the wind has held off. I worried about it so much that I ... I actually had the wildest dream."

"Go on."

She shook her head. "We don't have time for that now. When will the Toreros be here?"

Chris shrugged his shoulders. "What did you agree with Cedric?"

"Four o'clock, in suit and tie to help welcome the guests."

"Well, then …"

"Will you please follow up with them and …"

"Jules! Darling, there you are!"

They both spun round and Julie gasped "Greg?" as a tall, expensively dressed man with boyishly gelled sandy-colored hair strode towards them.

Greg was beaming like a Father Christmas who has managed to pull off the ultimate surprise present.

Julie got up to give him a hug. "Greg! What …"

"Surprise!" He planted a long kiss on Julie's mouth. She was the first to draw away.

"Man, it's hotter in Cape Town than I expected." He used a handkerchief to wipe the perspiration from his forehead. "I told you I'd come down for your gala, and here I am!"

Julie introduced the two men. Greg looked at Chris pensively.

"I have a feeling we've met before. Where … it will come to me."

Chris shrugged. He noticed Julie fidgeting with her hair; she seemed agitated.

Greg turned to Julie. "Shall we go and have some lunch? I'm dying for a cold beer."

"What? Now? Greg … I'd love to, but I have a million and one things to do."

"Hey, I'm not talking about taking the whole afternoon off … though I'd love to," he said, touching her waist. "But I also have things to do. Got a meeting lined up this afternoon with one of our big clients – these people insist on doing business on the golf course. It's a tough life." He winked at Chris, who had to fight hard to keep his expression neutral.

Julie looked at her watch. "OK, but we'll have to get something here on the estate. I have to be back in forty-five minutes. Chris, do you want to join us?"

Was it his imagination, or did her eyes actually plead with him? He couldn't be sure. Chris caught a whiff of expensive cologne. What did she see in this guy? Greg seemed at least twelve, perhaps even fifteen years older than Julie. Chris knew the type – the sort of man who always tried too hard to be "one of the boys", buying rounds of drinks for everyone in the pub, but who hadn't earned their membership on the field. Maybe that was it; Chris reckoned that he probably showered Julie with expensive gifts.

Greg smiled at the younger man, nodding his encouragement, but Chris found himself saying, "No, no, that's OK. I'm sure you have lots to catch up on. I think I'd better go and round up the Toreros. Bruce said he was going surfing in Camps Bay; he's likely to lose track of time." He forced a smile. "You two go and enjoy your lunch."

"We'll see you later," Greg said over his shoulder, as he put his arm around Julie and led her out into the light.

##

Chapter 10: Reaching for the Sky

Saturday afternoon

He found Bruce sprawled on a beach towel. Chris wrinkled his nose. "One can smell the tanning lotion a mile away. I thought you'd be out in the surf."

"Howzit, my mate." Bruce barely stirred, but the aspirant surfer next to him sat up and gave Chris a smile.

"Be a doll; find my friend a towel and give him a good coconut rub," said Bruce lazily, reaching for the girl. "He needs relaxing."

Chris couldn't vouch for the girl's surfing skills, but she knew how to give a good back massage. Twenty minutes later, he lay glistening on the white sands of Camps Bay beach, feeling the heat seep up through the towel. He kept his eyes shut and listened to the waves, the peculiar breathing of the ocean. It wasn't a steady in and out but rather an exaggerated, multi-stage breathing, like someone getting ready to blow out candles on a birthday cake: sucking in air, suck, suck some more, hold ... wait for it ... *crash* as a wave breaks, and *woosh* as it lunges up the beach. Then again, a long sucking sound as pebbles and shells get drawn back into the sea, before the process repeats. He loved the sound of the sea. It underscored a whole symphony of other sounds – chief amongst them, the squabbling of seagulls. Behind him, from beyond the beach's palm fringe, came the discord of cars and taxis, street markets, laughter, and squabbles of the human variety. A vendor shouted, "Ice *creeeam! Lekker, lekker* icy coca *colaaaa!* Ice *creeeam!"*

Chris's consciousness subsided into the rhythm of the ocean's breathing. His mind wandered to Julie. *He pictured her on the beach, the breeze playing with her hair, and the sun - reflecting off the ocean - casting a halo around her. Her eyes laughed at him, invited him. Then she came and lay down next to him and he could feel her warmth. He longed to hold her, protect her, and make her laugh.*

But no, she was with Greg. Chris felt a pang of guilt that he had found an excuse to walk away from the gala preparations. Then he thought of the way Greg had put his arm around Julie and his thoughts darkened. *OK, if that's how it is, let* him *help her.*

He rolled over and noticed that Bruce was gone – probably surfing. Chris surveyed the Beach Road where restaurants vied for attention with their blue, green, and maroon umbrellas. Behind them, set amongst lush gardens and mature pines, million-dollar homes rose in serpentine tiers up against the mountainside. There were quite a few construction sites and Chris ached with the desire to design a house. The area cried out for something bold, yet respectful of the natural setting. He pictured combining granite with sandstone; teak with steel; strong, angular lines. In his mind's eye, he moved effortlessly though his fantasy house, taking in the high ceilings and the views stretching unbroken from an infinity pool to the ocean. *One day... one day, I'll show them.*

He caught sight of a hang-glider, then another, and another. They meandered like exotic birds against the craggy backdrop of Table Mountain, then twirled and swooped above the pines towards the beach. He felt an urge to get into his car and go and find their launching spot. *To soar through the sky, that's living!* From the recesses of his mind, from a long-ago history lesson, Chris dredged a quote that had always intrigued him: *"Let me warn you, Icarus, take the middle way."* Daedalus' admonition to his son not to fly too close to the sun or too close to the water.

As he lay there, half-listening to sea, it was as if he could hear his own father's voice: *"Turn on the house alarm"; "Keep the car doors locked"; "Always have your cell phone with you".'* Bitterness descended on Chris like the shadow of an albatross. *Always stick to the trodden path, always do the right thing, play it safe.* His mind dragged him down a familiar path, a path he did not want to go down. *He saw his mother's hair blowing in the wind before she closed the car window; his mother racing up the stairs. Always play it safe – then, one day, you stop a bullet - and you've hardly even lived. He saw the gunman lift his arm; saw right into the barrel that seemed the size of a train tunnel. What was it he was supposed to have done? If only ... if only he had reacted. If he had blocked his mother and taken the bullet, if he had charged up and tackled that hoodlum. If only ... it was entirely his fault. His mother's life had been in his hands and he had failed; he'd played it safe – done nothing ...* And for the thousandth time in his life, Chris was overwhelmed by a sense of total and paralyzing guilt. He couldn't move, he could barely breathe.

He felt a chilling explosion across his chest and, for a second, thought a bullet had hit him. Then the icy wet sensation tipped him into full consciousness. "What the f ...." Chris swallowed his curses when he saw a young boy holding a bright-red plastic bucket. The boy pointed at Bruce and stammered, "Th... th... that man said I must do it."

Bruce grinned. "Didn't want you to get heat stroke, mate."

"You …" Chris lunged up at Bruce, who laughed and sprinted off along the water's edge. Chris tackled him into the surf and they both gasped as the icy waves crashed over their heads.

Suddenly, Bruce pointed to a spot behind Chris. "Hey, look, dolphins!"

Chris was not going to fall for that old trick. He grabbed hold of Bruce's shoulders and dunked his head into the surf.

"No, seriously," Bruce spluttered, when he came up for air. "Genuine – look!"

Indeed, a crowd of onlookers had gathered on the beach to watch a school of dolphins frolicking beyond the breakers. Bruce and Chris decided to brave the cold and swam towards them. Chris had expected the dolphins to shy away but, to his amazement, they didn't, and he found himself at the heart of the school. He could feel, rather than hear, the high-pitched noises that the creatures made. It felt like the sound waves reverberated through his chest. He had never experienced anything like it. One dolphin came to within touching distance and hovered for a moment. Up close, its skin was as smooth and shiny as stainless steel. Chris reached out but in an instant it slid away.

"*Awesome*," he whispered.

Bruce said, "My bollocks are freezing off, I'm going back."

Chris ignored him and stayed amongst the dolphins. On an impulse, he started swimming and immediately two dolphins broke away from the school and joined him. He tasted salt on his lips; he felt the sun on his back, and the presence of his two guardians to either side of him. Nothing mattered but this moment. *I'm alive*, he thought, *and to hell with playing it safe.* He savored the strength of his body as he headed out to sea.

Eventually, exhausted but exhilarated, he made his way back to the beach and through the throng of onlookers.

"That was so cool," a young girl said. "Do you often swim with dolphins?"

"No. In fact, that was the first time ever."

"Weren't you scared?"

Chris was about to answer when a blonde in a white bikini barged in. "Hey, Dolphin Whisperer, can I have my photo taken with you?" She flashed him a smile displaying perfect teeth in a mouth as wide as Julia

Roberts'. Chris looked to include the little girl he'd been speaking to, but the blonde possessively grabbed his arm and steered him off towards Beach Road. As she chattered away, Chris observed the bright lipstick and the bikini that did not do enough to hide her flat chest and pale, angular limbs. Her make-up was immaculate and even Chris, who was not much of an expert on perfumes, could tell that she was wearing something expensive. It occurred to him that she did not seem much like a beachy person.

"Oh, by the way," she said as they reached the road. "My name is Cindy. And you are?"

"Chris. Chris du Toit."

"Let me introduce you to my boyfriend, Lenny." An African man, his arms folded, stood in the shade of a palm. He had a thin moustache and a thick gold chain round his neck. Chris guessed him to be in his mid-thirties and thought that Lenny looked faintly ridiculous with his designer khaki pants, long-sleeved silk shirt, and Gucci sunglasses. Like Cindy, he didn't seem at all at home at the beach.

"Lenny, this is Chris. He was out there with the dolphins. "

The man nodded. Chris was surprised when his hand was shaken with bone-crunching force. It took all his willpower not to wince and he greeted Lenny through a frozen smile.

Lenny took out his cell phone to take a picture and Chris had the fleeting sensation that he had seen the man somewhere before. But Cindy, who melded herself against him and hugged his bicep as though it were a floating log in a raging river, distracted him. Chris dutifully smiled for the photograph and then hurriedly beat a retreat to his spot in the sun.

"Getting yourself fixed up for a threesome – you dog, you!" teased Bruce.

"Oh, piss off! Don't you ever think about anything but sex? Let's go find some lunch."

Bruce watched Lenny and Cindy disappear into the crowd. "That guy looks kinda familiar."

"That's strange." Chris looked up from where he was gathering his belongings. "I had the same feeling."

"Of course!" Bruce exclaimed. "He's the guy that was making a play for Julie at the De Waterkant Club. Remember? That's why Julie wanted me to dance with her."

"Do you really think it's the same guy?"

Bruce shrugged. "Look, it was dark at the club, but there's definitely something familiar about him."

Chris felt a creeping unease. Of all the people who had watched him swim with the dolphins, it had been this pair who had wanted to get his photograph. What earthly reason could they have had? He looked up and down the street but there was no sign of them.

The two men crossed Beach Road to Chris's BMW. Chris was annoyed to find that the vehicle behind him, a large black Pajero, had parked so close that he could not get to the trunk of his car. He opened the passenger door and chucked in the towel he'd used. As he turned, he noticed that the side of the Pajero was scratched and dented. There were traces of silver paint on the vehicle and Chris immediately thought of Bridget's encounter three days earlier. *She'd said that a large black SUV had forced her off the road.*

A car-guard, in bright-yellow vest and floppy hat, sauntered over from where she'd been sitting in the shade of a palm. She said, "I looked nicely after your car – no problems."

Chris explained that they were not yet leaving and asked the woman if she knew who the owner of the Pajero was. She shrugged her shoulders.

He handed her a tip. "My friend and I are going to have lunch there" - he pointed – " by the blue umbrellas. When the people come back for this car, I want you to come and call me, OK?"

"OK." She gave him a complicit grin from under her hat and quickly stuffed the money into a hidden recess somewhere in her bosom.

They were seated at a prime table on the terrace of The Sandbar. "This is the life," Bruce mused as he looked across the road to the beach and the ocean beyond. "All I need now is a Windhoek lager."

A pretty waitress with a ponytail approached. Bruce stared appreciatively at her tight-fitting T-shirt and cleavage as she leaned forward to wipe the table. After she had taken their orders and disappeared to the kitchen, Chris said, "Do you always have to be so damn blatant? It's embarrassing."

"Don't be such a prissy prick. Boobs like that are a real gift. I tell you, those babies are all natural goodness, not an ounce of silicone there. I'd love to get my hands on them."

"You're impossible." Chris shook his head, then asked, "How can you tell?"

"Tell what?"

"Tell whether they are natural or ... or enhanced." He blushed.

"Jeez, you know, sometimes I really wonder about you. Don't you know anything? These are the important things that you learn in the school of life, the ..."

"Spare me the lecture," Chris interjected.

Bruce shrugged. "Well, once you've felt some of those hard siliconies, you get to appreciate the real thing."

The waitress reappeared and brought their drinks. Bruce drained half his beer in one gulp whilst Chris sipped his Coke. Chris asked, "Is it true that you've worked as an escort?"

Bruce raised a quizzical eyebrow and finished his beer.

"Yeah. So what?"

"I was just wondering, I mean, just thinking about this stupid auction thing. I'm really annoyed about that."

"You've got nothing to worry about. No offense, but why would they go for you when I'm around? In any case, it's bound to be some rich old broad who can afford to pay the highest price. They usually don't even want sex, just the illusion of it. "

Bruce leaned forward conspiratorially. He was on to his favorite topic. "Look, the type of woman that goes and bids for a stud at a charity auction has very specific needs. She wants to be wanted, wants to feel special. Ten to one, she wouldn't expect sex. But she'd want to be seen in some fancy restaurant where you have to act gallant. She wants to show off her prize; all you have to do is *act* as though you find her attractive."

"How do you *act* as though you find someone attractive?"

Bruce rolled his eyes and shook his head in a gesture that implied pity and incredulity.

"It's easy. Pay her compliments; the art is to stay credible – you mustn't overdo it. If you look hard enough at any woman, you'll find something to admire. For older women, I always go for their hair, or their eyes, or their smile, or their manicured fingernails. If all else fails, you can compliment them on their exquisite taste in picking out jewelry. Jewelry is as precious to an old woman as her pet poodle ... or pug ... or whatever dog she's fallen in love with."

Chris snorted his skepticism.

"Well, you have to be subtle, weave it in with other conversation. Give me your hand?"

"What?"

"Just give me your hand. I want to show you."

Hesitantly, Chris reached his hand across the table.

Bruce took it in both of his and massaged Chris's fingers one by one. Chris felt acutely embarrassed but had to admit that the hand massage felt good. After a while, Bruce looked directly into his eyes. His expression was serious. "You have remarkable hands; I bet you play the piano?" Then his face registered mock surprise. "You don't? That's really surprising." He continued the massage. "What kind of music do you like?" Before Chris could say anything, Bruce continued the charade; he was hitting his stride now. "Tchaikovsky, *Swan Lake*? I should have known. Don't you just adore the scene where ..."

A waiter, bringing their food, interrupted them. Chris jerked his hand away as though it had touched burning coal.

"Hi, guys." The waiter put the plates down with a flourish and a broad smile. He straightened the salt and pepper shakers and wiped imaginary crumbs from the table. When he found that the table had a slight wobble, he went down on his knees and put beer coasters under one leg. As they started to eat, the waiter hovered, self-consciously playing with his earring. He turned the umbrella to ensure that they were fully in the shade. Finally, he said, "Well, chaps, if there's *anything* else I can do for you, just holler."

Chris thanked him gruffly and the waiter left, looking over his shoulder several times.

Bruce nearly choked on the fries he was eating. "You're actually blushing. I rest my case."

Chris frowned.

"A little bit of public affection draws a lot of attention. And that's what a mature woman wants."

Shortly after three o'clock, Chris looked up to see the car-guard with the floppy hat coming towards them at a run. She was breathing hard.

"They've just come back," she panted, gesturing across the road. Chris handed her another tip, slammed money on the table, and sprinted towards his car. In the distance, he could see the Pajero pulling out of its bay. He lengthened his stride but the sidewalk was congested and the Pajero was picking up speed. Chris veered off the sidewalk and ran in the street to avoid the vendors and ambling pedestrians. A taxi hooted in protest but he kept his head down and ran. In the distance, the traffic lights turned from green to orange. The Pajero showed no sign of stopping but, as it turned, Chris caught a glimpse of the occupants: Lenny and Cindy.

"Get in the car," he shouted to Bruce, who had followed. "Quick!"

"What the fuck are you up to? Watch out!" Bruce shouted as Chris maneuvered the BMW into the road, narrowly missing a cyclist.

"Following that Pajero."

"Why?"

"I need to see where that guy lives. I bet he's the one who tried to run Bridget off the road."

"What the hell are you talking about?"

"I'll explain later."

Bruce looked at the clock on the dashboard. "We'll be late for the gala."

"We'll be OK." Chris floored the gas pedal. The BMW roared up the winding mountain road and Chris felt the age-old adrenalin rush of a hunter locking in on a prey.

The French ambassador's wife peered through her fashionable glasses at the invitation printed on recycled paper and admonished the chauffeur, "Watch the bumps. I cannot read if the car shakes." The chauffeur merely nodded and proceeded up the driveway towards the Groot Constantia winery.

Madame Ambassador turned to her friend, the editor of a women's magazine. She pointed at the invitation and said, "Can this be right? '*Please join us for champagne and canapés under the oaks at Groot Constantia at four-thirty p.m. Dinner will be served at six p.m. pm in the wine cellar, followed by an evening of entertainment.*'"

"Why, what's the matter?"

"Dinner at six?" Madame Ambassador's finely penciled eyebrows rose to where they nearly touched her jet-black hair. "At this time, we have only just finished our *déjeuner*, our lunch! Look," she pointed across the vineyards. "The sun is 'igh up in the sky – it is the middle of the day." The friend glanced at her watch: 5.30 p.m. She suppressed a smile and made a mental note to get one of her journalists to do a piece on people who travel the world and expect the world to conform to their habits.

The large black Renault, with the French flag on its hood, slowed down and joined a line of cars waiting to offload passengers. Madame Ambassador sighed; she hated being kept waiting.

##

Julie nipped into the kitchen to assure herself that everything was under control. After a slow start, the guests were now arriving in droves. The chief caterer muttered about lack of space and the inexperience of the volunteer servers, but they seemed to be coping. Silver platters with cucumber-and-salmon sandwiches, tiny quiches, devilled eggs, caviar, and other delicacies were flying out of the kitchen. "They're really having a ball out there," one of the serving staff commented. "I swear, some of the old ducks are already getting tipsy."

Julie had changed into a sleeveless dark-green blouse with a matching pencil skirt that came down to three inches above her knee. The deceptively simple Chanel cut accentuated her perfect figure. The only accessories she wore were a gold bracelet and pearl earrings that she had inherited from her grandmother. She went out on to the lawns and mingled with the guests, who were chatting animatedly in groups around high bistro tables or sitting on teak chairs under the oaks. She greeted people, stopped to talk to those she knew, gently nudged champagne-carrying waiters in the direction of empty glasses, complimented the string ensemble on their playing, and directed security staff to deal with a couple of youths trying to gate-crash the party. She briefly joined a group of ladies including Cape Town's mayoress, who was gracious in her praise: "Miss Noble, looks like you've laid on a great event. It is so important for us to raise awareness." She lowered her voice. "And I believe you even managed to get the Minister of Health to accept an invitation – you'll have to share your secrets; I can never get her to attend anything I plan." Julie knew that the mayoress and the minister came from opposite ends of the political spectrum and there was not too much love lost between them. "I believe she'll be at my table, I shall have to be on my best behavior," the mayoress said. "Well, at least it's for a good cause."

A statuesque African woman in a boldly patterned dress with matching headgear approached them. Julie shook her hand.

"Madam Mayoress, may I introduce Ms Xindi Vuzela? She is on the board of the Red Cross Children's Hospital."

"Oh, I know Xindi … how are you, my dear?"

Julie excused herself and left them talking about the poor state of health funding. It was a gloriously warm afternoon, which allowed the guests, depending on age, to show off their tanned shoulders or their latest garden-party hat. Men were definitely in the minority and she noticed that most of them had discarded their jackets. Conversation flowed as freely as the sparkling wine.

"Julie, darling! Over here!" Her mother beckoned from where she was talking to a group of people. Bridget wore an elegant cream two-piece with matching shoes. She had toned down the jewelry to show off a ruby-encrusted AIDS "ribbon" brooch. When Julie complimented her on her appearance, Bridget flushed a little with pleasure. A minute later, however, Julie was embarrassed when her mother effusively introduced her as "The star who put this whole thing together".

"I can assure you, it's not all my work. We have a great team of dedicated volunteers helping us," she protested, gesturing to the group working in the reception tent. "And Wendy really has …"

"Yes, yes, but you are the brains behind it all," Bridget continued, beaming. Fortunately, she was interrupted by one of the other ladies - a woman who was older than Bridget, her silver coiffeur held down with so much hair spray that it gave the impression of a helmet. Julie visualized her on the back of Bull's Harley and had to suppress a giggle.

"Don't you just love these formal African dresses – so colorful." Discreetly, the woman turned her head a little, directing attention towards a neighboring group.

"That's certainly something for which we can thank Nelson Mandela …"

Julie was about to excuse herself when the woman addressed her directly. "Oh, do tell us what the surprise entertainment is? I'll *platz* if I don't find out soon."

"Probably a children's choir," one of her friends said drily.

"What's wrong with a children's choir?" Julie tried not to sound defensive.

"Oh, nothing, nothing. It's just that we get to hear a children's choir at *every* charity event. "

"It's a cross one has to bear," a third woman chimed in. With a note of irony in her voice she sighed, "*Noblesse oblige.*"

"Well, I trust you will enjoy yourselves," Julie said. "And we'll keep you in suspense a little longer regarding the entertainment." With a pointed look at Bridget, she added, "Won't we, Mother?"

Bridget, who had just helped herself to another glass of champagne, twittered, "Of course, dear, of course; my lips are sealed." As Julie turned away, one of the volunteers came running over. "There you are!" she said breathlessly. "I've been looking for you. The Khayalitscha choir mistress just called. The school bus broke down. They'll be late."

"How late?"

The volunteer shrugged. "I don't know, they didn't say."

"I told you, didn't I? A children's choir! They always *have a children's choir."*

Julie pretended she hadn't heard the comments from her mother's group, and headed straight to the reception tent where Wendy and a group of volunteers were welcoming guests. She was grateful to see that three of the Toreros, Cedric, Bull and James, dressed in smart dark suits, were amongst the welcoming committee. Cedric was air-kissing a tall, striking woman with jet-black hair who visibly enjoyed the fuss being made of the guests. As she headed into the crowd, Cedric whispered to Julie, "*That's the French ambassador's wife. This is so exciting! Maybe I'll get her to sponsor my next production.* "

"Good." Julie smiled. "You got your boys all ready to go, then?"

Cedric nervously tapped his fingernails on his watch. "All except Bruce and Chris. They should have been here an hour ago."

Julie felt a lurch in her stomach. "Well, where are they? Surely you can call them?"

"Neither is answering …"

He looked distinctly uncomfortable.

"Don't worry, man," Bull cut in. "They'll be here – or I shall personally wring their necks." He turned away to greet a celebrity Zulu talk-show host who had arrived with her entourage.

By six o'clock, there still was no sign of Bruce, Chris, the choir, or indeed the guest of honor, the Minister of Health. Julie's hands felt clammy. The guests, evidently having a good time, were making a good deal of noise. *God, if it was this noisy outside, what was it going to be like inside the hall?* She looked at her watch and scoured the crowd for any sign of Chris. She felt goosebumps on her arms; no one else appeared to be cold. She found Wendy.

"Wendy, what do we do?"

"If they all don't show up, we'll simply improvise. You can always get up and do a song-and-dance routine." Wendy dismissed Julie's horrified expression with a hand gesture. "Relax, we'll be fine. Let's start ushering people in for dinner; it'll take them at least twenty minutes to get seated, and by then our entertainers should be here."

Julie felt numbness rise from the tip of her spine. She knew the tell-tale signs of the icy fear that would rise to freeze her lungs, grip her heart, threaten to choke her … *"Breathe,"* the psychologist had said. *"When you feel it coming, breathe deeply; find something external to focus on, don't give in to the fear."*

Through a fog, she heard Wendy give instructions for the guests to be ushered into the hall. She saw a rusty bus groan up the driveway and come to a spluttering halt in a cloud of diesel fumes. A couple of volunteers went up to greet the Khayalitscha children's choir. But there was still no sign of Chris; something bad must have happened – she knew it. She did not dare look at her watch; it was like looking over the edge of a balcony, being pulled into a dark abyss.

Friday afternoon at the shopping center. What was it, nearly ten years ago? Julie had gone to a movie with a friend. Afterward, they had strolled through the shops, tried on jeans, killing time till 6.30 p.m. when her father was going to join her for dinner. This was a monthly ritual – the one sacrosanct evening when Harry Noble made it a rule to spend time with his daughter. The friend's mother had picked her up at 6.15 and Julie decided to wait on a bench near the clock tower where her father always met her. She watched people hurrying by, marveling at their tense expressions. The ornate clock at the center of the mall inched forward to 6.35 p.m. She crosschecked it with her wristwatch; they agreed. Julie felt the first stirrings of unease; her father was never late. The one time that he had been detained, he had sent his driver to fetch her.

Her gaze drifted through the crowd, willing his face to appear. A vendor at a T-shirt cart, fifty meters away, caught her eye and winked.

164

Julie quickly looked away and busied herself inspecting the special tea she had bought for her father: Chamomile and Primrose, his favorite. When she looked again, it was 6.38. Julie got up and walked in a wide circle, always keeping the clock tower in her sights, willing her father to come bounding along, full of smiles and with an apology for being late. She would sulk, certainly; it was not right to keep people waiting like this. She wished now that she had a cell phone - why wouldn't her mother buy her one? She looked at her watch again: 6.42; where was the nearest pay phone? She did not dare leave the area, in case her father arrived just as she had left and they missed each other. Another glance at her watch told her that her father was now fifteen minutes late. What was she supposed to do? After tonight, she would really insist that Bridget buy her a cell phone...

Julie nearly jumped out of her skin when someone tapped her on the shoulder.

"Hey, missie. You lost?"

It was the T-shirt vendor, an older man with a missing tooth and a furrowed forehead under a worn cap.

"No, no, I'm fine. My father will be here any minute now!"

Julie barely breathed. The man's gaze seemed to go right through her.

"Really, I'm fine." Her voice sounded squeaky.

The man gave her a final piercing look, then shrugged, and walked away. It was 7.03 when she settled back on her bench, now keeping a wary eye on the T-shirt vendor. If he came near her again, she would scream. She wiped her clammy hands on her jeans.

By 7.15, however, any anger she had felt had given way to plain anxiety. What was she supposed to do? Something like this had never happened before. She was always picked up on time from school, from art lessons, from shopping; either her mother, the driver, or one of the other staff members would be on hand to meet her when needed.

By 7.21, her anxiety was made even more intolerable by an overwhelming urge to go to the bathroom. She was still worried that she might miss her father if she left her bench, but finally she could wait no longer. She got to her feet and was just about to go in search of a bathroom when she saw someone slowly walking towards her. It was Greg. Julie ran toward him, threw her arms around his neck.

"Greg! God, am I pleased to see you! Where's my dad?"

"Let's go to the car; it's right outside."

"But it's dinner night with Dad. Where is he?"

"Julie, you ..." Never had she seen him at a loss for words. *"Your dad had a heart attack."*

"Oh ... so, is he in hospital? You must take me to see him at once!"

"Julie ..."

She knew then. She could see it in his eyes. Even before he said it, she knew that her father was dead.

Time had stood still in that moment, and then the horror had hit her. In some ways, it had never really left her. Even now, ten years on, those feelings were still just below the surface, ready to be triggered whenever someone was late, as Chris was now. She knew, as her grief counselor had frequently told her, that her fears were irrational, but she remained unable to control them.

Now, standing alone, uncharacteristically indecisive, she struggled to repress the rising conviction that something dreadful had happened. *Where was he?*

"Are you OK? You look awfully pale." A woman gently touched her shoulder.

"Yes, yes, I'm fine." Julie shook her head to make the fog lift. She looked across the lawn and saw a lone figure heading towards her, unhurried. It was Greg. She stumbled as she moved forward. The woman grabbed her elbow and steered her to a chair. Fearfully, Julie watched Greg approach. *What message was he carrying this time? Who had sent him to break the bad news to her?* A part of her brain felt sorry for him – why did he always have to be the one to break the bad news? At the same time, she admired his strength. He was her rock, the man who was always there for her in a crisis.

"Well," Greg said, rubbing his hands together, "I had a very productive afternoon." Then he must have noticed her blank expression. "The Malaysians, remember? I told you about them. We managed to get in nine holes and work through the last of the details to clinch the deal. Matt will be pleased."

"Oh ... that's ... good."

"Are you OK? You've obviously been overdoing it, Jules, you look totally washed out. If you want to be successful, you have to learn to delegate." He signaled a passing waiter and two minutes later had her drinking a vodka on the rocks, despite her protestations.

"You know I can't tolerate spirits."

"In this case, it's medicine. Drink up; you need it." He watched her like a stern nurse, ensuring that she drank her dose. "There, you look better already."

She had to admit to herself that the way Greg took charge was comforting. She did not want him to see that now she was fighting nausea as well as anxiety. She mustered a smile, which dissipated when she saw her mother approaching.

Bridget planted herself in front of Greg. "Well ... if it isn't Mr. Louw himself. What are you doing here?"

"Hello, Bridget." Greg's voice was even. "I promised Jules that I'd be here, so ..."

"Don't call her Jules, her name is ..."

"Bridget ..." There was an edge in his voice, though he spoke quietly. "Why don't you just mind your own business?"

Bridget drew back her head and looked directly at him. Her cheeks were flushed. "It seems to me that you are completely forgetting your place and ..."

"Mother, please! Not now!"

"Look what you've done!" Bridget pointed at Julie. "The girl's as white as a sheet. You always, always upset her."

"I upset her? That's rich Bridget; that's really rich."

Julie had had enough. She willed herself to her feet and went into the hall. She did not dare to think about having her mother and Greg at the same table for the rest of the evening.

##

Half an hour later, Wendy stood, microphone in hand, on the podium. The wine cellar was filled to capacity and she noted with satisfaction that the décor exuded the quiet elegance she and Julie had envisaged. Candles cast a soft glow over the white tablecloths and crystal glasses, whilst concealed spotlights highlighted the magnificent lily arrangements on each of the sixty round tables. The ancient cellar walls bore no decoration other than a frieze of red AIDS ribbons.

A helper appeared at the back of the hall and gave an excited thumbs-up. Wendy tapped the microphone and signaled to the sound engineer to stop the music. After welcoming the guests, and thanking all the volunteers, she concluded, "And now, please join me in welcoming our guest of honor, her Excellency the Minister of Health." Drumbeats erupted, and the cellar doors were flung open. Guests turned and craned their necks as James, in the splendid traditional dress of a Zulu praise-singer, led in a procession. He chanted, ululated, and danced energetically. Wendy was struck by how seamlessly James had achieved the transition from urban sophisticate to Zulu warrior, deeply connected to the ancient rituals of his people. He put his heart and soul into the intricate dance steps, his every move amplified by swishing leopard skins draped over his head and bare shoulders. The beaming minister, dressed in a boldly patterned traditional dress and matching turban, slowly followed as James danced ahead.

Everyone applauded when she and her entourage finally took their seats. The TV crew retreated to the back of the hall. Wendy welcomed the minister and then gave the signal for starters to be served. From then on, everything proceeded according to plan: the children's choir gave a solid performance and the audience applauded; the mayoress kept her speech short and to the point; conversation and laughter flowed freely; raffle prizes were awarded; the main course was served; plates were cleared, glasses refilled – and still there was no sign of Chris and Bruce.

Greg and Julie sat at a table near the stage with Bridget, Wendy, and a number of major donors. There was one empty seat – Chris's father had declined the invitation. The conversation jumped from art collecting to fashion, from finance to everyone's favorite topic: the trials and tribulations of airline travel. Julie admired the totally relaxed manner in which Wendy fulfilled her compere duties on stage and entertained the guests at the table. She herself, however, was finding it hard to concentrate. For Greg's sake, she smiled and nodded from time to time, but she barely listened to the conversation. Her insides had shriveled into a knot of anxiety. And to make matters worse, she had a new worry to contend with on top of her concern for Chris - her mother's alcohol consumption. Bridget had already reached that stage of bright, flushed gaiety that, in Julie's bitter experience, preceded loud belligerence or depression. At least she and Greg were ignoring each other for now, but how long would that last? Julie squirmed with anxiety as she envisaged various embarrassing scenarios.

As if on cue, Bridget raised her glass and loudly interrupted conversation at the table. "A toast!" She tapped her glass. "A toast to my daughter! Darling, you haven't eaten a thing. At least join us in a drink. This isn't a funeral, you know." Julie looked imploringly at Wendy, but there was no stopping her mother. "A toast to the bestest daughter a mother could have," warbled Bridget. The other guests politely raised their glasses and Julie inclined her head stiffly in acknowledgment, as she fought to contain the nauseous tension threatening to engulf her. For the umpteenth time, her gaze sought out Cedric, who had positioned himself near the back door. This time, to her delighted amazement, he gave her a broad smile and an eager thumbs-up. Julie leapt up and made her way round the table to let Wendy know the good news.

"Excellent." Wendy looked at her watch. "Tell them ten minutes max; the audience awaits."

Julie rushed out of the hall and across the yard to the makeshift dressing room in the manor house. She barely knocked on the door before entering.

"Hey!" Bruce said, startled. "We're getting dress ..."

"So what? You're going to get undressed in front of five hundred people in ten minutes. Why act coy now?!"

"You've got a point ..."

"Anyway, where the hell have you two been?" Julie interrupted, glaring from Chris to Bruce and back to Chris.

"It's a long story," Chris began. "We think we may have found the guy that tried to run ..."

"I'm not interested in a long story!" Julie exploded." You're the most selfish creature I've ever come across. What were we supposed to think?"

"She worried about us," Bruce said, with a grin. "Isn't that sweet ..."

Julie stood on her toes, her face inches from his, "You ... you ... conceited, self-opinionated twit," she flared. She rounded on Chris. "Couldn't you call? Couldn't you find one single minute to think of someone other than yourself?"

She could see from his expression that her words were finding their mark. She knew that she should stop now, that she'd made her point.

He tried to defend himself: "We were following someone and my cell battery had gone dead; if you would just let me …"

Julie knew she was being irrational but she could not stop herself. It was as if an overheated light bulb in her head had finally exploded and all the tension of the last hours was pouring out. In a cold, furious voice, barely recognizable as her own, she lashed out, hardly aware of what she was saying, only knowing that she wanted to hurt him for hurting her, for putting her back in touch with those intolerable feelings. "Yet another lame excuse. If you weren't so full of excuses, and stepped up when it mattered, maybe your mother would still be alive today."

Time stood still in the shocked silence that enveloped the small, crowded room. From afar came the sound of laughter and music, but all Julie was aware of was the thundering rush of blood in her own ears. As if in slow motion, she saw a bolt of deepest pain pass through Chris's eyes before his face turned into a mask and the dull blue eyes stared right through her. Julie had a flash of memory: *she was six, and she had accidentally dropped one of her mother's Lladro porcelain dolls. As it shattered, she had wished with all her heart that she could undo her clumsy mistake.*

"I'm sorry. I didn't mean …"

"Don't," he said quietly and held up one hand. Then he turned his back on her. She was about to apologize again when Cedric firmly interrupted. "We've got to get on stage," he said, taking her elbow and guiding her towards the door. "Julie, it's best if you leave."

In a trance, her eyes blinded by tears, she went back to her seat. Fortunately, the entrance of the Toreros distracted Greg, and everyone else. It seemed as if there was a fierce determination in their every movement. From the moment they unfurled their red cloaks, Julie saw that the crowd was enthralled. The TV crew, who had listlessly settled down for a free meal at a table near the back, scrambled for their equipment. When Bull rode his Harley down the red carpet and on to the stage, there were gasps of disbelief, followed by applause. The TV cameras appeared to weave a magic spell on Bull. He gave the performance of a lifetime, grunting, roaring, and beating his bare chest like Conan the Barbarian. James and Riaan wrestled with him like hunters trying to bring down a buffalo. Julie noticed women shouting, egging on the fighters; they seemed determined to see real blood. Bull got carried away by all the applause; when he tossed Riaan over his shoulder the dancer overshot the edge of the stage and landed between the tables.

A collective gasp went through the hall. "Oh my God! Is he hurt?" Julie was half out of her seat, frantically hoping that the paramedics would be at their post outside, when Riaan leapt up and, with a perfect somersault, catapulted himself back into the show.

"Aren't they great?" her mother shouted across the table, joining in the enthusiastic clapping.

The second dance number was one that Julie had not seen before in any of the rehearsals. All six Toreros appeared in beach gear, carrying surfboards, volleyballs, and towels. Julie's attention was caught by a group of eight women seated three tables away. She knew that they were the award-winning agents from a major real estate company. They were clearly in a party mood. As she watched, three of them jumped up and started chanting, "Off, off, off. We want it all off!" They turned to the neighboring tables and tried to entice others to join in with their chant. The neighbors, however, were not quite as inebriated. They merely applauded appreciatively when the Toreros peeled off first their shirts and then their tank tops. Julie's eyes wandered further through the hall – she saw quite a few middle-aged matrons chuckling, and even some old ladies. Bruce and Chris showed off their athleticism as they leapt, twisted, and turned in a game of volleyball, propelling the ball up to within inches of the stage lights.

Julie's roving eye settled on a pretty young girl, eighteen or nineteen years old, sitting with her parents at a table near the stage. Her hair was in a thick braid and even from a distance Julie could see her sizeable diamond earrings. She was following each of Chris's moves with rapt attention, and had a look of such raw longing and desire on her face that Julie couldn't help but feel jealous. *God, I've really blown it*, she thought suddenly.

Immediately, she chided herself and sought out Greg's hand. He gave hers a reassuring squeeze. "This isn't really my scene, but it looks like folks are having fun."

At that moment, Greg's cell phone started to ring. He ignored her withering look and spoke quietly into the phone.

"Something's come up …"

She pressed a finger against her lips.

He whispered, *"Look, I'm sorry, I have to go. You've done a marvelous job here, Jules."* He gave her a kiss on the forehead. *"I'll see you later."* With that he was gone.

171

The dancers fanned out into the audience and the music changed to "Let's twist again." It struck Julie as familiar – something she'd heard her father play many, many years ago. She was conscious of Greg's empty chair next to her; thinking of her father deepened her loneliness.

The woman on Julie's left nudged her and whispered, *"Look at her."* Discreetly, she pointed in the direction of the French ambassador's wife. *"Looks like a cougar on the prowl."*

The Toreros moved from table to table, inviting patrons to twist with them. There was an enthusiastic response. James, in particular, seemed to have the knack of dancing with three women at the same time. Julie was astonished to notice that members of the audience were now vying with each other to stuff ten- , twenty-, and even fifty-rand notes into the waistbands of the dancers' board shorts. Her table partner leaned over and asked, "Who gets that money – the dancers or the Khanya AIDS Foundation?"

"Good question. We'll have to see."

Bridget interjected, "Why, there's no question about it. A tip is a tip. The boys deserve something for their troubles." She tottered to her feet, clapped enthusiastically, and shouted, "Bravo, lads! Bravo!" This attracted Riaan's attention; he moved towards their table and gallantly held out his hand, inviting Bridget to twist with him. Julie observed her mother closely, fearful that she would trip and make a complete spectacle of herself.

Her neighbor piped up, "Your mother is a beautiful women; you're lucky to have inherited her looks." It might have been the alcohol, or the exertion, or both, but Julie had to concede that her mother looked quite radiant. She wasn't used to seeing her mother having fun. After a few minutes, Riaan escorted Bridget back to her chair; she sat down beaming and, despite his protestations and Julie's embarrassment, insisted on stuffing a wad of bills into his waistband

Fortunately, they were all distracted by Bull. He had made his way to the minister and was twisting enthusiastically, trying to entice her to join him. She laughed heartily but was not to be persuaded. Eventually, following the example of others at her table, she shoved a folded bill into Bull's waistband, gave him a slap on the backside, and said, "Go play outside. you naughty boy."

"That's going to make the ten-o'clock news," the woman on Julie's left observed drily. "I can just see the headline: *'Minister of Health announces doubling of annual contribution to the fight against AIDS'."*

Julie had to smile and Wendy commented, "This will get us great publicity; we can ask the TV station to air an appeal for donations when they report on this event."

The next number was the Tango and, to Julie's relief, Bruce kept his clothes on. After that, Chris and James led the dancers in the Cowboy routine. They performed flawlessly, exuding energy and sex appeal with their tight jeans, broad smiles, and loud *"Yeahs!"* Two members of the audience were expertly lassoed and only released once the mayoress had paid a ransom into the charity fund.

The show concluded with the triumphant dancers taking their bows in front of the TV cameras and a wildly applauding audience. Julie had to grudgingly concede that the Toreros had exceeded all expectations. She should have felt relieved, elated, pleased, proud – she felt nothing. She was numb – and acutely aware of the fact that not once, during the entire show, had Chris looked in the direction of her table. Her arms were leaden and it took an extraordinary effort to applaud; it took even more effort to maintain a smile and accept compliments from everyone who stopped by to say how much they were enjoying the event.

When dessert had been served and the guests were drinking their coffees, Wendy rose to announce the final event of the evening. "Ladies and gentlemen, we have one final treat in store for you. An auction!"

The auctioneer, a flamboyant white-haired man in a dark suit, strode on to the stage. Wendy said, "This is not just any auction. We are auctioning off a romantic dinner for two at the Mount Nelson Hotel."

Julie heard a few polite noises of appreciation. The women next to her said, "I could get that for my kids; they'd enjoy it."

Wendy continued, "Not only will you win dinner for two, you will also win the company of a charming young bachelor for the evening." At her signal, the six Toreros walked on to the stage – back in their dark suits and white shirts. A buzz went through the hall and, despite the microphone, Wendy had to raise her voice, "Ladies! I suggest you get your checkbooks out. And please give these fine young men a round of applause for their willingness to support the fight against AIDS."

"Forget the kids," the woman next to Julie said as she rummaged through her purse. "I'm going to get this for myself."

When the applause, including loud whistling from the estate agents, subsided, Wendy went on, "First, we will determine, via a draw, which one of these charming bachelors is to be auctioned off. Madam Mayor, if you please."

The mayoress made a good show of stirring the pieces of paper in the hat and shutting her eyes tightly before making the draw. She unfolded the paper and announced, "Ladies ... and, since we live in an age of non-discrimination, gentlemen ..." There was laughter in the hall. Cedric waved at the crowd and winked theatrically. The mayoress continued, "You will have the opportunity to bid for an evening with ... Chris du Toit."

Loud applause - the other Toreros high-fived Chris and congratulated him before heading to a beer-and-food-laden table near the back. Julie tried to read Chris's expression. He was smiling but the smile appeared a little too fixed. For an instant, earlier that evening, she had seen that mask slip; had seen how vulnerable he could be. Her insides were in turmoil; she was consumed by guilt, anger, self-recrimination. *What had possessed her?*

The auctioneer got businesslike. "Can I have an opening bid, please? We will start with one thousand rand, one thousand. Lady at the back in the blue dress," he pointed. "I've got one thousand. Do I have one thousand five hundred?"

The excitement in the hall was palpable and rapidly the bidding jumped in five-hundred-rand increments to three thousand, then four thousand. *That's a ridiculous amount of money for an evening out,* Julie thought.

At five thousand rand, the bidding stalled. "Ladies, this is for charity. Any pleasure you might get out of the evening is purely incidental. You are doing a good deed. Do I hear five-five?"

One of the estate agents had been bidding and Julie noticed that there was urgent conferring going on at their table. It looked like her colleagues were chipping in, egging her on. Indeed, as the auctioneer said, "Five thousand, going once ... going twice ..." the estate agent frantically raised her arm and shouted, "Five thousand five hundred."

Near the stage, the pretty young girl who had hung on to Chris's every move during the performance was in serious consultation with her parents. Breathlessly, she now turned to the auctioneer. "Six thousand rand." This earned her a smile from Chris.

"I have six thousand rand. Do I hear any advances on ..."

"Eight thousand!"

A collective gasp went through the crowd as everyone turned to look at the new bidder. Madame Ambassador looked distinctly feline, a cat that had its prey cornered.

"All for a good cause," the auctioneer said smoothly. "Madame, your devotion to charity is admirable. I have a bid for eight thousand rand."

Julie watched Chris. He kept fidgeting with a button on his jacket.

"He's so adorable," the woman on Julie's left said, sighing.

"Going once ... going twice ..."

"Nine thousand!" Bridget had leapt up, raising her arm. "I bid nine thousand rand."

"*Mother, no!*" Julie hissed. "*Stay out of this.*" She could have died of embarrassment.

"*I thought you liked him,*" Bridget whispered back. "*Do you want him in the clutches of that woman?*"

"*He can take care of himself!*"

She glanced up. Chris was looking directly at her. An infuriating, mocking half-smile, a raised eyebrow; all vulnerability had gone. *Oh God, how will this look to him?*

"Ten thousand!" said the ambassador's wife, with a triumphant air, looking defiantly at Bridget.

"Thank God," Julie sighed. She turned to Bridget. "Mother, please let it be! Don't you see how this looks? People will think we rigged it and Chris will think you're paying for him to take me out."

Bridget looked at her. "But, darling, that's exactly what I'm doing; a little present for my precious daughter." She blew Julie a kiss across the table, rose to her feet, and in a slightly unsteady voice proclaimed, "Fifteen thousand rand!"

The crowd was stunned into silence, Madame Ambassador tilted her head in gracious defeat, and somewhere in the distance Julie heard the auctioneer say, "Sold!"

##

Chapter 11: Into the Wilderness

Wednesday

Chris shielded his eyes against the sun to gauge the distance up to the ridge: two, maybe three kilometers? It was hard to tell. His boots crunched on the path - a dusty, serpentine ribbon winding in amongst *fynbos* and low shrubs that hadn't seen rain for months. He took a sip of water from his flask, aware that he had to ration the precious liquid.

After another hour of steady climbing, he felt the coolness of a sea breeze coming from across the ridge. He'd been on this trail several times before and yet, when he reached the top of the path, the view still took him by surprise. In the foothills below him, quaint farmsteads lay dotted like toys on a quilt of vineyards and wheat fields. Beyond them, the full expanse of False Bay stretched all the way to Table Mountain. Less than a week ago, he had stood at Groot Constantia, looking across the bay towards the very place where he was now seated on a rock. He felt the three-day stubble on his chin. Was he the same person as that young man? He wasn't sure.

He was surprised to feel the vibration of the cell phone in his pocket. There was a faint one-bar signal. He scrolled through the list of missed calls: Cedric, Desmond – finally - and Julie, two times. *Julie.* He sighed. He had embarked on this ferociously paced hike in an attempt to clear his mind and to gain some perspective, but although he was not ready to talk to Julie, he couldn't stop himself from thinking about her. For three days, he'd had a non-stop conversation with her in his mind. *Julie – the only person to ever say out loud what he had felt all these years: that, he, Chris, was responsible for his mother's death.*

'If you weren't so full of excuses, and would step up when it mattered, your mother would probably still be alive today.'

He couldn't hate her for speaking the truth. For years, everyone around him had been at pains to assure him that there was nothing he could have done, that it hadn't been his fault, to a point where he had almost believed it himself. But now the wound was ripped open. Her voice reverberated through his head and the words hurt; they hurt like Dettol antiseptic poured on a bleeding gash.

A couple coming down the path ahead of him interrupted his thoughts. Chris guessed they were early retirees, hiking mid-week when it was quiet on the trails. They looked experienced, with sturdy boots, high quality daypacks, and sensible hats.

"Amazing view, isn't it?" the man said. He was wiry, with a lined face. The woman had taken better care of her skin. She leaned on one of her hiking poles and peered at Chris over a pair of sunglasses. He sensed that they were inquisitive types who would happily settle in for nice chat.

The man expressed his envy at Chris for being out on the trail for several days; they were just doing a day hike, he told him. "We love to be out on the trails, but these days we draw the line at sleeping out on the hard ground."

"It's just not as safe as it used to be," the woman chimed in. "You never know who you might meet out here; are you sure you'll be OK all by yourself."

Chris nodded, touched by her concern. "What's the water situation like further up?" he asked. "Have to admit that I had expected to find more water. All the usual rock pools are dried up."

The couple lamented the lack of rain, global warming, and the impact of the weather on the wine industry. They insisted that Chris take some of their water.

He watched them disappear down the track, and was acutely aware that, these hikers aside, no one in the world knew where he was. After moping around his apartment the whole Sunday after the gala, he had simply heaved his gear into the car on Monday morning and driven out to the mountains without telling anyone. *Maybe not such a great idea.* He got out the cell phone and tried to send an SMS to his father. But by now the rogue cell phone signal was gone.

##

Julie had lost count of the number of times she'd tried to call Chris. She knew that a simple apology could not undo the hurt she had caused him, but at least she wanted him to know that she was sorry. On the other hand, if he was going to be childish and ignore her calls, and not even give her a chance to apologize, then so be it. She stepped out of her car and took the elevator up to Cedric and Desmond's apartment.

As always, Cedric was immaculately turned out – his black T-Shirt and pants had designer-torn holes and his streaked hair was crafted into tufts to create that "I-just-got-out-of-bed" look. It occurred to Julie that Cedric probably spent a lot more time on his appearance than she did.

She pulled an envelope out of her bag and said, "We've finalized the accounts – I hope it's OK that I just made out a single check to the Toreros? I wasn't quite sure how you guys split the money."

"Gosh, you *are* on the ball. Normally, we have to wait weeks and months to get our money! Come inside. Do you have time for a cuppa?"

Julie accepted the invitation and, whilst Cedric made tea, they chatted about the gala and the generally favorable comments that had been made in the press. Some write-ups had been predictably shocked or tongue-in-cheek, but Cedric had received a couple of enquiries for future Torero engagements.

Julie asked, "Have you seen Chris ... since the gala?" She tried to keep her voice casual.

Cedric busied himself pouring tea into delicate bone-china cups. Next, he rummaged through various cupboards to produce a plate of shortbread cookies. Julie wondered if he was going to ignore the question. Eventually, however, he said, "No, I haven't; guess he's licking his wounds."

"No need to rub it in; I've tried to ring him several times, but he doesn't return my calls."

"What is it with the two of you? I mean, Desmond can be difficult at times, and we have our differences, but you and Chris ..." he paused, looking at the ceiling as if trying to find inspiration. "You seem to have made a whole new art form out of pushing each other's buttons."

"I don't know. Maybe we're chasing something that could-have-should-have-might-have been a long time ago – trying to recapture the dreamy romanticism of fourteen-year-olds. It's probably just an illusion." With one fingernail, she traced the intricate rose pattern on the cup. It reminded her of her grandmother's house and a time long ago when life was simple and full of kindness.

He asked, "What are you going to do?"

Normally, Julie would have would have brushed off the question. But the sudden memories of her grandmother, and the genuine concern in Cedric's voice, breached her defenses. She looked out of the window without seeing the boats, the palms, or the midday sun playing on the water.

"With my life? What can I do? I'm going to grow up and live in the real world. I can no longer hide from my responsibilities at Noble

Enterprises." With some bitterness, she added, "It's bad enough that my mother simply runs away from it."

"I thought the company was in good hands with your stepfather and, what's his name – the bloke that came to the gala for about ten minutes?" Cedric said.

Julie ignored the jibe and said, "My stepfather is getting to retirement age and it would probably solve a lot of problems if he bowed out and spent more time with my mother. That just leaves Greg to shoulder the full burden. It really isn't fair on him." She sighed. "I've always assumed that one day I would marry someone and together we would run the company, as a team, the way my parents did. I just thought I'd have a little more freedom before stepping into that role."

"God, you should hear yourself. It's all about duty and responsibility and shouldering burdens. They call me a queen but you take the cake! "

Julie bristled. "My parents built that business. It is my father's legacy; I cannot just abandon it."

"Well, then, assuming that you have to take on 'the role', which, by the way, I seriously question, who says Mr. What's-his-name…"

"His name is Greg, as you well know." She was getting annoyed.

"Who says that Greg has to be the Queen's consort? It's none of my business, but isn't he … a little old for you?"

"Fifteen years is nothing. He's smart, he's funny, and he's competent. Greg knows what he wants in life and he's always been there when I've needed him."

Cedric shrugged.

"What?" she demanded.

"Nothing; like I said, none of my business." He drank his tea. "It's just … there seems to be such chemistry between you and Chris, and it sounds to me like you are sitting here trying to convince yourself why you should be with Greg."

Julie knew that she should stop trying to justify her position, but she could not help herself. Cedric was getting too close to the dilemma that she had been wrestling with all week. Greg was the perfect match for her, yet every time she thought of Chris, her emotions … She shut out the thought.

"Greg is very caring. Did you know that for years he's been volunteering, working with troubled youths and drug offenders from the townships? He and I can do great things with the company."

"Sounds more like a business relationship than a marriage." Cedric looked at her across the rim of his tea cup. "What about sex? If I picture Greg and Chris side by side, I know who I would ..."

Julie felt the heat in her cheeks. The memory of Chris's lips touching her breasts in the moonlight flashed through her mind. "You're right; this is none of your business! Thanks for the tea." Her voice was sharper than she had intended. She picked up her keys.

"Hey, don't be so touchy." He gave her his most engaging smile and gently took the keys from her hand. "I was just beginning to enjoy our talk. Why don't I open a bottle of champagne – to celebrate the success of the gala? "

"Now? In the middle of the day?"

"Why not? You and I have never had a chance to really talk. I think we have a lot in common."

Julie was tempted, but immediately all her defenses kicked in. Discretion, she knew, was not Cedric's strong suit. If she let down her guard, and told him even part of what was really on her mind, it would probably be broadcast to the entire world ... including Chris.

"Maybe some other time; I really do have to go. I have a couple more checks to drop off ..."

"Gosh, that reminds me!" exclaimed Cedric. "I still have all the money that those lovely people insisted on sticking into the Toreros' jockstraps." He reached behind a row of books on the shelf and handed her a thick envelope.

Julie said, "Oh ... I thought the Toreros were going to keep this ..."

"So did they, until Chris told them in no uncertain terms that all money collected was for the Khanya AIDS Foundation. He nearly came to blows with Bruce, but," Cedric looked directly into Julie's eyes, "Chris usually gets what he wants. He made me promise that I would get the money to Wendy. That's the last time I spoke to him."

She peered into the envelope. "This is a lot of money; I can't ..." She pushed the envelope across the table. "As my mother says, a tip is a tip."

"Yes, well, no disrespect, but when it comes to money, your mother appears to be as detached from reality as mine." He licked the envelope, shut it firmly, and handed it to her. "Please take it now before I get tempted to invest in another piece of art."

He walked her to the elevator and gave her a kiss on the cheek. "Do me a favor; try calling Chris just one more time. I know he's hurting."

The doors shut and she was alone.

Chris veered deeper into the mountains, away from the sea and the well-worn trails. He did not see another human being all afternoon. At nightfall, he found a sheltered spot, rolled out his sleeping bag, and lit a fire. He chewed on dried springbok *biltong* and waited for tea water to boil. As he looked into the flames, he remembered his Boy Scout days; others had complained about the food and the hardship, but Chris was always at home in the wilderness. When he was fifteen, and in his rebellious phase, the scoutmaster had sent them out in small groups on a four-day survival trek in these very mountains. Little did the scoutmaster know that Chris's group of boys had hidden bottles of booze in their packs. The four of them had built a huge fire and dared each other to drink the most awful mixtures of alcohol. They had shouted, shrieked, and stomped around the campfire like demented cavemen before passing out in the dust. It was a miracle that the forest had not caught alight. The next morning, Chris had woken to an epic hangover which had served to temper his desire for alcohol from that day forward.

He lay and listened to the lonely hooting of an owl. If Mama Mercy had been there, she would have been beside herself with fear and would have covered her ears to block out the portent of death. Chris gazed at the stars and tried to let their order influence the turmoil that was his life. He'd noticed the empty chair at the gala – *was his father really mad at him? And what was he going to do about a job?* Since Julie's outburst, he had also found himself thinking more about his mother's killer. In fact, he'd thought more about him in the last three days than he had in the three months before the gala. *Why had the police never found him?* Then Chris imagined having Julie next to him out here under the stars. *Did she like camping?* But maybe it was irrelevant now - she'd clearly lost all respect for him. She had tried to call him, certainly – but it was probably about Saturday's "prize" dinner at the Mount Nelson. He was sure she intended to cancel, yet part of him hoped she wouldn't, despite her outburst at the gala.

Eventually, he drifted into a restless sleep.

He and his buddies were laughing and drinking around the campfire. A girl with flowers walked by and Hughie made fun of her. Chris wanted to stop him but his throat was thick and his limbs leaden. Hughie was mean to the girl. Julie appeared. "You're always full of excuses," she chided him. "Why don't you step up when it matters?" She seemed sad.

Next, he was on the staircase at home. He looked straight into the barrel of the gun, saw the arm stretching behind it all the way to the face of the murderer, half-hidden by a hood. Chris could see the thin mouth, the wisps of a goatee. He wanted to shout, run, charge at the murderer, but something was tightly wrapped around him; he couldn't move. A shot rang out. He strained against his bonds and screamed. Then another shot rent the air, and another. He heard Nala scratching and growling. But Nala was dead...

He woke drenched in perspiration and sat up. The fire had burned down to a few glimmering embers. Chris became aware of a presence; he felt as though the breath of a *dementor* had gone down his back. He listened with every fiber of his being. Again, he heard the scratching; then he saw a pair of red eyes looming in the darkness. He could smell a rank odor of death and decay. Slowly, Chris extricated his arms from the sleeping bag, all the while keeping his eyes fixed on the two red dots. Again the animal growled, and the stench was overwhelming. Chris reached towards the fire and gripped a half-burnt log. With a wild shout, he threw it at the marauder. The creature scuttled off into the night.

Chris rebuilt the fire and retrieved what was left of his rucksack. He assumed it had been a wild dog or hyena that had mauled his rucksack to get at the *biltong*. As he examined the jagged gashes, he suddenly had a vivid recollection. He sat down with a thump. Whenever he dreamed about the day of his mother's murder, he was always a hundred percent focused on trying to make out the facial features under the hood. But now he remembered something he had never consciously taken in before: a tattoo on the murderer's forearm. It was the head of a snake, or maybe that of a dragon. Chris felt a surge of excitement – finally, after all these years, he had managed to extract a new piece of evidence from the darkest pit of his brain. He put more wood on the fire, got out his sketchpad and, as if in a trance, drew the tattoo.

Afterwards, he inspected what was left of the rucksack. His food supply was gone; it certainly was time to go home. With that decision made, he settled into his sleeping bag and sank into a deep, undisturbed sleep.

##

Chapter 12: Dinner for Two

Friday

The pilot looked over his shoulder. "We'll be taking off in about five minutes, Miss Noble. With this wind, it'll be bumpy, so it would be good if you stayed strapped in." Julie nodded. She saw a tiny version of herself reflected in duplicate in the pilot's sunglasses. She and the other Julie sat forlornly in their respective leather chairs. She felt guilty to be the only passenger in an eight-seater Lear jet. *What a waste.*

Through the open door, she saw the co-pilot walk across the tarmac; he was balancing three paper cups on a cardboard tray and ducked as he entered the plane. "Hell, this *bleddy* wind. Excuse my French. How do you put up with this weather?" He offered Julie a cup. "Hope you like coffee; afraid we didn't have time to load up any other refreshments."

She did not really feel like coffee but accepted the brew anyway. "Sorry to have dragged you out so early. What time did you have to leave Johannesburg?"

"*Agh,* don't worry, it's nothing; we're used to being called out at all hours of the day and night – all part of the job." He grinned and winked at the pilot. "Remember that time Mr. Greg called us for an overnight *jol* to Maseru? That was some party, I swear … "

The pilot interrupted him sharply: "I'm sure Miss Noble is not interested in your tall stories. Let's get this baby rolling." He resumed his pre-flight checks.

Julie's cell phone rang.

"Hi, Wendy."

"Good morning, Julie dear. Hope I'm not waking you?"

"Don't be silly, it's nearly nine o'clock."

"Well, I wouldn't have been the least bit surprised if you'd allowed yourself a little lie-in. You certainly deserve some time off, it's been such a busy week!"

Outside the porthole, Julie saw that the ground crew, bent against the southeaster, were reeling in the fueling hose. It really was a fierce storm. She felt queasy at the thought of going up in a small plane. The jets purred into life.

"Anyway," Wendy went on, "I was just calling to see if you wanted to come over tonight, and whether you could bring Chris. The segment on the gala, along with all the extra interviews, is going to be on the *Carte Blanche* TV program tonight, and I thought it would be fun to watch it together. I've invited a few other people, including an old friend who might be able to help Chris find a job. I've not been able to get hold of Chris myself, but I'm sure that you ..."

"Wendy, I ... "

"... are in contact with him. I know that you'll be going to the Mount Nelson with him tomorrow night, but ..."

"Wendy, I'm on the plane, leaving for Johannesburg in two minutes."

"On the plane? But why do you need to go to Johannesburg? How will you get back in time for your dinner with Chris tomorrow?"

"I have no intention of going to dinner with Chris, not tomorrow, nor any other night." Julie found it hard to keep her voice steady. "This last week has been very ..." – she groped for the right word – " ... illuminating. Greg and I had a good long talk a few days ago and decided to spend more time together. He sent the plane down to pick me up this morning."

"Oh, I see." There was a long pause. "I know your mother went a little overboard with the auction bidding, but don't you think you're perhaps over-reacting?"

"A little overboard!?" Julie's voice rose. *"A little overboard!* She made a laughing stock of me in front of half of Cape Town! How do you think it makes me look if my mother feels it necessary to pay *fifteen thousand rand* to get me a date? I don't want to be seen with Chris. I am perfectly capable of finding myself a date, if I want one."

"Julie, my dear, people would not interpret it like that – honestly. They might think your mother a little showy, but it will be forgotten by next week. You honestly read far too much into this."

Julie glanced at the pilots, who were both apparently engrossed in their instrument checks.

"In any case, I *have* to go to Johannesburg. Since Mother is not talking to Matt, I have to represent the family at a dinner with new overseas clients tomorrow night."

"Have you spoken to your mother? I'm sure if you explained how you felt ..."

"I left a message on her answering machine."

"What did you tell her?"

"To enjoy the evening with her gigolo." Julie had meant to sound light-hearted, but she could hear the bitterness in her own voice. "Anyway," she said, trying to finish the conversation, "I've got to go, we're about to take off. We can chat on Monday. Bye."

She snapped the phone shut. The pilot glanced over his shoulder. "Ready?"

Julie pulled an eye-mask over her faced and curled into the leather seat. The plane was buffeted by wind gusts as it moved towards the runway. The engine noise increased and Julie did not hear the co-pilot as he made a call on his cell phone. The conversation was brief: "We have the songbird on board. ETA at Lanseria: half-past-eleven."

Julie woke two hours later and spent some time putting on eye make-up and lipstick and checking her nails in readiness for her meeting with Greg. When the plane commenced its descent, she pensively surveyed the dusty landscape below, so different from that of Cape Town.

She slipped on high-heeled shoes and the crew helped her down the steps, before handing down her Louis Vuitton suitcase. Normally, she would have been embarrassed about using such expensive luggage, but the case had been a gift from Greg and she had felt that he would be pleased to see she was using it. She recognized Greg's waiting Jaguar, but not the uniformed driver who stowed her belongings and held the door open for her.

She acknowledged his greeting and smiled to hide her disappointment, resolving not to ask where Greg was. Fortunately, the driver obliged. "Mr. Louw sends his apologies for not being here in person. He's finishing up some work so that he can take the afternoon off. He asked me to take you to the golf club, for lunch with him and Mr. Baxter."

Julie felt cheered at the prospect of seeing her stepfather and ruefully reminded herself that she had lectured her mother on the demands of running a big corporation – and that that applied to Greg as much as Matt Baxter. *It was actually very considerate of Greg to get his work finished so that he would have time for her*, she told herself. The thought made her feel more positive as she waved good-bye to the pilots.

Twenty minutes later, her mood was further improved when she stepped into the air-conditioned lobby of the golf club, Matt was waiting for her, beaming. He gave her a fatherly bear hug and kissed her cheek.

"You look wonderful!" he said.

"So do you. Have you lost a little weight?"

He patted the silk shirt covering his stomach. "You think so? I don't know. I've been trying to cut back on the whisky – just don't get any time for exercise. Come, we can go through to the dining room – Greg should be here any minute. I don't mind telling you, that young man is worth his weight in gold. If he ..."

"You've told me that before, frequently." She hooked her arm into his. "You're making him work too hard – he wasn't even able to meet me at the airport."

"Ah, well - yes; as you know, this mega deal with the Malaysians ..."

"I'm just teasing."

The club's hostess greeted them warmly. "Your usual table, Mr. Baxter?"

She led them through the dining room to a table with a commanding view over the golf course. The placid water-hazards and saturated green of the fairways stood in stark contrast to the dry hills beyond. Inside, it was pleasantly cool, and strategically placed potted palms and giant ferns provided privacy for the diners. Matt pointed out various improvements that had been made to the golf course as they watched a couple of springbok that had ventured on to the fairways to nibble at the luscious grass.

"I tried to call your mother," Matt said. "She must have had the phone off the hook. I couldn't get through to her."

"She's had a busy time." Julie had to bite her lip not to add, "... and has procured the services of a young man to entertain her."

"Well, I'm always happy when you two girls have fun. It's a pity that you're so far away – your mother misses you. One of these days, we'll have to talk seriously about you getting involved in the business."

They'd been over this before. She was never quite sure how serious Matt was. She was tempted to find out, to shock him into a reaction by saying, "How soon can I start? What's my job?" For the moment, though, she decided she'd bide her time. Maybe she would try shock tactics later, once she was clearer about her feelings for Greg.

Matt now launched into a description of the renovations he was planning for the house and garden; then he spoke about his golf (going through a bad patch), following this with an outline of the business deal with the Malaysian clients. "That reminds me," he said, stopping mid-sentence. "We have some documents that your mother needs to sign. If you manage to speak to her before I do, please ask her to take care of this; it's rather urgent."

Julie nodded dutifully, though she thought it was hardly likely that she was going to speak to her mother soon.

Just then, Greg entered the dining room. Julie waved to attract his attention and he acknowledged her with a characteristic nod, his head tilted to one side. She watched his progress through the room, noticing how he stopped frequently to greet an acquaintance or business contact. When he laughed at some pleasantry, as he did often, his teeth showed the same brilliant white as his shirt.

"Seems like he knows everyone here," Julie observed.

Matt followed her gaze. "Ah yes, that's the beauty of golf; you truly can mix business with pleasure."

"Jules, you look great," said Greg, when he finally got to their table. He bent down to kiss her and she could feel his longing. She had to gently push him away.

They ordered lunch and, at Matt's prompting, Julie gave an edited account of the AIDS gala. Her assertion that Bridget had had a fun time seemed to satisfy him.

"I knew it was a good thing for her to get out - and she so enjoys spending time with you. "

Greg winked. "I'm sure she was a great support."

Julie rolled her eyes complicitly, then immediately felt guilty, and that she should be defending her mother, not laughing about her with Greg. "It might surprise you, but Mother actually did an excellent job in helping us welcome guests. It's just that ... she never knows when to stop."

"Ah, a mother's love," Matt said. "It knows no bounds. I remember when I was a boy and my mother ..."

"Don't look now," Greg interrupted in a whisper. *"Dr. Majola has just walked in."*

In answer to Julie's raised eyebrow, he said, "Surely you must know Dr. Majola? He is the chief director at the Ministry of Defense. He has more clout than the minister himself."

Matt shrugged, annoyed at having his story interrupted, "Yes, yes. So, anyway, as I was saying, I had come off my bicycle and ..."

Their food arrived. Julie noticed how Greg's whole manner had changed; he was alert, very focused on the new arrivals, who were seated at a table somewhere behind her. Then, having not touched his food, he excused himself. A few minutes later, Julie saw him coming from the rest rooms. He took the long route, past Dr. Majola's table.

"He's very good at building relationships," Matt said, as they both watched Greg engineering a "chance" encounter and being introduced to everyone in Dr. Majola's party. Julie could not hear the conversation but, judging by the smiles and laughter, it seemed everyone was getting on like best friends.

"Why would he want to build a relationship with the ministry of defense?" she asked. "We don't produce any weapons."

"No, but if you think about it, I'm sure you'll see the value." When she did not answer, he continued, "We produce high-precision medical instruments. Who has a major interest in buying those instruments?"

"Oh, I see," Julie said, feeling like a dimwitted schoolgirl. "The armed forces?"

"Exactly! And, unlike the provincial hospitals, they seem to have a pretty limitless budget. They are also often interested in trying out new things."

"New things? What kind of new ..."

Greg rejoined them, beaming. "Sorry for deserting you, but I couldn't pass up such an opportunity."

He cut into his untouched steak, put a piece in his mouth. Then he frowned, and waved towards the waiter. "This steak is cold; can you please find me a hot one – medium rare?"

As the waiter disappeared, Julie put down her fork. "How could you do that?"

"Do what?"

"You sent back the steak as though there was something wrong with it."

"But there was; it was cold."

"That's hardly the kitchen's fault." Julie was indignant.

"What do you want me to do? Eat cold steak?"

"If you're going to have it medium-rare, you might as well eat it cold. You could have just asked him to have it reheated."

"Oh, what does it matter? We give this place a lot of business, don't we, Matt? One steak is not going to bankrupt them." He softened his tone. "It's certainly not worth arguing over. If it'll make you happy, I'll offer to pay for a second steak." He reached across and lifted her chin. "Peace? Give us a smile."

His condescending manner irritated her, but she decided to let it go.

Matt replenished her wine and urged her to tell them more about the gala. She described the food and outlined some of the challenges in terms of logistics, security, and coordination – especially once the Minister of Health had decided to attend.

Matt lavished praise. "I never doubted you would pull it off, but I didn't realize quite how big this event was. You're amazing."

Greg nodded agreement, and mimed taking his hat off to her with an elaborate bow.

"National news! You're a natural at PR," Matt continued. "I can't wait for you to come and join our team."

Their compliments brought a flush to her cheeks. She began to feel that she had indeed done a pretty darn good job. The wine was making her less inhibited, and she found herself launching into a description of the bidding war between Bridget and the French ambassador's wife.

"That's my Bridget," roared Matt, causing a few diners to turn and look at him. "Trust her to put the Frenchy in her place."

Much later, when Julie reflected on the conversation, she found it odd that neither Matt nor Greg had asked what Bridget was going to do with her "prize". For the moment, though, Matt's laughter was infectious, and Julie started to wonder why she had been so upset about Bridget's behavior. It seemed pretty funny now.

When Matt excused himself to greet a friend at another table, Greg reached across and squeezed Julie's hand. "I love to see you laughing and happy," he said quietly, lifting her hand to his lips. "I've been thinking about you and me ... about us," he said, his voice husky. Despite the air conditioning, she felt warmth radiating from his hand to hers, all the way up her arm.

But the moment didn't last, because just as she was indulging in feeling appreciated and wanted, Greg again became distracted by something behind her. Julie had to control her annoyance - *this was the second time he'd done this.* She turned to see what had caught Greg's attention, and saw the hostess coming towards their table, followed by two Asian men.

"Excuse me, Mr. Louw, your golf guests have arrived; I believe your tee-off time is in ten minutes."

Julie spun around in surprise, about to question Greg. He, however, was already out of his chair and welcoming the guests: "Julie, let me introduce you to our business partners from Malaysia: Lim Wah San and Goh Yong Meng. Wah San, Yong Meng, this is Julie Noble, the daughter of the founder of Noble Enterprises."

"Pleased to meet you, Mr. Lim, Mr. Goh." Julie shook hands and observed the newcomers. Both men were of Chinese descent. Mr. Goh was shorter than Julie and it was hard to read his expression. He was the older of the two and held himself very erect. She thought he was probably more at home in a formal office environment; he certainly looked faintly ridiculous in his golfing outfit, with the pants pulled up too high. Mr. Lim, by contrast, was taller and stockier, with a thin moustache and a gregarious smile.

"It is an honor, Miss Noble," Mr. Lim said, and bowed deeply. Mr. Goh pulled his face into a smile and said something in Chinese. She was surprised by the firmness of his handshake, and appalled by the tobacco stains on his yellowed teeth.

Matt returned to the table, and jovially slapped both newcomers on the shoulder, then pumped their hands. "So good to see you again; hope you're feeling ready. We've got the caddies all lined up."

Both men nodded their heads enthusiastically, and Mr. Lim enquired courteously, "Have you had your lunch?"

"Yes, yes, we're all done here; time to get moving. Julie, I presume Greg has filled you in on the program for the next two days? The driver will take you home now – I'm sure you're tired after such an early start."

Matt led the way towards the lobby. Julie held Greg back and they followed the others at a distance. "What's with this 'program', then? Someone led me to believe that you were taking the afternoon off to spend time with me."

"I'm sorry, Jules, I couldn't change the arrangements. We've had this visit planned out for weeks."

"I never got any of the details. And don't call me 'Jules'. It sounds like the name of a butler."

"Oh, come on now, you're being childish."

She did not respond.

Greg continued in a matter-of-fact way, "Golf this afternoon, followed by drinks. Tomorrow we take them on a tour of our facilities. Two other colleagues will join Mr. Goh and Mr. Lim. In the evening, we have a dinner laid on in a private suite at the Michelangelo Hotel. There we'll sign the contract and celebrate our new partnership."

"And what is my role?"

"You represent the Noble family. You know what these Asians are like; they want to know that they are dealing with the people at the top." She wasn't sure whether he was being facetious, so she ignored the comment.

When the driver pulled up, Greg opened the door for her. "Look, Julie, I'm sorry, but this is really important. Why don't you go and buy a nice dress and get your hair done? Spoil yourself." He squeezed her hand. "I'll make it up to you."

As she got into the vehicle, he again lifted her hand to his lips and kissed it, but this time she felt no warmth. Then he shut the door and turned to catch up with Matt and the others.

She closed her eyes and settled into the upholstery. As the Jaguar sped away, she wondered what Chris was doing. *Was he still so mad that he wouldn't return her calls?* If she was really honest with herself, she couldn't blame him.

##

Saturday evening

The buzzer squawked. Chris looked at his watch: 7.30 p.m. on the dot. He swore silently as he tried once more to force a golden cufflink into place. The buzzer squawked again like some irritating parrot; he dropped the cufflink next to its mate near the basin, walked to the hallway, and pressed a button on the intercom.

"Yes?"

"Good evening, Mr. Chris," a tinny voice said. "There's a man from Five-star Limos down here to pick you up."

"Thanks, tell him I'll be down now-now."

He went back to the bathroom, put a splash of after-shave on his freshly shaven chin and used a dab of gel to tame a stray curl. With some determination, he managed to fit the cufflinks, before putting on a dark-navy blazer. His bed was strewn with shirts; uncharacteristically, he'd had trouble deciding what to wear. In the end, he'd settled for a white shirt and charcoal pants that sat low on his hips. He stopped in the hallway to adjust his tie, and remembered to pick up the envelope that had been sent by one of the Khanya volunteers: it contained vouchers for the limo, dinner, drinks; there was even a map to help direct him to the home of the winning bidder. He studied the contents as though looking for some hidden clue, some way out. Then he threw away the map and pocketed the vouchers.

Chris found the security guard outside, admiring the stretch-limo. "Mr. Chris, this is one big car," he said, awe in his voice. "It's come all the way from America."

The driver held the door and, with a flourish, pointed out a pair of crystal glasses and a bottle of chilled champagne. "D'you want me to open that now, or wait till we pick up your lady?"

Chris tugged at the unfamiliar tightness of his buttoned collar. His throat felt dry. "I'll wait. Do you have a bottle of water?"

"Sure. Hey, it's your big night; whatever you need." The driver winked. "D'you want a little whisky with your water?"

He accepted a whisky gratefully.

As they set off, Chris turned up the music to prevent any further conversation. A bunch of wrapped roses lay on the seat next to him; they really had thought of everything.

Going through Green Point, he distracted himself by playing with the light controls. A piped strip of light along the edge of the car's roof cycled through a series of lurid colors, from purple via pink to red and indigo, while tiny star lights twinkled across the roof. The driver beamed at him via the rear-view mirror. He had a gnarled face and the chauffeur's cap sat at an angle on his unruly mop of gray hair. Chris smiled wryly and wished the man would keep his eyes on the road. He looked out at the craggy face of Table Mountain, illuminated by floodlights. A full moon hung over Devil's Peak. *Under normal circumstances this could be very romantic,* he thought, *but traveling alone in an eight-seater limo just seems like a sad waste.*

The limo had been expected and was waved through the security gates. As the vehicle cruised to a halt in front of the Noble residence, Chris slugged back the last of his whisky. With a deep breath, he assumed a cheerful smile that would have scared small children, had there been any around to observe it.

The chauffeur opened the door for him. "Nice place," the man said, and smacked his lips as he looked up at the mansion, huge and imposing in the moonlight.

Chris mounted the steps, roses in hand, then hesitated. Scenes from the last few days played back and forth through his mind. The moonlight reminded him of the evening on the beach – *Julie's dimpled cheeks when she laughed, her tumbling hair. She had responded hungrily to his touch and he'd really thought they were on to something good. Then the scene changed to Julie at the Khanya center, surrounded by children who clung to her, adored her; Mercy's voice, "Our Miss Julie, she be an angel."* But these good memories were fatally undermined, because, try as he might to avoid it, he kept coming back to her raging comment on the night of the gala: *"If you would stand up when it matters, maybe ..."*

He wiped his palms and loosened the tie. All day, he had been waiting for a call to cancel the dinner. After that outburst, and the way she had stormed out right after the auction, he didn't really expect her to go through with it. *But then, why get her mother to bid in the first place? Was she just being spiteful? Or did she want to make peace, apologize? Or was this the final humiliation?* There was simply no telling.

He rang the bell. From deep within the house, a melodious chime rang out, but no one answered. He waited a minute or so, then rang the bell again. When the door finally opened, he was a little surprised to be greeted not by Julie, but by her mother.

"Good evening, Mrs. Noble, I mean, Mrs. Baxter."

"Hello, Chris." Bridget's voice sounded husky. "Oh, you've brought flowers; how lovely. Roses are my favorite!" She took the bunch and delicately inhaled their bouquet. "Come, come inside." She led the way to the lounge, where the roses were carefully placed on a sideboard. "Have a seat; would you like a drink?"

"Well," said Chris, looking at his watch, "that depends on whether Julie is ready."

"Julie?" Bridget gave a nervous little laugh as she smoothed her brow with one finger. Realization slowly dawned on Chris as he took in her carefully applied make-up, the plunging neckline. *Oh God,* he thought. *Oh shite!*

"Julie is in Johannesburg with Greg. No doubt having dinner, as we speak." She sat down, crossing her legs. The shimmering silver dress was slit right up to her thigh. "And," she continued, with a coquettish smile, "if I remember correctly, it was I who bid for you, not Julie."

"Of course." Chris fought to regain his composure. "I'm sorry, my mistake." His mind was in overdrive. *This changed everything; how could he have been so naïve? It explained why no one had called to cancel; Julie wasn't even in town.* He felt like a total idiot and kept tugging at his collar. "I think I *will* have that drink."

Bridget nestled back into her chair and pointed towards an enormous cherrywood cupboard. "Drinks are in the cabinet. Help yourself, and whilst you're at it, shake me up something exciting, would you?"

Holy cow! Chris thought, as he opened the "cabinet" and surveyed the selection. If his soccer mates had been here, they would have burst into raptures to rival those of any saint. He reached for a bottle of 27-year-old Laphroaig whisky.

"You must do a lot of entertaining." He looked up and met her eyes in the smoky mirror behind the bottles and glasses.

She pondered the question. "I've made it a rule with my husband that we only entertain friends at home - business associates can be dealt with in a restaurant. So we tend to go out a lot." Her debonair façade cracked a little when she added, "I can't remember when last we entertained here."

Chris was beginning to recover from the shock. Even though he felt let down after psyching himself up for the dinner with Julie, part of him was relieved – for tonight he could forget about the whole complication of trying to figure out what she wanted. *And, he told himself, an evening with Bridget might be an opportunity to find out a little more about Greg, and his supposed relationship with Julie.*

The smoky mirror softened Bridget's features. It struck him that this woman had made a major donation to the charity and was obviously looking forward to the evening. He did, at least, owe her a bit of fun, so he decided to lighten the mood, indulge in some harmless flirting.

"Let me guess," he said, fixing Bridget with a penetrating look. "You're the shy type; but deep inside there's a party girl, waiting to break free."

She blushed and laughed. He took off his jacket, picked up a cocktail shaker and expertly tossed it from one hand to the other. "We need something zesty for a hot full-moon night. How about I mix you my magic Margarita?"

"What's so magic about your Margarita, cowboy?"

"Ha! Wait till you taste it. It turns women into putty."

"You're not going to drug me, are you?"

"Why would I do a stupid thing like that? It would deprive me of your company."

The phone rang. Bridget hesitated. Chris sensed that she was enjoying the light-hearted banter and was afraid of breaking the mood. She let the phone ring three times before she finally got up and, with an irritated sigh, walked to the study. "Be right back, don't go away."

She did not bother to shut the door, and Chris could not help but hear one side of the conversation.

"For God's sake, Greg, it's Saturday night, I'm about to go out. What's so important that it can't wait till Monday?"

"No, I haven't signed the damn contract. I haven't even printed it yet. The computer's been giving me trouble."

"Don't get cheeky with me!" Her voice rose. "Of course I know where the on-off switch is. The wireless modem is playing up."

There was a pause.

"Well, if you or Matt would take the time to explain to me what's going on, I would have a better understanding of what is and what is not important, wouldn't I?"

"OK, look. I'm not promising anything. I'll try once more a little later; and if I get the damn thing printed I can sign and fax it to you."

She sounded calmer when she asked, "How's Julie?"

"Tell her ... tell her I'll catch her later." She hung up.

"*Augghh!*" Bridget was clenching her fists as she walked back into the lounge. "That man really needs to learn his place."

Chris silently offered her a Margarita.

"Chris, I'm sorry. I'm going to have to deal with this stupid contract. They need it signed this evening." She looked deflated as she sat down, took off her high-heeled shoes and rubbed her foot.

"This was a silly idea." Distractedly, she brushed a loose strand of hair from her forehead. "Your assumption was quite correct; I *did* bid in the auction to have you go out with Julie. Of course it wasn't for me ... God, I'm old enough to be your grandmother."

"That's not true," Chris began, but Bridget held up her hand to stop him. "I just don't get it; I simply do not understand her," she went on. "I really wanted to do something nice for her – show her how proud I was."

"Well, that makes me feel better." Chris gave her his half-smile.

"What do you mean?"

"If *you* don't understand her, and you are her mother, then I don't feel so bad about not being able to figure her out. I thought it was just me."

She sighed. "And now she's with Greg. It's one of the things Matt and I keep fighting over. Matt trusts him totally, but I have my doubts." She pulled her legs up on to the couch and appeared lost in thought. Chris noticed the plaster above her knee – the wound she had sustained when her car was rammed. She appeared so vulnerable; all his protective instincts kicked into gear.

"Look, I really don't mind if we skip the Mount Nelson. Why don't I rustle up something in your kitchen whilst you take care of whatever paperwork it is you have to sort out?"

For a while, it seemed as though Bridget had not heard him. When she finally spoke, it was in a whisper. *"You would do that for me?"*

He was embarrassed to see that her eyes had grown moist. "Hey, a man's got to eat. I'm not promising anything spectacular, but I can do a mean spaghetti bolognese. Let's go see what you've got in your freezer."

Chris was following her to the kitchen when he suddenly remembered the car waiting outside. "The limo driver! Shall I tell him to wait, or come back in an hour?"

"Just tell him to go. You can borrow my car to get home. Whilst you talk to him, I'm going upstairs to put on some jeans."

The driver was surprised. "Aren't you the randy one – skipping dinner and straight down to business, *eh, eh?*" he said, winking conspiratorially.

If only you knew. Chris gave the driver a tip and punched him lightly on the chest. "Just get lost and enjoy your evening off."

The kitchen was not nearly as well stocked as the bar, but there was mince in the freezer and the basics for a tomato-based sauce and pasta; he also found frozen shrimps that he thought might do for a starter. He set about defrosting the mince and rifled through the fridge – carrots, tired-looking lettuce, and celery that had lost its rigor. The pantry yielded a few useful cans: pineapple, various types of beans, *mielies.* He saw potential for a salad.

Bridget reappeared in jeans and a light-green top that picked up the color of her eyes and complemented the auburn of her hair. She opened a bottle of wine, settled herself on a bar stool at the counter, and watched him as he got rid of his tie, rolled up his sleeves, and started chopping vegetables.

"You know that SUV that tried to run you off the road?"

"Yes?"

"Was it by any chance a Pajero? I happened to see one last Saturday with silver paint scrapes."

She swirled the wine in her glass and studied it intently. "I don't pay much attention to cars, so I have no idea, really."

"Well, anyway, Bruce and I followed it; all the way out to near Stellenbosch. That's why we were late for the gala."

"And?"

Chris gave her a brief rundown of the chase from the beach in Camps Bay. "The driver must have noticed us," he said. "He eventually turned into a big, muddy construction site that was too much for my BMW; he gave us the slip through a rear exit."

"Do you remember the site?"

"It was one of Bob Richter's - but that doesn't say much. He's in charge of half the construction sites in the Cape. I did get the address, though, and the license plate of the vehicle."

"Good; we can pass that on to the security people at Noble." She refilled his glass. "But now I don't want to think about that incident anymore."

They chatted companionably and discovered a common interest in architecture and garden design. "The Rodin Museum in Paris," she said. "That must be one of my favorite places in the whole world. It's light and bright and on a human scale. Not too big. Don't get me wrong, the Musée d'Orsay is stunning, but it overwhelms. At the Musée Rodin, strolling through the gardens, seeing those magnificent sculptures, it just - I can't express it - but it's like you feel proud to be part of the human race; there's so much raw emotion and so much beauty!"

Her eyes were bright and her hands reached up to touch some sculpture visible only to her. Chris was struck by the mother-daughter similarity. Clearly, Julie had inherited much of her intensity and passion from her mother.

"What's your favorite modern building?" she asked.

He turned from the stove and paused to think. "I can't really name one specific building, but I love it when the daring and unconventional turn out to be defining. Maybe the Sydney Opera House – I know it's a bit of a cliché, but it is truly magnificent. There was enormous resistance to it when it was in the planning stage, and yet it really works, functionally and acoustically. Have you ever been?"

She shook her head.

Chris was getting into his stride. "And then there is the Gherkin, in London, another one of those defining buildings; a classic from day one – and it set a new standard for environmental design in the ..."

"Watch out!" she called, and pointed at the spluttering saucepan behind him.

"Damn!" Chris swore as he whipped the saucepan away from the high heat. Some of the hissing sauce shot up and splattered across his white shirt. He stirred furiously to prevent it from burning.

"Might have to settle for take-away pizza," he muttered. "What do you think?" He carefully blew on a spoonful before he let her taste it.

"*Mmmh.* It's delicious. But look at you. That sauce is going to stain badly – take off your shirt."

Chris started to protest, but realized she was right. He unbuttoned the shirt and handed it to her. She stood silently for a moment, then reached out and, with her middle finger, wiped a few splatters of sauce from his chest. Carefully, she licked her finger and looked directly into his eyes. Her hand returned to his chest, searching, pressing on his chest muscles as if to test their hardness. Then, without taking her eyes off his, she licked her middle finger and rubbed it around his right nipple, a tiny smile hovering around her lips.

Chris was taken by surprise and did not know how to respond without offending her. *Was she messing around or was she serious?* He stood motionless and held her gaze, half-excited, half-horrified.

Then suddenly Bridget seemed to change her mind, and broke away. "Maybe you should put on an apron. I think you would look quite fetching in an apron." He was relieved that she had returned to a lighter tone.

"Wouldn't know, I don't think I've ever worn one … without a shirt."

"Don't worry, I'll find you a shirt." She disappeared into the laundry room and he could hear water running into a basin. Chris felt shaken but also exhilarated; the evening was full of surprises. He inspected the wine bottle – *how much wine had she had?* He turned his attention back to the food.

Bridget returned with a shirt – presumably one of her husband's. He put it on and served up two plates. She steered the conversation back to architecture and he was gratified by her genuine interest in his ideas and aspirations.

Fifteen minutes later, Chris pushed away his plate. "Enough about me," he said. What about you? What are you … "

The phone rang. She picked up a receiver in the kitchen.

"Yes?"

"Matt, darling! How are you?"

Chris got up to leave the kitchen, but she motioned him back, mouthing that she would only be two minutes.

Fat chance, Chris thought, as he sat down and busied himself opening another bottle of wine. He savored the rich Cabernet. *Whoever buys the wine in this house really knows what they're doing.*

"Yes, I did get your voicemail this morning," Bridget was saying. "It was sweet of you to call. I had a frightful migraine and was planning to call you back later."

"It's much better now." *Pause.* "Yes, I decided to stay in."

"The contract?" Exasperation crept into her voice; she silently rolled her eyes at Chris, and then appeared to be mollified by something Matt said. "OK, darling. I'll go and do it straight away ... no, don't worry... Fine, give me the fax number at the restaurant." She jotted down a number. "Fifteen minutes, promise. Bye."

She put down the receiver. "Right, I'd better go do it. They're in a restaurant with a group of clients to celebrate this big deal and they need me to sign the contract."

She headed to the study and Chris bent down to pack dishes into the dishwasher. Out of the corner of his eye, he saw that Bridget had stopped in the doorway and was watching him. *Jeez*, he thought. *Is she teasing or does she really want it? Surely not!* He tried to remember his conversation with Bruce. This wasn't going at all the way Bruce had predicted. *She's just lonely*, he told himself. He straightened, turned and smiled at her. Bridget blushed and left – she seemed a little unsteady on her feet. Chris spotted an apron hanging on a hook next to the door. A bit drunk himself by now, he toyed with the idea of stripping and serving her coffee dressed in nothing but the apron. *That would certainly give the lady her money's worth,* he thought.

In his mind, he could hear those famous lyrics: *"And here's to you, Mrs. Robinson ... "*

He eyed the apron.

##

It was a cozy young girl's room, frozen in time: white furniture, the matching curtains and wallpaper off-white with a delicate pink stripe and tiny flowers. An army of stuffed toys was neatly arranged along the headboard – waiting for the girl that had gone off, first to boarding school, many years ago, and then to university.

Julie sat, as she had for hours and hours as a teenager, on the window seat. *The trees have grown*, she thought. Young kids were playing on a swing in the neighbor's garden. *Wonder what happened to the Shackletons? They must have moved. Or maybe those are their grandchildren?* She'd have to ask her mother.

Her knees were pulled up, arms hugged around them as she watched the sun go down. Thanks to smog and heat it was a fiery sunset, typical of the Highveld. As she looked down the driveway, she fell into a reverie.

Any minute now, her father's car would pull up, he would step out, wave at her and shout, "Hello, my princess, will you come down and let me into your castle?" And she would run down the stairs and hug him.

Her eyes grew misty; she wished she could have had just one hour to talk to him – just one hour. He would have been able to help her think things through rationally, to help her make sense of her jumbled thoughts and feelings.

Greg seemed sincere in his love for her; she was convinced that they could form a strong partnership. Together, they could run the company, and maybe even move into this house, have children of their own. The sense of continuity appealed to her, and it made a lot of sense. *Then why wasn't she more excited?* The sun disappeared behind the neighbors' roof. A slight breeze came through the window; she hugged herself more tightly and had a sudden flashback to her dream – Chris – because she was sure it had been him - hugging her, the deep sense of calm and belonging she had felt. Then she remembered his touch when they had been on the beach; the way the light of the moon had cast a glow over his bare shoulders, his lips …

And then suddenly a car *was* speeding up the graveled driveway after all – but of course it wasn't her father, it was Greg. He skidded to a stop and jumped out of the car, dressed for dinner in a dark suit and tie.

'Oh shucks.' She looked at her watch. 'I'd better move it.'

Twenty minutes later, she came downstairs to find Greg and Matt, whiskies in hand, in the library.

"Ah, there you are, my dear," Matt greeted her. "I was just about to send up a search party." He chuckled and winked at Greg.

"Sorry to keep you waiting."

Greg smiled. "Turn around, let's see what we've got here."

Julie was reminded of the days when she would show off her ballet costumes to her father. Dutifully, she twirled around. She loved the soft flow of the ankle-length cream-colored dress she'd borrowed from her mother's wardrobe. *"Hmm,"* Greg said.

"What? Don't you like it?"

"I like it, darling, but I was hoping for something a little more … a little more daring, to help distract and entertain our honored guests. At least show your shoulders and a bit of leg. This seems so … so buttoned up. What do you think, Matt?"

Matt refused to get drawn into this particular discussion. "I think she looks lovely in anything she wears," he said.

"Greg, our guests are from Malaysia - a Muslim country." Julie tried to hide her irritation. "I specifically chose something a little conservative to show respect. The last thing I want to do is offend them."

"Oh, but they are *Chinese* Malaysians. The only God they believe in is money."

"Honestly, Greg. I don't know how you can *think* something like that, let alone *say* it."

"Please, baby, do it as a favor for me. Put on something a little sexier. And you've got to lay on the jewelry. This is South Africa, the Chinese expect our women to be dripping with gold."

"*Our* women?" Julie raised an eyebrow.

"You could wear some of your mother's," Greg said, ignoring her comment. He turned to Matt and asked, "Do you think Bridget would mind?"

"Go right ahead, Julie," Matt said. "You know where your mother keeps her jewelry. We recently got her that necklace that looks like golden rose petals. That would fit the bill."

"Matt, I couldn't …"

"Why not? Don't you like it?" Matt looked hurt.

"Oh no, no, it's not that. It's the most exquisite piece of jewelry I've ever seen. But I thought you kept it in the vault at the office. I would feel nervous that something might happen to it."

"Don't be silly," Greg said. "It's exactly the sort of thing that would impress our guests and I'll be with you. Nothing will happen to the necklace."

"OK, OK." Julie gave a small sigh of exasperation. Greg lightly patted her bottom as she turned.

When she rounded on him, his face was all innocence. "Do hurry, we don't want to keep them waiting."

Upstairs, Julie quickly picked out a classic black dress – low cut at the front and back. Looking at herself in the mirror, she felt disturbed that her mother owned something quite so revealing. The dress would certainly excite Greg; he'd probably expect to get favors later. *Maybe she'd develop a headache; after all, he could have had fun with her yesterday afternoon, and instead he'd opted to play golf with the Malaysians!*

There was a three-foot-high safe in one corner of the dressing room. Julie had known the combination, based on her birthday, for as long as she could remember. She spun the lock and the safe door opened silently. Bridget was meticulous about her jewelry; it was all neatly arranged in a series of felt-lined leather drawers. Julie went through the drawers and found, to her surprise, that the rose-petal necklace was missing. She picked out a set of gold-and-diamond earrings with matching chain and pendant instead. On a whim, she also put on a finely crafted bracelet that had been passed down from her grandmother. The outfit was completed with a silver pashmina shawl.

When Julie re-entered the library, Greg gave a low whistle. They briefly discussed the missing necklace and concluded that Bridget must have taken it with her to Cape Town.

"I'm surprised she didn't wear it to the AIDS gala," Julie said.

Greg shrugged his shoulders. "You know how unpredictable she is."

##

They were eight at dinner in the plush, private room with a view over the lights of Sandton: Matt and Greg, Julie, two senior lawyers from the company, Messrs. Lim and Goh, and another Malaysian associate. Julie learned that Mr. Goh, the small, wiry man, was the CEO. He looked more at home in a tailored suit than in the golfing clothes he had worn previously. He sat in the erect manner of powerful men who are short in stature. Everything about him was understated and sparse, yet the others responded with deference to his every word and gesture. The associate translated between the CEO and the hosts. Mr. Goh extracted a pair of gold-rimmed reading glasses from his pocket and glanced at the menu. On seeing that it was only in English, he put away his glasses and listened as the associate labored to translate each dish.

Julie was relieved to have Mr. Lim on her right; he spoke fluent English and proved to be a charming table companion. Halfway through the main course he said, "You are wearing a very interesting bracelet."

"Thank you. It's been in the family for many years." She took off the bracelet to let him study it.

"It looks Egyptian."

"It's definitely from the Mediterranean region, but I'm not sure exactly from where."

He handed it back. "My wife, of course, expects me to bring back jewelry for her – gold, preferably with diamonds. She thinks one can just pick up gold in the street bazaar in South Africa." He paused. "Perhaps you would do me the great honor of helping me purchase a gift for her?"

Julie thought of the potential pitfalls: she had no idea how much money he was prepared to spend, or what his wife might like. She realized, however, that it would be rude to turn down the request. So she tried to sound sincere when she replied, "Of course, it would be a pleasure." She turned her attention to the ostrich steak and plum demi-glaze on her plate. The food had been so artfully decorated that it seemed a pity to eat it.

The lawyer on her left leaned towards her and said under his breath, *"God, it's tedious to have to talk through an interpreter all the time."* Greg must have overheard him. *"Be nice,"* he hissed. *"It usually just takes a bit of booze to loosen foreigners' tongues."* Julie shot him a disapproving glance, hoping that Mr. Lim on her other side would not have heard the comment.

Mr. Goh said something in Chinese to his associate. The man nodded.

"What did he say?" Greg asked.

The associate spoke in halting English: "Mr. Goh express surprise."

"Oh? At what?"

"In Asia, we sign contract first, then we eat."

"Ah, yes," Greg said. "Don't you love doing business with different cultures? One learns so many new things. In South Africa, we always say, 'Never do business on an empty stomach.'" He raised his glass. "To a long and productive partnership! Cheers." They all raised their glasses.

A few minutes later, Julie noticed Greg and Matt whispering urgently. Greg sounded agitated. She only caught a snippet: *"...you'd better bring her in line."* Then Matt got up, cell phone in hand, and excused himself.

Julie turned her attention back to Mr. Lim. "Do you, by any chance, have a photograph of your wife?"

Enthusiastically, Mr. Lim took out his wallet to show her a photograph of himself and his wife in front of Kuala Lumpur's famous Blue Mosque. Julie saw, with a jolt, that the woman in the photograph was wearing long robes and a *tudung* to cover her hair.

"Your wife is Malay?"

"Yes, I converted to the Muslim faith."

"So, pardon my ignorance, but does your wife wear any jewelry?"

He laughed. "Of course. My wife loves jewelry. Being a Muslim does not mean you take a vow of poverty. Look at this!" He handed her another photograph; this one showed a smiling Mrs. Lim next to a top-of-the-range Mercedes.

"I see. Doesn't she find it very uncomfortable to always wear these clothes, particularly in the tropical heat?"

"On the contrary; she's very comfortable. People don't understand: different cultures simply have different standards as to what is modest. I am sure you would feel very uncomfortable if you were in public wearing only your underwear. That is how my wife feels if she does not cover her hair."

Julie suddenly felt naked under his gaze. From across the table, Mr. Goh was looking at her too. *Had he been listening to their conversation? He couldn't have – he didn't speak any English.* She held his gaze till he turned to his associate to say something in Chinese. Both men laughed.

She turned back to Mr. Lim. "You're right; there are many things we do not understand about Muslim culture. I have heard about the wonderful Blue Mosque in this photograph. Would I be allowed to visit it?"

He shook his head. "No, on two counts. You are not a Muslim, and you are a woman."

"You see, that is hard for me to understand. It feels like a severe restriction of my freedoms ..."

"Ah, but what is freedom? A famous Western philosopher once said we can only be free when everyone obeys the rules. What happens to a child without boundaries? I'll tell you. They grow up disrespecting authority. The Americans place so much emphasis on the rights and freedoms of the individual, but where does that get them? Pornography, rape, murder, and violence are rife. No one is free anymore – they are all scared."

Mr. Lim had become quite agitated. All other conversation at the table had stopped. Greg shot Julie a glance that was hard to interpret; *did he want her to stop the conversation or continue it as a way of playing for time?*

"You should visit Kuala Lumpur," declared Mr. Lim. "It is a wonderful city. You could walk around anywhere without fear. Isn't that freedom?"

"There certainly is an appeal to feeling free from the threat of violence, but I would still find it hard to be dictated to ..."

"It is not a case of dictating," Mr. Lim interrupted her. "A parent has an obligation to enforce boundaries for their children; likewise the State and religious leaders have a responsibility to enforce good behavior, otherwise society will sink into anarchy."

They were interrupted by the arrival of the dessert trolley. Julie chose a crème brûlée from the decadent array and Greg used the opportunity to steer the conversation to safaris and other tourist attractions in South Africa.

Ten minutes passed, and Julie noticed that Mr. Goh had begun to look at his watch repeatedly. Again, there was an exchange between him and his associate. No one asked for a translation; Mr. Goh's impatience was obvious.

Just as things were becoming uncomfortable, the hostess appeared and handed a sealed envelope to Greg. He opened it and, with a flourish, presented a set of papers to the Malaysian associate. "Feel free to peruse it once more. Everything is as we agreed, and the document has been signed by our chairman. Please tell Mr. Goh that it is ready for his signature."

To Julie's surprise, Mr. Goh, not the associate, took the document from Greg's outstretched hand. "We certainly expect everything to be in order," he said clearly, in perfect English, before unscrewing a fountain pen and signing with a flourish.

The lawyer next to Julie, unable to hide his surprise, said, "You speak very good English, Mr. Goh."

Without a trace of irony or humor in his voice, Mr. Goh said, "Yes, alcohol does that – it loosens the tongues of foreigners."

##

"Chris!" Bridget called from the study. "Do you know anything about computers?"

He dried his hands and went to find her. She was peering through a pair of glasses at a "This page cannot be displayed" message on the screen. A quick bit of trouble-shooting revealed that the cable to the external modem was not properly connected. He clicked it into the place and Bridget sighed with relief.

"I can never remember all these passwords. Would you mind passing me the little leather-bound notebook from the safe?"

Chris looked around. The high-ceilinged study was as imposing as the rest of the house. Dark bookshelves covered two walls, while the books themselves looked like they had been bought by the meter – all matching volumes, many of them leather-bound. The third wall had floor-to-ceiling windows with velvet drapes; the desk was against the fourth wall. A wood panel in this wall had been moved sideways to reveal a safe. Chris gripped the handle and swung the door open. He had to rustle amongst several files and sheaves of paper before he found the small notebook.

"Is this it?"

"Yes, thanks." She found the password and put the notebook to one side.

Chris studied the bookshelves whilst Bridget printed out and read the contract. Occasionally, she frowned and made neat notes on a separate sheet of paper. When she reached the end, she remained seated, pen in hand, apparently undecided.

"What?" Chris asked.

She took off her glasses and tapped a manicured fingernail on the collated papers. "There's something here I don't understand." She flicked through the contract and motioned for Chris to have a look. "This is a diagram of a piece of equipment, a type of autoclave. We seem to be selling a couple of custom-built units to the Malaysians."

"That's good, isn't it? What is it used for?"

"Good question. That's what troubles me. I can't for the life of me understand what they want with it. One of my late husband's many obsessions was to find a cost-effective way to manufacture immunosuppressants. He wanted to make antiretrovirals so affordable that all AIDS sufferers could have access to them. I know that he and your father spent hours on this."

Chris was surprised, but said nothing. He nodded for her to continue, and Bridget gave him a brief outline of the research. Harry Noble had built a prototype autoclave and experimented for months, but the ultimate compound always proved to be unstable – there was no way to preserve it long enough to make it useful. Dr. du Toit, as a heart surgeon, was extremely interested in this research. Many of his patients had to take immunosuppresants for life following surgery, and if the cost could be brought down, then the benefits would be enormous. The two men had spent many hours discussing the chemistry and formulations. But, ultimately, they shelved the research.

"Harry was such a force of nature," said Bridget, smiling wistfully, her eyes focused on something Chris could not see. "He was intent on making the world a better place. Julie has inherited that drive from him." She sighed. "I wish you could have seen Harry and your father. They were as excited as schoolboys with a big secret. They brainstormed all manner of applications. Harry even had a cock-eyed idea that he could adapt this process to produce a synthetic compound that had the same properties as ground-up rhino horn. There would be no more need to hunt rhinos. They really were going to save the world!"

Chris sat down in a chair opposite her, searching his memory. He found that he did indeed have a vague recollection of his father and Harry Noble, holed up together in the upstairs study. He certainly hadn't thought about it at the time, though – he had had too many other things – his swimming and dancing, for example – to occupy him.

Bridget turned her attention back to the papers in front of her. "I didn't realize that the research had been resurrected," she said, frowning slightly. "In fact, it seems it's progressed to the extent that it has become commercially viable. Our scientists must have revived it and then cracked it. They must have found the answers that eluded Harry." There was no conviction in her voice.

"Why don't you phone your husband and ask him?"

She looked at her watch. "They're sitting at dinner, waiting for me to fax them the contract. I'd better get it to him. But I will ask him tomorrow. If it truly is what I think it is ..." She unscrewed her fountain pen and signed the contract, then punched a number into the fax machine, and watched as the pages chugged through, one by one.

"There, that's done!"

They settled in the lounge, Bridget on the couch and Chris in a chair opposite. She nipped at the Drambuie he had poured for her and he savored the bouquet of a very mature KWV brandy. Bridget seemed to need to talk, and Chris listened quietly as she told him about her first husband and the tough but fulfilling years when they had jointly built up the company. Then she spoke about how delighted they had been when Julie was born, after they had all but given up hope of having a baby. Wistfully, she described the wonderful years when Julie was at primary school and the company was growing.

"It all came crashing down when Harry died. I fell apart and I blame myself for not being strong for Julie when she needed me most. Unfortunately, that time defined my subsequent relationship with her. She's forever treating me like an invalid who could fall apart at any minute; she doesn't understand that I simply went through a very traumatic experience and needed time to recover."

Chris thought it ironic that, by contrast, his father had been very strong when Danielle died; strong to the point of not being accessible at all. There probably was no way to get through such trauma without damage.

"Matt and Greg run the business now. They have built it up way beyond the company we used to have, which is ... great." She swirled her glass, studying the rich liquid. "But, to be honest, I miss being involved. I miss the excitement of waiting to find out if we'll get a contract, or approval for a new product."

"So, why don't you step back into the company?"

"Oh, I don't know. It's become so big ... And Matt keeps telling me - in the nicest way possible - that I shouldn't worry my pretty head about it. He thinks that I should just enjoy spending the money, or do charity work."

"And?"

"I know it sounds awful, but it's amazing how quickly you can get bored spending money. As for charity work, it's one of those things you either love or you don't. I'm involved with a couple of charities, but it's a duty. It's not like Julie and her Khanya center. I suppose, at heart, I've always enjoyed business."

For a while, they both sat in silence. Bridget's tale had stirred up the past for Chris. He now remembered a time when his father had been full of excitement and enthusiasm. His mother must have been fully aware of it, because Chris remembered seeing her in his study, leaning over papers and drawings as he explained something to her. When he had popped his head in and asked what they were up to, they had both looked like children caught in the act of stealing cookies. It was painful to remember his parents as they were then – young, excited, happy.

Bridget said, "I've made up my mind. I'm going to go back to Johannesburg and I'm going to take an active role in the business. If Matt or Greg don't like it – tough luck. I have to do it, for myself and for my marriage. If I'm more involved with the business, it will give Matt and me more in common. Don't you think?"

Chris nodded. They chatted a while longer, and Bridget grew increasingly animated. "I should have done it ages ago ..." she kept saying.

Eventually, Chris could not suppress a yawn. Bridget looked at her watch, "Good grief, look at the time – you need to be on your way."

Having had a coffee to sober himself up, he followed her to the garage, where she handed him the keys to the silver Mercedes. "Thank you, Chris, for a wonderful evening," she said, turning to face him. "You're a fantastic listener and have really helped me straighten out my thinking."

He protested, embarrassed, that the pleasure was all his. She reached up and tousled his hair. It was a motherly gesture; there was none of the sexual innuendo of the early part of the evening.

212

"You know, had I had a son, I would have liked him to be just like you." Her voice dropped. "I'm so sorry that your mother is not around to see what a fine young man you have become."

She gave him a peck on the cheek and pressed the button to open the garage door.

##

Chapter 13: Rude Awakening

Monday

Chris breathed deeply and lengthened his stride as he jogged along the Sea Point promenade. The air was cool and he savored having the broad track to himself, with only a gaggle of seagulls for company. They perched on the guardrail like a platoon of soldiers facing the rising sun, watchful, ready for the day's fishing to begin. As Chris approached, they lifted off the rail, one by one – hovered, squawked – then returned to their positions. Chris envied them; they, at least, knew what they had to do.

He had spent Sunday going through his portfolio of sketches and plans, updating, discarding, and organizing. He needed to get serious about finding a job.

As his feet pounded the paving, he went through his options. He could approach architectural firms in the smaller towns outside Cape Town, which meant he'd probably spend his time upgrading garages and ugly shopping centers and becoming increasingly bored. Or he could work with Wendy on the Khanya project, but that was not going to pay the rent and could lead to awkwardness with Julie. Another option would be to try and find a job as a construction foreman, but work like that was very difficult to find during a recession. *Plus*, he thought wryly, *Bob Richter's hardly going to give me a recommendation and the man controls a hell of a lot of the building that's going on.* Finally – as a last resort – he could always work as a barman. *God, has it come to this?* he thought. *Five years of study and I end up a barman?*

He turned away from the sea and headed home. His top priority was to stop depending on an allowance from his father. That might mean giving up the apartment and moving in with a friend. But then again, maybe he needed to get away from Cape Town, maybe look for a job overseas. One of his classmates had landed a job in Saudi Arabia and was urging him to apply as well. From what Chris had seen on the Internet, they certainly had some spectacular projects on the go there. *There's nothing tying me to Cape Town,* he thought, a little bitterly. As his apartment building came into view, he resolved that his first action today would be to give notice on the apartment. That would give him maximum flexibility. Having made this decision, he bounded up the stairs into the lobby - where he found his path blocked by two men in suits.

"Chris du Toit?" An official-looking badge was thrust in his face.

"Yes?"

"I'm Inspector Musamil Ibrahim. This is Sergeant Vervey. We need to ask you a few questions."

"About what?" He looked from one man to the other and willed his breathing to slow.

The security guard behind his desk had dropped all pretense of updating his log. He had seen the badge and this was the most exciting thing to have happened in days. With an earnest, innocent expression he leaned forward to follow the conversation; after all, he too was in law enforcement, even if his training had been all of two weeks (part time).

The inspector looked at the guard and said to Chris, "It might be best if you could come down to the station with us. It won't take long."

"Right now? I need to shower." Chris glanced towards the elevators and then over his shoulder to the entrance door, fervently hoping that none of the other tenants would see him with the policemen. If they were to slap handcuffs on him, he would be too embarrassed to ever show his face here again.

The sergeant edged closer, as though he expected Chris to bolt. He was a middle-aged man who, in Chris's estimation, had spent much of his life boxing or playing rugby. His nose had been broken and he looked awkward in a suit that must have been bought before his once-muscular body started to shape-shift from fab to flab. His once-black hair had turned into a bushy gray mop that looked like it never had the benefit of a professional hairdresser. With a heavy Afrikaans accent, slowly, deliberately, as though he were addressing a moron, he said: "The matter is urgent ..."

Chris's mind raced through a myriad of possibilities. *Had something happened to his father? One of the Toreros? Julie?* A wave of nausea spread from his stomach and threatened to choke him. *No, in that case the police would not be wanting to question him; they'd just tell him. Maybe Bruce had been dealing in* dagga *again, or maybe someone got robbed at the gala? Or had something happened the other night at the De Waterkant Club? But then ...* The possibilities were endless and he stopped trying to figure it out.

"Am I under arrest?"

"No, no," the inspector said. "But it is a rather delicate matter, which is why we do not want to discuss it here. And it *is* urgent."

He looked at Chris's sweat-soaked vest. "I'm a runner myself. I know how it feels. We'd appreciate it if you could keep your shower brief."

"I can be ready in five minutes."

"Sergeant Vervey will accompany you ..." - the inspector tilted his head and gave a hint of a sardonic smile - "... for your own protection." He motioned in the direction of the elevator and tapped his watch.

A short while later, Chris was ushered into an unmarked police car. They drove in silence along the beachfront. Chris watched the familiar parade of newspaper sellers, school kids, joggers, and nannies. It felt surreal.

The inspector sat next to him in the back, texting on his cell phone; the sergeant drove. Chris caught a whiff of hair gel and studied the inspector's immaculate black hair and dark face. *This man takes his clothes seriously,* Chris thought, as he observed the inspector's tie and Oxford brogues - polished to perfection. The olive suit was casually flung open to reveal a "Fabiani 100% wool" label, an immaculately ironed shirt - and a holster under his arm. Chris knew that the Cape police department had been on a major drive to recruit Muslims to their ranks, and subsequently fast-track them, so that police demographics could better match the diversity of the population. What surprised Chris was the man's ostentatious display of wealth – a thick gold bracelet nestled against one of the heaviest Rolex watches he'd ever seen. He wondered if it was the genuine article.

He would have been even more surprised if he had known that Inspector Ibrahim held a Master's degree in History and had a deep interest in Comparative Religion. The inspector came from a wealthy family that owned a computer import business and he was the chairman of an organization that helped underprivileged Muslims with funding for their Hajj to Mecca.

As they drove, Chris was aware of the sergeant's watchful eyes, framed by bushy eyebrows and sagging skin, in the rear-view mirror. Dark and expressionless, they seemed to expect him to try and throw the car door open and leap out. Chris thought of the many movies he'd seen where someone jumped from a moving vehicle or train, rolling as they fell to absorb the shock. He could just picture the outcome if he tried it and some truck went right over him. Besides, he'd done nothing wrong.

"Do you watch *Law and Order*?" Chris asked, attempting to break the silence.

The inspector briefly paused in his texting, but said nothing. Neither did Vervey.

"So, what's this all about?"

"You'll find out when we get to the station," the inspector replied. His tone was polite but he did not even look up from his cell phone.

Chris looked out at the ocean to avoid the sergeant's constant gaze. He found the man disturbing, and, had he but known, his intuition was right, for Sergeant Vervey was a man on the edge. A devout Christian whose life philosophy could be summed up in the words: 'Spare the rod and spoil the child,' Jacobus Vervey, the son of a railway worker, had been a deacon in the Dutch Reformed Church for as long as he could remember. As he prayed to God to bring him justice and deliverance, he knew that God was testing him, testing him the way he had tested Job, and he didn't know how much longer he could take it. His wife had left him and two years ago his seventeen-year-old daughter had fallen pregnant. Despite Vervey's best efforts to persuade her to reveal the identify of the father (so he might blow his balls off), the girl had defied him. He'd wanted to throw the Jezebel out of his house but eventually the *dominee*, his pastor, had persuaded him not to, arguing that it would look bad to the congregation.

Vervey had just begun to accept his fate when God handed him the next blow – a Muslim boss! Now he had to put up with Friday prayers and halal food and God-knows what else. How was he supposed to respect a man ten years his junior, promoted over his head? Affirmative action would be the end of the white man in South Africa.

He looked again at the young man in the back seat. No doubt it was a cocky smooth-talker like this one who had impregnated his daughter. *Hedonists, the lot of them.* Hedonist was his new favorite word; he'd looked it up. It made him think of heathens and of Sodom and Gomorrah; no doubt those cities had been full of hedonists and, since even he knew that you couldn't go around calling people sodomites, it gave him satisfaction to call them hedonists.

Jacobus Vervey was getting impatient with the Lord. He knew that it was his duty not to question and to await God's will – *but,* he thought, as he drove towards the station, *If ever God needs a pair of hands on earth to sort out some of the scum that are polluting the place, then I'm ready and waiting.*

Ten minutes later, they parked outside the Camps Bay police station, a pale single-story building that looked as though it was permanently hunkered down against the wind. Chris had sketched it a few years ago for one of his projects; the incongruous building had intrigued him. Nestled amongst palm-fronted restaurants, and overshadowed by million-dollar apartments, it appeared more like a worn-out B&B than a police station. Now, on the front step, Chris turned, allowed himself to gaze back across the beach to the exact spot where he had swum with the dolphins. The car-guards were chatting to each other and in the distance he could hear an early ice-cream vendor: "Ice *creeeam, lekker, lekker* ice cream!"

The sergeant, however, was in no mood to let him linger. He gripped Chris's arm and guided him out of the light, through a dinghy charge office, and into an interview room. The inspector followed and Chris heard the metal door lock behind them. After the din of the road outside, the silence was suffocating.

The room was sparsely furnished: a government-issue table, four chairs, and a waste-paper basket – the heavy, wooden variety that looked like a storage crate for apples. The walls were bare, except for a faded map of the Cape Metropolitan area and a framed portrait of President Mbeki, smiling benignly down on the proceedings. On the far side of the room was a row of filing cabinets, with a dusty fan and boxes of paper stacked on top of them.

The sergeant puffed himself up like a rooster at dawn and pointed at one of the chairs. "Please, have a seat." There was, however, no "please" in his tone of voice.

Chris turned to look at the inspector behind him. The latter nodded his encouragement and Chris decided it was best to comply.

"How do you support yourself, Mr. du Toit?" Vervey began. He seemed to have difficulty with the word "Mister", dragging it out and letting his tongue roll around it as though he were avoiding a bitter taste.

"I don't see what possible relevance that ..."

"*We* will decided what is and what is not relevant."

Chris clenched his teeth, hesitated. Before he could even make up his mind whether to answer the question or not, however, the sergeant was off again, like a hound on the chase. He pressed his fists on to the table and leaned towards Chris. "Now, *Meneertjie*, you can work with us, and we can sort things out quickly, or we can do it the hard way. Which will it be?"

Chris felt instantly annoyed. There was nothing inherently wrong with calling someone *"Meneertjie"* – little man or little sir - but in this context it was condescending in the extreme. He was beginning to think that he was trapped in a bad cop flick. This was going beyond a joke. He struggled to control his anger and said, "It would help if you told me what the fuck is going on here …"

The sergeant's fist crashed on to the table. "Watch your language! I will not tolerate swearing in my police station. If you swear again, I'll rip your tongue out!" He breathed heavily, straightened up, and tugged at his jacket cuffs. "*You* might not go to church, but I do; and you'd better remember it."

Chris was completely speechless. Weighing his options, he eventually swallowed, half-raised his hands, and said, "Fine, no swearing. But I would still like to know what is going on. I thought I was supposed to be helping you."

The sergeant now adopted a very matter-of-fact, neutral tone of voice. "Just tell us where you've hidden her? Is she still alive? I promise you, if you've hurt that woman, you'll rot in jail till the day you die."

Chris turned pale and his eyes sought out the inspector, hoping for some clarification. "What is going on? Is this someone's idea of a practical joke?" Ibrahim didn't answer immediately, but he moved away from the wall and sat on a chair opposite Chris. He took out a pad and pen.

"Do you know a Mrs. Bridget Baxter?" he asked.

"Yes."

"When last did you see her?"

"Saturday night."

"What time?"

"It was quite late – around one o'clock in the morning."

"*Sies*," the sergeant interjected. "Aren't you ashamed of yourself, taking advantage of an older lady?"

Chris felt a hot rage bubble up from his gut. "Last time I looked, the constitution allowed us to associate with whomever we wanted to." Deliberately, he asked, "What the *fuck* are you accusing me of?"

The sergeant came raging at him, but Chris had expected it. In a flash, he was out of his chair and blocking the punch. He was about to let rip with a kick to the groin when the icy voice of Inspector Ibrahim cut in: "Vervey! *Los hom!*" Reluctantly, the sergeant stepped back, but he continued to glare at Chris and now there was life in those dark eyes – a menacing sparkle. Chris breathed deeply, still holding up his arms in a defensive position. He could not be sure that this man, who seemed to display as much rationality as a rabid dog, would actually listen to his master. A part of Chris marveled that someone who he had never met could hate him so intensely. It was incomprehensible , but also deeply disturbing.

With visible effort, Vervey managed to regain his composure; he plucked furiously at his jacket cuffs and spat out, "You cocky little ... I told you not to swear. The Lord ..."

"Mr. du Toit is here to help us in our investigations," the inspector said calmly, "Please sit, Mr. du Toit, or may I call you Chris?"

Chris nodded and sat down, but he continued to keep a wary eye on the sergeant.

"Now, Chris, it would appear that Mrs. Baxter has disappeared. We have reason to believe she was kidnapped."

"Kidnapped?" Chris was stunned.

"Yes, sometime between one a.m. on Sunday morning, when you allegedly left her home, and nine p.m. on Sunday night - last night - when her husband received a call demanding a ransom."

"But ... but that's insane. Who would want to kidnap her?"

"That, Chris, is exactly what we have to find out. As far as we can make out, you were the last person to have seen her."

"Are you accusing *me* of kidnapping her?"

"No, we are merely trying to establish Mrs. Baxter's movements. It is unfortunate that the time-window, between when she was last seen, by yourself, and when her husband received the ransom note, is rather long. I do apologize for Sergeant Vervey's zeal, but you will appreciate that, in a kidnap situation like this, time is of the absolute essence. Would you mind giving us an account of the evening?" He tapped his pen expectantly.

Chris thought for a moment, and then explained why he had gone to the Baxter residence. He gave the briefest background of the auction at the gala (which elicited snorts from the sergeant) and a general account of the evening. The inspector listened intently.

"So, let me see if I understand correctly," he said, when Chris had finished his account of the evening. "You are currently in possession of

Mrs. Baxter's car?" He gave Chris a penetrating stare. "And she just lent it to you – in the middle of the night?"

Chris nodded. For the first time, he was beginning to feel a little uneasy. He could see how this might look from the inspector's perspective.

"When were you supposed to return the car?"

"She was going to have her driver come round on Monday morning – today – to pick it up." Chris looked at his watch. "In fact, he might be there, looking for the car, as we speak."

"Are you in any sort of financial difficulties?"

"No."

"It's a pretty nice apartment you have there; expensive area. How do you support yourself?"

"My father gives me an allowance." Chris heard the sergeant snigger derisively and felt the color rising in his cheeks. "I only graduated a couple of months ago and am currently looking for a job."

"I see. You understand that we may need to verify this with your father. How can we reach him?"

"Do you have to? I really would prefer it if we left him out of this."

"It's just routine."

"You can reach him at Groote Schuur Hospital. Dr. Jacques du Toit."

"The heart surgeon?"

"Yes."

Chris always felt a tinge of pride and a good measure of embarrassment when people made the connection between him and the famous surgeon. That was part of the reason why he very rarely mentioned his father.

The inspector asked a few more questions, consulted his notes, and added to them with his careful handwriting. "What you have told us about the phone calls ties in with what Mr. Baxter has said. We'll obviously want to check with the gala's organizing committee and the limo company. I would appreciate it if you stayed in town and kept your cell phone on at all times, in case we need to reach you."

Chris nodded.

"Do you know anyone who might have a grudge against the Baxters?"

Chris shook his head, relieved that, for now at least, the spotlight was no longer on him. "I really don't know Mrs. Baxter that well, and I know very little about the family business."

"Well," the inspector got up, "for now, you're free to go. Would you like Sergeant Vervey to give you a ride back to your apartment?" He motioned for his colleague to unlock the door.

It was on the tip of Chris's tongue to say he'd rather have root-canal treatment, but he decided that smart-alecky comments would not go down well with either of the two men.

"I'm sure you both have a lot to do. I can get a taxi or call a friend to give me a ride. Inspector, may I call you later to see what you have found out? I still can't believe it. Maybe the whole thing is just a hoax," he added, a note of hope creeping into his voice.

"Maybe." The inspector led the way to the front office, briefly shook Chris's hand, and retreated. Sergeant Vervey merely grunted, then followed his superior.

Five minutes later, Chris sat on the terrace of a coffee shop, waiting for his double-espresso order. He had gratefully accepted a glass of water from the waiter and glugged it down the way a pelican eats a fish: one gulp. His hand was trembling and he spilt some water on his chest. *Kidnapping! How could anyone suspect me of kidnapping? Where could Bridget be?* And then his tumbling thoughts slowed for a second, and a single word thrust itself into his mind - *Julie!*

Deep in the recesses of Chris's mind was something he visualized as a dark stinkwood casket. It was the place where he had buried the thoughts of fear, hatred, and vengeance that had consumed him in the aftermath of his mother's death. He had worked hard over the years to keep that casket nailed shut, but every once in a while its writhing and squirming contents tried to break out. Now, as he thought of Julie, imagined the fear and anxiety she must be going through, his own demons rose up in sympathy – he could almost feel the creatures throwing themselves against the casket lid, desperate to break free.

The inspector had given him strict instructions not to speak to anyone about the incident, but Chris decided that this ban could not possibly include Julie. He dialed her number and was frustrated to find it going directly to voicemail. "Hey, it's me," he said, speaking into the void. "I just had the most bizarre conversation with the police. They told me that your mother has been kidnapped. I can't believe it ... How are you holding up? Is there anything I can do? Call me. Please." He hung up, feeling annoyed that he had not managed to express himself properly. He had really wanted to talk to Julie, and instead all he'd done was leave a message which would probably sound banal when played back.

His coffee arrived; he sipped without tasting anything, and watched the summer scene unfolding in front of him. During his time in the police station, Camps Bay beach had progressed from languid awakening to the full-blown frazzle of drivers hunting for parking, kids squealing, noisy street vendors, and hot sun. The smell of tanning lotion and coffee permeated the air. A group of surfers readied their boards and paddled off into the rolling breakers. Chris closed his eyes, but immediately he had an image of Bridget, bound and gagged, bleeding from a bullet wound. Her blood was dripping on to a white surface – white as the beach – white as the carpet on to which his mother's blood had dripped. The demons in the casket of his mind were rattling furiously. He pressed his fingers against his temples and tried to block out these unwanted pictures. He tried to conjure up a happy image of his mother, one of her smiling - but he couldn't. Instead, he felt again her weight as he caught her body, saw again how the light left her eyes, her strong spirt snuffed out ... Suddenly, Chris was filled with a murderous rage. It was as if the lid had finally come off Pandora's box. Images of himself hacking the murderer to death flooded into his mind, leaving him feeling repulsed but also strangely satisfied.

He slumped back in his chair, shaking his head to dispel the images. The thought of Julie acquiring her own stinkwood casket full of dark demons was unbearable. He willed his hands to be steady and picked up the phone to dial James Buthelezi's number.

"You're shitting me," James said, when Chris told him what had happened.

"It's true."

"I ... I don't know what to say."

"You don't need to say anything. You just have to give me a ride home."

"Sure, be there in ten minutes."

Chris finished his coffee, then dialed Julie's number again. It rang. He was about to give up when she answered.

"Hello?" Her voice was hesitant; he wondered if he had woken her.

"Hi, Julie, how are you bearing up?"

"I didn't get much sleep last night." She sounded evasive.

"The police just finished questioning me. I still can't believe your m ..."

"Where are you now?" she interjected anxiously. "We have to be very careful."

He looked around; there was no one in earshot but it was a very public place. "I'm at a coffee shop in Camps Bay. Can I call you later?"

"Yes, I'll be here," she paused. "How ... how was she when you saw her?"

Chris shrugged. "She was fine. We cooked a simple supper, chatted about all manner of things ..."

"This is such a nightmare – surreal. The police have set up a command center in the boardroom. I wish there were something I could do. I keep thinking ..."

"Julie, you sound tired. You must try to get some sleep – that's the only way you can keep your wits about you."

He heard the blast of a car horn and looked up to see James's black Mazda with its distinctive spoiler parked in front of the coffee shop. *Why did James always have to be so punctual?*

"My lift is here; I'll call you later. Please let me know if you hear anything, OK?" He hesitated. "And, Julie ... take care."

During the ride, Chris gave a blow-by-blow account of the events. James was grim when Chris described the sergeant. "Yep, that's what my people had to put up with for three hundred years: fucking Bible-punchers who want to *donner* their brand of Christianity into everyone."

At Chris's apartment building, they both ignored the inquisitive stare of the security guard and took the elevator. Chris fished the key out of his pocket and reached for the door handle, then stopped. He held up his hand and backed a step away.

"What?" James asked. "What?" Then he, too, noticed that the door was slightly ajar.

"Did you maybe forget to lock it?" James whispered. *"You were rushed out of here in one hell of a hurry."*

Chris gave him a disparaging look. "Does *anyone* in South Africa forget to lock their front door? Give me some credit!"

They both leaned forward and listened - *silence.* Chris carefully pushed the door open. James was right behind him, peering over his shoulder.

"Holy shit, Chris! What the hell have you gotten yourself mixed up in? This is bad, man." He shook his head. "This is not cool."

The apartment looked as though its contents had been forced through a giant shredder. Stuffing poured from gashes in the couch, drawers had been ripped out, papers, books, and clothes strewn everywhere. Even his favorite poster of the Getty Museum had been repeatedly slashed, and now hung in strips from the wall.

"What on earth were they looking for?"

James shook his head. "I don't think they were looking for anything." He pointed to what was left of Chris's CD collection, now reduced to scattered shards, strewn across the floor. It was clear that someone had deliberately broken as many as possible. "They're sending you a message."

Mechanically, Chris started to right the furniture.

"Don't touch anything! We have to call the police."

They were spared the trouble. On cue, Sergeant Vervey and two uniformed policemen barged through the open door into the apartment. There was something very close to glee in the sergeant's voice as he grabbed Chris and cuffed his hands behind his back. "Christopher du Toit, I am arresting you for the kidnapping of Bridget Baxter. Anything you say can and will be used against you in a court of law."

"What the hell? This is ridiculous! Look at my apartment. *I'm* the victim here."

The sergeant shrugged dismissively. "You and your friend probably did this to try and throw us off the scent. You all think you are so clever; well, sonny boy, we've got all the evidence we need now."

"What evidence?"

"We found traces of blood in Mrs. Baxter's car and I will bet you a hundred bucks that it is Mrs. Baxter's blood. And your DNA is all over that car."

Chris had to fight the urge to head butt the smirk off Sergeant Vervey's face.

"She'd hurt herself in a previous accident," he said, through gritted teeth.

"Yeah, yeah, yeah. What accident? We already checked. Nothing's been reported."

Chris felt his heart sink – they really were going to pin this on him.

Clearly enjoying himself, Vervey went on, "You are just like all good-for-nothing rich brats: swearing, drinking, drug taking, fornicating; never worked a day in your life. Your goose is cooked, man. As soon as Forensics have ID on that blood…" He shook his head in a gesture of mock compassion. "I feel sorry for you. A pretty boy like you in Pollsmoor Prison … He paused, his meaning obvious to all in the room.

"What you are saying is preposterous!" James interjected. "A man is innocent until proven guilty, as you should know. He has a right to protection."

"Is that so?" The sergeant's voice was heavy with sarcasm. "It seems that message did not get through to whoever is in charge of building more prisons; you should talk to your brothers in government. In the meantime, sonny boy here will have to take his chances." Yet again, he paused, relishing the effect he was having on the two young men. "Maybe you'd better start praying." The words shot out with such venom that, not for the first time, Chris wondered if the man was unhinged. His heart sank even further.

"Take him back to Camps Bay," Vervey said, turning to the two policemen. "Let's see if we can get a little more cooperation this time."

"Chris …" James gestured towards the chaos in the apartment. "What do you want me to do?"

Chris paused in the doorway. He shrugged. "Just leave it; lock the door." Then a though struck him. "James, could you please give Wendy a call? Tell her what's happened. Maybe she can help me find a lawyer."

##

Tuesday morning in Johannesburg

The twentieth-floor lobby of the executive suite at Noble Enterprises provided a commanding view over Sandton, with the skyline of downtown Johannesburg in the far distance. The horizon was suffused in a pale haze. *It's going to be a hot day,* Julie thought, and immediately chided herself for even thinking of the weather when there were so many more important things to consider.

She twisted a strand of hair round and round her finger, and stared out of the window. After a while, she became aware of someone behind her, and the next minute Greg had put his arms round her and was kissing the top of her head. She closed her eyes and leaned back against his chest.

"Did you manage to get any sleep at all?" he asked.

"A little," she lied, looking up into his stubbled face, taking in the lines around his eyes. She felt grateful that he was there with her during this ordeal. It had been – what? - thirty-six hours since they had had that awful phone call demanding ransom, and they had been the longest hours of her life. She did not know what she would do if something happened to her mother. She didn't want to think about it, but found she could think of nothing else.

"Who would do something like this to us?" Julie searched Greg's face, desperate for some answers. "Do you really think its money they're after?"

"What else?"

"I don't know. It's just … kidnapping. It's such a mean and vindictive thing to do to someone. My mother must be beside herself." She brought up her hand and pressed her eyes shut to stem the tears. "Do you think they'll drug her … hurt her? I just don't know how she's going to bear up."

"There's no point dwelling on it now. And if you keep twisting your hair like that, you'll end up looking like a plucked chicken." He untangled her hand from her hair and kissed her neck. "You have to keep your strength up."

"Have the police found anything new?"

"The captain is about to give us an update; come along."

He led the way across the lobby into the boardroom, which the police had taken over as incident command center. Three uniformed policemen were typing on laptops and talking into their cell phones. A tray of bagels sat in the middle of the large oval table next to an empty pizza box. The smell of coffee hung in the air. At the far end of the room, a young policewoman was carefully updating the time-line on a whiteboard.

Matt was in his usual seat at the head of the table. Normally, his expansive manner filled the room as he steered the corporate ship; today he looked forlorn and diminished. Julie noticed his crumpled shirt and the heavy bags under his eyes. She gave him a hug and sat down next to him.

The police captain appeared to be seasoned veteran – short gray hair, a neatly trimmed mustache and a deceptively languid manner. Both he and his lieutenant were in plain clothes. The captain acknowledged the arrival of Julie and Greg with a nod and continued his briefing to Matt.

"The forensics team are at your house in Cape Town, dusting for prints. The dog squad are searching the whole estate."

"I bet that will make the neighbors happy," Greg commented.

"We've spoken to the chairman of the homeowners' association and simply told him that there has been a break-in. Under no circumstances do we want to publicize the kidnapping. We've also confiscated all the video surveillance tapes from the estate. Unfortunately, it appears …"

"What?" Matt asked. "Don't tell me there was a problem with the surveillance cameras? We have just paid a fortune in extra levies to upgrade the system."

"It would appear that the contractors were in the middle of doing the upgrades and a number of cameras were not recording."

"*Urggghh!*" Matt exclaimed. "The incompetence! I'll sue them!"

Julie touched his arm. "You can think about that later. Right now, we have to concentrate on finding Mother."

He grunted, rubbed his eyes, and shook his head as if to dispel a fog. "What do we do now? Wait for the next call from the kidnappers?" He turned towards Greg. "Who's working on getting the ransom money together?"

"I've been in touch with our bankers; they are handling it very discreetly."

Greg turned to the captain. "Was there anything of use on the tapes that you *do* have? Do you have any other leads?"

"The young man who visited her Saturday night …" He cleared his throat and consulted his notes. It seemed like he was trying to buy time and weigh up how much he should share. His unspoken thoughts were clear enough: *Mature women, young male "friend", husband far away. A recipe for disaster, whichever way you looked at it. How much did the husband know?*

"… Christopher du Toit. We have taken him into custody."

Julie's hand, occupied with twisting her hair, froze. "You don't seriously suspect that he had anything to do with my mother's disappearance?"

"At the moment, it's our only lead."

"That's preposterous!"

The captain shrugged. "It is too early to say. We are following up on several aspects of the story he has told Inspector Ibrahim in Cape Town." He hesitated, then looked directly at Matt. "You *are* sure that you cannot think of anyone else with a motive?"

"I've told you," Matt said, his irritation evident. "It could be anybody. We are a high-profile company. My wife is frequently at charity events and has her picture in the society pages. She's a natural target."

"It could be a disgruntled employee," Greg suggested. "I've got HR compiling a list of recent terminations."

The captain nodded and, after running through a few more items, adjourned the meeting.

Matt looked dumbfounded; he was not used to being ordered out of his own boardroom, even if it had been couched in terms of a polite request. The three of them retreated to Matt's office, where they sat in silence, each lost in their own thoughts. After a few minutes, Julie reached across and touched Matt's hand. "You should get some sleep. It could be hours before we hear anything."

"You *both* should get some rest," Greg said. "You can go back to the house and I could call you as soon as …"

"No." Matt pulled himself up and ran his hands through his hair. "I'm staying right here." Julie knew there was no point arguing with him, but she definitely did not want to go back to the empty house by herself. Eventually, with promises of being called immediately if there was any news, Greg persuaded her to rest on the leather couch outside Matt's office. He took off her shoes and even found a blanket. She gave him a grateful smile, curled into a fetal position, and closed her eyes.

Sleep proved elusive, however. Her mind raced and darted about like a skittish gazelle. *Who, who on earth would want to inflict such pain on her mother, on the family?* The staff at the houses in Cape Town and Johannesburg had been with them for years. It *had* to be someone from within the company - or maybe some rival business? Or was it someone with a grudge? Who hated her mother? Or if not that, who was in financial trouble? Her mind wandered to the Toreros: James - full of entrepreneurial schemes that probably weren't making any money, but his parents had money; Bull - burning with ambition, while eking out a living as an unqualified gym instructor for some community organization. Then there was Bruce - he seemed to be someone who played fast and loose with the law, if she were to believe half or what she'd heard. And what about Cedric, with his extravagant plans for expensive productions? And Riaan? Maybe he, too, had hidden financial problems... If she thought about it, she realized that there was not much she really knew about any of the Toreros – but could it be that one of them might be desperate enough to kidnap her mother? It just did not seem possible. And as for Chris - she knew his pride was wounded by the fruitless job search, and she herself had given him little reason to think well of her family recently - but there was no way, surely ...

She was hovering on the brink of sleep when something stirred in the back of her mind. Wendy had made a throwaway comment about Chris's remarkable knack for making enemies. Maybe, maybe this was not about her mother at all. Maybe this was a set-up to get at Chris. It seemed uncanny how he suddenly found himself in this predicament, with all the evidence pointing at him. *What was the name of that construction magnate with the jilted daughter? Reardon, Reichert ... Richter!*

Julie tried to place herself in Sandra Richter's thousand-rand designer shoes. Maybe the girl was nutty, but what she saw and felt was her reality: humiliated, dumped, deserted. If she were Sandra Richter, she too would want revenge.

She was sure that she was on to something and wanted to test her theory. She sat up, found her cell phone, and dialed Wendy's number.

Chris had no idea what time it was when he woke up on Tuesday morning. A square shaft of light, surgically cut into slices by vertical bars, illuminated the tiny room. For a short while he lay still, feeling totally disoriented, aware of the hardness of the bench under the thin mattress. Then realization came flooding back - he was in jail. "Shit, shit, shit!" He sat up stiffly and put his feet on the concrete floor. Judging by the color of the sky behind the bars, it was still early. He scratched the stubble on his chin and eyed the toilet bowl, three feet away from the bed, with distaste. It had no lid or seat and was made of some sort of metal – but if it was steel, it certainly wasn't stainless …There was a matching basin. He got up and peered at his foggy face in the metal mirror and felt a strange sense of detachment from the figure looking back at him – uncombed hair above a tanned face; blue eyes; strong jaw with a stubble beard. If anyone saw this face in the street, they might think: *that guy's had a heavy evening.* They would not begin to fathom the turmoil that consumed him - mainly outrage, but also concern. His concern was for Julie as well as for Bridget, and on top of that he would have to deal with his father's reaction. He imagined it now, seeing in his mind the look of weary resignation on his father's face. *"What have you gotten yourself into now?"*

What had *he gotten himself into?* He had no idea, and he had no idea how it had happened. He splashed his face with cold water in an attempt to freeze the thoughts in his mind; if he could get them to stand still, then he might be able to order them.

He stood in the middle of the bleak cell and realized that there was nothing he could do except wait, and that he had nothing to distract himself with, no book, nothing. *God, what if they really pin this on me? What if I really end up in a hellhole like this for ten, fifteen, twenty years? How long do they give one for kidnapping? What if Bridget is dead? Life in prison – Pollsmoor…*

The walls closed in and despair unfurled from the core of his soul. He knew the warning signals; he had to stop it. If not contained, the witch's cauldron within him would bubble over and spread to every fiber of his being till he wanted to hurl himself against a wall.

So Chris did what he had done all those years ago on the night of his mother's funeral, the only thing which seemed to control the demons. He started to dance. First, he stretched up as far as he could until he was standing on his toes. Then, slowly to begin with, he started to turn. The space was tight but that did not deter him. He knew exactly how far he could extend an arm or a leg. His design professor had always marveled at his spatial perception, his ability to guess the dimensions of a room to within inches, and here in his cramped cell he instinctively put this skill to use.

He conjured up music in his mind, used the walls as props, leaned in, kicked; his arms and legs became coiled springs to bounce his body back and forth. He crouched, twisted, and turned. It couldn't really be called a dance but it was movement. The tension receded and he was able to think clearly. *Some bastard is out to get me, but who? Why?*

The sky was bright blue, and the morning well advanced, when one of the constables came and escorted him to the small room where he had been "interviewed" the previous day. Chris steeled himself for another round with the sergeant. Instead, when he stepped into the room, he had to stifle a cry of relief. There, in earnest conversation with the captain, was Wendy. She stopped in mid-sentence and came to give him a hug.

"Chris! I couldn't believe it when James called me yesterday."

"Thanks for coming," he managed to say, hoping she would not notice the moisture that had shot into his eyes.

"This is my chief legal adviser."

Chris shook hands with an affable-looking man, a few inches shorter than himself. The lawyer had his gray hair tied back in a ponytail and wore large tortoiseshell glasses that were either a leftover from the seventies or the latest in Italian eyewear, Chris couldn't decide which.

Inspector Ibrahim appeared to be oblivious to Chris's presence. He was at the table, studying a set of papers.

"I'm so sorry, Chris," Wendy said. "We could only get hold of a judge this morning. But now everything is OK. He's set bail, the inspector has gone through all the papers, and we're ready to go." She turned and asked, "That's right, isn't it, Inspector?"

"How much is the bail?" Chris ventured to ask.

"Three hundred thousand rand," the lawyer said.

Chris paled. He barely had three hundred rand, let alone three hundred thousand.

"Don't worry about it," Wendy said. "I've posted it for you. The key thing is to get you out of here so we can figure out what's going on." With a pointed look to the inspector, she continued, "I would hate the police to continue wasting time with you when they really need to focus their efforts on finding out who has kidnapped Bridget."

By now, the inspector had finished reading the paperwork. He signed the documents and sorted them into two neat piles –one he gave to the lawyer, the other to the constable at the door.

"You are free to go," he said to Chris, with a smile that did not reach his eyes. "I suggest you carefully study the conditions of the bail with Mrs. van Houten's lawyer. You are to report here every afternoon and keep your cell phone on at all times."

"Mrs. van Houten." He bowed slightly and gestured towards the door. "It has been a pleasure to meet you."

For the second time in twenty-four hours, Chris found himself stepping out of the dark little police station and surveying the bright Camps Bay beach scene. He breathed deeply, then turned back to Wendy and her lawyer. After a brief discussion, it was agreed that Chris should meet up again with the lawyer in the afternoon.

A couple of curious onlookers stood near the entrance. Their main interest seemed to be Wendy's Porsche – a late model Boxster convertible the color of vintage Shiraz.

Wendy maneuvered the car down Beach Road. Today, the aroma of the sea was tinged with a hint of decaying algae. If Chris closed his eyes, he could picture a dungeon with the sea lapping against it. He'd seen a place like that at the Castle of Good Hope. His History teacher told them that the damp darkness and the sounds of the sea, had driven many a prisoner crazy.

Chris savored the sun on his face and the wind blowing through his hair. "Thanks, Wendy. I can't tell you how relieved I am to be out of that place."

She nodded and swerved to avoid a group of laughing teenagers who had spilled into the road.

"Where are we going?"

"I could take you to your place, but I gather from James that it is in something of a mess. So, I was thinking that I'll take you to my home to freshen up; then we must talk and figure out what is going on. I'm deeply concerned about Bridget."

"What do the police say?"

"Not much; I think they *do* suspect you, very strongly."

Chris remained silent. He looked out towards the beach: kids frolicking at the edge of the waves, a dog chasing a seagull. He wished he'd had a dog in his apartment – a great big dog like Nala. That would have served the intruders right.

He turned to face Wendy. "I can't really blame them, it's just bizarre how so many innocent bits and pieces implicate me: my spending the evening with Bridget; the car; the blood in the car ..."

"What else are they going to find?"

He shrugged his shoulders. "I don't know. You don't think of these things when you are just out for an innocent evening."

"I hope Inspector Ibrahim is beginning to realize that it is maybe just a little too convenient and simplistic to blame it all on you. Hang on!"

The Porsche banked into a hairpin bend and appeared to roar with pleasure up the steep winding road. Chris caught glimpses of magnificent houses behind high stone walls and iron gates. They drove along the upper reaches of Camps Bay, where the buildings clung to the side of the mountain like jewels set in a crown, each vying for its share of the spectacular sea view.

Wendy slowed and parked in front of a three-car garage. Her house appeared to be held in the hollow of a giant granite hand and rose up multiple levels. The cliff face towered high behind the house. They entered a lobby next to the garage and took the stairs up to the open-plan living area. It was smaller than Chris had expected, expertly furnished in a minimalist, yet cozy style. Everything, from the pale drapes and white leather sofas to the exquisite Persian carpets, was designed to complement rather than detract from the sweeping ocean views.

His eyes were drawn to a painting above the open fireplace. The artist had captured the greens and blues of the ocean in sparse strokes. For a moment, it made Chris forget all about his predicament.

"Is that an original?"

Wendy nodded.

Chris sat at the kitchen counter and Wendy poured him a glass of orange juice. He took it gratefully and let the calmness of the setting enfold him like the *karos* – blanket – that Mama Mercy used to wrap him in.

"You have a stunning place here."

"Thank you, yes. I like to think of it as my eerie; my hideaway from which I can keep an eye on the world below." She followed his gaze to a number of sailboats cruising along the Atlantic seaboard. For a moment, they both sat in silence, and then Wendy said, "You know, Julie has an interesting theory."

He looked at her, his right eyebrow raised quizzically.

"She thinks that maybe this is not so much about her mother, or Noble Enterprises, as it is about you; that someone has set out to frame you and get you into trouble."

"The thought *had* crossed my mind." He gave a dry, derisive little laugh. "On the other hand, isn't it rather presumptuous to think that anyone would go through such an elaborate scheme just to get at me?"

"Well, it's a theory, and at this stage we need to consider all possibilities. Who might have a grudge against you? "

Chris thought for a moment and shrugged. "I might have pissed off someone here or there, but …"

"What about the Richter family?"

He looked at her.

"Hell hath no fury like a woman scorned …"

Chris leaned his head back, closed his eyes, and sighed. He had to admit, it was possible. The girl was nuts and her father a mean bastard.

"Anyway," Wendy was all businesslike, "what would you like first: a shower, coffee, breakfast?"

"That seems about the right order."

"The guest room is upstairs to your right. I'm going to give Julie a quick ring to tell her you're here and then make us an omelet whilst you shower."

He was halfway up the stairs when she asked, "I know it's none of my business, but don't you think you should let your father know what's going on?"

Chris paused.

"He's going to find out anyway. It's probably best if he hears it from you."

"I'll think about it."

In the shower, Chris felt like he needed one of the power jets used to blast the grime off old buildings and monuments in order to wash the smell of the cell from his body. He turned the shower on as hot and as hard as he could tolerate, and scrubbed himself with soap from head to toe.

After his shower, a towel wrapped around his waist, Chris stepped out on to the balcony. He let the sun soak the moisture off his skin. His whole body hungered for the cleansing rays that would help erase the surreal memories of the past twenty-four hours.

What a mess. Maybe Julie is right. Maybe it is Old Man Richter still trying to teach me a lesson. He thought back to Richter's angry face at the building site when he'd warned him about sub-standard building practices. *What if there truly is something rotten going on with his constructions and Richter is shit-scared that I'll call in the building inspectors?* The more he thought about it, the more plausible it seemed.

The view from the balcony was even more sublime than from the living area. The balcony was completely private and overlooked an Arcadian scene of trees, mountains, and ocean. Chris knew there were other houses close by, but they were tucked away in ravines behind conifers. *Man in harmony with nature*, he thought. He wondered what it would be like to wake up to such a view every day.

Longingly, he looked at the lounger on the balcony. He was tempted to drop the towel, stretch out, and simply let the sun bleach away all his imaginary jailbird tattoos. Only for a moment, though; then he stepped back inside to get dressed.

##

Chapter 14: Lazy Afternoon

Tuesday afternoon

In her kitchen at the Kanya center, Mama Mercy wiped down the counters while keeping an eye on the volunteer packing away clean dishes and cutlery. The volunteer was a short woman with a bookish demeanor. The nearsighted manner in which she peered through her glasses reminded Mama Mercy of the moles that made such a mess of the lawns.

Just the other day, Mercy had said to Julie, "Don't get me wrong. I appreciate the volunteers' efforts - but they have a way of creating 'Easter-egg hunts' for me. Last week, I spent fifteen minutes searching for my rolling pin and eventually found it amongst the vegetables. Some volunteer had used it to crush garlic!"

Mercy hung the cloth over the edge of the sink and helped pack away mugs. "Thank you very much for coming today, Mrs. Richardson."

"You really must call me Becky."

Mercy put a hand over her mouth and gave an embarrassed little chuckle.

"Yes... Becky."

What would her grandmother have said if she had caught her addressing a white woman by her first name? Mercy could almost feel the force of the smack that would have hit her ears, almost hear her grandmother scolding, *"Show some respect, child!"*

Mrs. Richardson gathered her bag and the bunch of keys that seemed to dwarf her – *Why do white women always carry so many keys?* – and left, with a promise of being back for the lunch shift next Tuesday.

Mercy made tea for herself, sat at the kitchen table, kicked off her shoes, and stirred four spoons of sugar into the mug. She was glad to take the weight off her feet. How she relished this time after lunch when the kitchen was clean and quiet. It took her back to her childhood in the Transkei, when the only time she was free from chores – and the orders of her grandmother, *Meme* - was after lunch. Otherwise, from the first crow of the rooster, she and her sister would be busy: milking goats, fetching water, carrying firewood, or working in the vegetable patch behind the hut. But at lunchtime, when the midday sun was at its hottest, *Meme* and all the other grown-ups in the village would be inside their huts. That was when Mercy and her sister were free to go and play by the stream, or make necklaces from the seeds of the blue gum tree and pretend to be wives of the chieftain.

Mercy reached for a tub of lard and rubbed some on the sides of her knees and the top of her toes where the arthritis was causing most pain. She remembered how *Meme* had sworn by lard, claiming it could cure anything. Of late, *Meme*'s spirit, and many others, had visited a lot in her dreams. Even the fuzzy ghost of her father had made an appearance. When she was a child, he had worked in the far-away mines and only came home for a few weeks a year. Mercy and her sister had dreamed of how their father would come home one day with a whole herd of cattle and a sack of coins. And why should he not? After all, he worked in Egoli, the city of gold.

But he came back in a black box after a mining accident, and their mother had to go off to Butterworth to find work as a maid. Then she only came home to help with the maize harvest or when one of Mercy's brothers died. Mercy shook her head, but the wheezing, coughing faces of the three young boys would not be dislodged. It was her duty to carry their memory. Not one of them had made it to manhood. "Bad spirits," the medicine man had said; "weak lungs," the nurse at the clinic had said. Neither the medicine man's *muti* nor the nurse's pills could make any difference. Every winter, for three years in a row, they had buried a young brother. "God's will," the preacher had said.

Mercy did not mind the company of the spirits; in a way, they were comforting – they were her family. But the recent visits of so many of them was concerning her, because when the dead became so active it meant that they were preparing a welcome, that someone close to her was going to die. The last time Mercy had felt so much spirit activity was just before her mother had died of the TB. Now, as she sat in the kitchen, looking out of the window into the garden beyond, she sighed deeply. She knew it was not her place to try and guess at the Lord's mysterious ways, but she could not stop herself wondering who it was that He was planning to call home.

Maybe it was Grace – Thabo's mother. *Where was that boy, anyway?* She had noticed that he had not been there at lunchtime, and it had made her a little uneasy. She wished that Chris would come again; he was a good influence on Thabo, got him to play with the others.

She found herself staring at a faint reflection of herself in the kitchen window. Could it be that the Lord was preparing to call *her* home? The prospect held no fear for Mercy; her only regret was the thought of leaving the children at Khanya – and Chris. The Lord had not seen fit to give her children of her own but she had been there for that boy from the day he was born, even helping his mother nurse him the day he was brought home from the hospital. What a day that had been! *Pure joy!* Mercy smiled at the memory of the proud parents and their infant son.

She took another sip of her tea and engaged in one of her favorite daydreams: visualizing life after death.

She approached her village on the narrow path leading up from the river. The air was fresh and the earth smelled of rain. All her family stood outside the hut and waved: her parents, her sister, Meme. Her little brothers, too impatient to wait, ran down the green, green slopes. They hugged her and laughed without wheezing. Then everybody sat down to a big feast and Mercy, the guest of honor, was offered the goat's eyes and brains. But she did the right thing and respectfully passed these delicacies to her father. Meme's pinched face broke into smile and she said, "Mercy, my child, you have led a good life and you have made us proud."

After the feast, her family draped her in a brand-new karos and led her up to the throne of the Lord Jesus. There, foremost amongst his most beautiful angels, she found Madam Danielle. And they sat down together and talked, the way they used to when Chris was young.

"Why are you crying?"

Mercy hadn't noticed Prudence come into the kitchen.

"Onions," she said, and wiped her tears with the apron. A blue envelope slid out of the apron pocket on to the floor.

Prudence pounced on the letter. "What's this? You have a secret lover?"

"Don't make me laugh. You can read it – it's from my niece."

"Is she in trouble?"

Mercy shook her head, "No, but as always, she is looking for money. Now she wants to go to university."

Prudence scanned the letter. *"Atatat!* This is a lot of money she wants. Who does she think you are? One of the fat cats in the government?" She made herself tea and sat opposite Mercy. "What are you going to do?"

"I don't know. I'm thinking about it. I have a bit of savings for my retirement. Maybe …"

"Retirement, you? Never! They'll carry you out of this place in a box. Why would you want to retire?"

"Some days I dream of going back to the Transkei, to my village. I could build a hut and have a few goats. I miss the goats."

Prudence looked at the older woman. Her face brightened. "Why don't you ask Miss Julie to get some goats here? There's plenty of space and the children would enjoy it."

"Fresh goat's milk." Mama Mercy closed her eyes and licked her lips as though she were tasting wine from Jesus' very own chalice.

"I wonder when Miss Julie will be back?"

Prudence shrugged. "She's with her boyfriend, up in Egoli…"

Mercy frowned. "It's not like her to be away like this." Her thoughts strayed to the immediate problem of a bare pantry. "The big gala; did they make any money?"

"Oh yes; Miss Wendy, she said maybe we can start building soon."

"Maybe we go shop at Macro first." Mercy smiled.

Just then, both women were distracted by the sound of vehicle lumbering up the rutted track from the main road. Soon a panel van came to halt outside the kitchen window.

"Noble Enterprises again," Prudence declared, smiling. She patted down her hair, straightened her skirt, and walked to the kitchen door.

"They are here almost every day now," Mama Mercy said. "Stirring up dust!"

The driver opened the back of the van and lifted out a cardboard tray with two fish on it. Prudence led him into the kitchen and Mercy wrinkled her nose at the unmistakable smell of smoked *snoek*. The man lifted his cap respectfully in Mercy's direction but his eyes never once strayed from Prudence as she fussed about, admired the fish, and bent down to find tin foil.

"Fresh from the harbor," the driver declared. "I saw them there and thought of you … and the children, of course."

"Oh, Lucas." Prudence touched his arm. "That is so wonderful. You take care of us."

He grinned broadly, showing gaps in his teeth.

"Just trying to be good neighbors."

"Thank you," Mama Mercy said, though she kept her eyes on the red-haired man slouched in the passenger's seat of the van. He acknowledged her with a slow half-wave of his hand. For a moment, their eyes locked.

Mercy turned to Lucas. "What is it you do down at the barn? We see a lot of you these past days."

"Just storing extra inventory. They are still fixing the warehouse."

Mercy nodded and busied herself at the sink. She pretended not to notice the way Lucas had his hand on Prudence's backside. It was none of her business, but in her mind she could hear her grandmother snorting: *"Men - trouble, nothing but trouble."*

Prudence escorted Lucas back to the van and waved the men good-bye as they drove towards the barn.

Mercy turned around and examined the gift. Fish, with their downturned mouths and glassy eyes, always reminded her of grumpy old men. Fish eyes were tasteless, not like goats' eyes. Who in their right mind brought *snoek* to an orphanage, anyway? *Snoek* had lots and lots of bones that could choke a child, although she had to admit to herself that it was a good fish for building muscles.

Prudence bubbled back into the kitchen. "Isn't that Lucas the sweetest man? And so thoughtful to bring fish for the children."

Mercy said nothing. *Meme* had always told her that if you had nothing nice to say, then it was better to say nothing at all.

"What you looking at?" Prudence asked.

"Fish bones; get me the meat grinder. We'll turn them into fish patties."

#

Thabo had his head resting on a patch of soft grass. Dappled light, filtering through the boughs of a weeping willow, camouflaged his still body. His feet dangled over the riverbank into the coolness. From far away came the sound of laughter and shouting: kids playing soccer at the Khanya center; beyond that, the muffled sound of traffic on the main road. Down here, in his sanctuary, the predominant sound was the gurgling of the river and the chirping of insects in the afternoon sun.

Thabo noticed none of it. He was reading, totally immersed in a different world. Like him, the hero of the story had a sick mother who he worried about. But the boy in the book was off on a daring quest, and had fought a wizard to obtain a magical knife that could vanquish almost any enemy, and heal any wound. How he wished he had a knife like that.

The rattling noise of the van intruded on Thabo's world. He dragged himself away from a battle with a group of soul-devouring specters, rolled over on his stomach, and watched the van stop outside the barn just twenty meters away from him. Lucas, the big African driver, hummed as he opened the rear doors of the van.

"You've got the hots for that Prudence woman," the redheaded man said, opening the passenger door and getting out too.

"Maybe I do, maybe I don't."

"Your girlfriend will cut your balls off."

"She won't find out." Lucas reached into the back of the van, grabbed hold of a wooden crate, and gave it a hard tug.

The other man – Thabo had nicknamed him Red Hair - came over and stood next to his colleague, looking as if he was getting ready to help carry the crate. "She will, if I tell her," he taunted.

Lucas was no longer humming. He fixed his gaze on Red Hair and said, "If you breathe one word, I'll call my friend the magician."

The threat did not have the effect he had intended. Red Hair simply raised an eyebrow and smirked.

Lucas tried again. He gestured with his right hand, kissed the tips of his fingers and spread them open into the wind. "The magician," he said, nodding his head, his eyes wide and hypnotic, "he makes people disappear. *Poof!* You think about that."

Red Hair ignored him, and bent to pick up his end of the crate. Scowling furiously, Lucas grabbed at the other end, and in doing so, yanked it out of the other man's grasp. With a crash, the crate fell to the ground and shattered.

"Fucking moron!" shouted Red Hair, clutching at his hand, in which a thick splinter of wood had become embedded. "*Eina! Fok! Donner!* Look what you've done! Jesus! If this equipment is broken …"

Lucas glanced around in panic. "It's all your fault! Why didn't you hold on to your side?"

"My fault? You moronic cunt, how could I? You yanked it without warning." His face was suffused with anger and pain. "It's because you've got fuck-all blood in your brain, it's all in your prick. All you can think about is screwing that slut. If you ..."

"Shut up! Don't you dare call her a slut."

"The boss will use us for fucking shark bait." There was hysteria in his voice.

The top of the crate had come loose and, with his uninjured hand, Red Hair attempted to lift it. "Help me get this *bleddy* lid off," he barked. Lucas stepped forward and prized it free. Red Hair started removing layers of polystyrene, clearly anxious to check the contents.

"Seems to be OK." He clasped his bleeding hand again. "Shit, this is killing me. Look, not a fucking word about this to the boss, you hear me? He'll kill us if he knew we'd dropped this. I'm going to go back there and get them to bandage up my hand. You go find that old *boer* - the handyman. Get a hammer and some nails from him, and we'll just close up the crate. They'll never find out."

Thabo ducked low in the grass as the two men, still squabbling and cursing, set off up the track towards the Khanya center.

##

"Are you sure you want to go back to your apartment? You're very welcome to stay in the guest room for a few days," Wendy had said.

"Why, are you scared that I'll abscond and you'll forfeit your bail bond?" he'd teased.

"No, of course not, you're your father's son. I trust you implicitly. I just thought you might need a few days to sort out the mess in your place."

He knew that her unspoken concern was for his safety. *What if the thugs who had trashed his apartment were to come back?* He understood her concern and he was grateful that she did not voice it. By leaving it unsaid, they could pretend to keep that particular genie in its bottle. He had enough to worry about, so he'd made light of it. "I thought you knew that 'trashed' is the latest trend for bachelor apartments. I'll be fine."

She'd dropped him outside his apartment building. Now that he was filling the third garbage bag, he regretted his bravado. The place was a mess; even the bathroom had been ransacked. Shaving gel drooled down the mirror as if to impart a cryptic message that Chris could not decipher. The most disturbing thing, however, was in the bedroom. His only suit, together with a white shirt, had been laid out on his bed. Someone had made a deep gash above the left breast pocket and had cut out the area around the crotch.

Chris winced and tried to push the image out of his mind as he worked his way through the CD fragments. A few had escaped unharmed, and he put James Blunt's wistful "I Saw an Angel in the Subway" on as he sorted. Unfortunately, it did nothing to lift his spirits. He wondered how Julie was coping.

From somewhere under the debris, he heard his phone ringing. When he finally managed to find it on the fifth ring, the voice at the other end was tinny and faint. Chris wondered what had happened to the phone, but was grateful that it was still connected. He whacked the receiver and Julie's voice grew clearer, the words pouring out: "It's just been the most surreal nightmare; I keep going over things in my mind, over and over again; and then, of course, I feel terrible that I quarreled with my mother the last time we spoke - what if I never see her again? Oh God, Chris, I just wish there were something I could actually do. I feel so, so ..."

"Hey, hey, slow down. Look, there's no point beating yourself up. We just ..."

"Yes, but I feel so useless ... there has to be something we can do."

"What are the police saying?"

"They don't have a clue. They seem convinced that you have something to do with this."

"And you, do you believe them?"

She hesitated only a second. "Of course not! It's *preposterous*." He loved the way she pronounced the word – like an English teacher.

"Wendy told me your theory - that this might in fact be an attempt to get me into trouble. She said you suspect Bob Richter - thinking that he is still mad about me jilting his daughter."

"What do you think?"

"I think it's far more likely that, somewhere along the way, Noble Enterprises made some enemies. Or that someone simply wants to get a million bucks out of ..."

"Yes, but it's possible?"

Chris sighed. "I agree, it's possible." He thought of his mutilated pants and crossed his legs.

"So what can we do about it? Should we tell the police?"

"No, definitely not! It would just be a distraction for them. God, can you imagine how seriously screwed I would be if I accused Richter of kidnapping, and he was innocent?" He paused and shuddered at the thought of the consequences. Richter would probably have him beaten up and drowned in a vat of concrete.

"Don't tell anyone," he went on. "Meanwhile, I'll see if I can snoop around Bob Richter's study at his home a bit – I do know their place quite well."

Julie's voice registered alarm. "You mean, you want to break in?"

"*Shhhh!* Just pay a visit. Please, Julie, not a word. I'm doing this for you and for your mother. If there is the remotest chance that Richter is behind this, then we have to be very careful. He is one mean bastard. But I'll find out, and then we can tell the police."

"Chris ..." She paused. He waited. When she continued to say nothing, he began to wonder if she had been cut off. But then came the soft whisper, "*Please, please be careful.*"

"I will, I promise."

She hung up. For the first time that day, Chris felt his spirits lifting; *she truly cared.* As he reached to replace the receiver, he heard a faint click on the line.

He was startled when the phone rang again. Julie sounded breathless. "Oh, there was something else I meant to tell you. Completely unrelated."

"What's that?"

"I saw Desmond, here in Johannesburg."

If her intention had been to surprise Chris, she certainly succeeded. "Are you sure? He's in Hermanus, visiting his sister. You must have made a mistake."

"No, I promise you, it definitely was him. I'd nipped down to a supermarket to buy some toiletries when I saw him just across the road from Noble Enterprises. I waved like mad, and for a moment I thought he'd seen me. But then he turned and I lost him in the crowd. Isn't that the weirdest coincidence?"

"Really weird." Chris's mind was in overdrive. What possible connection could there be between Bridget's disappearance and Desmond? But then, it had been Desmond persuading him to fill in at the gala that had set off this crazy chain of events. He refused to believe Desmond would willingly lure him into trouble, so that must mean that his old friend was acting under duress... *but what?* More and more, Chris felt like a pawn in some giant game.

Now, however, his main concern was not to alarm Julie, and so he kept his voice light as he said, "I'm sure there's a perfectly logical explanation. Maybe he's got a lover on the side and is off for a dirty weekend."

"Do you ever *not* think of sex?"

"I'm so glad to hear you sound more like yourself."

She actually laughed. "Thanks, Chris. I have to get back to Matt. Talk to you again soon; let me know if you find out anything."

"You too."

This time he did not hear a click, but he sat with the receiver humming in his hand for a long time. The phrase *"puppet on a string"* came into his mind. He clenched his jaw and was about to dial Desmond's number when the door buzzer squawked. "Hi, it's me, James."

Chris was grateful to have his friend's help with the clean-up. Bit by bit, they managed to restore order, sorting books back into the shelves, packing clothes into the cupboards, sweeping up broken debris. By some miracle, Chris's laptop had slid under the couch and survived the onslaught. After a couple of hours, James suggested they take a break and get some exercise. Chris had just put on his running shorts when his cell phone rang. He picked it up and was startled to see the caller's ID: Sandra Richter. *Why on earth would Sandra be calling?* He let it ring a few more times before pressing the green button.

"Yes?" `

"Chris! Why do you not pick up? I tried and tried to call you."

He was relieved to recognize Thabo's voice. He had completely forgotten that he'd given his ex-fiancée's phone to Thabo.

"Thabo, sorry; my battery was flat. Good to hear from you. What's up?"

Excitedly, Thabo told him the story of Lucas and Red Hair: their arrival at the barn, their squabbling, and how they had managed to drop the crate between them.

"I wished that I had had a knife. Then I could have fought those nasty specters," Thabo said.

Chris expressed his alarm and confusion.

"It's a book I am reading about a magic knife." He paused. "Anyway, I went to have a look at that box."

"Jeez, Thabo; I don't want you to get in trouble with those guys. You be careful." He paused. "What was inside the box?"

"I never see anything like it. Looks like equipment from a Science class."

Chris was puzzled, but before he could ask any more questions, Thabo went on, "I don't have a knife but I *do* have a powerful weapon – the cell phone you gave me, with the camera. I took pictures." There was triumph in his voice. "Do you want me to SMS them?"

"Yes, please do; I'll have a look. Do you know how to SMS pictures?"

"Of course." Thabo sounded indignant and Chris feared he might have offended his young friend. But a moment later, Thabo had already put it behind him and his mind had moved on to something else. "Will you come and practice soccer with us this Thursday?" he asked.

Soccer practice seemed like an eon ago and Chris had to think. He did not want to mislead Thabo. "I can't promise, but I'll try my best."

"What should I do about these men and the box?"

"I want you to be very careful. Those men could be dangerous, so please, please don't do anything stupid. But, if you could spy a bit from a distance and find out what they are up to, then let me know. OK?"

"OK, we are like partners, like *CSI*, no?" There was pride in his voice.

Chris smiled. "Catch you later, partner. Be careful."

Moments later, the cell phone beeped and James looked over Chris's shoulder as his friend scrolled through a number of photographs.

"It *does* looks like lab equipment – that thing there looks like a fancy pressure cooker," James said.

"I think they are called autoclaves," Chris said, as he scrolled to another photograph. "This looks like a gas spectrometer. It's hard to see. Let me just quickly download this to my laptop."

They studied the pictures on the bigger screen. James said, "We're not going to get any wiser staring at this. Is there anyone we can ask? What about your old man?"

Chris sighed. His father was the obvious choice. Few people knew that his father was not only a leading heart surgeon, but also advised the South African Defense Force on medical matters.

"You know I hate asking him for anything."

"Right now, you don't have the luxury of indulging your silly feud with your father. You need your family."

Chris looked at him, taken aback. It was the closest James had ever come to berating him.

He tapped out a brief note and forwarded the photographs to his father. Then he shut the laptop, locked his front door – James double-checked that the door was indeed locked - and followed his friend to the elevator.

They were halfway through the lobby when a voice startled Chris: "Why - hello! If it isn't the Dolphin Whisperer!"

Chris blinked before he recognized the bleached blonde he had met on the beach a few days earlier. Her sullen boyfriend was with her. He tried, in vain, to remember her name as she sauntered towards him. She wore white –again - and her bright-red lips looked like a separate lifeform against the pallor of her face and hair.

"Aren't you going to introduce me to your friend?"

"Hi, great to see you again," Chris lied. "This is James; James Buthelezi."

She shook his hand. "Are you related to *the* Buthelezis?"

James flashed an embarrassed smile and nodded.

"Since *Chris* here," she emphasized his name, "has obviously forgotten my name, I'm Cindy. Do you guys live in this building?"

"Chris does," James said.

"Do you really? We were just making enquiries about possible vacancies because we like this location so much. Isn't that a coincidence? Do you like it here?"

Chris smiled to hide his disbelief. The woman certainly deserved full marks for sheer brazenness. She had first engineered the encounter at the beach and then, when he had followed her and Lenny in their black Pajero, they'd given him the slip. Now she was there again, by pure "coincidence".

She turned to her companion, who was talking to the security guard. "Lenny, come over here. You remember Chris? He actually lives in this block! Come meet his friend James."

Lenny pushed his sunglasses up on to his head and shook hands.

Cindy had her hands on James's arm and presented him as though he were a prized possession. "We will want to get to know James here better. He belongs to *the* Buthelezi family. Next time there's a Zulu royal wedding, he might get us an invitation."

Lenny merely grunted.

Chris said, "Well, we'd best get going. Good luck with your apartment search."

"Bye," she said, and gave a little wave. "We must have a drink sometime. You can fill us in on who's who around here."

Out on the street, Chris spotted the Pajero. One look showed him that the dents and scrapes had been repaired. *Damn!* How was he going to get the police to believe that someone had tried to run Bridget off the road when there was no longer any evidence?

They jogged in silence along the Sea Point promenade. White clouds cascaded over the edge of Table Mountain; halfway down the craggy cliffs, they dissolved into the swirls that helped to create the iconic image of a gigantic billowing tablecloth.

"Looks like we're in for a nasty southeast wind," Chris said.

James looked up at the clouds and nodded. "Yeah, it's going to blow a gale, might even get some rain. Look how choppy the sea is out near Robben Island."

The ocean appeared steely gray, like beaten metal. There were no sailboats today – the only vessels in sight were a clutch of container ships and the foreboding hulk of a heavily laden oil tanker.

The forces of nature were set to mount an assault on the Mother City, but Chris and James were protected from the wind where they were, in the lee of Lion's Head. As they ran, they had to concentrate so as not to collide with skateboarders, rollerbladers, kids on bicycles, and the senior citizens who militantly defended their turf, walking and talking in slow groups, never budging an inch for anyone else.

Chris felt the blood pumping through his body. The rhythm of his feet on the asphalt helped him to focus; step-by-step, he formulated a plan for getting into the Richter home. As far as he knew, Sandra and her mother were still overseas. He knew from his previous visits that Bob rarely stepped into the kitchen – that was a woman's domain – so the chances were that he would regularly be out of the house at dinnertime. *Yes, Bob would definitely eat out; the best time to "visit" would be right after dark.*

They veered away from the sea and, turning up Millner Road, passed Richter's Stadium View. Chris resisted the urge to stop and inspect it, though he wondered for a moment whether Bridget might be hidden at the construction site. He dismissed the thought; *It's too busy with workers swarming all over. It would be impossible to keep her hidden. I'll have to go to Richter's house and hope to find some kind of clue in his study.*

James interrupted his thoughts. "That Lenny character - where do you know him from?"

"I don't really know either of them, but they seem to keep popping up wherever I go. She accosted me at the beach the other day, and I think, though I am not quite certain, that he was eyeing Julie at the De Waterkant Club the other night."

James slowed his pace. "Do you really think it is coincidence that they are hanging around your apartment block?"

Chris shook his head, and the two friends spent the next ten minutes speculating about possible connections between Lenny, Cindy, the Pajero, the attempt to run Bridget off the road, and the kidnapping; but they could not reach any sensible conclusions. Chris wondered privately if the two were working for Richter, but he did not share this thought with James. He had toyed with the idea of asking James to come with him on the Richter "visit", but decided that it would be unfair to drag his friend deeper into the whole mess. He accepted that he had to do this alone.

"You must be careful," James said. "That guy is bad news. Did you see the tattoo on his forearm?"

"What tattoo? He was wearing a long-sleeved shirt."

"Hell, Chris. Some days I wonder how you, with zero street-smarts, have managed to live to the ripe old age of twenty-three."

Chris stopped and looked at James expectantly.

"When he shook your hand, his sleeve was pushed back an inch. I swear I saw the anchor tail of the Dragon Boys. Of course, I didn't see the whole thing, but the tail is very distinctive."

"Of what?"

James rolled his eyes. "The dragon is the symbol of one of the most notorious gangs on the Cape Flats. You can only join if you've killed someone."

"I didn't see anything."

"That's because you don't know what to look out for. Now me, when I see a man like that wearing a long-sleeved shirt on a summer's day, then I know he's trying to hide a tattoo. So I look for it." He paused and then continued, "By the way, we're being followed."

"I knew that."

An unmarked police car, Sergeant Vervey in the passenger seat, slowly overtook them. The sergeant did not even try to be discreet. He grinned and nodded as the car rolled by, clearly wanting them to know that he was keeping his eye on Chris.

"Moron," Chris swore under his breath, but it registered with him that he was by no means a free man. The police saw him as a suspect. Another thing to think about when he went to the Richters'; it wouldn't do to be followed there by the police.

At the Health Line Club, they picked up sweat towels from the reception desk. The young girl on duty greeted them in a shy manner.

Chris nodded and tried to read her nametag. *She must just about live here*, he thought. *She's always on duty.* He remembered that she was on duty the day Desmond had met him here at the club. *Desmond, what the hell is Desmond doing in Johannesburg? If it weren't for him, I wouldn't be involved in any of this.*

He followed James to the weights section, where they went through their standard routine, spotting for each other. After half an hour, Chris feigned exhaustion and said he wanted to get home to make the place habitable for the night. They agreed to meet the following morning to finish their workout routine.

"You get some sleep," James said. "Tomorrow we'll figure out who the hell is trying to set you up and then we'll kick some serious ass."

Chris appreciated James's attempt at bravado, but he suspected that his friend did not have the slightest clue as to where they would begin.

"Thanks, buddy," he said, as their fists touched in a good-bye gesture. Then he turned to jog home.

##

Chapter 15: A Visit to the Richters'
Tuesday night

Chris kept his eye on the rear-view mirror as he drove through the quiet Constantia suburbs. The Richters' home was close to where he had grown up, and he deliberately chose a route that took him past his father's house. If anyone were following him, they would think he was going there. He slowed as he drove by the wrought-iron gates of what used to be his home. A solitary window was lit – his father's study. For a moment, he felt an overwhelming urge to turn up the driveway and ask for his father's advice. Pride forbade it, however - this was something he had to figure out himself. He put his foot down and minutes later was driving past the Richter residence. With relief, he noticed that only the outside security lights were on.

He drove around the block and passed the house again, slowly this time. All was quiet. A few hundred meters down the road, he pulled in, extinguished the lights, and sat for a while, watching the deserted street and going over his plan. He kept telling himself that it was not that different from an attack move in soccer: *stay focused on the goal, but be nimble when encountering the unexpected.*

As he stepped out of the cocoon of his BMW, the force of the southeaster hit him. He opened the trunk, rummaged around for his dark jacket, and put it on with the collar folded up. He was about to sling on his backpack when an approaching vehicle slowed, did a U-turn, and stopped behind him. Chris had to shield his eyes against the headlights.

The driver stepped out. "Is there a problem, sir?"

Chris noticed the driver wore a uniform. *Damn.*

"Good evening," Chris said, stepping out of the direct light. On the side of the bottom-of-the-range Toyota, he read the words: "PPP - Peninsula Private Patrols".

"I thought maybe you had a flat tire or something."

"No, no, I'm fine. I'd left my cell phone in my backpack in the boot of the car and it started ringing so I just stopped to answer it, but I was too late."

"You've got good hearing." The man seemed to hesitate. He appeared disappointed - probably he'd been hoping to come across something suspicious to break the monotony of his shift. "So, you know your way around?"

"Yes. In fact, I'm on my way to meet some friends at Christ Church Constantia, just down the road. Thanks for stopping; it's good to know the security patrols are so on the ball."

The guard tipped his cap, got back into his car, and drove off slowly. Chris watched him disappear. It struck him that it was rather difficult to be taken seriously as a security guard if you drove around in a little bubble car. *Still, he's going to remember me.* He sighed, slammed the trunk shut, and drove to the church. He was relieved to see lights on in the church hall, probably some Bible-study group, or choir practice. He parked the car in front of the church, so that the security guard would be sure to see it if he drove past, and, keeping to the shadows, set off on foot back to the Richters'. Checking his watch, he realized that he was already twenty minutes behind schedule, and he had not even reached the house. He hastened his steps.

The wrought-iron fence, with its intermittent concrete pillars, was more a visual deterrent than a real obstacle. Chris chose a dark corner under a tree and easily heaved himself over one of the pillars. He landed softly in a flowerbed on the other side. He waited, listening. *Where was the dog?*

He sprinted across the lawn and slid along the side of the house, looking for a door or window that might have been left unlatched. He tested a few, but was not surprised to find them all locked. As he approached a corner of the building, he saw that there was light up ahead. Reluctant to leave the shadows, he crouched low, his hands touching the ground like a sprinter preparing to uncoil out of the starting blocks.

He peered around the corner and surveyed the broad verandah and the swimming pool beyond. The wind rippled across the pool and the underwater lights cast the verandah in an eerie glow. Chris remembered how he and Sandra had lounged by the pool. His eyes lingered on the large patio sofa ...

Concentrate! he admonished himself. He crossed the verandah and tried the sliding door, which he knew led to the family room. Suddenly, a spotlight burst into life; he ducked behind a wicker chair.

Chris cursed the motion detectors and waited for the thumping of his heart to subside. There was no other sign of life, however, so he moved on to the side of the garage, took a small rubber hammer from his backpack, and smashed the garage window. In the silence, it sounded to him like a cathedral window crashing down. He held his breath and counted slowly in his head ... *twenty-five, twenty-six, twenty-seven, twenty-eight, twenty-nine, thirty ... No alarm.* Silently, Chris thanked the expert who had lectured him and his cohort of budding architects on security. He could still hear him saying, *"The weak spot in ninety percent of our homes is the garage; people are focused on protecting themselves and their family, and hence don't extend the security perimeter to their garages."*

He pulled on a pair of gloves, reached through the jagged pane, slid open the window, and climbed in. By the glow of his flashlight, he picked his way past bicycles, golf bags, and garden implements to the inner kitchen door. *This is going to be the tricky one,* he thought. If the alarm was active, he'd have less than four minutes before the security guards arrived. With a silent prayer, he pulled the door open and waited. He eyed the escape route back to the window ... *twenty-five, twenty-six, twenty-seven, twenty-eight, twenty-nine, thirty ... Nothing!* He found the light switch and flicked it on.

There was a loud yelp, followed by a growl. *The dog, damn!* Chris had expected to encounter the dog outside. When she wasn't there, he had completely forgotten about her. The Alsatian had been asleep and was as startled as Chris. She leapt from her bed, crouched, and growled again.

"Here, Tessi, good Tessi. You remember me, don't you?" Chris tried to soothe the dog. He reached for a side pocket in his backpack. "Good dog." She bared her teeth as he stepped forward, a low rumble rolling from her throat. "Look, I brought you something." He held out a stick of beef *biltong.* The dog sniffed, undecided; then her growling stopped.

"You know you want it. It's all for you. Yummy, yummy *biltong.*"

Moments later, the dog was chewing happily and taking no notice of Chris. He proceeded to the front of the house. A soft glow came from the lounge; he inched towards the door and peered around the doorframe. There was no one; the glow came from a light that illuminated a larger-than-life portrait of Sandra. The artist had managed to capture the mixture of arrogance and exuberance that characterized his ex. Chris turned and hurried to the study; Sandra's smiling face would probably haunt his dreams for the next few nights.

He closed the drapes and rummaged through the papers on the desk, looking for something – anything - that would give him leverage over Bob Richter; maybe even just a phone number to connect him to that thug Lenny. Richter was evidently a tidy man, and his papers were arranged in neat piles. Chris spent ten minutes flipping through plans, proposals, and contracts: nothing out of the ordinary. He looked at his watch; Bob Richter could be back at any time. Chris tried the desk drawer and found it to be locked. He tried to yank it open and cursed when it would not yield.

He let his eyes roam around the room. Against the far wall, he noticed a small antique drinks cabinet. It was a beautiful piece of furniture, walnut with intricate ebony and mother-of-pearl inlay. Chris guessed it was French. He opened the cabinet and saw a glass filled with whisky – a stiff tot, at that. *How strange.* Next to the glass lay an official-looking document. Chris picked it up and had to suppress his excitement as he read – it was a citation from the city building inspector for *repeat* safety violations at Stadium View. The inspector was shutting down the site.

"Holy Moses," Chris mumbled. This could cost Richter's company hundreds of thousands. No wonder Bob had poured himself a stiff drink when he studied the citation. Someone must have surprised him, which is why he shut the half-drunk whisky and the document in the drinks cabinet. *But who?*

Chris heard a noise and spun around to see a woman standing in the doorway.

She had a large pistol pointed straight at him and said, "What on earth are *you* doing here in Daddy's study?"

"Sandra!?" It sounded like a croak and Chris nearly knocked over the drinks cabinet. He cleared his throat and tried to keep his voice conversational, "I … I thought you were overseas; I didn't expect you to be here."

"That's pretty obvious." Her expression was grim; nothing like the smiling face in the portrait next door. She wore a dressing-gown, her hair looked disheveled, and her face was devoid of make-up. She held the gun with both hands and lifted it, taking aim. "Give me one good reason why I shouldn't blow your brains out."

He felt a cold sweat forming at his hairline, but did not dare wipe his forehead. There were dark rings under Sandra's eyes and she looked scarier than he had remembered. He gulped. "I … I can explain …"

She kept the gun pointed at him as she slowly stepped into the room. "I don't want to hear any of your excuses. I heard enough of them when you broke off our engagement."

"Sandra, please, look ..."

"I said, I don't want to hear it!"

He watched as she came around the desk and stood in the middle of the room, looking at him. He did not dare say anything. For a long time, she just stood there watching him. He felt like a mouse in a maze being watched by a mad scientist. *What does she want me to do?*

Then he noticed that the gun had begun to shake. He became increasingly alarmed. Were her arms getting too tired to hold it steady? But her expression had changed, too; it had softened and there was a quivering around her mouth as if she were trying to suppress laughter. She brushed her hair back with one hand and the gun swung dangerously. Chris lurched to his right to try and avoid a potential bullet.

"You are a strange one, Chris du Toit. All the time I wanted you to come and visit, you found every excuse under the sun to stay away. And then, when you think I'm overseas, suddenly here you are."

"Look, Sandra, I know this must seem weird to you ..."

"Weird doesn't even begin to describe it." She sat down on the edge of a sofa.

"Please, put the gun down."

"What, with a sex maniac stalking me in my own home?" Her tone was mocking. For a fleeting moment, Chris was tempted to say, *"Calling me a stalker or a sex maniac is rather rich, coming from you,"* but he remained silent.

Now she looked like a cat, ready to enjoy playing with the mouse she'd just caught. Chris understood how weak his position was; she held all the cards. If she shot him, she'd walk away scot-free. After all, he'd broken into her house. He could picture the headlines and it pained him to think how the Richters would spin it: *"Jilted groom, crazed by jealousy, breaks into lover's home,"* perhaps?

He had to engage her, distract her.

"I don't understand where you've suddenly sprung from," he said. "I thought you were somewhere in Switzerland or Italy."

"I'm recovering from the flight; we got in this morning so I was catching up on my sleep when some noise woke me. I thought you were a burglar." She settled more comfortably into the sofa and folded her legs. A smile creased her lips. Then she started to laugh.

"What ... what's so funny?"

"You," she spluttered. "You should've seen your face. I've never seen such a shocked expression." She gasped for air. "Priceless!" The gun shook in her hand.

Chris measured the distance between them. Should he rush and grab the gun before it went off - either accidentally or intentionally? But rushing at her might startle her.

"I'm glad you find it amusing," he said smoothly, all the time watching the gun. Sandra was clearly as unpredictable as ever. "Where are your parents?"

"Gone to dinner, they should be home any time now. But seriously, what *are* you doing here?"

"I'll tell you, if you put that gun down. It's making me nervous."

"I like to see you nervous." Again the mocking tone; she closed one eye and aimed straight at his head. He put up his hands.

Then she lowered the gun and placed it on a coffee table. "You didn't think I'd actually shoot you, did you?"

He said nothing.

She patted the seat next to her. "So, come, tell me all about it."

Chris decided that the best way out would be to give her at least a bare skeleton of the truth. Without mentioning Bridget's kidnapping, or his arrest, he focused on the suspicion that Bob Richter might be waging a vendetta against him.

"That's preposterous." Her tone was suddenly serious. "How can you suspect my father of being so mean?"

"What about this, then?" He held up the citation. "I bet he blames me for the building inspectors stopping work at the site."

"Oh – that. God, he was mad about that. But it had nothing to do with you. One of the foremen ratted on him. The guy's been fired and my dad has taken care of things with the inspectors. They're back on track."

Chris decided not to pursue what "taken care of things" meant. He hesitated. "And what about … you know, us? Is he still mad at me?"

She looked at him pensively for a moment; then her expression changed in a way that took Chris totally by surprise. Pure joy spread across her features. "Oh, Chris, I'm the happiest girl alive."

He stared at her. Her mood swings were astounding.

"I'm getting married!"

He glanced over his shoulder, measuring the distance to the door.

"And I have *you* to thank for it."

"Me?"

"Well, sort of, you know … in a cosmic Karma kind of way. It was, after all, our … our little tiff that made me decide to go overseas for a while. And there I met the most wonderful, wonderful man." She clutched her arms, hugging herself.

"Really?"

"Yes! He's just gorgeous, and he's French. When he speaks … I can't describe it, I just … want to drown in the sound of his voice. So, you see, you just played your part as a pawn. You helped the queen find her king."

Chris wondered whether she was on medication. She must have sensed his disbelief, because she picked up an iPhone and scrolled through a series of photographs. Indeed, there she was, with the Frenchman, at a restaurant, on a boat, in full ski gear somewhere in the Alps – the white of their teeth rivaling the snow: both beaming, laughing, clearly in love.

"I'm very happy for you," he said. And he meant it. If Sandra had found love and happiness, he didn't have to feel guilty about her anymore. It felt as though at least one of his burdens had been lifted. "How did you meet?"

"I met him on the ski slopes. He is a financial adviser from Geneva. It was love at first sight; it was just meant to be." She sighed and closed her eyes. "Anton's the one!" She held up her hand for Chris to see her engagement ring. He made admiring noises – the ring held an impressive diamond and he felt a pang of inadequacy; it would be years before he could afford a ring like that.

"Anyway, Mummy and I have come back to start planning for the wedding. So you see, really, Daddy has many, many things on his mind, but you are definitely not one of them. And besides ..."

A car could be heard coming up the driveway.

"Mind you, he's going to blow a gasket if he finds out that you broke into the house and rifled through the study. And you know his temper." She laughed nervously, grabbed the gun, and slid it under the sofa.

Chris rushed to the window and peered through a crack in the drapes. He tried to assess whether Mr. and Mrs. Richter would come in through the front door or through the garage into the kitchen. He asked Sandra, but she just held up her hands and shrugged her shoulders. Then his eyes fell on the citation. He leapt across the room to put it back in its place in the drinks cabinet, where he nearly knocked over the whisky. He couldn't hear the car anymore, and so he decided that they had probably driven round the back to the garage. He rushed down the hallway, making for the front door. As he reached it, however, a shadow fell on the frosted glass panes and he could hear someone fumbling with a key.

"Shit," he swore under his breath, as he looked around for cover. Before he could move, however, Sandra came up behind him and pulled him into a hall closet.

"Sandra, darling, we're home!" her mother called.

Bob Richter's gruff voice said, "She's probably still asleep."

"But her light is on."

"Where did the dog get *biltong* from?"

"I don't know; you must have left it lying around."

Chris tried not to breathe. Sandra had pressed herself against him in the pitch darkness. Her scent was intoxicating and brought back memories – *there had been good times, very good times*. He felt her hand slide down his back and squeeze his buttock. He could hear steps receding from the hall; it sounded like Sandra's mother was going upstairs and her father into the kitchen. Chris allowed himself to relax a little; then, suddenly, Sandra's hand was cupping his testicles, and she was squeezing hard.

"Got you where I want you," she whispered.

"C'mon, Sandra. This isn't funny."

"It is to me." She paused. *"I need you to do me a favor."*

"What?" To his embarrassment, his voice was squeaky.

"Anton doesn't know anyone here in Cape Town. I need you to be best man at our wedding."

His mind reeled – but he nodded in the darkness. He would have promised anything to get out of this madhouse. Sandra, however, could not see what he was doing, and her grip tightened.

"Promise you'll be best man at my wedding."

"OK, I promise."

She let go, opened the door a crack, peered out, and then motioned for him to follow. With an impish peck on the cheek, she dispatched him.

"Remember your promise," rang in his ears as he jogged across the lawn and heaved himself over the fence.

##

Chapter 16: Where to Now?

Wednesday morning

Julie had a blanket draped around her shoulders and her hands clasped around a mug of tea. From the high perch of Matt's office, she looked out across the awakening city.

Matt had freshened up, though she noticed the bags under his eyes. He joined her at the window and placed a fatherly arm around her.

"Did you get any sleep?" he asked.

"A little. You?"

"I'm OK."

"Where's Greg?"

"He was up most of the night. I sent him home to get some sleep. He'll be back at nine for the next update with the police." He paused, looked down, and sighed. "Everybody going about their business as though this is just another normal day."

Julie watched minibus taxis weaving in and out of traffic as though they were engaged in some crazy dance ritual. A bus stopped and disgorged a kaleidoscope of people: children in school uniforms, men heading off to a nearby construction site, and a few women dressed for the office. An arthritic old woman stepped from the bus with difficulty. She stopped to speak to a man who was rolling up his blankets in a doorway.

"I suspect many down there have a cross of their own to bear," Julie said.

Matt shrugged. "I want to bring this to an end. I'm told that the staff are beginning to ask awkward questions about the police presence. It's getting everyone spooked." He passed his hand over his eyes, drew a deep breath, and said, "There was another ransom call last night."

"Why didn't you wake me? Did you speak to Mother?"

He shook his head. "It was very brief; Greg spoke to the kidnapper." Matt explained that, according to Greg, the kidnapper had sounded nervous - in a hurry. Greg even managed to negotiate the ransom down. The money was to be paid in Cape Town. Greg and the captain had been working with the Cape Town police through the night, planning for all possible scenarios.

"So, are we definitely going to pay the ransom?" Julie asked.

He explained his reasoning. The police had not come up with any particularly helpful ideas and he couldn't bear to think of Bridget suffering in captivity for another twenty-four hours. He conceded that Greg was worried about losing all negotiating power once the ransom was paid, but Matt felt they had no other option.

She squeezed his arm. "I trust your judgment on this."

Just then, Julie's cell phone rang. She dropped the blanket on to the couch where she had spent the night and picked up her phone. Her spirits lifted – *it was Chris*. She excused herself and stepped out of Matt's office.

The reception area exuded efficiency and opulence, with cherrywood fittings and leather chairs. Julie saw none of this; she only felt relief that it was deserted. She listened intently as Chris gave her a rundown of his visit to the Richters'; how he had broken in, placated the dog, what he had found in the study. She gasped when he sketched Sandra's gun-in-hand appearance. He made light of it, but she shuddered at what could have happened.

As she listened to his voice, and bathed in the rays of the sun, Julie felt some of her tension ease. Chris shared his belief that, even though Richter was a crooked wheeler-dealer and a mean bastard, there definitely was no connection to Bridget's kidnapping. Julie laughed out loud for the first time in days when he told her how he had been coerced into being best man at Sandra Richter's wedding.

"She's clearly still got feelings for you."

"Does that make you feel at least a *tiny* bit jealous?" he asked, only half-teasing.

Jealous? She didn't know. But she felt the warmth of his voice, his genuine concern, and talking to him soothed her, eased the exhaustion and anxiety in a way that nobody else could.

As if sensing her feelings, Chris asked, "How're you holding up?"

"It's hard. Do you … do you think they might have … harmed my mother?"

"Don't even think that, Julie. The kidnappers can gain absolutely nothing by harming her. And your mother is smart; she won't do anything to antagonize them."

"So what are you going to do now?" she asked.

"I'm going to see what I can find out about this Lenny guy. There's got to be a connection. I know he is the one who tried to run your mother off the road."

"You actually believe that story now?"

"No doubt in my mind."

She sighed. "Well, Matt has decided to pay the ransom."

"I'm glad. We need this whole mess to be resolved. I just hope to God the police don't screw it up." He paused for a moment. "They're going to try and catch the kidnappers during the hand-over, aren't they?"

Julie told Chris as much as she knew from her conversation with Matt. "But I don't know any of the details." She lowered her voice and looked around to make sure that no one was within earshot. "I probably shouldn't be talking about this, anyway. Oh, Chris! I'm so scared ..." She struggled to control her voice. Tears blurred her vision, began to trickle silently down her cheeks.

"Hey, you've got to hang in there."

"I was so mean to her the last time we spoke." She was crying properly now, although quietly. She couldn't help it.

"What would you say to her if you could talk to her now?"

Julie looked through the veil of tears at the little figures in the street below. "I'd tell her how sorry I am about all the time we've wasted bickering and arguing," she said. "I'd tell her how much I love her even ... even when she exasperates me. Oh, I don't know. I just want to hug her."

"Well, you hold on to that thought. Concentrate on staying positive."

She fished for a tissue in her pocket and blew her nose. *He's right, I've got to stay focused.* She pulled herself erect and blinked to clear her vision. Then she took a deep breath and said: "In answer to your question – yes, I am."

"What?"

"You asked me if I was jealous. Well, I am – a little ... just a little." She felt herself blushing.

"You look after yourself," he said, and she could hear the smile in his voice.

"And you. Be careful … Bye."

She held the phone, not wanting to break the connection. Only when she heard the click of him hanging up did she reluctantly press the red button. She leaned her forehead against the windowpane and replayed the conversation in her mind. There was no denying that Chris had a wonderfully calming effect on her - but that in itself was unsettling. Her mind darted about like flock of birds roused by gunshot: *her mother in captivity; Greg and the police; Chris with Sandra; what was Mama Mercy up to right now –serving breakfast? And Wendy, I must call Wendy.* She also could not stop thinking about Desmond's weird behavior. *What was he doing in Johannesburg?* She had meant to ask Chris whether he had spoken to Desmond.

The sun, now a mega-spotlight, threatened to give her a headache. She stepped away from the window and studied the faded outline of her own likeness in the glass. A reflected movement caught her attention and she spun round, strode across to the door leading out into the corridor, and yanked it open. A white-haired man, his startled look magnified by thick glasses, blinked at her.

"Charlie? What are you doing here?" She tried to keep her voice even.

"I'm sorry, Julie." He held up soft white hands in a gesture of surrender, and his eyes darted about as he continued in an urgent whisper, "*I was hoping to talk to you. I was just waiting for you to finish your conversation.*"

Short and round, with a white beard to match his hair, Charlie always reminded Julie of Father Christmas. He had been with the company from the early days and worked in the computer operations group. Three years earlier, when Julie had been doing an internship at Noble, her computer hard drive had crashed. Charlie - who cheerfully admitted to being an *über*-geek - had spent hours retrieving the data. Despite his love for drama, he had subsequently kept his mouth shut about what he had done – and had thus saved Julie from the embarrassment of admitting to Greg that she had ignored his advice to back-up regularly.

Now, standing at the door to Reception, Charlie was clearly anxious. He looked over his shoulder, then whispered, "*I have to talk to you. It's about your mother.*"

"What about my mother?" Julie pulled Charlie into the room.

"I've been hearing things – people are talking. They say she has disappeared, been kidnapped."

Julie paled but said nothing, waiting for him to go on.

"I've known your mother longer than anyone in the company," he began. Julie massaged her wrists to hide her impatience, dreading a lengthy preamble. However, she knew that it was pointless to try and rush Charlie.

"Whenever she needed help with her computer, she would call me personally," he continued. "But you see, it was quite strange - she called me the other night."

"When? When was that?"

"Saturday night; late, after midnight."

"Saturday!?" If this were true, Charlie would have been the last person to speak to her mother. "But why did she call you?"

Again, he looked over his shoulder. He leaned a little closer.

"She wanted access to someone's emails. She seemed very agitated."

"Agitated? How do you mean? Did she ... did she sound scared?'

"No, more like ... angry."

"Whose emails?"

The *ding* of the elevator startled them both. Matt's secretary, a statuesque African woman with intricately plaited hair and a smart, tailored suit, stepped out. When she saw them, her face broke into a broad smile.

"Good morning, Miss Julie. And Charlie, what brings you up here? Don't tell me the boss is having trouble with his computer? That'll make him grumpy, and I don't need that man to be grumpy."

She winked as she sauntered past them and placed her bag on the desk.

Charlie's eyes darted in all directions and Julie jumped to the rescue. "Matt's computer is fine, Felicity," she said. "I was just prodding Charlie for advice about what laptop to buy." She exchanged a glance with Charlie and watched with frustration as the secretary settled in behind her desk and flicked an imaginary speck of dust from the cherrywood surface.

Julie said, "I do think Matt might appreciate some coffee."

Felicity, however, made no move to get coffee. Instead, she fished a lipstick from her bag and touched up her lips with the aid of a little mirror glued to the edge of her computer monitor.

She caught sight of Julie's questioning expression, and said, "He drinks far too much coffee for his own good." Then she inspected her fingernails whilst her computer booted up.

Julie turned to Charlie and said, "Well, we'll have to find some time for you to share your wisdom with me. Do you still work in the computer ops room?"

He nodded.

"Great, I'll come and see you there - soon."

Charlie retreated to the elevators. As Julie walked back into Matt's office, Felicity smacked her lips and called, "Bye, Charlie. Don't let the viruses bug you!" She laughed at her own joke. Julie was reminded of a horse neighing and immediately felt guilty for having such an uncharitable thought.

##

At the gym, Chris and James did shoulder and biceps exercises, followed by bench presses. Chris tried to get into "the zone" to clear his mind, but he found it difficult. The fact was, he shared Julie's fears more than he had let on. In particular, he kept on asking himself why the kidnappers had not let anyone speak to Bridget.

He wondered what would happen if he simply ignored his bail conditions and went up to Johannesburg to be with Julie. That thought was immediately rejected. It would just instantly land him back in jail and he shuddered at the thought of having to ask his father to refund Wendy the squandered bail money.

"Come on," James said, snapping him back into the moment. "You're being a wuss; you can do more than that."

The crossbar felt like a slab of granite that was threatening to come down on his chest and crush him. His muscles ached and his face was contorted with effort. Using an old motivational trick, Chris told himself, *OK, she'll kiss me if I reach fifteen.* He closed his eyes, visualized Julie, Julie who had confessed to being jealous. He imagined her cheering him on, bending down for a deep, lingering kiss. With a primeval grunt, he pushed up the crossbar to secure his imaginary reward.

"That's more like it," James said, and counted off the last three reps: "Thirteen, fourteen, and fifteen! OK, my turn."

Chris got up and stretched his shoulder muscles. He noticed a commotion at the reception desk. "What the ...?" He swore silently as he watched Sergeant Vervey and two uniformed constables barge past the astonished receptionist. Chris lowered his arms and stood motionless, his chin jutting forward. The sergeant homed in on him like a camel sniffing water after two weeks in the desert. He was flushed with excitement when he drew himself up in front of Chris and said, "Your bail has been revoked; I'm here to re-arrest you, *Meneertjie*."

A tiny, irrational part of Chris's brain had hoped that the sergeant was there to tell him it had all been a mistake and the matter was cleared up. Beyond that, he'd thought there might be more questioning. *But to have his bail revoked...* He fought to keep his voice neutral: "Would you care to explain why?"

"New evidence." The sergeant gestured, and one of the constables gripped Chris's wrist and handcuffed his hands behind his back.

"We would like to inspect your locker," the sergeant said.

"My locker?"

"That's what I said, you parrot. You *do* rent a locker here, don't you?"

Chris nodded.

"Well, in that case, please lead the way."

Chris tried to remember when he had used the locker last. He certainly hadn't used it this morning or yesterday. On both occasions, he had jogged from his apartment and had not used the locker at all. *But what was all this about? What on earth were they hoping to find?*

He sensed every pair of eyes in the club following him as he led the strange procession - made up of the sergeant, two constables, and James - towards his locker. His skin felt on fire with shame and rage. In the changing rooms, he turned down a narrow aisle between two rows of metal lockers. A club patron, who was busy changing, hurriedly picked up his things and moved away when he saw the policemen approach.

Chris nodded and said, "This one's mine." He made an attempt to reach the key that was tied to his shoelace but, with his hands cuffed behind his back, it was an impossible maneuver. The sergeant directed one of his men to stay at the open end of the aisle to keep James and a number of curious onlookers away, whilst the other policeman was instructed to get the key. The man unlocked the metal cabinet and rummaged through Chris's T-shirts and other clothes. Disdainfully, he dropped underwear and a Speedo on to the ground before reaching to the back of the locker. After further searching, he turned triumphantly, holding up a leather case, roughly the size of a hardcover book.

The sergeant snatched the case and weighed it in his hands. "And what do we have here?"

Chris was reminded of the time a teacher at school had done inspections and found a packet of cigarettes in James's locker; the self-satisfied smirk had been just the same.

The sergeant opened the case to reveal the most stunning piece of jewelry that Chris had ever seen: a necklace of delicate golden petals studded with diamond "dewdrops". Chris wasn't an authority on jewelry, but he could tell that this was an exceptional work of art; the diamonds appeared to concentrate light on to the mirrored gold surfaces of the petals. The sheer beauty of the necklace took his breath away. He wondered who could possibly be the owner this amazing object.

The sergeant carefully shut the case and handed it to the constable. He straightened up and asked, "And what do you say now? That necklace happens to match the description of one that went missing from the Baxter household."

"Any number of people could have planted that. I leave a spare key at Reception."

"*Ja, ja.* Excuses, excuses. It's always someone else."

Without warning, he suddenly brought up his right knee and slammed it into Chris's groin. Chris gasped as the wave of pain exploded and spread. It felt like every nerve in his body was frazzled with electric shock waves. His instinct was to clasp and protect, but his hands were held in cuffs behind his back. He was doubled over forwards when the sergeant's right fist connected with his face and threw him up and sideways. Unable to steady himself, Chris slammed into the row of lockers and gashed his eyebrow on a latch. There was a deafening clatter from the reverberating metal. The noise seemed to overpower all Chris's other senses. He tried to focus on the sergeant, but there was an irritating liquid veil in front of his eyes. He kept blinking and shaking his head. Then he tasted the blood that ran down his face.

"You'll think twice before you try and kick me in the balls again," Vervey hissed.

Chris fought to regain his breath, while silently willing James and the other club patrons to come to his aid. But they couldn't see him – the sergeant's bulky frame blocked their view. Chris realized that he was on his own. He primed himself for defense, years of martial arts training kicking into gear. He lowered his head to avoid direct eye contact, tried to ignore the pain, and observed the stance of his opponent, as well as the position of all objects around him.

"Now, what have you done with her?" The sergeant's voice was cold. "Did your little sex games get out of hand, *heh*? Or did you just want to rob her? Or maybe you've already killed her?"

Chris used his shoulder to wipe the blood from his eyes.

"My patience is finished now, *op, gedaan.*"

The sergeant's fist came straight at his face, but this time Chris was ready. He managed to evade the blow and sidestep to place the constable between himself and Vervey. The space was very confined, and when the sergeant tried to barge past his constable to get at Chris, the uniformed underling intervened. With some hesitation, he said, in Afrikaans, "Sergeant, the people are watching."

Chris saw the internal struggle in the face that glared at him over the policeman's shoulder. Eventually, Vervey tugged at his jacket cuffs, his habitual gesture, and said, "We have enough evidence to put you away for a long, long time."

"Fabricated evidence, like this necklace in my locker," Chris said, with more bravado than he felt. "Don't you see that this is a set-up?" he continued, trying to sound more conciliatory. "You are going to look like a fool when the truth comes out."

Too late, he realized that the word "fool" was clearly a trigger for Sergeant Vervey. The man's expression reverted to one of fury, and he looked ready to try another punch.

With a visible effort, however, he reined himself in. He evidently had more to say. "If you think you are so clever, then explain to me why there were no ransom calls whilst we had you in custody? Big surprise, *heh*?" The sergeant smirked – he was in control again. "Then, when you were out on bail, there was another ransom call. Is that a coincidence, or what?" He spat the words out contemptuously. "But wait, that's not all," he went on, his tone now that of a TV salesman. "We searched Mrs.

Baxter's home - and what should we find? Your bloodied shirt in the laundry room!"

"That wasn't blood. That was tomato sauce."

"Tell it to the judge. We also happened to find your fingerprints all over the safe."

Chris groaned. *Of course, I opened the safe and rifled through it to hand Bridget her notebook of passwords. Damn, damn, damn.*

"Then, finally," the sergeant continued, "we had an anonymous tip-off that we might want to look here in your locker for Mrs. Baxter's missing jewelry."

Chris shut his eyes and said nothing. It was useless. He knew that he had been so thoroughly framed that it was pointless to try and argue. *But why?*

He did not resist when the constable took him by the shoulder and led him away.

James, and the other onlookers, gasped when they saw Chris's bruised and blood-smeared face. The constables, however, both had their hands on their holsters to pre-empt any trouble.

"Your friend here fell and hurt himself," the sergeant announced, to no one in particular. "If he went to a proper boxing gym, instead of this poofter parlor, he wouldn't be so winded by a little fall."

As Chris walked by, James touched his shoulder. Although his left eye was beginning to swell and he was finding it hard to see clearly, Chris could make out the deep concern in his friend's face. He managed to whisper, *"I have to find out who's behind this. You've got to get me out."*

As he was led out of the changing rooms, and once again faced the gauntlet of gawkers, Chris thought, *Damn it all, I've done nothing wrong, I have nothing to hide.* He ignored the pain in his groin and drew himself erect.

In some ways, it was as though time stood still during the long walk to the gym exit. And yet during that time, Chris became aware that something had changed fundamentally. *This was no longer a little misunderstanding to be cleared up; this was a fight for his survival.* Despite the swelling around his eye, his senses were on heightened alert. He was aware of the constable's body odor, heard the noise of a fan in the corner, a noise he had never picked up consciously before. He could sense when someone stopped their exercise to stare at him – he noted the change in their breathing - and slowly, deliberately, he looked them straight in the eye until, one by one, they turned away. As he passed the reception desk, he turned to the girl on duty. She was pale, her fist clasped to her mouth. *Why have I never noticed that she's besotted with me?* Completely unbidden, her name sprang into his head. "Keep my locker, Diana. I'll be back," he said calmly, before he was hustled unceremoniously into the street outside.

This time there was no unmarked vehicle, no civilized Inspector Ibrahim. Chris was roughly shoved into the back of a police van that smelled of urine, sweat, and fear. He had seen people being loaded into the back of police vans before. They were usually drunks, vagrants, or petty thieves, although he had once seen a man in a suit - a white-collar worker, maybe - being ushered into one of these vehicles. Yet it had always seemed completely beyond the realm of the possible that he, Chris du Toit, would end up in a police *bakkie* cage.

He managed to pull his legs clear just before the panel doors were shut with a bang. He had to duck his head to sit on a small bench, from where he peered out at the street through wire mesh. James stood outside the club, his fists clenched and his face inscrutable. But then Chris saw something that made his blood turn cold: Lenny, cool as can be, sauntered out of the club. As he passed the van, Chris noticed that he looked directly at Vervey, who was still standing by the vehicle. The sergeant nodded his head and Lenny acknowledged him with an almost imperceptible motion of the hand.

Shock gave way to rage. Chris hammered against the side of the van. "You bastard!" he shouted in Lenny's direction. "What have I ever done to you?"

The driver revved the engine of the van.

Seeing that Lenny was about to disappear from view, Chris shouted, "James! It's him! The bastard framed ..." but his words were drowned out by the roar of the engine. The police van lurched towards the main road and swung across the traffic with squealing tires. Chris pulled in his head and spread his legs to brace himself, otherwise he would have been flung about like a rag doll.

He heard laughter from the cab as the van picked up speed.

##

Chapter 17: "Oh How I Want To Break Free"
Wednesday midday

The midday heat hung oppressively over the police station. The charge office at the front, affectionately known as "the parlor", was deserted. A passage led to the rear – three holding cells on the left, and a series of offices, plus a tiny kitchen and bathroom, on the right. The duty officer had dispatched the constable to go and buy cold drinks, leaving only two people in the building: himself and Chris.

"Shut up; stop that racket!" The duty officer, laboring over paperwork at his desk, was becoming irritated.

Chris rattled the bars of his cell door again. "Come on, man. Just give me some ice." His bruised face hurt.

"*Vokof* and shut up. Can't you see I'm busy? You call me one more time, and I'll come over and *donner* you." He glared at Chris from his office across the passageway. Perspiration glistened on his dark forehead. He appeared permanently uncomfortable in the uniform that was two sizes too small for his expanding midriff; the collar and tie cut into his neck. His shorn marine-style haircut served to accentuate the roll of fat that lay across his neck like an outsized slug.

The officer tugged at his collar. "Can't wait for them to come and take you away to Pollsmoor. Those guys don't take any *kak*. Just you wait. You rattle your cage there, and they'll just throw you in solitary."

He turned back to his paperwork. After a minute or two, he looked at his watch and sighed with exasperation. "How long does it take to buy a *bleddy* cold drink? Where is that dumb *doos*? "

Chris retreated to the bunk and leaned his head against the wall. The coolness of the stone was at least something. He listened to the eerie creaking of the tin roof as it expanded under the merciless beating of the sun. Looking up in the dim light, he saw that there was no insulation under the sheets of corrugated tin. He felt a trickle of perspiration run down the back of his shirt. By tonight, he would be in Pollsmoor, with his head shaven and wearing gray prison garb. He shuddered and tried to steady his breathing. He could hear the cry of a seagull; the distant *ding-a-ling, ding-a-ling* of an ice-cream van, and the vendor shouting, "Ice *creeeam*, ice cream for a hot day!" He licked his cracked lips and gingerly touched the swelling around his eye. *What I wouldn't give for an ice cream right now.* Leaning to one side, he could look through the bars of the cell door, through the charge office, and the front door beyond, to get a sliver of a sea view. The sky was almost painfully blue; a palm swayed lazily, and the sun reflected off the water – sending taunting little messages of light from the outside world into this ante-chamber to the gates of hell: *Pollsmoor.* He closed his eyes.

What a balls-up! In his mind, he kept seeing Lenny strolling from the club, smug as a pimp on payday at the men's hostel of a gold mine. Chris was convinced that Lenny had planted the jewelry in his locker – there had been that unmistakable look of acknowledgement between Lenny and Sergeant Vervey. *But why? Why, why, why?* Chris felt as though he was moving in a thick fog where he kept bumping into large puzzle pieces. If only he could get some distance, he would be able to see how the pieces fitted together. He felt an overwhelming urge to move, to run or to swim; his brain needed motion.

He clasped his head between his hands and worked backwards through every interaction he'd had with Lenny. *They'd met in the lobby of his apartment building, he'd noticed Lenny's car and followed him the day of the gala. Before that, the first time they'd met was when the girlfriend, Cindy, had chatted him up on the beach. Had that been a coincidence? Probably not.* His head hurt.

Hang on, he thought. *That night at the De Waterkant Club, Wendy commented that some guy was eyeing me. Was that the same person who photographed me and Julie?* Now that he thought about it, Chris was convinced that it was Lenny that evening at the club. Lenny had tried to run Bridget off the road. *Why?* Somewhere, there had to be a connection to Noble Enterprises. He thought about this for several minutes, piecing together the scraps of information he'd picked up from Wendy and Julie. Then he remembered something else that Julie had mentioned, something to do with the Khanya center: *"Noble Enterprises provides us with a security guard*

At the time, that had struck him as strange. Considering all the basic needs at an orphanage, it seemed odd to provide security and, what's more, the security seemed to focus on a barn by the river, rather than the main center. For a moment, Chris felt as though there was a tear in the fog, as though he got a glimpse of ...

Ding-a-ling, ding-a-ling. " Ice *creeeam. Lekker, lekker* ice cream!"

It sounded as if the ice-cream seller was right outside the station. Chris opened his eyes, frustrated to have his train of thought interrupted.

He caught a glimpse of the boxy white van in the street. *Why is it stopping there?* he wondered. Evidently, the officer on duty thought the same. Chris heard a chair scraping and watched the officer walking to the charge office. From behind the counter, he addressed someone whom Chris could not see.

"*Wat de vok* do you want here, with your *bleddy* ice cream? This is a police station."

Chris pressed his head against the bars to get a better view. Three figures had entered the charge office. They looked like they were dressed for the Cape Carnival, in garish glittering shirts, green-striped white pants, white gloves, and green top hats that would have done them proud at a Mad Hatter's tea party. All three wore big sunglasses and paint on their faces. Chris had spent many a hot, beer-fueled New Year's Day with friends watching similarly dressed "Minstrels" winding their way through the center of Cape Town. He was half-expecting the three men to whip out the traditional carnival instruments: a trumpet, a banjo, and a penny-whistle.

He squinted against the sun to get a better look. One man towered above the others. The most bizarre-looking of the three, he reminded Chris of a cheese stick being squeezed out of its plastic wrapper; the top buttons of his shirt had ripped off and the next few were about to do the same. Chris would have recognized him anywhere. The burly frame was unmistakably that of Bull Khumalo! He drew in his breath and stopped himself from calling out Bull's name just in time.

Not one of the three men had uttered a single word. Swiftly, they shut the front door to the police station and, without the glare, Chris recognized James and Bruce under the layers of make-up. Anxiously, he peered towards the surveillance camera above the front door, but the three had their backs to it. Chris was astounded by his friends. *Had they seriously decided to come and break him out of jail – in those ridiculous outfits?* It looked as if, rather than going to Wendy or his father to try and see if they could arrange bail, James had taken his whispered *"You've got to get me out"* literally. A part of Chris was appalled, horrified that they were taking such a risk. *Did they have the faintest idea what it meant to break a prisoner out of police custody?* And yet another part of him was exhilarated, uplifted. *I should have expected this – this was what Bull was talking about that morning of the gala dress rehearsal – this is* ubuntu, *this is brotherhood. "Your need is my need, we are one."*

Meanwhile, the duty officer was becoming apoplectic. "Hey, you can't just close the door!" he shouted, reaching for his holster. "This is my…What do you think …?"

"Have an ice cream," James said in a distorted voice, opening the cool bag he was carrying. But what he lifted out was not an ice cream, but a small canister containing a foul-smelling liquid, which James sprayed into the man's face. As the officer spluttered, cursed, and tried to protect his eyes, Bull moved forward and grabbed him. Chris watched in awe as Bull's white-gloved hands – *there would be no fingerprints* - fastened round the man's fat neck in a vice-like grip and his gun fell to the floor.

Chris was beginning to fear that Bull might accidentally kill the policeman, whose eyes were beginning to bulge dangerously, when the big man relaxed his grip a little. *"Keys?"* he hissed, and the duty officer pointed with a shaking hand in the direction of his desk.

Just then, a banging on the front door startled them. "Hey, what *de vok* is going on? Open the door!" shouted a voice from outside.

The three men in their carnival costumes froze. Chris was reminded of the white-faced drama students, pretending to be statues, who sometimes performed at the Waterfront.

"Open the door," Chris whispered. *"It's the constable; if you don't let him in, he'll radio for help immediately."*

Bruce opened the door wide and, as the startled constable crossed the threshold, he walked straight into a dose of mace spray administered by James. Bruce slammed the door shut and locked it. The constable dropped a six-pack of cold drinks and howled in pain. Unlike his colleague, however, this officer was young and athletic, and he wasn't going to give in without a fight. Spinning round, he lowered his head, and charged at Bruce, who was standing between him and the door. The force of the impact caused both men to crash to the ground, and Chris could see that Bruce was heavily winded.

Using this moment of distraction, the duty officer bit into Bull's arm and managed to free himself. He lunged towards his gun.

"Watch out!" Chris shouted.

"No you don't!" James bellowed, and rugby-tackled the man, who hit the ground hard. James immediately straddled his back and pressed his neck and head to the ground. The officer yelled in pain.

"I'll break your neck," James hissed. *"Lie still!"* The man capitulated.

Meanwhile, Bull had swung around and focused his attention on the second policeman. As the constable attempted to get up, Bull caught him with a right hook that sent him reeling backwards across the room. Crumpled into a heap against the back wall, the constable held up his hands in whimpering surrender.

"Hurry!" Bull commanded, and pulled Bruce to his feet. With blood running from a split lip, creating a vivid gash across the white mask of his face, Bruce looked grotesque as he glared at the man who had winded him.

Bull asked, "Is there anyone else here?"

Chris shook his head.

The others sprang into action. James and Bull dragged the two policemen into one of the empty cells, whilst Bruce rummaged across the duty officer's desk for the keys. Once he had found them, he locked the two policemen into their cell, and came over to Chris. "Say 'pretty please'," Bruce coaxed, waving the key in front of his friend's face.

"Stop fucking around!" Bull bellowed, and Bruce unlocked the door with a flourish.

Chris hesitated. Suddenly, he was very aware that crossing the threshold of the cell was a step into a world he had never even imagined – the world of an outlaw. In the eyes of the judiciary, his guilt would be confirmed. *There will be no mercy, no bail, no nothing - if I get caught.*

"C'mon!" Bull was at the front door, peering up and down the street. "It's clear."

But then again, though Chris, *the judiciary have completely failed me. They thought I was guilty anyway. If I don't get out and find the real culprits, I'm going to rot away in Pollsmoor and Julie ...* He didn't dare to think of how devastated she would be if the kidnappers harmed Bridget. *I have to find Bridget – for Julie's sake - and to prove my innocence.*

Without looking back, Chris joined his friends. The policemen's threats– something involving a blunt butcher's knife and testicles stuffed down his throat – rang in his ears, as the four men jumped into a waiting get-away car: the ice-cream van.

"You're shitting me," Chris said as he clambered into the back of the van and the other three squashed into the front, with James driving. "This thing can't go faster than a lawnmower."

"Perfect disguise," James said, laughing, as the van crawled slowly away, playing its merry tune. Despite his bloodied face, Bruce leaned out the window and bellowed, "Ice *creeeam*, ice *creeeam!*"

The three in the front were in high spirits as they went over the events of the last ten minutes. They yelled, high-fived, and punched each other like schoolboys who had won a soccer match. Chris worried that the wave of relief and unspent adrenalin would wash them into trouble, and, sure enough, James nearly lost control of the vehicle as he mimicked the constable's "mace face".

"What do you think of our plan, Chris?" Bull asked, turning round.

Chris had been peering out of the back window to see if they were being followed – he didn't think they were - but he tried to enter into the spirit of things: "I have to say, you guys get full marks for … for sheer bloody chutzpah. In the middle of the day!"

They trundled their way down Beach Road. At one point, James even stopped for a group of kids who he saw hopping from one foot to the other on the hot asphalt, waving at the van. Chris opened a freezer box and passed wrapped ice creams to the front.

"No charge today," Bull said, and his clown's grin, combined with free ice cream, elicited a mixture of surprise and exuberance. One of the kids curved his forefingers into the corners of his mouth and pulled hard, baring his teeth to emulate the extra-wide grin.

"Cool hat," another one shouted.

Eventually, James turned up a quiet side street and parked behind two waiting vehicles. Chris recognized one as Bruce's VW camper. The other was a nondescript old sedan with "RENT-A-WRECK" stenciled on the side; the sort of vehicle hired by hundreds of backpacking tourists. He was impressed; his friends had done a good job in planning the escape.

They were still huddled in the van as James dropped the casual demeanor, together with the ridiculous hat. His tone was urgent. "Chris, this is as far as we've planned things. Now we've got to split. What's your next move?"

Chris was aware how much he owed his friends – his crazy, dumb, brave, heroic friends who'd taken a ridiculous risk to get him out of jail. They needed to see that their efforts had not been in vain, that he had a firm plan.

A tight knot had taken up residence in his abdomen ever since this nightmare began; he felt it tighten even more now with the realization that he was on his own, but he forced himself to visualize it as a coiled spring, an inner force that would propel him forward.

"I'm going after Lenny. He planted that necklace in my locker and tipped off the police."

"Yeah, but where will you stay?" James asked. "You can't go back to your apartment. That cockroach, Vervey, is bound to have it under surveillance."

James had a point. *Where* can *I go?* He thought. The police would be looking for him everywhere. He couldn't go to his father's, he couldn't stay with any of the Toreros – they were potentially in enough trouble for helping him, as it was. *Cedric's flat? No. Or what about Desmond's mother, Josie Andrews?* He rejected that idea, too. In fact, he realized that anyone who cared about him was off-limits. A wave of self-pity washed over him as he had visions of himself sleeping under a bridge, eating corned-beef out of can. But then self-pity gave way to anger, an anger that slowly grew until it became a glacial fury that made him cold and calm. Whoever had conspired against him was going to pay. *If I have to sleep amongst the homeless in Cape Town, so what?* It was nothing compared to the indignity and injustice he had suffered already.

Bull interrupted his thoughts. "You must come with me to Mandela Park," he said, matter-of-factly.

"Are you crazy?" Bruce looked incredulous. "A white boy will stick out like a tree in the desert. He'll be robbed and beaten up in no time."

"Bruce, my man." James shook his head as though he were addressing a dimwitted child. "You're so full of stereotypes. It's not *that* bad; they even have tours going through Mandela Park and the other squatter camps. You should try one sometime."

"Yes, but still …"

"Well, do you have any better ideas?"

"It's a good idea," Chris intervened. "The police will not expect it, unless ..." he hesitated and looked at Bull. "Won't they come looking at your place?"

Bull grinned his scary-clown grin. "My shack is too small, anyway. We'll keep you at the old boxing gym. There's a pack room at the back. You can sleep there."

James clutched his hat in front his chest and simpered with mock contrition, "Sorry, my boss, it's the best we can do at such short notice."

"Beats Pollsmoor," Chris said. "It actually suits me very well. Thabo lives up in that squatter camp and I want to get in touch with him. And I can walk down to the Khanya center."

"What do you want there?"

Chris tried to briefly outline his suspicions, and the connections he had begun to formulate whilst in the cell. He explained that he expected there to be a link between Lenny and the two characters from Noble Enterprises who made deliveries to the barn. Perhaps, he suggested, Bridget had found out what was going on and they first tried to scare her off by attempting to run her off the road and then, when she wouldn't stop, kidnapped her.

The more he thought and spoke about it, the more convinced Chris became that he was right, "Something at that barn ain't kosher and Lenny is at the hub of all this."

At any other time, the three blank clown faces, that now looked at him as though he spoke Ovambo, might have amused Chris.

"It's complicated, but I'll get it figured." He wished he felt as confident as he tried to sound. "Come on, Bull. I'll fill you in on our way to Mandela Park."

He turned to the other two. "Thanks, guys. I owe you big time." He clasped their hands and gave them fist punches. James gave him a brief half-hug and handed him the keys to the rent-a-wreck.

Minutes later, Chris and Bull were heading down the coastal road towards Hout Bay. They drove for a while until they reached a secluded cove, where Bull stripped and strode into the surf to wash off the make-up, before shaking himself dry and putting on his standard T-shirt and sweat pants. Chris splashed the waters of the Atlantic on to his bruised face. He looked at the beach, a strip of warm whiteness wedged between sea and mountain. He longed to lie down on his stomach, bury his toes in the sand, and just feel the sun on his shoulders ... and Julie next to him. *Julie...*

"Bull, hurry up, man. We've got to go."

Julie sat on a hard little visitor's chair. Charlie had tried to create some order on his desk, but had given up; piles of computer manuals and stacks of paper created a tableau of organized chaos. The two monitor screens behind him made Julie think of some square-eyed alien keeping watch. They were alone in his world: a corner in the vast neon-lit computer operations room. For once, Julie did not mind the droning of the air conditioner because it provided extra privacy. But she did have to try hard to ignore the little green and red flashing lights on the computer banks that traced the lifeblood of Noble Enterprises: its information flow.

She sipped tea from a mug with a photograph of a Chihuahua on it ("Buster Junior", apparently) and said, "I still don't get it; you say my mother called you at one a.m. because she wanted access to certain emails? Did she call you at home, on your cell? How did she even know your number?"

He coughed and looked sideways. "That's ... that's private."

"Charlie, please! My mother is in real danger. We don't have time to play games."

He cleared his throat. "Your mother and I go back a very, very long time," he began, and Julie resigned herself to yet another account of Charlie's long career at Noble Enterprises. He reminded her that he had looked after the company's computers from day one. He evidently regarded them as surrogate children - they could be temperamental at times, he said, but they did his bidding. Then he embarked on a description of the phenomenal growth in computing capacity and explained the data security challenges which he had had to overcome. Throughout all this, it was he, Charlie, whom Harry Noble, and latterly Bridget, had trusted to take care of the company's systems and information.

Julie nodded and smiled, while inwardly she seethed with anxiety and impatience. "You were saying that my mother called ..." she prompted finally, unable to take any more.

"Ah, yes; I was just trying to explain why your mother trusts me ... more than any other employee." He sighed. "About two years ago, we met, by chance, at an Alcoholics Anonymous meeting."

"My mother went to AA?" Julie spilled a few drops of tea, quickly wiping them off Charlie's desk with the palm of her hand.

He nodded, then rapidly continued, as though to get this part of the story out of the way as fast as possible: "It was quite embarrassing that we should both turn up at the same meeting. I offered to leave, but she insisted I stay. Afterwards, we talked about it and she said it would help her to have someone there that she knew and trusted. So we used to go to AA together." He paused and wiped imaginary dust off a book on his desk. "Being an alcoholic is a tough, lonely business." He avoided her eyes as he said this, then reached for a water bottle, took a swig. "Anyone who hasn't been through it can't understand. The battle that rages in your head – it's so exhausting."

Julie nodded in silence. Charlie took out a big crumpled handkerchief and mopped his forehead. "Sometimes, late at night, when she felt like the demons would overcome her, she used to call me. We'd talk – well, she'd talk and I'd listen." He smiled a little and Julie's heart went out to this man. Longwinded he might be, but here was someone who had been loyal and supportive to her mother when she herself had only ever been impatient. Tears welled in her eyes.

"I had no idea," she whispered.

"Oh, I enjoyed listening to your mother. She'd talk about the old days. I think she really missed the excitement of running the business, signing up customers. Your mother was a marvelous dealmaker. I've had the opportunity to watch her negotiate; she was a real pro. She was respected because she was tough but fair. Of course, when you were born she very much scaled down her involvement in the business – and once your father died, she stopped altogether."

"Did she …" Julie hesitated. "Did she ever say that she resented having to give it all up when I was born?"

"Oh, no, no! I'm sorry if I gave you that impression. Your parents had nearly given up hope when you came along. They were ecstatic. God, the day you were born, they paid all staff a bonus so that everyone could share in their happiness. I think they would have declared it a public holiday, had it been in their power!" He chuckled and for a moment was lost in his memories. "No, if ever there was a child that was wanted and loved, then that was you. But just because your mother wanted to be there for you, it doesn't mean that she didn't miss the business.

"Anyway, where was I? Oh yes. Because we often spoke at all hours of the night, I wasn't surprised when she called last week. What did surprise me, though, was her manner."

"Yes – you mentioned earlier that she seemed angry."

"Angry, certainly – but also very much her old self: sharp, in control." Charlie went on to explain that Bridget had been reading the fine print in one of the company contracts and was outraged – she'd felt that the principles of Noble Enterprises - Harry's principles, her own - had been betrayed. She wanted Charlie to dig into the email system to check out certain correspondence.

"But surely that's not possible? What about all the information protection systems and passwords we have in place?"

He smiled, and peered at her indulgently over the rim of his glasses. "Give me *some* credit, Julie. Who do you think wrote all those information protection systems? There is not a bit nor a byte of information in this company that I cannot access – you mother knew this."

"OK, so you helped her gain access to certain emails. Then what?"

"It took me quite a while, I had to keep filtering and searching till I found one particular email thread. That seemed to be what she was looking for."

"What did she say?"

He paused, touched his temple and thought hard. "Her exact words were, *'I knew it, I knew it; always trust your gut, Charlie.'*"

"This email thread, can you show it to me?" She knew she was breaking any number of company rules, but this new information could be vital. She prayed Charlie could be persuaded to trust her as he trusted her mother.

Without a word, he swiveled round and extracted a print-out from the middle of one particular pile. When he turned round again to face her, his expression was serious. He held the printed sheets close to his chest and she could see the deep concern in the magnified eyes behind the thick lenses.

"I won't tell anyone," she said. "I promise …"

"I'm not worried about me." He coughed and his voice was a hoarse whisper when he continued, *"It's you I'm worried about."* He looked around the computer room and kept clearing his throat. Finally, he said, "Julie, I don't know whether I'm doing the right thing. I don't think it is fair to burden you with ..." His hand fumbled across his desk and unearthed a key. He unlocked the bottom drawer. "These papers could just put you in danger."

Julie was aghast. *Why has he changed his mind? Is he going to lock that print-out away and not tell me what's in it?*

She felt desperate. "Charlie, no! Look, you've come this far. If that email thread has even the *remotest* chance of helping us find my mother ..."

He avoided her gaze. His coughed again, followed by a bout of wheezing, and struggling for breath. *God, what if he has a heart attack?* She measured the distance across the desk. *Could I grab the papers from him before he has time to lock them in his desk? No – it's too risky. Better to keep him on side and try persuasion.*

She clasped her hands around the mug and willed herself to calmly take another sip of tea. "Charlie, if my mother were sitting here right now, and it was me who had been kidnapped, what would you do?"

He looked at her for what felt like an eternity, but was probably only a few seconds. Then he silently handed her the print-out, touching it only with one thumb and forefinger, as though it were a soiled rag.

"Thank you, Charlie." Julie tried to contain her relief as she started to skim the thread of emails. *What? It makes no sense. Surely this can't be right?* She read the emails through a second time, then a third. She was vaguely aware that her hands felt clammy. She wiped them on her jeans.

"There must be some mistake," she said, more to herself than to Charlie. She turned the papers over but they were blank on the reverse side. Then she read the emails yet again, from bottom to top this time - all the way up to the unmistakable name of the sender: *Greg Louw*. She might struggle to accept what was in front of her, but in the end there was no getting away from it: these dangerous, arrogant emails had been sent by Greg, her Greg.

"Are you OK? I'm so sorry, I knew this would be a shock to you, that's why ..." Charlie broke off, looked at her anxiously. "What are you going to do?" he asked finally.

"There's no one I can trust. No one," she whispered.

"That's how I felt," Charlie said, sighing. "That's why I came to you."

"If this is true, and my mother found out, she would have been a real threat to ..." She had to swallow. Saying his name out loud somehow added an extra layer of confirmation to what she had read. "She would have been a real threat to Greg and his 'business partners'."

She folded the print-out and left it on the desk in front of her. For a while, she just sat there looking at it, mesmerized by the sharp edges of the paper, waiting for ... *for what? For the paper to burst into flames? Waiting for it to turn purple and reveal some hidden ink message that said this was all just a big hoax? There had to be a mistake somewhere; it just seemed too bizarre.*

She looked at Charlie. "Could this be some kind of set-up? Someone wanting to falsely implicate Greg?"

He shook his head.

"But you read about it in the papers all the time; malicious people hack into computers and plant all sorts of false information to cause trouble. Isn't that what might have happened?"

He shook his head again.

"You've had more time to think about this than me, Charlie. Do you think ... Greg ... actually engineered her kidnapping?"

He seemed to ponder for a moment, then he shrugged. "Greed is an enormous motivator. He wants control of the company. With this," he pointed at the print-out, "your mother would have had him out on his ear. Like I said, she sounded like her former self that night – like someone ready to take back full control of the company. If she had confronted Greg, he would have had to move fast."

Julie felt close to tears. *If only Mother had come to me, told me what she'd found out ... But then, how would I have responded if she had?* Ruefully, she had to admit to herself that she would not have believed a word of it, and would probably have accused her mother of being spiteful, vindictive, and ... worse. And of course she'd been up in Johannesburg when her mother found out all these details.

"I've been a terrible daughter," she said softly. "I should have paid more attention, allowed her to talk to me."

"Yes, well; I'm sure there'll be plenty time for self-recrimination later. The question is, what are you going to do *now* to make it right?"

Julie looked at him in surprise. There was a tough edge in his voice; she had expected sympathy.

He must have guessed her thoughts, because he leaned forward, took her hand in his, and looked at her intently. "I've had to deal with many a crisis over the last thirty years. Believe me, it's not pretty when you lose power to the data center or the global network hub goes down, or whatever. And you know what I've learned?" He didn't wait for an answer. "The worst thing to do in a crisis is to start recriminations and blaming. What you've got to do now is focus … focus!" She thought his eyes would bore right through her.

For the first time, Julie realized that she, too, was now in danger. She would have to be very, very careful. The magnitude of the deceit was hard to comprehend. Her parents' company - *her* company - usurped for shady and illegal dealings of the worst kind. Noble Enterprises *stood* for something - for top-class biomedical engineering, for helping people. *And now … now what? But Charlie's right, I need to focus, to stay strong.* That much was clear.

"Can you get me a copy of that contract, please, Charlie? The one between Noble Enterprises and the Malaysians? It's the one my mother read and signed on Saturday night."

"Sure." He swiveled round and tapped away on his keyboard.

Julie leaned forward, cupping her chin in her hands. The only advantage she had was the element of surprise; Greg didn't know that she had discovered the truth. She was convinced now that her mother was being held in Cape Town; no wonder Greg had wanted keep her up in Johannesburg – out of the way. The more she thought about it, the more she found her shock giving way to anger as the monstrousness of the deceit began to sink in. She straightened in her chair, suddenly impatient. She had to find a way to get to Cape Town, fast.

Then, as she watched Charlie at the computer, a realization struck her that almost stopped her from breathing. Throughout their conversation, Charlie had referred to her mother in the past tense: "We *used to* meet at AA …"; "We *used* to talk …" Was that just a slip of the tongue, or something more sinister? Could it be that Charlie knew much more than he was letting on? Or was he in cahoots with Greg, and carefully feeding her information? *But if so, why?* She had to force herself to breathe.

Charlie reached for the contract he had printed out, and handed it to her.

"What are you going to do now?" he asked again.

She got up, forced a smile . "I really don't know, Charlie. I'll have to think about it."

"Be careful."

"I will. Thank you, Charlie. Promise you won't say a word to anyone about this."

He lifted two fingers and touched his temple. "Scout's honor. I promise."

Julie made her way out of the huge room, passing banks of computers bathed in the eerie glow of artificial light. Right now, there was only one person in the world she wanted to talk to and he was a thousand miles away, in Cape Town.

She did not notice the small remote-controlled camera that silently swiveled to follow her every move. Down in the basement of the building, a man watched her receding back intently. "Nice ass," he muttered appreciatively. Then he picked up the phone, and dialed a number he knew by heart.

"What is it?"

"We have a problem with the songbird. She's just been talking to the *über*-geek."

"Damn! That bloody geezer just doesn't know when to keep his mouth shut."

"Do you want him to have … an accident?"

"No, we need him. But teach him a lesson. See how well he taps his damn keyboard when his fingers are broken."

"It will be my pleasure."

The phone went dead.

##

Chapter 18: On the run

Wednesday afternoon

The car crawled up a narrow dirt road through Mandela Park. A scraggly chicken squawked and scurried out of the way. Children waved and then stopped to watch the unlikely pair: the white man and the big African. A woman, carrying a heavy load of washing, reluctantly pressed herself against the splintery raw wood siding of a shack to let the car pass. She nodded when she recognized Bull.

The sun beat down on shacks that looked as though they had tumbled from a tear in the sack of some giant bag-lady. Made from "pre-owned" metal, plywood, plastic sheeting, tarpaulins, and other assorted materials, a uniform feature of these low structures was that each had rocks and bricks on its flat roof – without this ballast, the vicious southeaster would have blown the roof away. Most of the shacks consisted of a single room; they leaned against each other like drunk grape-pickers on a Friday night. Occasionally, there was an alleyway between shacks, just wide enough to let a person get through to the shared outhouse toilets behind.

Bull gestured to the sweeping curve of Hout Bay harbor in the distance. "It gets windy up here, but we have a million-dollar view."

Chris, the architect, was taking it all in, whilst trying to avoid fist-sized rocks in the road and potholes as big as washbasins. "It's a pity there aren't any trees for shade. It must be hot inside these … these houses."

"The trees – they've been chopped down for firewood."

"I'd hate to see what would happen here if a fire broke out."

"It's better now we have electricity," Bull said, with some pride, pointing to the chaotic web of wires that crisscrossed over the shacks. "Before, when people used paraffin for everything, there were lots of bad fires." He shook his head to dispel the memories.

Chris tried to avoid driving through a trickle of murky-looking liquid that meandered down the road and collected in puddles. As he navigated round it, a woman, with a baby on her back, emerged from one of the shacks. Chris saw her stoop to get through the door and was surprised when she emptied a basin of dishwater into the street right in front of the car. Cheerfully, she smiled at Bull and revealed a gap between her front teeth that reminded Chris of Mercy.

"The sanitation is better now," Bull observed. "The council has built more toilets and provided more taps. But it's still a problem."

Chris slowed to a crawl, then stopped to let a group of ragged kids, chasing an old tire, get by. Each one of them patted the car as they ran past, as if it were a ritual, or someone had dared them to touch this "metal beast". Chris shook his head. "It must be tough growing up here."

Bull shrugged. "They play outside, have friends; that's all a child needs to be happy. Main thing is to prevent them joining gangs." His voice was grim, and Chris, with a quick sideways glance, noticed that his friend looked exceptionally serious.

Bull looked straight ahead and said, "Some days, I just feel like giving up. But then I see the guys who come to the gym. They work out, they box, they do something useful – and they stay out of trouble."

They passed a small open area dominated by a single water tap. A group of women and children stood about with buckets and plastic bottles, waiting to collect water. Some had brought basins and sat on their haunches to do the weekly washing. To Chris, the atmosphere around the tap seemed sociable and relaxed. He heard laughter and chattering. An old woman admonished him to slow down with flapping hands.

Further down the road, they passed a man constructing a shack on a site the size of a single garage. Four wooden posts had been planted into the ground and the man was breaking up old wooden pallets to form the walls. He paused and looked at them with a sullen expression as they drove by. Despite the snail's pace, Chris was conscious of the car's dust trail. He slowed even more as he looked in his rear-view mirror and saw the homebuilder cough and spit.

"Watch out!" Bull shouted.

A chicken, squawking loudly, came charging out of one of the alleyways, followed closely by a yapping dog. The next second, there was a loud thud and Chris slammed his foot on the brake.

As if by magic, people appeared from everywhere. They swarmed around the car, talked excitedly and gesticulated. Chris was appalled at the thought that he might have hit and killed someone's dog. He was about to get out and see what had happened, when Bull commanded, "Stay in the car!"

Chris sat where he was for what seemed, to him, like hours. When he looked into the rear-view mirror, he saw more people coming up the road to join the crowd. Amongst them, he noticed the homebuilder, who had left his pallets behind. The man still carried his crowbar in one hand and tapped it into his other hand as if to set a drumbeat. When he drew level with the car, the man looked at Chris and their eyes locked. For an instant, Chris saw himself through the other man's eyes: the white boy, cowering in his car – the ultimate symbol of protected privilege – while his friend had to face the crowd and deal with the whitey's mistake. Chris could almost feel the other man's crowbar in his hand; imagine his urge to smash the windscreen.

Without further hesitation, he opened the door and stepped out. The crowd paid no attention; a circle had formed in front of the car and the people were absorbed by whatever was going on inside that circle – it sounded like a fight. Chris heard two women screeching; others whistled, jeered, and even laughed. He edged his way forward and managed to join his friend in the front row. It soon became clear that he had not hit the dog, but the chicken. The dog had pounced upon the stunned chicken and was now refusing to give up his prey. The two screeching women were the respective owners – one gripping the dog by the scruff of his neck, the other pulling the chicken by its legs. The crowd was highly pleased with this unexpected entertainment and egged on the combatants.

After a minute, Bull stepped in and prized the dog's mouth open to release the lifeless chicken. Its owner was beside herself with indignation and anger; she gesticulated at Chris and even he could make out enough of her Xhosa torrent to understand that she was holding him responsible. The mood seemed to change as the dog's owner and others in the crowd loudly voiced their agreement. Chris kept his eye on the man with the crowbar. He resisted the temptation to look behind him. He knew there was no escape route, and to search for one would be a sign of weakness that would further embolden the bubbling cauldron of humanity around him.

Without warning, Bull hammered his flat hand on the hood of the car. The sound echoed like gunshot round the shacks and momentarily the crowd was stunned into silence. Calmly, in a mixture of Xhosa and Afrikaans, Bull told them that the chicken lady would be compensated, that the show was over, that they should go home. After some rapid negotiation, Chris paid the woman fifty rand and she carried off the chicken – presumably to prepare it for dinner. The crowd dispersed after this, although a few youths lingered in the hope that some form of conflict might yet be reignited. One of them took a deep drag on the remains of his self-rolled cigarette and flicked the stub towards Chris's feet. It landed far enough from Chris not to be an outright challenge, and yet close enough to be a mark of disrespect. As the man exhaled, Chris picked up the unmistakably sweet smell of *dagga*. He felt the muscles in his knees tense, ready for a swift kick, but he kept his hands relaxed the way he'd been taught in martial arts – *maintain an element of surprise, don't warn the opponent.* He looked at the young man intently until the latter decided to retreat - with a few cackling jibes about the beat-up car.

If that's what he needed to do to save face, Chris wasn't bothered. He and Bull watched the young men saunter down the street.

Bull grunted. "Now everyone in Mandela Park knows you are here." It was the closest he had ever come to reproaching Chris.

Getting back in the car, they drove on till they reached a low-slung brick structure, public-works-department turquoise, which stood out amongst the ramshackle homes. The words "Community Center" had been hand-painted on the side in uneven red letters.

"Don't park here – too obvious - carry on," Bull said. Chris obeyed, and five minutes later they reached a fence that marked the end of the squatter camp. The shacks here seemed to have been professionally built, and some had multiple rooms. There was enough space between them to squeeze in a car.

"Put her here. I know the man who owns this place. I'll explain to him."

They walked back to the community center and entered through a back door. A boxing gym, roughly the size of a triple garage, took up most of the building. The concrete floor was painted gray and the equipment was sparse. Four men sat on upturned beer crates, watching a couple of boxers in the ring. A few more patrons were pummeling an assortment of punch bags.

When Bull and Chris entered, the fight in the ring was briefly suspended and everyone greeted Bull. Chris could feel their eyes on him, the stranger, but could not understand the rapid Xhosa. Whatever explanation Bull gave for his presence must have been a joke at Chris's expense, however, because two of the younger men laughed heartily. Then the fight resumed, and Bull led his friend to a small pack room at the back of the gym.

"What did you tell them?" Chris asked

"Your girlfriend beats you up and you are hiding from her."

Chris was not amused, especially when he surveyed the dark, dusty closet that housed a row of stacked folding chairs, a few old punch bags, and a pile of floor mats. The remains of a rusted exercise bike were heaped in a corner.

So, this is what it's like to be a fugitive, he thought. It occurred to him that he had nothing to put down in his new digs. He'd traveled light in the past, hitchhiking through Asia, but never *this* light. It felt strange to not even have a change of underwear. As if seeking reassurance, he patted the pocket containing his cell phone and wallet, which James had brought for him. A moment of weakness was enough, though, and then he was scolding himself for his self-pity and ingratitude. Bull was putting everything on the line to help and protect him. He turned to his friend and meant it when he said, "Thanks, man, this is great. I really appreciate you taking this risk for me, Bull."

"There's a shower and a toilet on the other side of the building."

"OK."

"So, what's your plan?"

Chris scratched his stubbly chin. "Do you know where Thabo and his mother live? I'd like to go see him.'

"Not far, I can show you how to get there. Then I'm going to find us some food." As an afterthought, he added, "James said he would come by later and bring some clothes and things." He cracked a smile. "Mine would not fit you."

As Chris turned to leave the pack room, he found his path blocked by a stocky man whose muscular build was a testament to many hours spent in the gym. His arms crossed, the man's dark features were expressionless.

"We don't want you here. You're trouble."

"What's your problem?" Bull asked from behind Chris.

Another man, equally muscular, a younger version of the first one, had silently joined the group. "Why you bring him here - trouble with the police?" he said, making no attempt to hide his suspicion and hostility.

Bull's voice was soft and low, but had the power of an approaching storm. "You should have understanding for that. I say he stays. Get out the way."

The first man held his ground for a full minute. Then he dropped his gaze and muttered a curse. He took a small step to the side, stretched his arms forward, and cracked his knuckles only inches in front of Chris's face. As he did so, Chris noticed a distinctive tattoo on the man's right forearm. He tried not to stare. *Where have I seen that serpent shape before? Why does it seem so familiar?* His mind groped, fumbled, and reached deep into a murky swirl of memories. Had it been somewhere in Tibet? On one of the monks? Like the fragmented images of an old ripped movie spool, he unearthed snippets: *an intricate mural, a snake writhing in the dust, a cloaked face.* He tried to remember the emblems and images he had studied as part of his Cultural History course, but everything remained vague and shadowy. Then he remembered that Lenny, too, had a snake tattoo on his arm. Chris had not actually seen it, but James had commented on it the day they had met Lenny and Cindy in the apartment lobby.

As he and Bull walked past, the second man, the younger one, leaned in to let his shoulder touch Chris's. They locked eyes. Bull was there immediately and guided Chris along towards the exit. At the door, Chris turned and looked hard at both men – the younger one smirked derisively. Again, something stirred in Chris's memory. Something was coming into focus. It felt as if his mind contained a hawk, a hawk circling over a field, glimpsing a movement, before finally homing in on the patch where the rabbit was hiding.

One of the men lifted his arm, fist clenched, in a black power salute. The hawk in Chris's mind swooped down, but the prey was not a rabbit. He lost all sense of time as he hurtled through a kaleidoscopic tunnel - *down, down, down* – until he could see the prey clearly: *it was a snake.* Chris's legs went numb and he felt as though a giant fist had grabbed him to squeeze the very life out of him. He struggled to breathe and felt the numbness rise; a wave of nausea swept over him as he stared at the outstretched arm with the blazing snake tattoo.

Then survival instinct kicked in. *Don't show weakness. Don't let them see!* He tore his eyes away and followed Bull outside, where he leaned against a wall and gasped for air like a man whose head had been held underwater. Bull looked on in alarm.

"Hey, man, you OK? Don't let those punks upset you." He slammed the door shut. "They won't dare touch you – they know you're my brother."

Chris shook his head. *"It's not that,"* he whispered, slowly regaining his composure. Bull looked perplexed.

"I ... I remembered where I'd seen that tattoo before. My mother's killer had one like it." He stared into space. "I can see him. Eyes in shadow under his hood, but his mouth is visible - young, barely started shaving." In a trance, he lifted his right arm. "The gun is pointing straight at me. I'm waiting to see the bullet, thinking that will be the last thing I'll ever see. My mother's shouting." Chris pressed one hand over his eyes. "I was so focused on the gun, but now … I can see his arm, behind the gun - and I see the tattoo. I swear, it's that very same tattoo." He was there again, in his nightmare; he could hear the shots, smell the gunpowder. It had never seemed so real; he let his head fall back hard against the wall and the pain was a relief; it brought him back into the present.

Bull said nothing.

With the first shock wearing off, Chris felt the numbness yield to a lava-bed of boiling rage.

He made for the door. "One of those bastards killed my mother!"

"Don't!" Bull gripped him round his chest. "They're just waiting for an excuse to rip you apart."

"I don't care! Let go! I'll throttle them with my bare hands!"

"Shut up!" Bull hissed, and dragged Chris into an alleyway between two shacks. A passing woman looked at them, shook her head, and made *cluck-cluck* noises.

"You're attracting attention. People will call the police!"

Again, Chris struggled to break free. "Murderers!"

"You shut up now or I'll knock you out."

The look on Bull's face, a mixture of deep concern and anger, persuaded Chris that he meant it. He stopped struggling. Slowly, cautiously, Bull loosened his grip. Chris closed his eyes, leaned against the side of a shack, and slowly slid down into a sitting position. He heard Bull breathing hard as he crouched down beside him. The struggle had obviously not been a pushover for the big man.

Chris said, "It's definitely the same tattoo. I remember it exactly."

"It's the sign of the Dragon Boys gang."

Chris felt an old bitterness rise like bile. "I can't understand why the police never found the murderer. They should have tried harder!"

Bull looked at his friend. Slowly, he nodded. "I'm sorry, man. Of course they should have tried harder. But the Dragon Boys are powerful and they never rat on each other. It's one thing to know that a member of the gang did it; very difficult, though, to pin anything on a specific individual."

"Why do you allow a bunch of gangsters in the gym?"

"Like I said, we try and steer them on to a different path. We don't judge. Besides, I am sure these two are too young to have had anything to do with your mother's murder. When was it, again?"

"Eight years ago." Chris breathed more calmly now. "You'd better tell me all about this gang. I need to understand my enemies."

Bull gave him an overview of the gang that had started, like most others, as a group of thugs who dealt in illegal firearms and defended their drug patch in Langa, one of the townships. In the 1990s, after the euphoria of the first free elections in the New South Africa, many young people became disillusioned. There were still no jobs, there was no longer an enemy to fight, and the country was awash in illegal weapons after decades of conflict. What set the Dragon Boys apart from other gangs, however, was their initiation: to become a member, you had to have killed someone. This bestowed a notoriety on the gang that grew steadily, particularly as they let it be known that they were for hire as assassins. In 2004, the police Special Branch killed a number of the leaders, and the gang morphed into something else – it became almost like a fraternity, with a network of cells in various townships across the Cape Peninsula. This new group appeared more sophisticated and avoided direct confrontation with the police; they went about semi-legal activities such as "providing protection" for taxis, *shebeens,* and other township businesses. Bull was convinced that the Dragon Boys were still fully into drug dealing and weapons trading, but had become smarter and better organized.

Chris listened in silence. There was nothing very surprising in what Bull said. The gangs were an integral part of life in Cape Town, and he had heard it all before – on the news. But the squalid life of the townships had never before reached out and touched him, as it did now.

Chris caught the smell of mutton stew and burning paraffin coming from one of the shacks. It reminded him of Nala, his golden retriever. Nala would go crazy whenever Mercy cooked mutton stew; *Nala, who had died in a hail of bullets when the murdering Dragon Boys had invaded the house.* Suddenly, Lenny's image flashed into his brain. *Lenny's about the right age.* And then Chris remembered something else: Lenny seemed to really hate dogs; that day at the beach, he had cursed at a dog owner who let his dog come to within a few feet of him. Whoever had shot Nala must have either hated dogs, or been petrified of them. Why else would anyone blast a whole hail of bullets into a dog?

"Bull, are the gang members all Xhosa?"

"It started with Cape Coloureds. You will not remember, but there were a lot of very angry Coloured youths in the nineties. They felt cheated: under apartheid, they were "not white enough" and under the new regime they were "not black enough". But, as I say, now the Dragon Boys have become a big network that includes Coloureds, Xhosas, and even Zulus."

Lenny was a Cape Coloured and Chris was once again doing mental gymnastics with the chess pieces in his mind. Julie had first come up with the idea that someone was out to frame him, but after his visit to the Richters, they had discounted that idea. But what if Julie was right? Perhaps someone *was* trying to frame him - and that someone was a Dragon Boy. Chris had been at a complete loss as to why anyone would hate him enough to get him landed in jail. But what if, inadvertently, he had gotten too close to his mother's killer and spooked him? What if the killer had set this whole train of events in motion, thinking that Chris was about to unmask him?

He had to find Lenny; the first step was to see if Lenny had a Dragon Boys' tattoo. *And then?* He did not dare let himself think that far.

Quietly, he said, "For years and years, I dreamed of finding my mother's killer. I dreamed of revenge, of all the things I would do to him, how I would make him suffer."

Bull looked at Chris, nothing but concern on his face.

"It used to eat me up, but eventually, slowly, I learned to let go. I had given up on ever finding him. But now..." He looked towards the gym.

"Whatever you do, don't confront them. You can't beat them at their level. You have to use your brains and the patience of the spider that waits for its prey. Can you do that?"

Chris closed his eyes, took a deep breath, and nodded. "I know those two are too young; I need to find Lenny."

Bull said, "I'll make some enquiries – see if I can find out anything. You, though, you must stay out of trouble. Do you still want to see Thabo?"

Chris nodded.

"Come on, then." Bull got up and held out a hand to lift Chris out of the dirt.

Avoiding the muddy puddles in the road, Chris followed Bull down a lane that was too narrow for any cars. Two old men, their faces sunken and shriveled, sat on cracked plastic chairs, soaking up the sun. One of them was rolling a cigarette; the other lifted his hat as they approached.

"Molweni!" Bull greeted them and they both responded with beaming toothless smiles. Bull stopped to chat. Chris tried to follow the conversation. He cursed himself for not having paid more attention during Xhosa lessons at school. Mercy had tried to help him, but he'd simply had no interest. He could follow the general gist of the conversation, but not any of the specifics. The old men appeared to be retired fishermen and were keen observers of the weather and everyone passing by. One of them *cluck-clucked* and looked up at the bright-blue sky. The men held the view that it was too hot for this time of year, there were no more fish in the sea, the sheep were getting cataracts and going blind, and the world was going to hell in a woven wicker basket. Bull steered the conversation to the youth of today. This unleashed a flood of *cluck-clucks* and much shaking of balding heads. *Talk about the world going to hell in a basket!* Bull let them vent. Chris stole a look westward towards the harbor; the sun was beating down on the sea. He wished Bull would get on with it. After a few more minutes, however, Bull casually enquired what the Dragon Boys were up to. Had there been any new gang members in the area, or just the usual suspects? At this, the old men became quiet. In low tones, they whispered to each other. One of them nodded in Chris's direction and muttered something that he could not understand.

"They don't know you, so they're a bit reluctant to talk. Why don't you go ahead to Thabo's? See that shack with the blue door?" Bull pointed. "That's the one. I'll catch you later – you've got my cell number?"

Chris nodded.

He turned to the old men, bowed slightly with the palms of his hands touching each other in front of his chest, and bid them *"Molweni, iluphala."*

The old men were visibly pleased with this sign of respect. They beamed their toothless grins and wished him prosperity and many children. He heard them chuckling as he walked down the path towards the shack.

Thabo opened the door on the second knock. His face registered surprise and then broke into a broad smile. "*Meestar* Chris! How you find me here?"

"Bull showed me the way."

"You want to come inside?"

Chris hesitated. *What exactly* do *I want?*

Thabo said, "Come, come. My mother, she is resting. I must give the baby food. Then we can talk."

Chris had to stoop to enter the single-roomed dwelling. He took in the cramped quarters: a kitchen dresser, a chest of drawers with a plastic water *balie* on it, a single bed that doubled up as lounge furniture. Since all the family's activities were condensed into this single space, there was a potpourri of smells that confused Chris's senses. He could smell onions, as well as washing powder, cough syrup, and the oppressive sweat that accompanied hot days and tight spaces.

Thabo's mother lay on the bed, propped up by pillows. She looked at Chris, smiled weakly, and nodded her head. His eyes took a while to adjust to the dim light provided by a postage-stamp window. He could see the beads of perspiration on her forehead.

Thabo said, "*Umama*, you remember *Meestar* Chris from Khanya? He is the one who coach us soccer." He picked up a washcloth, dipped it in the basin of water, and gently mopped his mother's forehead. She smiled appreciatively and heaved herself into a more upright position. Chris approached. "Good afternoon. It's a pleasure to meet Thabo's mother. How are you feeling today?" He shook her offered hand carefully. It felt hot and fragile and reminded him of the time he had picked up a tiny bird, a *mossie*, which had fallen out of its nest.

Her head swayed slightly back and forth as she considered the question. "Today, not so good; tomorrow will be better." Again she smiled and Chris found himself mesmerized by her eyes – deep brown pools in the half-light. Looking at the perfect teeth and high cheekbones, he thought she must have been a very beautiful woman before AIDS had gripped her. Now her lips were visibly dry and cracked. She withdrew her hand and seemed to have trouble breathing. Chris saw a look of alarm flash across Thabo's face as his mother broke into a coughing fit. The frail body shook and shook, as one spasm after another wracked her. Her lungs heaved in her sunken chest and seemed to rattle the very bones of her skeleton in their desperate quest for air. Eventually, the coughing subsided and Grace lay back against the pillows with her eyes shut.

The baby began to cry. Chris hadn't noticed it before, as it lay in a makeshift crib between the chest of drawers and a big carton of washing powder, inscribed with the words: "Mama use Omo, makes the washing so bright".

Thabo took charge. He picked up a bottle from the dresser and poured out a measure of lurid green liquid. He helped his mother drink the medicine, then moved the pillows and got her to lie on her side. Expertly, he started to pat and massage her back.

"I have to make her lungs loose," he explained. "Please, pick up the baby and sit there," he nodded towards the only other significant furniture in the room: a small, spotlessly clean kitchen table and two chairs.

Chris picked up the crying baby and rocked her. She peered at him in amazement and fell silent. She had her mother's eyes. As he kept rocking the child, Chris had a chance to observe the room. There was something very cozy about it, despite the family's poverty. The walls had been plastered with layers of newspaper to provide some insulation. A cheerful pink curtain hung in front of the window and there was an assortment of photographs, some curled at the edges, carefully stuck to the wall above the chest of drawers. The room, with its low ceiling, reminded him of his tree house. The only difference was, when he got tired of his cramped tree house, he used to go back to the main house with its running water, kitchen, and TVs. For Thabo, this *was* the main house.

He remembered the hours he and his father had worked together on the tree house. Jacques seemed to get immense satisfaction from it, and thinking back now, Chris couldn't remember a time when the two of them had been so happy together. They had sawed and hammered and varnished; kitted the tree house out, put in place the rope ladder ... He had forgotten all about that. Now, it seemed like the last time he'd been really close to his father. He wondered where Thabo's father was.

The baby started to cry again.

"She's hungry," Thabo said. He reached into the kitchen dresser and fished out a jar of Purity. With one fluid twist, he popped off the lid and handed Chris the jar and a spoon. Chris tried to hide his ignorance; he'd never fed a baby before, and felt a little rattled by the crying. The first spoonful was spluttered and spat out all over the kitchen table.

Thabo laughed. "Got to stop her crying, then she can eat." He dipped a finger into the jar and gave it to the baby to suck.

Chris tried. It was the most surprising sensation to have his goo-covered finger sucked. He would never have thought that a baby could suck so hard. After a few minutes, he progressed to the spoon, and from then on, the whole operation was easy. He felt a great sense of accomplishment when, five minutes later, the jar was empty. Thabo showed him how to lift the baby against his shoulder and burp her.

Grace had fallen into a fitful sleep. Chris put Thabo's sister back into her cot. Then they went outside.

"Thabo, I hope you don't mind me asking, but where do you get money?"

"When my grandmother gets her pension, she send us money from Transkei. And other people here help."

"I see."

Thabo took out his cell phone. "I'm happy you came. I want to show you more pictures I took last night."

"Last night? What were you doing out last night? Thabo, I told you, I don't want you getting into trouble."

"My mother was not well yesterday, so the nurse said we must stay at Khanya for the night. When everyone else was asleep, I went down to the river. Just to think."

"*Ah ha!* Just to think, eh?"

Thabo nodded his head, all innocence. But he couldn't hide his excitement for long. "Those men, they came again."

"What time was that?"

"Late, maybe eleven o'clock. I saw them take the big box out of the barn. Same box I took the picture of the other day. They put her on the rubber boat on the river."

"You saw that?" Chris was excited. "And then, did you see where they went with the dinghy?"

Thabo was expertly pressing the buttons on his phone. "Something else. Here, look." He flashed through a number of dark, grainy pictures. "They went back and carried something else to the boat … a body."

"A body!?" Chris was stunned. "Are you sure?"

Thabo nodded his head vigorously. "Look, look at the picture."

Chris focused on the little screen and, indeed, one could make out two shadowy figures carrying something that looked distinctly like a body. *Could it ... could it be Bridget? Very likely.* The barn would have been an ideal location to hide her. Who would ever suspect it? Chris felt vindicated. All along, he had thought that there was a connection between Noble Enterprises and Bridget's kidnapping. It dawned on him that the connection was closer than expected. It appeared like an inside job, with Noble employees involved. That would explain it: disgruntled employees - a bunch of amateurs. A thought struck him – *God, has something gone wrong? Have they accidentally killed her?*

"Thabo, did she ... did the body seem to be alive?"

Thabo nodded.

"How do you know?"

"The one man say, 'Man, she's heavy. You should not have drugged her, she could have walked by herself.'"

Chris felt immensely relieved. *It must have been Bridget, and she was alive.*

Thabo continued, "I saw where they went."

"What!?"

Wordlessly, Thabo led the way, up the narrow path, back towards the two old men. They turned left and reached a patch of ground from which there was a clear view of the harbor.

Thabo pointed. "That big, big boat."

Chris followed his finger and saw a super-sized yacht lying at anchor far out in the harbor.

"Thabo, you're amazing. I should be very, very cross with you. But I'm not. You followed the rubber dinghy down the river to the beach?"

Thabo nodded and smiled.

Chris was very excited. "OK, so now what we have to ..."

There was a commotion up the street. Loud voices could be heard shouting and arguing. Someone cried out in pain. Instinctively, Thabo crouched down low against the side of the nearest shack and peered around the corner. He jerked back his head and drew in his breath, as if a viper had stung him. Chris looked at him, puzzled. Then, cautiously, he inched past Thabo, crouched low, and also looked around the corner. A gang of six men, led by the two Dragon Boys from the gym, swaggered down the street. Two had guns stuffed into their belts – they made no effort whatsoever to conceal these weapons. The old men had started a fight, loudly taunting the Dragon Boys. Abuse was being hurled back and forth. Thabo had regained his composure and, lying flat on the ground, stuck his head out next to Chris's.

The Dragon Boys' second-in-command clearly had had enough. He grabbed one of the old men, whipped out a knife, and held it against the man's neck. Thabo gasped. Several onlookers scurried away or averted their eyes. The gangster yelled at the old man and flung him to the ground. Then the group continued on their march down the path.

Thabo tugged at Chris's shirt. They withdrew and Thabo led the way down a narrow alley, away from the Dragon Boys. When he deemed it safe, he stopped, shook his head, and tapped his finger against his temple.

"The sun has made the old iluphala *crazy,"* Thabo whispered. *"You cannot speak like that to the gang men."*

Not crazy at all, Chris thought. *They were doing this deliberately to warn me.* He was overcome with a sense of gratitude. *You never know what form your guardian angels will take.* He promised himself that he would come back and thank the old men properly. They'd laid it all on the line for a perfect stranger. He was deeply relieved that neither of them had been seriously hurt.

"Thabo, listen. I've got to get to the car and get out of here. You must do me a favor – this is very important. You must send those pictures to Miss Wendy. I will meet with her later and can look at them properly on her computer. Then I can decide what to do. Will you do that for me?"

Thabo nodded.

Chris continued, "Can you please also tell Bull that I have gone to follow up a lead? I don't know when I'll be back."

He looked at the earnest upturned face. "Thank you, partner," he said, giving Thabo a fist-bump. The boy grinned broadly, and then he was gone. Chris turned and, with all his senses on high alert, zigzagged his way through the shacks till he reached his rent-a-wreck.

Julie had fled the building and found a corner in a coffee shop, where she sat down with a cappuccino and tried to collect her thoughts. It was pleasantly cool inside and she was grateful to hide in the cloud of anonymity provided by the hissing coffee machines, the chatty baristas, and a never-ending stream of customers. She looked out of the window at the crowded street. Queues were forming at the bus stop for the afternoon commute. A minibus taxi stopped abruptly in the middle of the road, resulting in a cacophony of angry hooter blasts; the taxi's co-driver leaned out of his window and cheerfully insulted the impatient drivers behind him, while soliciting business from people in the bus queue. After hurried negotiation, three women and a teenager broke away and squashed into the taxi.

"Dog eat dog; it's all about business." How often had Julie heard Greg say that?

Her eyes were drawn to the sheaf of printed emails that lay on the table next to her empty cappuccino cup. She felt the same sensation one gets when looking over the edge of a very high bridge; you know you shouldn't, and yet you cannot resist subjecting yourself to the siren attraction that threatens to pull you down into a dark abyss. The contents of the emails were seared into her brain and it hurt; it hurt like she imagined it would hurt to be branded with a red-hot iron; branded a fool – as a trusting, gullible, naïve, stupid fool. All Greg had ever wanted was Noble Enterprises, *her* company. He had deceived them all and she was acutely aware of what was at stake: everything her parents had worked so hard to achieve, not to mention the livelihood of several hundred loyal employees.

"You OK, miss?" The waitress sounded concerned and Julie managed a nod. She had to snap out of it. Like Charlie had said, there would be plenty of time for recrimination later.

"I'm fine, thanks." Julie pointed at the cup. "Can I have another, please?"

She read the papers once more, and this time she was able to contain her anger and emotion and be more analytical. It was clear from the emails that Greg's relationship with the Malaysians, Mr. Lim and Mr. Goh, went much deeper than a normal business relationship. The two men appeared to be very well connected in Hong Kong, and Greg had worked with them to supply merchandize that they could not buy legitimately. Her skin felt hot. *Not only had Greg stooped to an unthinkably low level, but he had also used the resources of Noble Enterprise to develop and manufacture....*

Her cell phone rang and she saw from the caller ID that it was him – it was Greg. She closed her eyes and let the phone ring three more times before greeting him in a calm voice.

He sounded hurried and there was concern in his voice. "There's been another development – can you meet me in Matt's office?"

"Oh my God, what's happened to my mother?" Julie couldn't breathe – it was as though a see-through sound barrier had sprung up around her. She could see the baristas talking to customers, but heard no sound; another taxi had stopped, but this time its occupants were mute. Through a pin-hole in the sound barrier, she heard Greg's voice: "Nothing to do with your mother; it's Matt. He's been taken ill; we think it might be a heart attack. The ambulance left twenty minutes ago."

She gasped. "What ... how ...? You should have told me! Immediately!"

"I'm sorry – it's just been so crazy. " She could hear weariness in his voice. "The paramedics seemed to think he was not in imminent danger. We'll know more in an hour." Quickly, he added, "I am sure it is just exhaustion."

Julie hurried back to the office. All the way up in the elevator, she chided herself for feeling relieved that it was "only Matt having a heart attack". She caught up with Greg outside the boardroom.

"Darling, you look done in. I'm worried about you." Greg sounded genuinely concerned.

She avoided his attempt to hug her by launching into a barrage of questions about Matt. There really was nothing much more to tell, however. Matt's secretary, Felicity, had raised the alarm and, even though Matt tried to protest, he had been taken to the Sunninghill hospital. Greg assured her that a top cardiologist was on the case.

Julie did not trust herself to look him in the eyes; she was afraid that he would see her anger and contempt. Instead, she looked out across the city and asked what the latest plans were with respect to her mother.

He pointed to the door behind him. "The board are assembled for an emergency meeting; we can no longer hide the fact that your mother's been kidnapped. For one thing, we need board approval to free up the money for the ransom."

She had a strong impulse to march past him, straight into the board meeting. It was intolerable that, with both Bridget and Matt out of action, the company be left in the hands of Greg – a scheming crook, a liar, and … and – she still found it hard to acknowledge - a supplier of rhino horn, an accessory to the brutal mutilation and annihilation of an endangered species. She could expose him to the board right there and then with the print-out that was sitting in her handbag like a ton of toxic waste.

Julie reined in her thoughts and kept her eyes on the horizon. She needed to keep a cool head. Nothing would be gained by throwing all her cards on the table at this point. Greg, fortunately, seemed to interpret her detached demeanor as a sign of stress and tiredness. "You really should go home and lie down a bit," he said, the picture of solicitude. "I can call you …"

Julie thought, *The company is facing its biggest crisis ever, and I'm supposed to go home and lie down!* It was almost too patronizing to bear. But, at the same time, she realized that Greg's arrogance was also his greatest weakness. He would underestimate her; he always had. And that gave her room to maneuver.

As if partially reading her thoughts, Greg said, "Julie, you know I only have your very best interest at heart. If you are not comfortable with this arrangement …"

"No, no, of course it's fine." She forced a smile and, for the first time since learning the horrible truth, summoned the courage to look him directly in the eyes. "I'm just absorbing the shock about Matt." Her mind was racing. *I have to get out of here, back to Cape Town.* Every minute spent in Johannesburg was a minute wasted.

"How's the ransom money getting to Cape Town?"

He looked at his watch. "The money is already on the plane with the pilots on stand-by. The board's approval is a mere formality," he said, raising his hand in a dismissive gesture. "The plane should be leaving within the hour." He looked at her sharply. "Stop worrying; I've got it all in hand."

"What happens when the plane gets to Cape Town?"

"One of our people will meet it. Then we wait till we get final instructions from the kidnappers."

"Who is this person in Cape Town?" Julie asked innocently.

He put a finger under her chin and lifted it so that again she had to look into his face. *Why did I never notice how greasy his hair is? And he's far too old for all that gel.* She noticed, too, the crow's feet extending from the edges of his eyes. As for those eyes, she couldn't read any expression in those deep gray pools.

"My, my, we *are* full of questions," he said.

She took a step back, but held his gaze. "That shouldn't surprise you. My mother's life is at stake here. I do believe I have a right to know."

"It's a man I trust implicitly – he's worked for me for many years. I believe it might be better if we keep his identity secret for the moment." His tone was abrupt, brooking no argument.

Julie had to summon all her guile and acting skills to suppress her anger. *How dare he treat me like a child?* But she realized that, right now, she had to put on the performance of a lifetime. She dared not let him suspect that she was on to him. Hence her voice was diffident when she fluttered her eyelashes and said, "You know, Greg, you're right. I *am* feeling exhausted and I think there's no point in me sticking around here; you obviously have everything well in hand. I think I might just drop by the hospital to see how Matt is doing and then go home."

"That's my gal," he said, his voice all solicitous sweetness again. "Shall I call a driver?"

"Oh, no, no; you have enough on your mind. I'll take Matt's car."

"Call me from the hospital," he said.

"I will ... darling." She leaned forward and kissed his cheek. The stubble touching her lips used to feel so manly, mature, and exciting. Now it seemed to be the hallmark of unfeeling roughness. She had to close her eyes to deal with the flood of conflicting emotions: loathing and anger, certainly, but also a hint of sadness. Greg had been a pillar in her life for as long as she could remember. She had trusted him, relied on him, imagined a future with him – and now all that was gone for ever.

She watched as Greg turned, slicked back his hair with both hands, and paused before shoving open the heavy double doors to the boardroom. He had always believed in a grand entrance.

Julie didn't even wait for the doors to close behind him. She raced to Matt's office, where Felicity interpreted her hurry as a mark of concern for Matt's health. The woman willingly handed over Matt's car keys and shouted after Julie, "Don't go breaking your neck, now. He's a tough old thing. He can wait for you – the doctor says it's not all that bad."

She had to rein in her impatience through several red lights. Mercifully, the traffic eased up once she got on to the highway and, as the speedometer needle inched towards 150 kilometers an hour, she said a silent prayer, *Please God, keep the traffic cops away.* When the turn-off for the Sunninghill hospital came into view, though, she ignored it. Instead, she put her foot down and kept going till she reached the signs for the airport.

Julie dropped the car with valet parking, and purposefully strode through the small terminal building and out on to the tarmac. The Noble pilot had just signed for his fuel and was about to board the plane when he saw her. He greeted her and peered into the distance behind her, as if to look for a porter or someone carrying luggage.

Julie forced a broad smile and kept her tone light as she said, "Do you have space for one more? I have no luggage - last minute decision. I want to surprise a friend in Cape Town."

The pilot tipped his hat. "It will be our pleasure. You are, in fact, our only passenger today; just flying down a briefcase with documents."

As she boarded the plane, the co-pilot turned in his seat. "Hi there; had enough of Joey's already?" He smirked. "Afraid I don't have time to get coffee. We've just had the all-clear; Cape Town's waiting for those papers." He nodded in the direction of an aluminum case, wedged underneath one of the seats.

If only you knew... Julie thought, and settled into the seat furthest from the cockpit. She never expected any of the Noble staff to be diffident, but she felt the co-pilot was a touch too casual towards her. She watched him flick quickly through the switches above him. He seemed a bit slapdash – and it did not inspire confidence.

"Do I have time to make a quick call?" she asked.

"Knock yourself out," the co-pilot said, and earned himself a disapproving look from his superior.

Julie desperately wanted to speak to Chris and tell him what she'd learned. But she hesitated, undecided. She was beginning to wonder if her phone was being tapped, and she didn't want to put her mother or Chris in even greater danger. Or maybe she was just being paranoid? She stole a glance towards the cockpit. The pilots weren't paying any attention to her.

The plane began to taxi towards the runway. Late afternoon was a busy time at Lanseria and they joined a queue of other planes. Julie decided that the muffled sound of the jet engines provided a perfect sound screen; the pilots would not be able to hear her conversation. She dialed.

#

In the cockpit, the co-pilot took out his cell phone and made a call. The sound screen worked both ways; hence he knew that Julie would not be able to hear his conversation.

He said, "The songbird has joined us for the flight to Cape Town."

"Is that so? The cunning little minx; I didn't think she had it in her."

"What do you want me to do?" the co-pilot asked

"Nothing – Lenny will take care of it on arrival."

"OK."

The pilot looked at his colleague and asked, "What was that all about?"

"Oh, nothing, nothing. Just checking if my buddy wants to meet me at the airport. He's been wanting to meet Miss Noble here for a long time." He made a gesture with his thumb, jerking it over his shoulder.

The pilot gave him a sharp look and said, "That is completely unprofessional of you, how …"

"Don't get yourself all twisted – my buddy is busy, anyway, and can't make it."

The pilot was about to respond, but at that moment the control tower crackled over the radio.

"We'll talk about this later," the pilot said, and opened the throttle.

##

Chris managed to find his way out of Mandela Park without further incident. He decided that it was too early to go to Wendy's house; he wanted to wait for nightfall before visiting her. *Where should I hide?* he wondered. Phrases from various TV programs and books shot through his mind, 'Hiding in plain sight', 'Security through obscurity', 'The most obvious place is the last place anyone would look for you'. He steered the car towards Hout Bay beach, which was packed with Capetonians trying to escape the afternoon heat.

The car park was arranged as a one-way system and stretched for a mile along the beach. Slowly, he drove the full length, but had no luck in finding an empty spot. At the exit, he was forced to get back on to the main road. He stopped, undecided as to whether he should loop back to the entrance and try again, or go someplace else. For a fleeting moment, Chris again felt the unnerving sensation of being an outlaw – always on the move, nowhere to go. He couldn't go home, couldn't visit his friends. With some longing, he looked at the crowd on the balcony of a beach bar. He couldn't even sit in a pub and have a beer!

A car behind him hooted. Chris resisted the urge to show the driver the finger. The last thing he needed now was a road-rage confrontation. He swung right and drove back to the entrance to the car park. This time he was lucky; a car pulled out right near the entrance and one of the ever-present car guards motioned him into the spot. He gave the man five rand – not too much, not too little; hopefully, the car-guard would not remember him.

Chris took off his shoes, rolled up his jeans - just another guy enjoying a stroll on the beach. The smell of tanning lotion and watermelon hung in the air. He passed a group of eight young people, settling in for an evening barbecue. A brown-haired girl strummed a guitar whilst two of the guys worked on getting a fire going. The others, beers in hand, were offering advice. To Chris, it seemed like decades since the last time he and a group of friends had had a spontaneous *braai* on the beach. A glance at the group's packets of chops and sausages made him feel hungry.

Out, beyond the breakers, a group of surfers bobbed on the water. Beyond them were the usual mix of sailboats, windsurfers, and kayaks. Chris looked out to towards the large boat, which sat serenely amongst the swirling minions. Yachts around the Cape tended to be built for fishing or racing in rough seas – they were generally less than thirty meters long. This particular boat was an unusual site. It was a sleek, ocean-going yacht, more like a small cruise ship, with three decks. He guessed her to be about the length of a tennis court. Her name was painted in cursive script along the bow: *Moonflower*.

When a pair of kayaks came close to the *Moonflower*, the crew gesticulated and shooed them away. Chris wondered whether the crew were armed - and guessed that they probably were.

The smell of grilled meat, drifting from a vendor cart, attracted his attention. He realized that he had not eaten anything all day, other than a few slices of bread and jam, which the police had shoved into his cell nearly twelve hours ago. He sauntered across to the cart and bought a *boerewors* hot dog.

The vendor had the weather-beaten skin of a fisherman or farmer, and teeth that bore testimony to a lifetime of smoking. He inhaled deeply on his cigarette as he turned the sausages on the grill and said, "You're lucky. I'm nearly sold out."

"Yeah, I suppose it's the nice weather that brings everyone to the beach."

"Not just that. See that big boat out there? They're my best new customers. Can't seem to get enough of my *boerewors* and chicken *sosaties*."

Chris kept his voice casual. "I've not seen the boat before."

The vendor squinted into the setting sun, turning his forehead into a set of deep ravines above a forest of bushy eyebrows. "Never seen anything like it here in Hout Bay. That is one fucking beautiful bitch of a boat. I'd give my left testicle to cruise away on that baby."

Chris asked, "How long have they been here?"

"Came last Tuesday. Every once in a while, they send a couple of guys on a dinghy to get food from me."

"Have you had a chance to talk much to them?"

The man was a treasure-trove of information. It did not take much prompting for Chris to find out that the *Moonflower* belonged to a tycoon from Malaysia. Some of the crew spoke passable English, but they mainly kept to themselves.

The vendor said, "The crew are pissed off because their captain won't give them shore leave. They're looking for a bit of action." He grinned and made a lewd gesture. "The owners are off somewhere, no doubt getting *their* piece of action, so I can understand why the men are unhappy."

Chris took a bite of his hot dog and looked out to sea, where jagged sunlight reflected off the water. It occurred to him that the afternoon would be a very bad time to approach the yacht from the beach, but early morning would be a different story; then the light would be in the eyes of the ship's crew.

310

A slight breeze unfurled the flag of the boat; *what was a Malaysian registered vessel doing in Hout Bay harbor? And more to the point, what did Malaysians have to do with Bridget Noble-Baxter?* He hoped that Wendy might be able to shed some light on these questions.

"How many hot dogs do they buy at a time?" Chris asked.

The vendor jerked up his head and narrowed his eyes. "What's it to you? You trying to take away my business?"

"No, no. Just asking. Hey, no big deal. I was just thinking what pressure it is for you when there is suddenly a big order like that."

The man seemed mollified. "Pressure? Man, you have no idea. They rock up here and then they want twelve or fifteen chicken *sosaties* all at once. And, of course, it all has to be halal. *That's* pressure, man. Hectic, I tell you. I like the business, but I'll be pleased when they're gone."

"When they're gone?" Chris was alarmed.

"Leaving tomorrow – so, you see, there's no business for you steal, anyway."

"Don't worry," Chris said. "I don't think I'd be up to it. As you say, too much pressure."

He bought a second hot dog and picked his way amongst sandcastles, sunbathers, exuberant dogs, and groups of kids playing soccer till he got down to the gleaming sea. The cool water swirled around his feet. He curled up his toes and tried to prevent the sand erosion from under his feet. The irony was not lost on Chris; the life he knew, like the sand he stood on, was rapidly eroding away.

His phone rang; it was Julie.

"Chris, are you OK? I heard you'd been arrested and escaped."

"Who told you?"

"The police, of course. Remember we have regular briefings. But, listen, I have something really important to tell you." Her voice dropped. "I have found out ... certain things."

"Can you speak up? I can barely hear you."

"I can't really talk," she said, her voice an urgent whisper. "I'm on the plane back to Cape Town. Should be there in a couple of hours."

"Shall I come to meet you?"

"No, no, no. That would be much too dangerous – I have found out … certain things. The deceit in the company goes right up to … the top – and the police are in cahoots. I have documents to prove it. I'll call you once I've landed."

He could hear the anxiety in her voice. He wanted to tell her that he was on her mother's track, to say something reassuring, but he was also worried that their calls were being monitored. He had to be careful what he said.

"I keep thinking of that night on the beach," he began.

"Are you on the beach right now? I thought I heard waves in the background."

Bugger, Chris thought. He covered the mouthpiece and hastily jogged away from the sea to a nearby dune.

"Chris, Chris? We're about to take off. I'll have to go now … Chris?"

"Sorry, lost signal there for a minute. Just remember, we have to end where we started." Even as he said it, he thought it sounded like the corny stuff one hears in crappy movies. But he couldn't think of anything else that might tell Julie where to find him.

After a pause, her voice came in a whisper: *"I've also thought about that night on the b... under the moonlight... a lot. Be careful ... I miss you."*

He slipped the phone back in his pocket and looked out to sea, savoring the moment. An old couple walked past. She was one step ahead, a deep – and probably permanent - scowl on her face. The husband, stooped with arthritis, struggled to keep up.

"Great evening, isn't it?" Chris said to them, smiling broadly, Julie's final words singing in his head.

The husband focused his milky eyes on Chris. Then he turned around awkwardly to see if there was someone behind him. Having ascertained that Chris was indeed addressing him and his wife, he was about to say something when his wife cut it, "Come along Herb!" She nodded curtly in Chris' general direction. As they walked off she spoke to her husband in the insolent manner of some old people, "Must be an imbecile to stand there smiling. What's there to smile about? Should mind his own business."

Chris had a mental flash of him and Julie, old and wizened, walking on the beach together. *Would they be as grumpy? Never!* He closed his eyes. The breeze tugged at his hair and cooled his chest; the late afternoon sun cast a glow on his face. It seemed crazy, but he felt as light as a cloud, happy. *Is this what it felt like to be in love, truly in love?* To think think that he might have caved in to the temptations of that devil Bob Richter. He could have ended up married to Sandra, and would have cheated himself of these strange and wondrous feelings. At this moment, his escape from the Richters seemed far more significant than his jailbreak.

He inhaled the tangy smell of ocean spray and listened to the symphony of surf and seagulls and laughing children and ... the sound of a police siren.

His eyes flew open. From atop the dune, he saw them coming: an official police vehicle with blue lights flashing and an unmarked car close behind it. Chris immediately recognized Sergeant Vervey's dirty gray Camry. He willed himself to remain calm and started walking in the direction of his car. How had they found him so quickly? He'd underestimated Vervey.

The police vehicle mercifully turned off its sirens, drove the length of the car park, and took up position at the exit. The uniformed officers got out and proceeded to stop a vehicle that was aiming to leave. They peered inside, then waved the vehicle on. Sergeant Vervey joined them; he appeared to be looking intently up and down the beach.

Chris reached the nearest row of cars and bent down, pretending to wipe sand off his feet. He measured the distance to the police with his eyes. If he drove up slowly, and then suddenly accelerated, would he be able to surprise them? Surely they wouldn't actually *shoot* at him? The biggest risk was that there might be a slow vehicle ahead of him, preventing him from racing past the police and out of the car park. The gap was narrow; they had half-blocked the entrance with their vehicles. Still, he thought he might have a chance.

He got into the rent-a-wreck. For a while, he just sat, gripped the steering wheel, and pictured the path he would take. *Reverse out slowly and approach the police at a measured pace; don't arouse suspicion. Once close enough, floor the car, and veer to the gap on the right.* In his mind, he could feel the wheels leaving the asphalt, moving on to sand. This would be the tricky bit; too far to the left, he'd hit the police car; too far to the right, and the sand would stop him. Chris summonsed up memories of the hours he'd spent with friends at the go-kart track when he was sixteen. He'd enjoyed the thrill of the race, the squealing tires, and the smell of rubber. And he was good at racing. He'd usually finish in first or second place - except, of course, for the time his father had come to watch and Chris had miscalculated the hairpin bend on the third lap. He could still hear his father's disappointment, those damning words: *"Well, you tried ..."*

Focus! You can do this.

He started the engine and put the car into reverse.

A bang on the roof made Chris jump out of his skin. A face appeared right next to him: the car-guard. He motioned for Chris to open the window and said, "Hey, boss, the fucking police is screwing around that end. *Naai hulle.* This is bad for business. Just reverse her out this way."

He gave the car roof another pat and jogged to the entrance of the car park, where he stopped a vehicle that was about to turn in, gesturing expansively. Meanwhile, Chris didn't need any encouragement to swiftly reverse the rent-a-wreck out towards to the main road. A vehicle had been waiting patiently to turn into the car park, and as he passed, he nodded his thanks to the driver ... and froze. The driver was Inspector Musamil Ibrahim. Their eyes locked and Chris felt a chill run down his spine as he looked at the man's cold, expressionless face.

"Damn!" He slammed the car into first gear and floored it so hard that it lurched forwards with a shuddering squeal.

In his rear-view mirror, he could see the inspector do a rapid three-point turn.

As Chris hurtled up the street, he felt as if he was having an out-of-body experience. A part of him was back on the go-kart track, expertly cornering at maximum speed and enjoying the thrill of the race. The other part of him was like the eternal prey, trying frantically to outpace and outwit a predator.

How the hell can I shake him off? And where am I going to get another car from? In the movies, it always seemed so easy. People jumped on a motorbike that conveniently had its engine running, or hijacked a car – the keys, remarkably, still in the ignition –at a petrol station.

He took a sharp right and had barely gone three blocks when he saw the inspector's car behind him. He gritted his teeth and pushed the wreck to its limit; a sharp left, followed by a sharp right, through the car park of a church, and back down to the main road. He bore down on the traffic circle with such determination that two other vehicles came to a screeching halt and let him pass. A quick look in the mirror showed him that he had gained a couple of seconds. The inspector was caught at the circle.

In a flash, Chris remembered that Riaan, of the Toreros, lived in Hout Bay with his parents, who had sold their farm a few years earlier and retired to the coast. The house was very close to where he was now, set back from the road, and surrounded by a high hedge. And he remembered that there were garages at the back of the property. It seemed a heaven-sent opportunity.

He took out his cell phone and found the number. The maneuver nearly sent him flying into one of the oak trees that lined the narrow street. Riaan's mother answered after the fourth ring.

"Chris, what a pleasant surprise! You've been much too scarce."

"Hello, Nina. Is Riaan there?" He tried to control the urgency in his voice.

"No, but I have a wonderful *bobotie* in the oven. There's more than enough for ..."

"Nina, look, sorry, I need your help. There are some bad people chasing me."

"What? I don't understand. Where ..."

"I'll explain later. It's ... er... some road-rage maniac." Chris felt bad about the white lie, but didn't want to complicate things by telling her that the police was chasing him.

"I'm about to turn up Valley Road. When I tell you, can you please open your gates?"

"Chris, what ... "

"Please, Nina, do this for me! Have you got the gate's remote control?"

"Yes, yes, I'm going out on to the balcony now."

"Immediately, when I'm through the gate, you must shut it."

"OK. I think I can see you, are you in that little white ..."

Chris looked in the rear-view mirror; there was no sign of the inspector.

"Open the gate! Now!" he shouted.

The heavy iron gate was three-quarters open when he got there, Nina, on the balcony, aiming the remote like a laser weapon from *Star Wars*. Chris barely slowed; with a quick prayer, he shot through the gate and up the driveway to the garages.

Nina came rushing over to where he sat, breathing heavily, at the wheel of the car. "This is so exciting!" She put her plump arms around him and gave him a huge hug. He smelled the aroma of freshly-baked scones and felt enveloped in an invisible cloud of hominess.

"We should call the police!" Nina said, releasing him.

"No, no, that's not a good idea. Nina, I have to tell you, it's actually the police who are chasing me."

Her eyes grew wide and her mouth formed a matching circle as she said, "Oh?"

"I'm sorry, I didn't know where else to turn."

"Chris, you don't need to explain, and I'm glad you came to us. Whatever it is, I'm sure we can sit down and figure it out. Riaan should be home soon. I've just baked some scones. Come, I'll make you a nice cup of tea."

Chris was deeply touched by this unquestioning support. He smiled ruefully. "There's nothing I'd rather do than have one of your scones, but it'll have to wait for another time." He paused. "Do you think you could lend me a car?"

She eyed him for a moment. "Judging from the way you came through that gate, I'm not letting you drive my Benz, but you're welcome to take the old *bakkie*." She pointed at a blue pick-up.

"That would be perfect." He followed her inside and she handed him a set of keys, along with a suitably concealing wide-brimmed cloth hat.

"One more thing, Nina. You must give me about a ten minutes start, and then I want you to put the rent-a-wreck in the street and call the police."

"Why? I really don't like doing this. And what shall I tell them?"

"You've got the vehicle of a fugitive sitting in your driveway, Nina – you need to get it off your property and then explain why it's in the street outside. Call the police and tell them that you were in the *bakkie*, waiting for the gate to open, when someone jumped out at you with a knife and hijacked your vehicle. Then you can say that the hijacker left that wreck standing in the road."

"Oh, Chris. I don't want to get you into more trouble."

"I'm in so much trouble already that one extra car hijacking doesn't matter. But the police must think that I took the *bakkie* from you by force. Otherwise you'll be an accessory." He saw the doubt on her face and decided to play on one of her great passions: amateur theatre. "Nina, if the police come to question you, it will be a chance to really put your acting skills to some good use. Think of it as an audition."

She looked at him for a moment, then started to hyperventilate, fanning herself with both hands. "Oh, officer, it was too terrible! Such things aren't supposed to happen in this neighborhood!" She rolled her eyes. "I was so scared, I didn't even get a good look at him, I think maybe there were two ... or three of them. Wearing sunglasses. He had blond hair, no ... wait, maybe it was brown, or more like reddish-brown." She winked.

"You're good," he said, and smiled.

She gave him another hug. "I want to hear the full story later, OK? And if you need help, you always know where to find us."

A couple of minutes after this, Chris watched her standing on the balcony, waving, as he drove the *bakkie* down the driveway. He had a lump in his throat; Nina's willingness to help him had restored his faith in human nature, something that had been sorely tested in recent days.

He pulled the hat lower over his forehead as the *bakkie* trundled along at a leisurely pace, still pinching himself that he had got away with it – so far. Now, he just had to hope that the belching diesel clouds from his exhaust didn't attract the attention of any cops.

##

Chapter 19: Catch You Now

Wednesday evening

The Pajero was parked in a distant, dark corner of Cape Town airport's car park. Cindy's eyes swept the area in front of the vehicle like a set of prison-yard searchlights. Without looking down, she reached to an ankle holster, pulled out a knife, and started to polish the blade with a piece of cloth. It was a treasured possession, this cloth, hand-woven in Brussels. She'd bought it in a shop next door to the unassuming little place where she had acquired some of her most prized knives.

Next to her, Lenny was on his cell phone. When Lenny was angry, his voice tended to rise, and that was happening now. "How the fuck could you let him get away?" he shouted, sounding like an enraged fishwife. "I ask you to do this one little thing, one thing ..."

In the confined space of the vehicle, Cindy could hear both sides of the conversation. The underling, who had raised Lenny's ire, was sullen. *"Sorry, boss, but ..."*

"Don't 'sorry, boss' me! You're such a dumb *doos*; the most pathetic *lamsak bleddy* excuse of a Dragon Boy I've ever come across!" He punched the steering wheel in frustration and ignored Cindy's frown. "I have a good mind to cut your balls off – except you probably don't have any!"

He ignored the man's protest and raged on: "I thought you and the boys might enjoy this. I give you a present on a platter – what did I say to you ... *heh, heh?* What did I say?"

"You said we should have a bit of fun with the white boy; teach him a lesson."

Lenny continued, "Yeah ... that's exactly what I said. When last have you and your friends had a gift like that? Tell me? *Heh?* I look after my brothers. But what do I get? *Heh ... heh?* Bugger all - nothing! That's what I get. Sweet fuck-all! You let the cunt escape. If the police catch him before we do, I swear, I'll personally make you pay ..."

"Lenny..."

"What?" He covered the mouthpiece and turned to look at Cindy.

"You're wasting your time with those morons," she said. "You're just going to give yourself a heart attack."

"Stay out of this, woman! This is between me and ..."

She did not look at him, but held up the blade to inspect its surgical edges in the dim light. Her voice was as icy-blue as the blade when she spoke: "You will not speak to me in that tone. I am not one of your baboons." She spun the knife around her index finger and looked straight ahead towards the control tower.

He was immediately contrite. "Sorry, look, I'm really sorry. Let me just deal with the guys ... OK?"

Cindy ignored him; her attention was now consumed by the lights of a small plane coming in to land.

Lenny uncovered the mouthpiece and said, "Now, listen. You and your boys get your asses down to the harbor. Sooner or later, that meddling son-of-a-bitch will show up there. I don't care what you do with him, but you make sure he does not get anywhere near the *Moonflower*. You hear me?"

"Yes, boss."

"Stay out of sight. So far, the big boss is making sure that the police are diverted away from the harbor – but we don't know for how long. We don't need any crap with the cops, OK?"

"Yes, boss."

"Call me once you've dealt with him."

He flipped his phone shut.

"They're here," she said. "Let's go."

As they drove past the terminal buildings, Lenny stayed in the outside lane to avoid the lights. They stopped at a gate marked "VIP", where a guard approached and motioned for Lenny to lower his window.

Cindy leaned across and smiled. "Good evening – we're here to pick up the pilots from the Noble plane." She handed over two ID cards.

The guard studied the IDs before he walked into the cone of light from the headlights and started to write down the number on the license plate on a clipboard. He frowned. Cindy's face was a smiling mask, while her hand rested on her knee, inches from the holstered knife. The guard rifled through various sheets of paper on his clipboard, and then disappeared into his booth.

"What the fuck ...?" Lenny muttered.

"I bet you the old bitch reported the license plate number to the police after you gave her that fright on the road near Camps Bay," she said.

"Greg is convinced that she hadn't."

"Greg doesn't know everything. The old bag could well have lied to him. Oh God, if they have a warrant out for the car ... that's all we need."

"I told you ..."

"And *I* told *you* that it was a dumb idea to try and run her off the road. There are many far more subtle ways to scare a person. You are such an imbecile, at times. What if he calls the police?"

"He won't," Lenny said. He opened his jacket, to let it hang loose, and reached for the grip in the holster under his arm.

"Look at the cameras," she hissed, through clenched teeth. *"And try not to do anything stupid ..."*

The guard re-emerged, handed back the ID cards, and said, "Sorry for the wait. We have a new guy on day shift and he put the authorization form in the wrong place. I just found it."

He stepped aside, opened the gate with a flourish, and watched them pass.

Cindy looked at the guard's beaming face in the side-view mirror and muttered, *"What does he expect? A frigging medal?"*

##

When the plane started its descent, Julie woke with a start. She was surprised to find that she had dozed off and it took her a moment to realize where she was. The pilots were silhouetted in the eerie glow from the cockpit. The plane banked and she got a striking view of Table Bay and the city. The sensuous line of the bay was made visible by the twinkling of thousands upon thousands of lights that flowed like a river. Following the curve of this "river", one could see the fountainhead: the high-rise buildings of central Cape Town nestled against Table Mountain, which provided a craggy backdrop for the exuberant play of light and life.

Where is Chris now? She wished she'd asked him to meet her at the airport, because she did not dare use her phone again; she was now convinced that it was monitored, and it could therefore lead Greg's people - or the police - to Chris. Hopefully, they would somehow be able to meet up, either in Hout Bay or at Wendy's. Julie thought through the logistics; she'd left Johannesburg without thinking about her next steps. Normally, Greg would have ensured that there was a driver to meet her at the airport; now there would be no one, and she certainly was not going to entrust her life to some unknown taxi-driver. Better to rent a car.

Julie's initial shock had started to wear off, and she found that she was now able to periodically block her feelings of hurt and betrayal. It was like pushing the coats of dinner guests into an overstuffed closet - not a permanent solution, but sufficient to allow her to function for a while. In one such clear-minded moment, just after the plane had taken off, she had tried to piece together what was going on. Greg had masterminded her mother's kidnapping, this she knew for certain. She was also convinced that he had bought off the investigating police officers. Their lack of urgency, and the fact that they persisted in running the investigation from Johannesburg when her mother had been kidnapped in Cape Town, indicated delaying tactics. This thought made her clutch her handbag, with its incriminating print-out of emails, tightly in her lap. She knew that, in themselves, the emails were probably insufficient proof to convict anyone, but they ought to be enough to get the attention of someone in law enforcement. The snag was, who? *How high up did the corruption go?* She was going to need Wendy's help. Wendy, through her lawyers, would be able to get through to the Special Crimes Unit.

As she sat in the plane, going over and over what she now knew, Julie had desperately wanted to take out the papers and study them properly. But she did not dare do so till she was alone. She still did not trust her emotions - and, of course, there was no telling who had been coerced into doing Greg's dirty work, or who was paid by him to do it.

There was one email, however, that she did not need to look at again, because it was imprinted on her mind. It had been written a few days earlier:

From: Gregory.Louw@noble.co.za

To: SK.Goh@asianenterprises.com

Dear Mr. Goh

I look forward to our meeting on Sunday and trust that you and your colleagues have had a comfortable cruise so far. I do so much admire the way you manage to combine business with pleasure and trust that the seas will be calm for your journey home.

The next crate of our delivery is ready and waiting in Hout Bay and can be brought to the yacht at your convenience.

A delicate matter has arisen in which we require your assistance. The wife of our managing director has not been in good health of late and has suffered a nervous breakdown. Our MD would like to spare her the prying eyes of the media. We believe a period of seclusion on a cruise, followed by some time spent in comfortable surroundings on one of the Malaysian islands, would help her recover in body and spirit.

You would do us an inestimable honor, and further cement the strong ties between our enterprises, if you would consider taking her as a passenger on board the Moonflower. *Two caregivers, whom I hold in very high regard, would accompany her, and we would obviously credit a suitable discount on the merchandize ...*

The plane lurched as it neared the ground. Julie looked out at the desolate sea of squatter huts that washed right up to the fence of the airport, and her anxiety kicked in again. The settlement below, dimly lit by wood fires and kerosene, seemed to exude an atmosphere of menace that reflected her own situation. Julie could actually smell the acrid smoke that added to the gloom. She was suddenly acutely aware of her own vulnerability. *Am I going to be safe in my apartment? But surely Greg wouldn't dare do anything to endanger me ... or would he?* She suddenly remembered the bugging device that Chris had found on the picture rail, and how she had naïvely dismissed it as something left by a previous occupant. She shivered. Maybe she could go to her mother's house in Constantia - at least that was within a security estate, and she could alert the guards if she needed to. But the thought of her mother's cavernous, empty house made her shiver even more.

As if he read her mind, the pilot turned and asked, "Miss Noble, how will you be getting home?"

"I'll just rent a car."

"Are you sure? I have my car parked at the airport; I'll be heading towards the southern suburbs."

The co-pilot said nothing.

"That's really kind of you. But you've had a long day; I don't want to take you out of your way. I'll be fine." Under normal circumstances, she would have happily accepted the pilot's offer. He was an older man, and he reminded her a little of her father. But what had happened today had turned the world she had known on its head. Greg's deceit had shifted the tectonic plates on which her perceptions, especially her perceptions of men, had been founded. It was safer not to trust anyone.

Steeling herself for what lay ahead, she fastened her seat belt for the descent.

##

The co-pilot reached up to give Julie a hand down the steps. She emerged into night air that was tainted by the smell of jet fuel. The plane was parked far away from the bustle of the terminal.

"Thanks, I'm OK. I've done this before, you know." She smiled.

"Oh, but I insist."

His grip on her wrist seemed firmer than necessary, and he did not let go when she set foot on the tarmac, despite her attempt to pull away. A shaft of light fell from the plane's door and illuminated the figure of a woman waiting a few meters away. Silently, they looked at each other. Then, with a shock, Julie noticed another shadowy figure in the dark, a few meters behind the woman. *Who are these people?* Julie looked at the co-pilot and tried again to free her arm from his grip.

The woman, eerily pale, with bright-red lipstick, stepped forward. She tossed back her platinum-blonde hair and said, "Julie, I presume? Greg asked us to look after you."

"Greg?"

"Yes, Greg; you know, your fiancé? He's concerned about you."

Julie had come across her fair share of meanness hiding behind cosmetic smiles; but, even in the limited light, she could see that this woman was in a class of her own. The lips were pulled wide, but the face did not smile.

Julie held herself erect and was relieved that the light was behind her; the woman had hopefully not noticed her shock. Somehow, she had not expected Greg to react so fast. *How has he found out that I'm on to him?* She blamed herself for underestimating him and resolved to be more vigilant. Then she mustered her most mannered, finishing-school tone of voice: "That is so like Greg. How very thoughtful of him. But you really should not have troubled yourselves."

Julie's senses were on high alert. Time seemed to have slowed down. She was conscious of the strong breeze lifting a few strands of her hair and tossing them about. She felt the smooth strength of the co-pilot's grip on her wrist. She smelled the wood fires, heard the wailing of an ambulance siren on the highway. She strained her eyes to make out the dark features of the man who kept in the shadows a few meters behind the woman. There was something familiar about him. It took her a few moments to make the connection: *he's the man in the white suit who stalked me at the De Waterkant Club!* She drew in her breath and felt a numbness spreading. *What had the woman said? "Greg asked us to look after you ..."*

For an instant, all sound around her appeared wiped away. It was as though her brain had to shut out any new information whilst she processed the realization that this man – this stalker - worked for Greg. How long had Greg had her under surveillance? How long had he been plotting against her family? *Was there no limit to his treachery?* A bubble of fury started to rise in her chest. What a fool she'd been to ignore all the signs ... But then her mind jerked back into the present, and to the imminent danger she found herself in.

A man in yellow overalls, who had been clamping the jet's wheels, was walking back to his van which was parked a short distance away. As he got into his vehicle, Julie realized, with a sickening jolt, that once he had gone, so too was all hope of rescue. Throwing her handbag to the ground to free up her arm, she began to wave frantically, shouting at the man to stop. But the breeze, and the sound of the van's engine, drowned her voice. The man waved back and drove off.

"Let go of me!" Julie said to the co-pilot, trying hard to keep any tremor out of her voice. The smell of jet fuel was making her feel nauseous.

"Let her go," the dark man said from the shadows. "She's not going anywhere. Where's the money ... I mean ... the case with the documents?"

"Asshole!" the women hissed at him.

"Shut your mouth, woman," he retorted.

Just then, the pilot appeared at the top of the steps. Julie had completely forgotten about him. "What's going on here? Miss Noble, is everything OK?"

"No, it's not ... *ouuww!*" She howled in pain and shock as the co-pilot yanked her arm and twisted it behind her back.

Julie's eyes stung. She turned, her eyes pleading with the pilot. All her hope was now concentrated on him, as she realized that he did not seem to be part of this outrageous group of Greg's lackeys.

The pilot looked in disbelief at his colleague. "Have you gone crazy? You realize that this is the boss' daughter? You're going to get yourself fired. "

"Don't be such a puss, Arthur. We'll cut you in on the money. No one will ever know," the co-pilot said.

Julie was shaken by a further wave of horror, as she realized that the three figures on the tarmac were planning to split the ransom money. It wasn't going to be used to free her mother and that meant ...

She struggled again to free herself. "Help me!" she called to the pilot.

"Shut up!" The blonde said, and let the back of her hand land hard on Julie's cheek. "You don't always need to be center of attention." The blow hurt.

"Lenny, go get the case with the ... documents," she commanded.

Lenny made for the steps, but now the pilot had overcome his shock. He had the advantage of height and, as Lenny came up the steps, he kicked him in the chest. Lenny swore, but he managed to get hold of the pilot's leg, and to yank him down the steps. Julie could see that the pilot was fit for his age, taller than Lenny. She hoped fervently that he, like most pilots in South Africa, had a military background. It certainly looked that way as he got back to his feet, and, charging like an enraged buffalo, knocked Lenny to the ground. The two wrestled on the tarmac and Julie shrunk back as she watched them both trying to land punches. The pilot forced Lenny against the plane, but the younger man slid sideways and managed to hook his leg behind the pilot's, pushing him down on his back. It was difficult to see in the darkness, but she could hear both men panting and grunting. Then Lenny staggered to his feet, breathing hard, and the pilot followed. The two men locked, as if in a strange dance. As they passed through the shaft of light, Julie saw blood trickling from the pilot's nose. She noticed that the woman licked her lips, mesmerized, enjoying the fight. Then she noticed Lenny reach for one of the heavy wheel chocks and bring it up in a wild arc.

"Watch out!" she screamed.

The pilot sidestepped and Lenny lost his footing as he swung and hit nothing but air. Gasping now, evidently struggling, the older man crashed his knee upwards and Lenny went down. Summoning what remained of his strength, the pilot reached down and grabbed Lenny's shirt to drag him up. As he pulled his right fist back ready for the knockout punch, he did not see Lenny, his face contorted by rage, reaching under his shoulder...

The gun in Lenny's hand looked like the head of a snake that had uncoiled itself from its hiding place in his jacket. One muffled shot; and then the pilot's hand unclasped, and he fell silently to the ground. Blood splattered all over Lenny's silk shirt.

"Oh, jeez..." the blonde said. "Now what?"

"Shut up!" Lenny bellowed. "For once, will you just shut up? Let me think." He made futile attempts to wipe the blood off his shirt.

Julie seized the moment. She thrust her free hand into the co-pilot's face and scratched with all her might.

"Bitch!" he cursed, and let go. She ran. Within seconds, she realized that her sandals were a hopeless encumbrance – they slowed her, and their clacking on the tarmac was a dead giveaway. She kicked them off in mid-flight and looked back to see the blonde screaming orders and the co-pilot setting off in pursuit. Julie turned towards the lights of the terminal building. The darkness was her friend; calling for help would be counter-productive, there was no one around to help her and it would only serve to guide her pursuer. Better to save her breath.

She ran for her life. She had witnessed a murder and had no doubt that she, too, might be killed if it suited Lenny and his gang's purposes. She felt the wind on her skin and could hear her blood pounding in her ears. Her lungs started to burn, but the lights were getting closer. Just as she was beginning to hope she might have got away, however, she sensed the presence of her pursuer behind her. She felt his footfall before she heard the rasp of his breath. She turned her head briefly to confirm her fears; he was gaining. Julie bent her head down and did a quick zigzag to the right. There was nowhere to hide. She zigzagged back to the left, following the runway lights.

Just then, a vehicle approached. By its silhouette, she could make out that it was a refueling tanker.

"Help!" Julie called and waved her arms. "Help!" He voice sounded dry and disembodied.

326

"Shut up, bitch!" The co-pilot was not far behind her. She thought she could feel his breath. Her lungs burned but she forced her body onwards and onwards, commanding it to obey her. And then, just as the pain in her lungs reached the point of agony, she felt, rather than heard, that the panting had receded. A quick glance over her shoulder confirmed that the co-pilot could not keep up. *She was getting away.*

The dark SUV seemed to appear out of nowhere, screeching to a halt in front of her. Desperately, Julie changed course to sprint around the vehicle, but it had effectively slowed her enough for the co-pilot to catch up. He crashed her into the side of the car. At first, she was only aware of his hot, heavy breathing, as if he had taken from her own lungs the air they so desperately craved. Then she felt a searing pain in her shoulder.

In slow motion, she saw the tanker pull up - her last chance. She clenched her teeth against the pain and was about to catapult herself off the side of the vehicle when the pale ghost of a woman slid out of the passenger seat. Julie felt the knife in her back even before she took in the scent.

"Play along, now. One word, and I'll filet your face."

The truck stopped and the driver rolled down his window. "Hey, are you's crazy? You're not supposed to be out here on the runway."

"Yes, we know," Cindy said smoothly. "We are so sorry. The pilot thought he saw some debris on the runway as he landed, and we just wanted to make sure there was nothing that could damage some other plane."

"You should report that."

"Yes, of course. We will."

As the driver rolled up his window, Julie opened her mouth and wet her lips. The knife pierced her skin and she could feel a trickle of blood. *It was no use.* She allowed herself to be bundled into the back of the SUV.

They drove back to the plane and stopped. Lenny, in the driver's seat, flicked open his cell phone and made a call.

The woman polished her shiny knife with a piece of cloth and gave directions as the co-pilot tied Julie's wrists and ankles with duct tape. Despite her protests, he then wrapped tape around her head several times to cover her mouth, before bundling her back into the car like a piece of baggage. Her shoulder throbbed and her feet hurt like hell from the barefoot run on the rough surface.

"Get the money," the woman commanded. The co-pilot went to the plane and returned with the aluminum case. He slid it into the back of the vehicle; the case hit Julie's knee where she lay curled up. She groaned.

Julie could hear Lenny shut his cell phone. He sighed.

"What?" the woman asked.

"What do you think? The boss is seriously pissed about the pilot."

"Can you blame him? What does he want us to do?"

"We are to put the pilot on the plane and Sunshine here is to take it up, head for Johannesburg, and ditch the plane in the mountains. It's insured."

"What, are you fucking out of your mind?" The co-pilot was aghast.

"Why? You've done parachute jumps before, haven't you?"

"Yes, but this is different, this is nuts! And how do I get my money?"

"You'll get it. Don't you trust the boss? Look, he knows he owes you, big time. You have the scoop on all of us. You'll be paid. Just do it."

Julie could hear grunting noises, and assumed it was Lenny and the co-pilot dragging the pilot's body on to the plane. She thought about his wife, waiting with dinner somewhere in the southern suburbs. *It was monstrous, outrageous.* Then she heard the plane's engine start. Lenny got back into the SUV and slammed the door shut.

"God, this is such a royal fuck up," the woman said. "Will the tower even let him take off at night?"

"Sure. They fly these jets at night all the time."

"There's blood on the tarmac. If only you used your brain sometimes. Why did you have to go and waste him?"

"You're so full of bright ideas now. What would you have us do, *heh ... heh?* Anyway, Greg's really pissed off with you, too."

"With me?" Julie could hear the indignation in the woman's voice.

"He didn't want his *songbird*" – he emphasized the word derisively – "to be hurt."

Is that how that bastard thinks of me? A songbird? A tiny little vulnerable ornament, set in a cage to twitter on command? If ever I get out of this, I will...

"So now it's my fault?" The blonde's voice was icy. "He doesn't have the balls to deal with her himself. He should actually thank me - the little bitch needs serious breaking in. Anyway, he'll get over it. What does he want us to do with her now?"

Julie held her breath.

"Mother-and-daughter reunion. He wants them both shipped out to Malaysia."

"Do we get paid extra for babysitting two rather than one?"

Lenny snorted. "If you want to call him and suggest that, be my guest."

Malaysia?! But at least her mother was still alive. In the midst of all this horror, Julie was overcome with a sense of tremendous relief. At least Greg had shied away from killing her mother. And he didn't want her harmed, it seemed. So maybe they were both safe, for now, if she could just wait it out until … and then she remembered. Her evidence against Greg, the print-out of the emails, had been in her handbag, and that handbag was gone, dropped when she had tried to get away from the co-pilot. With the emails lost, there would be no evidence against Greg, because he would surely be canny enough to delete the originals. The pilot was dead, Matt was incapacitated, Chris a fugitive, the police bribed, unknown numbers of staff members at Noble in Greg's private employ – and now herself and her mother conveniently out of the way. *Until what? Until Greg had seized total control of the company?* A wave of despair washed over Julie, and she groaned audibly, despite the duct tape round her mouth.

"Shut the fuck up," yelled Lenny from the front of the SUV. "There's a gate ahead. If you so much as breathe, I'll blow your brains out. I swear I will."

##

Chapter 20: Discovery

Wednesday evening

It was dark when Chris parked the old pick-up half a kilometer from Wendy's home. He extinguished the lights, slid down low in the seat, and waited. All was quiet. The moon had not yet risen and he could barely discern the gloomy silhouettes of trees against the outline of Table Mountain on his left. There was a delicate scent of wild flowers in the air that made him think of Julie's perfume.

To the right, the inky waters of the Atlantic, fringed by a myriad of twinkling lights, stretched in a graceful curve for miles into the distance. It reminded Chris of a ruby and diamond necklace he had once seen in a jeweler's shop window: the contrast of sparkling gems against the black velvet of the display dummy had stuck in his mind. His thoughts wandered to the thin gold necklace that Julie often wore. He longed to hold her, to explore the curve of her neck. Her skin had the smoothness of polished marble, yet it was warm and yielded to his touch like a flawless peach. He could still remember the first time he had touched her skin when, as a twelve-year-old, he had unclasped her necklace with fumbling fingers at his mother's dance class.

He turned his attention away from the sea. In the street in which he had parked, lights were on in many of the houses, and he imagined families having dinner, watching TV, and discussing the day's events. *Could Julie and I ever be like the families living in these houses?* He pictured himself coming home, being greeted by Julie, by their children … For a few minutes, he allowed himself to wallow in a fantasy of domestic and sensual bliss …

But then he shook his head; there was no time to indulge in fantasizing. A final look in the rear-view mirror confirmed that the street was deserted. Chris got out and was immediately struck by the balminess of the night. So incongruous; this was weather for a beach party, not for ducking around in the shadows to outwit the police. He walked up the street and was grateful for the absence of streetlights. From far below came the muted din of traffic and bars along Camps Bay's Beach Road. Up in the avenues, where Wendy lived, however, even the squeak of Chris's running shoes disturbed the rarefied silence. He lengthened his stride and was within sight of Wendy's home when, without warning, a blinding set of lights bore down on him. Instinctively, Chris lifted an arm

330

to block the light, pressed himself against an ivy-covered wall, and crouched down. He held his breath, aware of his pounding heart, and waited for a police command or a barking dog.

After a few seconds, he relaxed. He realized that he'd merely tripped the motion detectors around the gates of someone's driveway. He allowed himself a few deep breaths, cursed his amateurish negligence, and managed to avoid the motion detector arcs of the other houses in the street.

Wendy's Porsche was parked in the driveway. *Good,* he thought, with a sense of relief. The beach vendor had said that the yacht was due to leave the harbor in the morning, and he urgently needed to talk to Wendy before then. She was the only person he could think of who might be able to give him the information he needed on the Noble business set-up. As he got closer to the car, he was surprised to see that Wendy had left the convertible's top down. *Must be nice to live in an area where car burglary is not a concern,* he thought,

Reaching the house, Chris rang the bell. There was no response. He stepped back and looked up to where light spilled from the lounge across the balcony. He heard voices. *Oh, damn.* It hadn't occurred to him that Wendy might have visitors – possibly even a boyfriend. *What a nuisance.* Still, he couldn't wait. He rang the bell again.

When she opened the door she appeared flushed, her blue eyes vivid. She was barefoot, wearing a loose-fitting T-shirt and shorts. Her hair was tousled as though someone had played with it. Looking at her now, Chris was not surprised that she should have a man in her life.

There was only momentary surprise on Wendy's face. "Chris! We've been so worried about you. Where have you been? Why didn't you call?"

He peered up the stairs, but did not see anyone else. Feeling vulnerable in the brightly lit doorway, he furtively looked over his shoulder. All seemed quiet in the street.

"It's a long story."

"Come in, come in." She took his arm and pulled him inside. "Oh God, what happened to your face? You look a mess!" The concern in her voice felt like the warmth of a log fire on a winter's night. She beckoned him to lead the way upstairs and continued to be solicitous as she followed him. "Have you eaten anything? Gosh, when we got to the police station and found that you had escaped … we just didn't know what to think."

He was puzzled as to why she kept saying "we", but before he could ask her, a voice called from the kitchen, "Who is it, darling? Everything OK?"

Chris, at the top of the stairs, stopped so abruptly that Wendy bumped into him. He stared in disbelief at the man pouring wine at the kitchen counter.

"Dad?"

"Chris!"

For what seemed an eternity, Jacques held the bottle in suspended animation. Then, carefully, he put it down next to an open laptop, and approached his son.

"That's a nasty cut above your eye. Has someone taken care of it?"

"It's nothing, I'm OK," Chris said. He hadn't given the cuts on his face any thought since this morning in the police cell. *Was that only this morning?*

"Here, sit down," Wendy commanded. "Let your father take a look at that." She steered him to a bar stool, turned up the lights, and produced a first-aid kit.

Chris let Jacques inspect his cuts, trying not to wince at the pain.

"This one should have been stitched." His father rummaged through the first-aid kit. "The magic tape will have to do, but first I'm going to have to clean it."

As he sat there, having his father tend his wounds, Chris felt he had fallen into an alternative universe. His world had imploded, he was a fugitive, and here he was, sitting in Wendy's house, having his cuts attended to by her lover – his father!

The Dettol burned like hell and brought tears to Chris's eyes; he gritted his teeth. Part of him wanted to explode with frustration. Did his father have any clue at all that his son's life had been heaved off its foundations and was teetering on the edge of a precipice? And yet, at the same time, another part of him found it deeply reassuring to have the doctor take charge, to feel the firm competence of his father's hands.

Jacques had finished. "There," he said. "It will probably leave a small scar under the hairline, but at least it won't get infected."

"Thanks."

There was a pause. Chris looked from his father to Wendy and back again, letting the truth of their relationship thoroughly sink in. Wendy, he now noticed, looked flushed and embarrassed, like a teenager caught out by her parents. She busied herself repacking the first-aid kit. The silence stretched uncomfortably. Then Chris remembered the purpose of his visit. He said to Wendy, "Did you get an SMS with a bunch of photographs from Thabo?"

"I just showed them to your father."

Wendy turned around the laptop and continued, "In one of them, it looks like a body is being carried; we were most concerned. Thabo is not answering his phone. We were just about to contact the police ..."

"Don't call the police," Chris said. He quickly filled them in on everything he had learned from Thabo. They were relieved to hear that Bridget was likely to be alive, and that at least there was a clue as to where she was being held - on the yacht in Hout Bay.

"Where did Thabo take the photographs of that crate of equipment?" Jacques asked.

"In a barn at the Khanya center. I assume the crate has by now also been loaded on to the yacht. Why? Do you know what it is?"

"I am not hundred percent sure, but I have a pretty good idea."

"So?" Chris had to control a rising exasperation. *Why does he always have to be so careful and circumspect about what he says? We haven't got time for this.*

Still Jacques hesitated. Then he said, "If it is what I think it is, we really have to alert the police."

"Not the police!" Chris reiterated.

"Chris, you have to give yourself up. This is ridiculous, surely you can explain to ..."

"Dad, please!" Chris was too agitated to sit. He jumped up and starting pacing the room. "The police don't believe a word I say. They think I kidnapped Bridget, or even murdered her. Can you imagine that? How do I begin to have a rational discussion with them? They punch first and ask questions later." He paused, took a deep breath, and looked directly at his father. "They're either in on this, or they are being manipulated by whoever has set me up."

"That is absurd, outrageous," Wendy intervened. "We will vouch for you, explain to the police …"

"Wendy, the only way I'm going to clear this up is if I can find out who has kidnapped Bridget myself. You need to give me more detail on what kind of business Noble Enterprises is involved in."

"I told you, medical equipment. They produce and supply …"

Jacques had been looking at the computer screen while Chris and Wendy were talking. Now, he suddenly interrupted: "That's it! They must have developed the Rhino-S without authorization. Bridget probably found out; she would never have allowed it."

Chris and Wendy looked at him.

"Rhino-S? Would you care to explain?" Wendy asked.

He did not appear to have heard her but continued to page through the images. "Son of a gun, they've actually commercialized it." He looked up and said, "There's a colonel in the Special Branch who I've worked with; he'll understand the implications of this. I'm sure he'll listen. I'll give him a call."

"No," Chris said, very deliberately, leaning forward on the kitchen counter. "For once, you are actually going to listen to me!" He barely recognized the commanding tone in his own voice as he continued, "First, I want you to tell me what you know. *I'm* the one who's been framed and beaten up by the police. *I'll* decide whether we call them or not."

Their faces were inches apart. Never in his life had Chris spoken like this to his father and he half-expected a slap across the face.

"Dammit all," he said. "The only way we'll sort this out is if we can figure out what happened to Bridget and who's behind it. I don't trust the police. They're a bunch of fucking assholes."

"Don't swear," his father said mechanically.

"Fuck, fuck, fuck!" Chris said in a cold and deliberate manner. "Swearing seems to be the only way to get your attention. I've tried everything else."

He thought that this time he really was going to get a slap. The two men stared at each other.

Jacques' voice was as cold and clipped as his son's when he said, "*You've* tried to communicate with *me*? That's …" He clamped his mouth shut.

Many years on the trauma ward had taught Jacques du Toit to control his emotions, but he had become quite pale and Chris could see a vein bulging over his left temple. Blood pulsated through it; he could almost feel it - because the same vein in his own temple was throbbing too. He could hear hard breathing, but was not sure if it was his or his father's. Chris had the weird sensation that he was looking in a mirror; he was his father and his father was him. *How can I be at war with myself? What is going on between us?*

"Will you both just drop it? We need to concentrate." Wendy looked from father to son, exasperated.

Eventually, Chris brought his breathing under control. "Please, Dad," he said. "Please tell me what you know about this … this Rhino-S."

The doctor drained his wine glass and Wendy took this as a cue to start brewing coffee. Chris sat back on his bar stool and waited.

His father turned and looked straight at him. "Eight years ago, Harry Noble, Julie's father, came to me with one of his inventions. He had a brilliant mind and was one of the most thoroughly decent people I've ever known. He really wanted to make the world a better place …"

Jacques went on to explain how Noble Enterprises had been at the forefront of developing all manner of medical equipment and processes: heart-lung machines, artificial limbs, and defibrillators. They had also done research into cost-effective vaccine-production methods. Harry had spent a lot of time in Angola, the Congoes, Uganda, and other countries dealing with the ravages of war. He was passionate about trying to find creative, affordable solutions for the problems of Africa. Some of his research was focused on the prevention of malaria and tuberculosis. His prolific interests and passions also extended to wildlife preservation. He was very aware that the trade in rhino horn and elephant tusks was an integral part of many of the conflicts in the region, since the proceeds were often used to buy weapons.

Chris nodded and tapped his fingers on the counter. None of what his father had said was new to him.

The doctor continued to explain that Harry and one of his researchers had come up with a process to manufacture artificial rhino horn – or rather, a way to take a quantity of real rhino horn, process it, and "multiply" it into a larger quantity with the same properties. The process was borrowed from the mechanisms used to grow cultures of vaccines.

"Sort of like having a yeast dough that grows and rises?" Wendy asked.

"Think more of growing algae in a sealed tank. It was tricky, and required very carefully controlled environments. They experimented endlessly with various substrates and raw materials, faced all kinds of technical challenges. The problem was that a whole batch could easily become unstable and get spoiled. But think of all the possibilities – satisfying Asia's demand for rhino-horn aphrodisiacs."

Jacques was becoming more animated as he spoke and his passion was infectious. Wendy chipped in, "I guess the idea was to flood the market with this artificial rhino horn and hence stop the slaughter of endangered animals."

"You've got it," Jacques said. "Harry dubbed the substance 'Rhino-S', short for Rhino-Saver. He was very excited when he came to me with the plans, and even a small prototype for manufacturing it."

"And what happened?" Chris asked.

"Well, Harry, being the man he was, grasped very quickly that his invention was problematic. For starters, it still required the real thing. That is, to produce five kilograms of Rhino-S, you needed to have one kilogram of real rhino horn to start with. Much as he tried to just keep multiplying, it would not work. Every batch needed to be seeded with genuine rhino horn. So, he recognized that he could actually end up legitimizing rhino-horn trade and endangering the species even more."

Chris nodded. "Like the ivory trade. The only way to stop is to go for 'zero'. *Every* tusk is illegal. "

Wendy said, "Duerrenmatt's dilemma."

They both looked at her without comprehension.

"You must have heard of it," she said. "Duerrenmatt wrote a play about the physicists who first discovered how to split the atom. They realized the potential for good and for destruction ..."

"We all know how that turned out," Chris said.

Jacques turned to the laptop and pointed at one of the images. Chris thought that the greenish glass tubes, plungers, syringes, and other paraphernalia appeared far more ominous on the computer than they did on the little phone screen.

"You think this is the equipment needed to produce Rhino-S?" Chris asked.

"I am convinced of it – it looks very similar to the prototype; except ..."

"Except what?"

"I've spent a fair bit of time as a military consultant, and whoever modified the design and built this unit definitely borrowed heavily from military design principles." He rubbed his chin and muttered, *"Surely not?"*

Chris leaned in closer. His father flicked through a number of the images. Thabo had done well. One of the images, taken from a little further away, showed each component, resting in a carefully crafted foam compartment.

Jacques pointed at the screen. "What does this look like to you?"

"A whole lot of syringes?"

"Exactly! The original was meant to be in the form of tablets. But due to the unstable nature of Rhino-S, one of Harry's researchers had suggested injecting the substance rather than making tablets."

Wendy said, "That sounds pretty horrible!"

"Well, you'd be surprised what people inject themselves with in the hope of youth and virility. But you are right, Harry wouldn't hear of it. It seems, however, as if someone has gone ahead and developed a very elaborate kit to manufacture an injectable form of Rhino-S. But they clearly have not solved the basic problem, - look at that – that's real rhino horn to seed the process."

They sat in silence for a minute, and then Jacques said, "Harry came to me because he was hoping that I might have suggestions on how to get the military to take over this research. It was getting too expensive for him to fund and, since the South African military expend vast resources in trying to prevent poaching, he'd hoped that they could progress with this idea."

Wendy asked, "So? What did you advise him? What happened?"

Jacques got up and walked across to the picture windows. He sighed deeply. "The prototype device was ... lost. Shortly after that Harry died, and as far as Special Branch and I could make out, that was the end of it - until I saw these pictures."

"What do you mean, 'lost'?" Chris asked.

The doctor hesitated. Chris had never seen his father like this – pensive, and somewhat uncertain, as he seemed to dredge through a sludge of memories that he would have preferred to leave untouched. He was clearly considering how best to answer his son.

Meanwhile, Wendy put three steaming mugs on the counter, and Jacques returned from the window. Chris noticed that Wendy knew exactly how his father liked his coffee – half a spoon of sugar and a dribble of milk. There was a time, long ago, when *he* had made coffee for his father.

Jacques nodded his thanks. Then he turned to Chris. "Remember the day your mother died?" he started, his voice tentative.

Chris felt his throat go dry and his pulse rise. *What sort of a question was that?* The mere sight of blood made him nauseous; the smell of roses, which he always associated with his mother and her studio, put a vice around his chest and threatened to choke his heart; once he'd nearly crashed his car when he thought he'd seen his mother's murderer boarding a bus; one of his girlfriends had left him because his vocal dreams had "freaked her out". And now, of course, not a day went by without him experiencing flashbacks of a thin arm with a distinctive tattoo …

The bile of indignation rose in Chris's stomach. He was about to erupt when Wendy's hand touched his arm - like the stroke of a butterfly.

He managed to hide his emotions behind a sip of coffee and simply nodded.

His father continued, "The police came and ascertained that nothing was stolen; that it had been a random act of house-breaking and that the burglars had been surprised by you and Mom."

Chris nodded again. "I remember."

"Well, that wasn't entirely true. The burglars had been there with a very specific purpose – to steal the Rhino-S designs and prototype that were in my study. Those were the only items missing - and they were never seen again."

"Were the police informed at the time?" Wendy asked.

"Believe me, once the police heard what had been stolen, they put a complete gag on everybody associated with the case. Special Branch got called in; that's where I got to meet Colonel ..."

"You should have told me." Chris felt his hand trembling and he put his mug down hard on the counter. He was oblivious to the drops of hot coffee splashing over his hand.

"You were fourteen years old," his father said. He sounded weary.

"I had a right to know," Chris said quietly, the calmness of his voice belying the anger that was coursing through him, stronger now than ever. *How* could *he not have told me?*

"Chris, I could not possibly burden you with the knowledge of a project that the police had classified as top secret. Anyway, what good would it have done?"

"For all these years, you allowed me to be burdened with the thought that my mother's killing was completely random, senseless." He was breathing hard now, with the effort to stay calm. "Meanwhile, there was nothing senseless about it. *You* had brought a highly dangerous piece of equipment into the house; *you* laid the bait that attracted those murdering bastards."

"Chris, that's not fair," Wendy said. "Your father could not have known ..."

"Who the hell can I trust when the people I'm supposed to be closest to hide things from me?!" Chris looked from one to the other, his eyes accusatory, his voice rising as his fought-for calm finally evaporated. "What else aren't you telling me?" He was shouting now. "What other surprises lie in store for me? I've had quite a few tonight, already!"

The silence that followed this outburst was broken by the chime of the doorbell. Whoever was at the door was clearly impatient, a second and then a third ring following fast on the first. Both men turned to Wendy, who walked across to the window and peered down into the street.

"It's the police," Wendy whispered. "Chris, you must hand yourself over. My legal team will sort it out in no time, and they can work with the police to find Bridget."

As she turned to go downstairs, Chris leapt up and caught hold of her arm. "Wendy, if you want me to ever speak to you again, you'll let me do this my way."

She looked him square in the eyes. It struck Chris that, after what he had just said – or shouted, rather - maybe she would see it as a blessing if he never spoke to her again. Then she pointedly lowered her gaze to the vice grip of his hand on her arm. He loosened his hold and she left the room. Chris turned to look at his father, who was sitting, still as the Sphinx, at the kitchen counter. He found himself desperately hoping for some sign from the man, some indication of what he thought his son should do - or, indeed, of how he felt. But Jacques merely nodded. Was it encouragement? Or was it a gesture that said "You're going to have to face the music,"? Chris simply didn't know. *Why is it so damn difficult to get into his brain – or his heart?*

The two men listened in silence as Wendy opened the door.

"Mrs. van Houten, sorry to disturb you so late, but we need to ask you a few questions."

"Really? I think we met at the police station, Sergeant...Vervey. Did I get that right? I am terrible with names."

Vervey! How the hell has he found me so quickly again? A chill ran down Chris's spine as he tried to listen for any sounds that would tell him how many men were with the sergeant, but his nemesis was the only one that spoke.

"Have you any news of the kidnapping?" Wendy was asking.

"I really cannot comment on the case," the sergeant replied pompously.

""Of course, I understand; it's just that Mrs. Baxter is a dear, dear friend of mine and I am the godmother of her daughter. And I am, of course, extremely concerned about her, and ..."

"Yes, yes." Vervey's tone expressed impatience as he cut Wendy off mid-sentence. "But I am here tonight on a more pressing matter. Do you mind if we come in and take a look around?"

Wendy's tone remained polite, but acquired a boardroom edge. "I'm happy to answer any questions you might have," she said slowly, "but I cannot imagine why you should want to search my house. Am I suspected of doing anything wrong?"

"No, of course not. We're looking for the fugitive – Chris du Toit. Since you bailed him out yesterday, we thought he might have come here."

Wendy gave a little laugh. "Honestly, Sergeant, you should give Chris a little more credit. Wouldn't coming here be rather obvious? Dr. du

Toit and I are in constant contact, anxiously waiting for Chris to call either one of us. If he does, we will urge him to hand himself over to the police immediately."

"I see. I still would appreciate it, however, if we could have a quick ..."

"Sergeant Vervey, if you want to search my home, I suggest you find a judge to issue a search warrant."

"This is a very urgent matter ..."

"In that case, I'm sure the judge would be happy to provide you with a warrant. Now, unless you have any further questions ... good night."

Chris heard the door shut and moments later Wendy appeared at the top of the stairs. He gave her a silent hug and mouthed "*thank you*".

"I'm sure they'll be back soon," she said. "We don't have much time. What is it you wanted to know?"

Chris gave Wendy and his father a rundown of his conversation with Julie. He explained that she had discovered something important – she had not been able to tell him what, for fear of her phone – and his – being tapped. He told them that Julie was on her way back to Cape Town, and that she had said she would be in touch once she had landed. As he said this, a thought struck him, and he looked at his watch. "That's odd. Her plane should have landed over an hour ago. You haven't heard from her, have you?" He looked anxiously at Wendy.

Wendy shook her head and the look on her face ramped up his burgeoning concern for Julie's safety. He looked from Wendy to his father and back. He needed to find out anything they knew that might shed light on what was going on, and quickly. Trying to contain his impatience, he went on: "There's obviously something very fishy going on with Noble Enterprises, and it must be something to do with this Rhino-Saver. Julie sounded very distressed during our short call, but she said one thing that really stuck in my mind: '*The deceit goes right to the top – and the police are in cahoots.*' I am now convinced that Bridget found out about it, and she was kidnapped to shut her up."

Wendy was looking pensive. "We know Bridget would have been violently opposed to this business with Rhino-S," she began. "Maybe you are right, maybe she needed to be silenced, got out of the way. And who would be behind that? Who is it who basically runs the show at Noble? It's Greg." She paused, allowing her words to sink in. "Bridget has never trusted him. She has tried in the past to clip his wings but, since both Matt and Julie trusted him implicitly, she was outnumbered. She confided in me a few months ago that she was deeply frustrated. Her battle with alcohol has always made her vulnerable, and it has allowed Greg to undermine her with the board at Noble."

Jacques was indignant. "That's really low, considering how Bridget and Harry built that company from nothing. I have always admired Bridget; she's intelligent and very principled."

Chris noticed how much emphasis his father put on the word "principled". He knew that in Jacques' eyes to be "principled" was to be in possession of one of the noblest of qualities. As if reading his mind, Wendy said, "Yes, of course, but I'm sure Greg would describe it more as 'obstinate' or 'pigheaded'. He tried to have her ousted, but, out of respect for Harry, the board would not support such a drastic step. But the bottom line is that Bridget is now merely tolerated, not taken seriously ..."

She stopped. They'd all heard it: a faint *click* from the scullery. Someone was breaking in through the back door.

Jacques was the first to react. He raced through the kitchen into the scullery, slammed shut the door between the two rooms, and confronted the intruders.

"How dare you break into Mrs. van Houten's home?" Chris heard him say. "The police commissioner will hear about this."

"Get out of my way!" It was Vervey, all pretense of civility clearly gone.

Chris realized what his father was doing – he was protecting Wendy. If Chris were caught in her home, she'd be deeply implicated. Silently, he stepped on to the balcony and looked down. One policeman was stationed at the front door. He had no idea how many others were with Vervey, but he knew his father wouldn't be able to fend them off indefinitely. *I'm trapped*, he thought. Then his eyes fell on Wendy's Porsche, its hood down, parked in deep shadow right below the balcony.

He hissed, *"Your keys, throw them!"*

Wendy reacted immediately; she picked up her keys, and tossed them to him. Without a sound, Chris slid over the side of the balcony. For a moment, he hung at full stretch, peering past his feet to the ground. He cursed silently; it was higher than it looked. But he had no choice, so, taking a deep breath, he let go. Luckily, he landed well, and after a moment's crouching in the dark, he crept over to the open Porsche. The noise of a passing car gave him enough of a sound shield to slide into the driver's seat, and put the key in the ignition. The engine sprang into life and Chris flicked the headlights to full, blinding the policeman at the door.

The next second, he had put the Porsche into reverse and was shooting down the driveway, praying that there would be no passing traffic. He turned sharp right, braked hard, and yanked the car into first. Two shots rang out above the squealing of the tires as he careered around a curve in the road. He felt the deep exhilaration of escape and for a few instants savored the smell of leather and the handling of the vehicle. It almost seemed as though the Porsche enjoyed being unshackled from its usual pace. The rev counter hovered in the unfamiliar red zone.

By the time Chris reached the T- junction at Beach Road, he had a plan. He veered left towards Hout Bay, without slowing. He was determined to find hard evidence, and the only place he would get that was at the Baxter residence in Constantia. But first he had to line up some diving equipment. *"Before dawn ..."* Where had he read that? *Attack on Pearl Harbor* or some similar war history. *"The best time to attack is before dawn."*

He could sense, rather than see, the cliff falling off to the sea on his right. It was cool with the top down and the wind pushing up against his face. He did not care. The Porsche held through the curves as though guided by a rail. This was the very stretch where Lenny had forced Bridget off the road.

"Bastard!" Chris shouted out against the wind and the crashing breakers. "Bastard murdering Dragon Boy; I'll get you!"

He fought the urge to press his foot down harder on the accelerator. There was no sign of any pursuers and it would be the biggest travesty if he wiped himself out in an accident of his own making.

The clock on the dashboard indicated that it was just past ten p.m. Chris got out his cell phone and slowed down while he dialed Bruce's number. It rang several times before Bruce answered.

"Chris, my man, where are you? I can hardly hear you."

"I'm driving," Chris bellowed above the sound of the wind.

"What's up? I thought we were going to chill it and not contact each other for a while."

"Sorry, Bruce; bit of an emergency. I need your help – again."

"No sweat, man. If it's half as much fun as this morning, I'm all for it."

"Listen, you know that mate of yours with the diving shop at Hout Bay harbor?'

"Yeah?"

"Is there any way I can get hold of some gear?"

"Now?"

"No, for Christmas … of course now!"

"OK, OK, don't get fucking mad with me. Jeez – you're the one who keeps getting himself into the shite."

"Sorry, man. It's just …"

"No worries. I'll see what I can do. Where are you now?" Bruce asked.

"On my way to Hout Bay."

"I'll meet you there. If you are in such a damn hurry, maybe we'll have to just … borrow some stuff. I think I know the code to his alarm system."

"Thanks, mate," Chris said, grinning in the dark. This was just the kind of ingenuity he had hoped for from his friend. "I owe you."

"Oh yes. You owe me big time; lager for life, or something like that. See you there." The phone went dead.

He was about to put it down when it rang. He looked at the number and pressed the green button. "Thabo? What are you doing up so late?"

"Meestar Chris! You must come! You must come quick!"

"Why, what? What's happened? Are you OK?"

"Come, come quick. They're going to hurt her!"

"Slow down. What? Who?"

"It's *Meez* Julie!"

Chris felt an icy chill rising from the pit of his stomach; its tentacles spread in an instant and threatened to choke the air from his lungs and entwine his heart. He forced himself to breathe.

"Thabo, where are you?"

"I'm at the harbor; I was watching the boat, like you asked me to."

"And?"

"I saw *Meez* Julie, she was struggling. They hit her! They hit *Meez* Julie!" Chris could hear the panic in the boy's voice.

Dear God – that was why she hadn't been in touch earlier..."OK, Thabo. I want you to stay hidden out of view at the harbor entrance. You hear me? Don't do anything! I'm on my way; I'll be there in a few minutes. Look for me – red Porsche."

He flung the cell phone on the seat next to him, gripped the steering wheel, and let his foot go down on the accelerator like a sack of cement.

##

Chapter 21: All I Need Is ... Evidence

Wednesday night

The Porsche nearly lifted off the road as it crested Suikerbossie Hill and bore down on Hout Bay. At night, the village and harbor lacked their touristy charm. The smell from the last remaining fishmeal factory permeated the air and Chris felt the salty chill of fog rising from the ocean. The dampness muffled all sound except the car's engine. In the distance, he saw a fishing boat leave the harbor. Its lights glowed through the mist like flickering candle flames, as it gradually receded into the darkness of the Atlantic Ocean. The mournful wail of a foghorn bade the vessel good-bye.

A wind-blasted sign helpfully proclaimed "800 Meters to The Wharf and the Best Crayfish in Africa".

Chris slowed and glanced at the low-slung buildings on his left; he nearly did not see the figure that appeared from nowhere in the road ahead of him.

"Pisscat!" Chris cursed and swerved, narrowly avoiding a collision. His heart thumped and he was thankful for the car's wide spray of light; without that, he probably would have hit the man. As he shot past, however, he realized that it was not a drunkard at all - it was Thabo.

Chris stomped on the brakes and the seat belt cut into his shoulder. He leapt out to meet the boy running towards him.

"Thabo, I nearly killed you! You're going to give me a bloody heart attack!"

"Shhhh!" Thabo held a finger to his lips, his eyes wide and white in the darkness.

"What? Why?" Chris whispered.

"The Dragon Boys; they know you coming."

"But how?"

"I crept up and heard them talk."

"Thabo, don't you ever listen? I told you to hide and be careful." Chris shuddered at what might have happened if the gangsters had caught Thabo eavesdropping. He couldn't help but raise his voice, which prompted Thabo to wave his hands. Chris had never seen the boy so animated.

Thabo pointed to the car. "You must hide it; they know you are driving red Porsche. They are waiting at the harbor entrance."

Chris was shocked. He knew that the police were in cahoots with the kidnappers. He had suspected it from the moment that he had seen Lenny and Sergeant Vervey acknowledge each other outside the health club. Everything he had learned since then had confirmed his suspicions. But, even so, the efficiency of their cooperation continued to surprise him.

He parked the Porsche in a dark side street and listened in silence as Thabo gave him a quick rundown of how he had come by his information. The boy described how he had hung around near the gym in Mandela Park to see what the Dragon Boys were up to. After dark, three of them had come out, looking very excited. He overheard them talking about "action at the harbor", and decided to follow them down there. When Thabo explained, matter-of-factly, that he had hitched a ride, clinging to the back of a minibus taxi, Chris had to suppress the urge to once again admonish him. The kid lived in a different world from him, and knew its ways, so who was he, an outsider, to tell him off? *And*, he thought, *he certainly uses his initiative.*

Thabo went on to explain how the three gangsters had met up with a Coloured man and a woman who scared him because she looked like a ghost - even though, he stressed to Chris, he did not believe in ghosts; not like Danny and other kids at the Khanya center who believed anything. Thabo had watched as they hauled Julie out of the back of a vehicle and, when she struggled, the woman had hit her. Then they had all got into a speedboat. Because of the mist, he couldn't be completely certain, but he was pretty sure that they had gone to the big yacht. Thabo had waited, and, after a while, the three gangsters had come back alone. They were now sitting and smoking just inside the harbor entrance, where Thabo had listened to them talk before setting off to warn Chris.

Chris and Thabo avoided the harbor's main entrance, instead getting down to the beach by crossing a low sand dune. A short sprint brought them up against the harbor's breakwater. The old concrete structure was pitted and worn, showing signs of rusty rebar. Over the years, the harbor authority had piled tons and tons of rocks up against the breakwater to protect it from the ocean's might, and now Chris and Thabo clambered over these rocks and on to the pier. They crouched and allowed their eyes to adjust to the gloomy light. To their left, the main pier jutted out into the darkness; it was a solid structure that allowed small trucks and vehicles to drive up and down and service the fishing boats. Dim light emanated from the portholes of some of the boats moored alongside.

They had to watch their step to avoid the day's debris: empty beer bottles, coke cans, and polystyrene boxes overflowed from rubbish bins, while fish guts, abandoned by seagulls, created an additional hazard. The smell of kelp and fishmeal hung in the air. It was quiet, save for the sucking noise of waves receding from the bollards and a plaintive seal barking into the night.

Chris thought of the lonely yacht moored out in the bay, away from the harbor's protection. He conjured up the memory of what he had observed from the beach that afternoon. The *Moonflower* had three decks. *Where would they be keeping Bridget and Julie?* He needed a plan of the yacht.

"Someone there," Thabo whispered, and halted, ready to bolt. A figure stepped down from the boardwalk of a quaint Victorian building that sported a sign proclaiming, "The Surf and Sea Shop - Diving School".

It was Bruce. He greeted them with exasperation: "Where've you been? I bust my gut getting here, as you tell me it's an emergency, and then you come sauntering along, as if you're out for your evening stroll!"

Chris gestured for Bruce to lower his voice and whispered, *"There's a group of gangsters that you really don't want to meet near the harbor entrance."*

"You're shitting me."

"No, it's true."

"How do you do it? I mean, how does one person attract so much trouble?"

"I suppose I hang out with the wrong people. Can we get in?"

"Sure thing, but I don't want Security asking me any questions. We'll go round the back. Can your young friend here stay and keep guard?" He turned to Thabo. "You just need to whistle if you see anyone coming, OK?"

Thabo nodded and uttered the low-pitched mating call of a loerie.

"Pretty good," Bruce said, and gave a thumbs-up. Thabo disappeared into the shadows.

A few minutes later, under the jaundiced light of a single bulb, Chris and Bruce surveyed the equipment in the diving school's storeroom.

Chris worked his way along the neatly packed shelves and picked what he needed: wet suit, flippers, oxygen tank, mask, flashlight, and more.

Bruce looked at the mounting pile of equipment and said, "You'll need a ride back to your car. My VW Kombi is parked right outside."

"No, I saw a good spot amongst the rocks at the breakwater. We'll hide it there."

"Jeez, I don't know. If this stuff gets stolen, I'm going to be in so much trouble ..."

"Technically, it's already stolen – or it will be, the moment we walk out the door."

"Borrowed, my friend, borrowed. I hope you know how to use it. This is expensive equipment."

Chris did not even credit the comment with a response. Instead, he lifted the tank with one hand and brought it over to the large oxygen cylinders. Keeping his eye on the pressure gauges, he filled the tank in minutes.

"OK, OK, you've made your point," Bruce said. "Where'd you learn this?"

"Diving holiday in the Seychelles, with my father."

"Oh, for the life of the rich and idle," Bruce quipped.

They both heard it at the same time: the sound of the loerie, low and urgent. Bruce was first to react - with three strides, he reached the wall and flicked off the light. Chris remained motionless and listened. A car went by. In the distance, he could hear a foghorn. He bent down and felt amongst the pile of equipment at his feet till his hand closed around the grip of the flashlight. He hoped it would allow him to surprise and blind anyone walking through the door. It wasn't much of a weapon but, if necessary, it could be used to clobber someone over the head – better than nothing.

His eyes grew accustomed to the dark. Carefully, he shifted backwards, aiming to take up position behind the door. He heard boards creak outside and Bruce's breathing right next to him. A light shone through the front window and bobbed across the display dummies, with their snorkels and bathing costumes.

"Did you disable the alarm?" Chris whispered.

"Of course, but with all your clanging about ..."

"Shhhh!"

The light disappeared. Moments later, it came in through the window of the storeroom – much closer now. They pressed themselves against the wall. From the sound of the steps, Chris deduced that there was only one person – probably a security guard. He wondered whether the man would be armed. The light disappeared again, but now they could distinctly hear the steps progressing towards the back of the shop. If the guard reached the back door and found it unlocked ... Chris firmed his grip on the flashlight; he could feel Bruce tense up next to him.

The sound of crashing glass, followed by the incessant scream of a car alarm, startled both of them. Then they heard Thabo shouting, "Run, Joey!" He appeared to be answered by a loud whistle. Seconds later, his voice came from a different direction, and again he shouted, "Run, guys!" The heavy thudding of boots told Chris that the security guard had set off to catch the suspected car burglars.

Chris exhaled and whispered, *"That boy is something else."*

"Let's get out of here." Bruce picked up the oxygen tank.

"Hang on just one second." Chris reached up to one of the highest shelves and grabbed a harpoon.

"What the ...?"

"Don't ask."

They crept along the side of the building as best they could with their load. The car alarm still blared, but there was no sign of the security guard. When they reached the front of the building, Bruce stopped short and cursed under his breath, *"The little fucker! That's my Kombi. He smashed the window of my Kombi."*

"Oh, get over it. Your insurance will pay."

"Insurance? You've got to be kidding ..."

Chris said, "Look, you'd better stay and deal with this; act the aggrieved victim when the guard comes back. Gimme the tank."

"You sure you can manage?"

"Of course – hey, thanks, mate."

Bruce got out his car keys and pressed a button. The ensuing silence was a relief. Chris shouldered the oxygen tank and was swallowed by the fog. He retraced his steps to the breakwater, where he found a cavity amongst the rocks. It would do, as long as he retrieved the equipment before sunrise. His watch read 11.32 p.m.

A slight breeze had sprung up and torn a hole in the fog. Chris could see the yacht now, lying serenely at anchor, her red warning beacon beating a steady pulse. *What's Julie doing now?* Again and again, he told himself that the kidnappers had nothing to gain by hurting her, but he worried about her temper, and whether she might not provoke them. After all, Thabo had told him that he had seen them hit her. He had to fight the overwhelming urge to commandeer a boat, any boat, and charge out to the rescue.

##

With one last look at the yacht, Chris turned and jogged to the Porsche, leapt over the side of the open vehicle, and sped up the valley towards Bridget's house in Constantia. Every time a car's lights appeared, he watched for signs of a patrol vehicle. The road was narrow and twisted its way up the valley through thickets of trees. The familiar smell of blue gum hung in the night air as he drove past the turn-off to the Khanya center. He thought of Mercy and the children, all fast asleep in their beds, unaware of the intrigue and deceit that had been swirling around them. Mercy would be furious when she found out. He smiled in the dark as he pictured Mercy tearing strips off Lenny and his gang.

Chris had come out of a series of bends and was on a stretch of straight road when he noticed lights in his rear-view mirror. The vehicle was some way back, but gaining. The blue gums were so close to the road that their roots lifted the asphalt and made the road uneven. Chris accelerated and, leaving the straight road behind, gunned the Porsche through a number of tight curves. He felt like he was in a pinball machine, trying to avoid the thick trunks that kept appearing in the car's icy spray of light. When he finally stole a glance in the rear-view mirror, however, he could not see any lights.

"They've turned off, I saw it," a voice said, from three inches behind his head.

Chris nearly lost control of the car and narrowly missed an oncoming delivery truck on its midnight run.

"Thabo! You have to stop giving me such frights!"

"I knew you would come back to the car, so I hid in the back seat," Thabo said, with disarming logic.

Chris shook his head. "You should be home in bed," he said, but without much conviction.

"I also knew you would say that. Is why I keep quiet. Now is too late, we have passed my house." There was satisfaction in his voice.

"Well, stay down; I have to see if I can talk my way past the security guard."

A few minutes later, Chris pulled up outside the guardhouse at Silver Pine Estate. He saw the guard peer through the window, then pick up his clipboard. The man seemed remarkably alert; he walked around the vehicle and made a note of the license plate.

"You're late," the guard said.

Chris's throat felt like sandpaper and his voice, when he managed to speak, came out hoarse: "Sorry, man, I know it's late, I don't want to cause you any trouble. You see, I want to surprise my girlfriend and ..."

"I didn't say '*It* is late', I said '*You* are late'."

The guard towered next to the car. Chris was stupefied. *How could he have been expecting me?* Did Vervey and the police have *everyone* in their pockets? But how could the police have known that this was where he was going to come? Surely neither Wendy nor his father would have told them? *It doesn't make sense.*

"Oh ... really? You were expecting me?" he managed, trying to sound bright and innocent.

The man looked at him intently. "Is this Mrs. van Houten's car?"

Chris was so surprised that he was unable to answer. His instinctive response, however, was to get the hell out of there. He shot a glance into the rear-view mirror to see if he could back out. *The security guard's not visibly armed, maybe if I slammed the Porsche into reverse ...*

"Mrs. van Houten; is this her car?" the guard repeated slowly, as if talking to an idiot.

Chris was just about able to nod.

The man reached into his pocket. Chris, still primed for escape, watched his every move.

"OK then, you can go. Mrs. van Houten called a while ago to say she was sending you to pick up something from her friend – very urgent, she said. I was expecting you an hour ago."

The heavy gate lumbered open.

Chris, still stunned, but amazed at Wendy's foresight, put the car in gear.

"You go surprise your girlfriend," the guard said, and a broad grin spread across his face.

Chris raised his hand in salute as he let the car glide into the estate.

They parked in the driveway of the Baxter residence and got out. Chris looked up at the imposing façade and was reminded of that evening, just a few days ago, when he had arrived here in a limo, thinking he was going to pick up Julie for dinner. *Instead, I ended up spending the evening with Bridget.* He wondered how she was holding up after several days in captivity. *Well, at least she has Julie with her now for moral support,* he thought grimly.

"Where's the key?" Thabo was impatient to get moving.

"No key. We have to find a way in."

"What about alarm?"

"I know the number – I think."

"You *think?*"

Based on his previous experience at the Richters' house, Chris started at the garage. However, they had no luck – the side door was solid wood and the garage had no windows. Thabo peered up at the balcony.

"I could get up there."

Chris thought it looked awfully high, but it was a distinct option. *"Let's first go around and see what's on the ground floor,"* he whispered.

The grass felt damp underfoot and absorbed the sound of their steps as they moved to the garden side of the house. Chris tested various windows – all locked. He looked around at the silhouettes of Greek cypresses outlined against the moonlit sky. The fragrance of roses and wisteria hung in the night air.

Thabo sneezed.

They held their breath, waited. Nothing stirred.

"Do we break a window?" Thabo asked.

Chris measured the distance to the neighbor's house with his eyes.

"Better not - they might hear. Let's keep looking."

They crept up the broad marble steps and were swallowed by the darkness of the colonnaded verandah. Chris tested one sliding door, then another. When he tried the third door, though, it yielded. He felt a rush of exhilaration as the door slid open noiselessly – but after a few inches, it would go no further.

"Damn, it's got some stopper." He yanked hard, but the slider would not budge beyond a six-inch gap.

"I can squeeze through that," Thabo said.

"Never!"

The boy grinned and proceeded to slide his left arm and leg into the gap.

"Wait! The alarm."

Thabo froze.

"Look, this is the family room. If you *do* manage to get through, you'll set off the motion detectors. You'll have thirty seconds to get through the room and down the passage to the entrance. The alarm panel is next to the front door."

"What's the code?"

"Double-O-seven, seven."

"Easy."

Chris watched Thabo contort his body through the gap, then turn his head sideways and force it through. His skin stretched and his ears pressed flat against his head, like those of a dog with its head stuck out of the window of a speeding car. Then he was gone. Instantly, Chris heard a soft, high-pitched noise – the alarm system was in countdown mode; thirty seconds and all hell would break lose.

He started to count the seconds: *A thousand and one, a thousand and two.* What should he do if the alarm went off? He looked over his shoulder towards the cypresses. Was the fence electrified? Probably. ... *A thousand and fifteen, a thousand and sixteen, a thousand and seventeen.* He'd have to make for the car. But what about Thabo? *A thousand and eighteen, a thousand and nineteen ...*

"Thabo," he whispered into the dark void. *"Can you find it? Hurry up!"* He yanked at the door but it was futile. Wiping his forehead

with the back of his hand, he continued the mental countdown: *a thousand and twenty-seven, a thousand and twenty-eight...*

The high-pitched noise stopped. *Silence.* Chris heaved a sigh of relief.

Moments later, Thabo opened the door for him and they crossed the family room to the study. Chris closed the drapes, turned on the lights, and went straight to the safe. He was disappointed, yet hardly surprised, to find it locked. Next, he tested various drawers of the desk – a few were unlocked and he started to rifle through papers. Thabo slid into a leather chair and watched; with his fingers, he drew patterns in the gray fingerprinting dust that the police had left on the desk.

"Hey, stop that. You'll leave fingerprints."

"What about you?" Thabo said, trying to stifle a yawn.

"Mine are already all over the place. I can't really get into more trouble than I'm in already." Chris paused and looked up at the boy. He noticed how tired Thabo was.

"You've done an incredible job, partner. This will probably take a while. Why don't you lie down on the couch next door for a bit?"

Thabo shook his head vigorously to dispel the tiredness and said, "No, I keep watch."

Chris leafed through a stack of papers but couldn't find anything of real interest, so he turned on the computer. The Windows jingle announced the machine's readiness and he was prompted for a password. He rubbed his chin and wished he'd paid more attention the last time he was in the study with Bridget. Tentatively, he tried "Julie" and received a "password incorrect"; a similar message was elicited for "Bridget", "Noble", "Julie007", and a few others.

Chris was becoming concerned that the computer would freeze on him if he tried too many passwords. Then he remembered that Bridget had needed a notebook to remind her of the password. *Where is that notebook?* He went over to the safe and twiddled the combination lock, his ear pressed to the metal door, the way he'd seen it done in the movies. He couldn't hear anything. What a Catch 22: he needed Bridget to give him the computer password, and he needed the password to rescue Bridget. He pounded his fist against the metal door of the safe.

Turning round, he noticed that Thabo had fallen asleep in the chair, his arm and head dangling awkwardly over the side. Chris stooped down and lifted the boy. The chair moved back a little to reveal one corner of a small dark slab. He recognized it immediately – Bridget's notebook. Quickly, he carried Thabo to the family room and settled him under a blanket on the couch. Thabo mumbled something and smiled in his sleep as he curled up in the luxurious nest of leather and mohair.

Chris retrieved the notebook and, paging through it, had to admire how meticulous Bridget was. Various user IDs and passwords were neatly laid out. She regularly changed her passwords, crossing out the old ones and noting the dates on which she changed them. Chris fleetingly thought how out of keeping this behavior was with the slightly distracted, scatterbrained impression he'd had of her. The passwords were all combinations of place names and dates. *Quite clever,* Chris thought. He would never have guessed any of them in a million years. He tried the latest password: "Paris2007-08". He felt a rush of excitement as the screen changed and the whirring sound from the hard drive indicated that the machine was finally getting ready to do some work. As he waited for the computer to boot up, he reflected on what a sloppy job the police had done: they'd missed the notebook with the passwords, and they hadn't even bothered to take away the computer. Clearly, they'd been completely convinced that they had their man and just needed to squeeze hard enough to get a confession. Even the fingerprint dusting seemed cursory – just enough to prove that a certain Chris du Toit had been there.

The computer beeped its readiness and Chris was immediately in an element that was almost as familiar to him as water or the dance floor. Systematically, he identified documents that Bridget had reviewed on the evening of her disappearance. He copied a whole batch on to a memory stick and sent one document to the printer. Then he went into Bridget's emails. She'd been busy that night; someone called Charlie had forwarded a slew of emails. He opened them, one by one, with the intention of scanning quickly through them, printing anything that could direct his next moves, and copying the rest to the memory stick. He knew he could not stay in the house too long. But, as he opened the third email, he got absorbed and couldn't help but slow down to read the pages. As with the earlier emails, it was from Greg Louw, and was addressed to someone called Mr. Goh:

...The merchandize is ready for shipment. End destination is of no concern to me, but the equipment will only be released once commission payment is received in the following account...

The text was carefully worded to avoid anything incriminating, but Chris was convinced that the account details were for an offshore bank

– illegal foreign exchange dealing would at least get the police's attention. He hit "print" and continued. The next few emails got more heated. In one, it appeared as though there were delays in the transfer of funds and Greg's correspondent wanted to have more information regarding the effectiveness of the "merchandize".

Again, Chris printed the email. The emails that Charlie had forwarded seemed to cover very recent email exchanges but also older correspondence that Bridget had specifically requested from Charlie. In one of these older threads, Bridget asked Greg for more details regarding a certain overseas business transaction. Chris was intrigued; he hadn't realized that Bridget was actively concerned with specific business matters. She certainly had not given him that impression. Judging from the string of exchanges, Greg had not welcomed her interest. His first response, although polite, had been to the effect that she should enjoy her well-deserved retirement and leave the details of the business to him. The final one, however, was couched in very different language: *"I have slaved to build this two-bit near-bankrupt little business into an empire of note. Please do not continue to waste my time."*

No wonder Bridget disliked the guy. She appeared to have assembled a whole string of documents to build a case against him. The next email was again addressed to the mysterious Mr. Goh.

"Holy…" Chris whistled softly under his breath.

Here it was - clear proof that Greg had been plotting to have Bridget kidnapped. *He must have a God-complex or something to think he can get away with it,* Chris mused, staggered by the brazen arrogance of the man. *How could the police have missed this?* Chris printed the email, then sat back in the chair, and re-read it slowly. Gone was the circumspection of the earlier emails - this was the writing of a man who felt supremely confident that he was in control; he was simply removing an inconvenient obstacle.

Although Chris had not yet found hard evidence that the police were in Greg's pocket, he was convinced of it. There was no other explanation. He sighed, leaned back, and closed his eyes. If he handed the police this evidence, what would they do? Destroy it and simply lock him up again? How far up the ranks did the rot go? He felt despair creeping over him. *Maybe this is all futile,* he thought, and for a few seconds he gave in to dark imaginings. But then he shook his head like a dog, as if to dispel the encroaching negativity. *There had to be a way.* He just didn't know what it was yet.

He opened his eyes and was so startled that he banged his knee against the desk. A man had appeared in the doorway. Chris recognized him immediately; it was the large African driver he and Thabo had seen unloading a crate at the Khanya center's barn. The man held a knife in his hand and looked nervous.

"Hey, Ginger," he called over his shoulder. "He's here." The thick carpets swallowed all sound and Chris couldn't hear any footsteps. But, seconds later, another man materialized in front of Chris – Ginger, presumably, if his hair was the reason for his nickname. Chris remembered not only his hair, but also the pale skin and bored expression. He'd been the one who did not want Chris and Thabo to look around the barn. Chris thought of the photographs Thabo had taken, and wondered if these two had even the slightest idea what the contents of that crate really were. The idea flashed into his mind that maybe he could shock them with that knowledge, appeal to their better selves. But then he looked more closely at the pale, indifferent face of Ginger and decided that the chance of that working would be like that of the proverbial snowball in hell.

"Just like the boss told us," Ginger smirked. "You think you're so frigging clever and then you go tap into the company network. The boss picked it up like that." He arced his arm through the air and snapped his fingers so loudly that the African driver actually jumped a little. Chris had a second or two to study the big man's demeanor; he was far more nervous, he realized. *There might be a better chance ...*

"Don't *do* that," the African said.

Ginger waved away the protestations. He had swopped his lab coat for dark jeans and a fisherman's sweater, but there was something about his current outfit that seemed strangely familiar. And suddenly Chris remembered: *I've seen him somewhere else, not just at the barn... That night at the beach with Julie, those two men who I helped get their dinghy afloat ...* He felt anger rising, but kept his voice even when he said, "So, we meet again."

"Yeah. That day at the barn, we told you politely to stay away. But you wouldn't listen."

"I'm not talking about the barn; I'm talking about the night at the beach when I helped you get the dinghy from the river lagoon into the sea."

"Oh, that." Ginger laughed. "I wondered if you'd recognized me."

"What was in that dinghy – Rhino-S?"

"If that's what you want to call it – yeah. So what?"

"Ginger, shut up!" The black man took a step forward.

Ginger seemed unfazed. "Doesn't matter. He's history anyway." He laughed again, but without mirth.

"You can't talk about the … the merchandize. The boss will kill us!"

The African was clearly becoming agitated, and, for an instant, the two would-be assailants were not watching Chris. He had the desk between him and them; that gave him a brief advantage. With one powerful motion, he swiveled the chair around, and propelled up and away from the two men, towards the heavy drapes that concealed a sliding door. Ginger was halfway round the desk as Chris yanked the drapes apart and got his hands on the latch. He tried to flick it back - but it was locked. Thwarted, Chris crouched, swung around, and adopted a judo pose to confront them.

"You might as well come quietly, or I'll have to use this," the black man said, wielding the six-inch blade.

"You're out of your league …" Ginger sneered, certain of Chris's helplessness.

The words were scarcely out of his mouth before Chris was upon him, launching a sharp kick right in the man's stomach. It was a move he had practiced many times in martial arts, but he had never done it wearing heavy shoes before. The effect was striking. Ginger made a sound like a balloon losing air. His eyes bulged and his skin turned an ugly shade of red that clashed with the color of his hair. As he doubled over, clutching his stomach, Chris stepped forward and followed up with a hard chop on the man's neck that caused him to fold like a sack.

The big driver looked at his partner on the carpet. He seemed momentarily bewildered, uncertain, even, and Chris seized the moment to try and reason with him. "Look, I know you work for Greg. In the end, though, he's just going to drop you and let you take the blame for whatever goes wrong. I have no problem with you. No one needs to get ..."

Before he could finish his sentence, something snapped in the African's eyes. With a loud noise, somewhere between a growl and a scream, he lifted the knife and lunged forwards, half-tripping over his prostrate partner.

Chris sidestepped and tried to land a chop on the man's neck. But the driver had expected this and the blow glanced harmlessly off his back. He turned and lunged again, barely missing Chris's shoulder. They both stepped back, breathing hard, circling each other. Chris kept his eyes on the knife. Every time the African made the slightest mock attack motion with the knife, he reacted. He desperately needed a shield. He did not dare take his eye off his assailant, but mentally he took inventory of everything in the room: the paintings – *too flimsy* - the chairs – *too heavy* - books – *too small.*

They continued circling, and Chris felt the velvet drapes brush against his back. Without taking his eyes off his adversary, he half-turned, grabbed the drape, and yanked it with all his might. For a second, he thought the whole wooden pelmet would come crashing down. The driver must have thought the same; he took his eyes off Chris as the hooks gave way and the heavy fabric tumbled down. The drape was still in mid-air when Chris grasped it. He flung it at his opponent, launching himself after it like a human bulldozer. The other man instinctively stepped backwards, his knife was entangled in the fabric. Chris bore forward – *just a couple more feet to the door.* He knew that if he could just get past the big man, he could easily outrun him.

But then the African seemed to recover himself. He yanked hard at the drape, causing Chris to lose his balance. Then, managing to free the knife, he thrust it at his opponent. Chris felt a searing pain in his arm. In that split second, he was aware of two things: the triumphant look on the face of the driver and his own blood dripping on to the carpet.

Chris was forced to retreat; his eyes were fixed on the knife and he knew his only chance was to use his feet – they were protected. When he felt the desk behind him, he grasped the edge and lifted himself into a half- roll and kicked like he had never kicked before. The other man had seen it coming, though; he avoided the kick.

Step by step, Chris moved backwards until he felt the coldness of the glass door behind him. He could see a gleam in the driver's eye just before the man rushed forward. Ignoring the pain in his arm, Chris ducked, got in under the blade, and grasped the knife-wielding arm with both his hands. Gripping as hard as he could, he turned the arm like a giant screw. The African let rip with a grunted scream, but his other arm was still free, and he managed to plant a thunderous punch from behind on Chris's left kidney. The pain was blinding. Chris let go of the arm and staggered back against the sliding door.

Both men were doubled over, and for a few seconds their panting was the only sound in the room. But the driver, the bigger man, seemed to recover first. Lumbering to his feet, he stretched himself to his full height, lifted the knife for the final blow. *I'm going to die,* Chris thought, through a haze of pain. He closed his eyes, and a kind of resignation swept through him as he prepared for the knife to find its mark ... and then – nothing. Instead, he heard the sound of something whistling through the air, and then a sickening thud. Opening his eyes, he saw his adversary lying face down in front of him. Next to his head was a small, round object. It looked like a paperweight. *What on earth ...?* He struggled to his feet – and then he saw him. Standing in the doorway, a big grin on his face, was Thabo.

"Where did you learn to throw like that?" Chris couldn't fully take in what had just happened yet, but it looked very much as if his young friend had played David to the driver's Goliath.

"Killing snakes."

Chris shook his head. "You're something else, you know that? Thank you, partner; don't know what I'd do without you. I think just saved my life back there."

But there was no time to lose. Both men were out cold for now, but for how long? Swiftly, Chris gathered the print-outs. They needed to get out as fast as they could.

Thabo remained near the door. He stole a furtive look at the still figure of the driver on the floor. "Do you think he's ..?"

"No, he's just knocked out – don't worry. Look, his chest is moving."

Thabo watched for a moment, and then let out a sigh of relief.

"You did great," Chris said. "We'll have to get you a place on the national cricket team." He found a large envelope for the print-outs and added the memory stick - the evidence that would get him out of this nightmare.

"What are you going to do with this?" Thabo asked, pointing at the envelope.

"I've got to get this to Miss Wendy. Her lawyers will know what to do – they know people high up in the police. Let's go!"

"Stop right there!" It was Ginger. He still lay on the floor but now he held a gun in his hand, the barrel pointed straight at Chris. Slowly, he picked himself up, never letting his eyes off his target. With his free hand, he rubbed his neck where Chris had chopped him. "It's going to be such a pleasure to get rid of you," he said.

Chris watched intently; imperceptibly, he moved his body a little sideways to ensure that he was squarely between the gun and Thabo. The gun trained on Chris, Ginger inched to where his partner lay on the floor. He nudged his toe into the man's ribs. "Wake up, fat ass." Chris glanced over his shoulder; Thabo was behind him. The big man on the floor stirred and groaned, and dragged himself into a sitting position. He looked groggily in the direction of the door, trying to figure out what had hit him. Ginger reached down to help his partner up.

Chris reacted instantly. Spinning round, he tossed the brown envelope towards the door, and shouted, "Thabo, run!"

He just had time to register that both boy and envelope had gone before the two men were upon him.

Minutes later, Chris found himself once again flung into the back of a panel van. This time, however, it was not a police van, but the windowless white vehicle which the men had used to deliver their crates to the barn. The doors slammed and he could hear a padlock snap shut.

"What about the boy?" the driver asked. "Should we call the boss?"

"He said not to contact him till we've gotten rid of this guy."

"But what if the boy goes to the police?"

"Look, I'm tired of arguing with you. Do you think the police are going to believe some skinny little black kid that walks in full of stories? Never! If you want to call the boss, though, go right ahead."

They both got into the van. Chris could feel the vehicle sag under their weight. Then he heard the doors shut. Their voices were muffled, but he could still hear the conversation.

"Where to?" the driver asked.

"The quarry at Kontermans Kloof. Once we're finished there, we'll call the boss and see what he wants done about the boy."

Chris felt a cold chill that numbed even the pain in his arm. They must mean to take him to the quarry and kill him there. There was a smell of rusting iron and already he felt entombed.

Then he heard the driver say, "If we're going all the way to the quarry, I'll have to stop for petrol."

"Oh, for fuck's sake! Why?"

"How was I supposed to know that we'd be chasing around the whole damn peninsula tonight? I was going to fill her up tomorrow morning."

"Just shut up and drive. Don't fill up here in Constantia – too much light, too many people. There's a small petrol station where …"

Chris could not hear the rest of what he said above the noise of the engine. As the van moved forward, he felt his way around in the darkness. Finding the doors, he steadied himself and kicked against them with all the power he could muster. They did not budge. Again he kicked, and again.

Chapter 22: Thabo

Thursday early morning

Thabo, his senses on high alert, crouched under a row of shrubs. A dog barked into the night and he shrunk deeper into the shadows. The smell of fresh-cut grass was unfamiliar, luxurious. It was nothing like the smell of dusty dryness that he was used to from Mandela Park.

He kept his eyes on the front door and strained to listen. What were they doing to Chris? *Please God, please, don't let them hurt him. Please!*

The envelope was safely tucked into the front of his shirt and he knew he ought to get to the main road and find a way to contact Miss Wendy. That's what Chris had told him to do. But he couldn't just abandon his partner. What if they hurt him?

The door opened and a shaft of light lit the pathway. Thabo ducked and held his breath. Instinctively, like a blind man reading Braille, his hands felt across the ground, searching for a sturdy rock. But there was nothing but soft, loamy soil.

Thabo peered through the branches as Chris was led out of the house and bundled into the back of a delivery van. The doors of the van slammed shut and Thabo heard the click of a padlock. If only he had a weapon, any weapon – a brick, or even just some nails to flatten the tires. He cursed himself for not having thought of sabotaging the van earlier. Bent on all fours, he made a tentative move towards the vehicle. Could he creep underneath and rip out some wires?

Too late - the two men got into the cab and started the engine.

Again, Thabo touched his shirt and felt the envelope. Chris had been very clear; his partner was counting on him. He really ought to … Then the van began to move, and Thabo immediately knew what he had to do. He shot out from his hiding place and sprinted after the van, catching up with it after ten paces. He reached up, gripped the back door handles, and swung himself up on to the bumper. Had anyone been there to see him, they would have marveled at the fluid ease with which he executed the maneuver – as practiced as someone stepping on to a bus.

Just then, there was a violent thud from inside the van, and Thabo nearly lost his grip. He clung on as Chris kicked the door again and again. Hot exhaust fumes swirled around his legs and he tucked his nose into the crook of his elbow to avoid breathing them in. He heard laughter from the cab and then the kicking stopped. As the van picked up speed, there was only the rushing wind.

Julie's head hurt; her mouth was dry and her eyes leaden. She was aware of a rocking motion and thought she might be on a train. She remembered the time she and her parents had traveled on the Blue Train from Johannesburg to Cape Town. She remembered the starched cloth on their table in the dining car, and how the glassware sparkled like her mother's diamond necklace. The waiter had poured her a little wine, and it had smelled of church, and the good-night-kiss scent of her mother … And her parents had laughed as she tasted her thimbleful of wine. How happy they had been …

The soles of her feet hurt. *Why?* For some reason, she knew that she had been running barefoot, but why? *And where?* The memory faded and she became aware of a cool dampness– the salty smell of fog and seaweed.   And there was something else; a scent she distinctly remembered. She opened her eyes.

"Thank God … thank God, you're awake." Bridget clutched one of Julie's hands and dabbed a damp cloth against her daughter's forehead.

Why is Mother crying? A minute ago, we were so happy.

It took Julie a while to register that she was in a ship's cabin, her head resting on her mother's lap. Her mother! Her mother was alive! Tears streamed down her face as she struggled into a sitting position and wrapped her arms around Bridget, holding on to her as if her life depended on it. For a few minutes, the two women held each other tightly, as if neither quite believed that the other was really there, and might vanish if they let go. Finally, Julie loosened her grip and allowed herself to look into her mother's eyes. Despite the dim light, and the veil of tears, she could see the exhaustion in Bridget's face. Without make-up, Bridget looked pale and vulnerable, and Julie was overcome by tenderness. She reached up and gently smoothed the furrows on her mother's forehead, pushed back a strand of hair.

When she could trust herself to speak, she said, "I was so worried. Are you OK? Did they hurt you?"

"I'm fine. They wouldn't dare ..." Bridget's tone did not convey as much conviction as the words suggested.

"When I thought that ... that something had happened to you, that I might never see you again ... I just couldn't bear it."

Again the tears flowed, again she and her mother held each other tight. "It will be fine, darling. It will be fine. Don't worry about a thing." Bridget's voice was soothing,

How Julie wished she could believe it, the way she used to many, many years ago.

"I'm just so relieved that you're awake," her mother went on, quietly. "When they brought you in, I could see you'd been drugged, but they wouldn't tell me ..." Her voice cracked.

By now, Julie's head was beginning to clear. As the ability to focus returned, so too did the realization of the gravity of their predicament. She peered into the darkness outside the porthole. "What time is it? How long have I been here?"

"It's after midnight. That dreadful blonde woman looked in once, about an hour ago; didn't say a word. And as for that Lenny character – he's the one who abducted me, you know." Her voice was laden with outrage. As if to reassure herself, she continued, "Matt will sort him out. I can't wait for Matt and the police to get here. They'll ..."

Matt! Julie sat bolt upright. "We have to get out." She crossed to the door and yanked at the handle until her shoulder hurt. The porthole was bolted shut from the outside. Julie moved around the cabin, testing the wood paneling, the ceiling. She even opened the small closet and tried to kick out its back panel – it was solid.

"Believe me, I've tried," Bridget said. "There's no way out. There's nothing to do but sit and wait for the cavalry."

Julie swallowed. *What cavalry?* "I don't think Matt or the police are going to be coming any time soon." She paused, wondering how to go on. "Matt ... Matt's in hospital. He's had a heart attack."

Bridget's hands flew to her face. Slowly, she got up and moved to the porthole. With unseeing eyes, she stared into the darkness.

Julie touched her shoulder. "I have every reason to believe he'll be OK. Felicity's spoken to the doctors, they say it's a minor attack, probably stress-related ... I wanted to visit him before I left, but ..." She paused, suddenly feeling a heel for not visiting her step-father. "But I had to get away, quickly, before ... before ..." She found herself almost chocking on the words. "Before Greg found out I knew what he was up to."

Bridget slowly turned to face her daughter. "So you know about Greg?"

"Yes." Julie's voice was almost inaudible. She thought of all the times Bridget had tried to warn her about Greg, and how she had refused to listen, thought she knew better.

But if Bridget had any feelings of being vindicated, she did not show them. She simply sighed, and said, "At least that's a relief. I've been sitting here, agonizing about how I was going to tell you. I assumed you wouldn't believe me."

Julie said nothing; she knew it was true. If her mother had told her, a week ago, that Greg was scheming to take over the company, that he had dragged Noble Enterprises into illegal dealings with an international cartel, and that he had been ruthlessly exploiting them all, she wouldn't have believed a word of it. He had had her totally fooled. A wave of shame and fury welled up in her, and she crossed the cabin and pounded her fists against the door.

Bridget gently took her daughter's hand and led her back to the bunk, offered her a glass of water. Then she said, "Tell me all you know. Let's see if together we can figure out exactly what's going on here. It's just you and me now ..." She paused and swallowed.

Julie knew exactly what the unspoken words were that were left hanging in the air. *"It's just you and me now, just like when your father died."* She was aware of feeling an overwhelming sense of connection with her mother. Yes, they were prisoners, yes, the future was horribly uncertain, but they were together, united by adversity as they had been united by grief all those years ago. Somehow that made all the difference in the world.

Bridget broke the reverie, and when she spoke, there was a glint in her eye that reminded Julie of the fearless businesswoman her mother used to be. "I'll be damned if we give up without a fight. We'll figure something out. Now tell me, how did you find out about Greg?"

Thabo's arms ached, but he hung on. He had frequently traveled the two kilometers from Mandela Park to downtown Hout Bay clinging to the back of a van or minibus, but this was different. He guessed they had driven for at least half an hour; the streets were completely unfamiliar to him. A couple of times, he had tried to communicate with Chris by tapping against the metal door, but it was useless. The van rattled so much that Chris had not noticed, and Thabo was scared he might attract the attention of the men in the front. *What am I going to do when they stop?* he wondered. He still had his cell phone, and had thought that he would call for help as soon as they stopped, but now he was getting concerned. They were so far away from anyone he knew that help might not get to them in time.

Anyway, who was there to call? The police? Never!

Miss Julie? She was locked up, no good.

His mother? She had a cell phone that was one of her most prized possessions. The phone was only used once a month to call her sister in faraway Umtata. Thabo had never met this aunt. He felt a pang of guilt. His mother thought he was spending the night at a friend's house. She had tried to hide her surprise when he told her, but he knew that she was delighted to think he had a friend to stay with. She had urged him to go, told him she was fine, and that the neighbor would help with the baby. If he called her now … He had a fleeting sense of how reckless his actions were. If something happened to him, what would become of his mother? He banished the thought and shifted his weight to lean up more against the van. Gripping more firmly with his left hand, Thabo used his right one to carefully take the phone out of his pocket. He'd made up his mind – he was going to call Miss Wendy; after all, that was what Chris had wanted him to do in the first place.

The streetlights were intermittent and his hand was unsteady, but he managed to turn on the phone and enter the PIN. Impatiently, he waited for the device to respond. *Come on, come on.* His left hand started to cramp, and he did not notice the van slowing a little. Then the driver made a sharp left turn and Thabo, caught by surprise, lost his balance. The phone shot out of his hand and bumped along the tarmac into the bushes at the side of the road. For one awful moment, he thought he might follow it, but then he managed to get a grip with both hands and restore his balance.

Then van slowed again, and lurched to the right as they pulled into a petrol station. Thabo saw that it was not like the shiny service station in Hout Bay, where he sometimes went to buy toffees. This place was dimly lit; there were tires piled high and a lot of broken trucks and cars. He did not wait for the van to stop; as it slowed, he leapt off the bumper and ran in a straight line away from the vehicle, hoping the driver would not see him in the mirrors. Blood pounded in his ears as he raced towards the edge of the lot and slid in amongst the vehicle carcasses.

Red Hair and the driver got out, stretched, and looked around. There was no sign of a pump attendant anywhere. From his hiding place, Thabo saw Red Hair bang against the side of the van and whisper something – probably threatening Chris to stay quiet. Thabo inched forward and let his hands do their Braille dance across the ground to detect any obstacles. The smell of rust and oil was familiar to him. Carefully, he crawled around a tire and moved a couple of cans out of the way. His eyes never left the two men in the distance.

Suddenly, Thabo touched something hard. He looked down and saw a crowbar next to a stack of wheels. His hand firmed around his find as he continued to watch. The driver had gone inside the darkened kiosk and was cursing loudly. It sounded as if he had found the pump attendant fast asleep. Red Hair, meanwhile, had walked to the far end of the building and could be heard relieving himself.

Thabo seized his chance. Staying in the shadows, he circled to the left until the van was between him and the two men. Then he took a deep breath, and sprinted the thirty yards to the vehicle, wielding the crowbar like the baton of a relay runner.

Reaching the van, he pushed the crowbar under the riveted clasp and yanked hard. He grimaced when the rivets protested with a screech that echoed through the quiet night. The clasp resisted the pressure, however, so he swiftly repositioned the crowbar.

This was the moment Chris chose to resume kicking against the van door. It caught Thabo by surprise; he fumbled and the tool nearly slipped from his sweaty hands. Now he could hear footsteps and Red Hair shouting. In a panic, Thabo looked over his shoulder. *If I run now, I might still make it back... But – no.* He banished the thought, rammed the crowbar back into place, and pulled with all his might. The clasp yielded and Thabo barely managed to get out of the way as Chris kicked the doors open.

Thabo stifled a scream when Chris leapt at him with the fiercest expression he'd ever seen. Clearly, his partner had no idea who was opening the doors and was spring-loaded for a full-on attack.

"Thabo!?" The expression changed immediately.

"Come! Come, this way!"

Together, they ran for the cover of the car wrecks. Thabo could hear loud voices behind them; he didn't turn to look – he just ran like never before in his life. He'd done it! Right next to him was Chris, his partner. He'd done it; he'd freed him. If anyone could have seen his face, they would have marveled at the broad grin of the boy who ran like an Olympic champion.

As the first shots rang out, they ducked behind an old truck. Chris took the lead; since he'd been cooped up in the van, his eyes had become accustomed to the dark and he had no trouble seeing where to go. They picked their way through the scrap and sprinted across a dimly lit street. Thabo heard tires squeal as the van charged out of the petrol station and careered down the street they had crossed seconds earlier.

They continued to run, through an alley, past a row of dark rundown shops, and a row of dumpsters, the smell from which bore testimony to the heat of the last few days. Crossing another street, they jumped over a low wall into a churchyard. There they sank down at last, backs against the wall, panting, listening. Chris peered around the edge of the wall and waited; *no sign of the van.*

"Thabo ... how ... how the heck did you follow us?"

"I hitched a ride on the back of the van. And I had to hold on very tight when you kicked against the door." He lifted his tightly clenched fists to show Chris how hard he had held on.

Chris shook his head. "All this way? Man, do I owe you. I've never been so glad to see anyone in my whole life."

Thabo beamed in the darkness.

Chris asked, "Do you have any idea where we are?"

"The last sign I saw said 'Kontermans Quarry'."

Thabo noticed that Chris shuddered at the words. "Are you cold?"

"No, I'm fine. But if you hadn't come along, I would have been very cold ... permanently cold."

They sat in silence and listened. All remained quiet.

"They took my phone," Chris said. "You don't happen to have yours, do you?"

Thabo shook his head. He wondered whether Chris would be cross about him losing the cell phone. Then another thought struck him and he said, "That paperweight thing that I threw at the big man ..."

"Yes?"

"I think I broke it. Will I get into trouble for that?"

Chris looked at him, and then he couldn't help himself, he began to laugh. Thabo did not understand why, but then he, too, started laughing. Everything was crazy; the world was crazy, mad. But they had managed to escape, and so they laughed ... laughed in the darkness of the graveyard.

Eventually, Chris wiped the tears from his eyes and said, "No, Thabo, I'm sure you won't be in trouble. Now, tell me," he said, as his voice returned to normal, "were you able to get that envelope out of the house?"

Thabo nodded, and pulled it out of his shirt.

Bloody hell, this kid is a complete superstar! "Man, if only we could clone you, the world would be a better place." Thabo hadn't a clue what Chris was on about, but he judged that it was something positive because his partner looked so happy.

"Well, then, let's go find ourselves some wheels."

The streets were utterly deserted – no hope of any form of public transport or a taxi. They stayed in the shadows and walked back to the service station. The petrol attendant was wide awake now, still shaken up by the encounter with two gun-wielding maniacs. He had watched them chase off after Chris and Thabo, and realized that things might have gone badly for him, had they not lured the two madmen away. He was therefore more than willing to look the other way while they "borrowed" an old Corolla. It was severely dented, only had one headlight, and the rear window had been smashed, but it had air in all four tires and the engine started on the first try.

##

Julie and Bridget looked at each other and drew closer when they heard a key in the door. Cindy stepped in, without knocking.

"Ah. I see you're awake. Mother and daughter reunion, how touching."

As always, her smile did not reach her eyes. Julie tried hard to keep her own face expressionless, and not betray any fear or weakness. Cindy had changed into a dark tracksuit with a turtle neck that served to accentuate the pale skin and wide red mouth.

Her eyes fixed on Julie. "Come," she commanded, with a slight jerk of the head.

Julie rose slowly and extricated her hand from her mother's concerned grip. Bridget rose to follow.

"No, not you. Greg only wants to talk to his *little songbird*," she sneered.

She followed Cindy down a narrow, carpeted passage. As they walked, Julie tried to take in every detail of her surroundings: three cabin doors left and three right, *no exit behind them*; a narrow staircase ahead. Julie registered that she and her mother were kept in the cabin furthest away from the stairs. She wondered who the occupants of the other cabins were.

They went up the stairs and emerged into what appeared to be the yacht's main reception area. Despite her anxiety, Julie marveled at the unashamed splendor of the vessel – it was hard to picture this as a boat. The double volume space reminded her of the lobby in a boutique hotel: Persian rugs on the floor, two leather sofas with Chinese lacquer coffee tables. Everything discreetly anchored to the floor. Pleated lampshades cast a soft glow on the walls that were adorned with oil paintings of tropical scenes.

On her left, the main portal to the outside appeared to be firmly shut. Through the glass, she could see part of the lit deck. A man in uniform stood smoking at the railing. Julie thought he carried a gun, but she couldn't be certain. The man suddenly turned towards her. He took a drag on his cigarette and, for an instant, the glow turned his face into an eerie red mask with thin eye-slits. It felt as though the eyes behind the mask were staring straight through her. Julie's insides twisted into an even tighter knot.

"Will you please move along?" Cindy asked, in a regal tone of exasperation. She was already halfway up the stairs to the next deck, and looked down over her shoulder as though Julie were her miscreant subject.

Julie shot Cindy a cold stare. Deliberately, she remained unmoving, firmly planted in the middle of the lobby, continuing to take in her surroundings. The curved staircase on which Cindy stood wound its way up to a mezzanine deck. Under the mezzanine area was a built-in bar. Fleetingly, Julie thought how cozy this would be under normal circumstances, although she thought the heavy, low-hanging chandelier was faintly ridiculous on a yacht. In a storm, it would be a serious liability.

Then Cindy impatiently beckoned again, and Julie followed her up the stairs. On the mezzanine level, she caught a glimpse of the bridge. Two Asian men in white uniforms stood silhouetted against the blue glow of instrument panels. It struck Julie that there seemed to be even more displays than in a plane. *A plane!* The though jolted her back to the events of earlier that night, to her barefoot flight from Lenny and his gang, to the rough hands of the co-pilot as he slammed her against the SUV, to the pilot, the only one who had tried to help her, lying dead on the tarmac. A shudder ran through her body, and she had to suppress an involuntary gasp.

Both men glanced up to look at her with some curiosity as she headed away from them down a long corridor. She noticed that one tipped his hat. At the end of the passage, she saw another portal – *a possible escape route? There* must *be lifeboats somewhere out there.* She never got near the portal, however, as Cindy had stopped and was knocking on a wooden door. They entered a large cabin that reminded Julie of Matt's office in Johannesburg. There was a cherry wood desk and a built-in bookcase running the entire length of one wall. Off to one side was a boardroom table with six chairs. Two men sat at the table. She recognized them immediately – Lenny, and the recipient of Greg's shocking emails, the man with whom she had had dinner so recently - Mr. Goh.

Mr. Goh, his face an inscrutable mask, got up when she walked in and said, "Miss Noble, it is a pleasure to meet you again." *No pretense, now, of lack of English,* she thought grimly. He bowed slightly, the absolute minimum that good manners would demand, and touched the tips of his fingers in front of his chest. "Please allow me to welcome you aboard my ship." His arms spread in a jerky movement, like a bird testing its wings for flight.

Although she now knew full well the extent of Mr. Goh's involvement in Greg's treacherous and illegal dealings, Julie still found it hard to know how to react in the face of such mannered politeness. Her main feeling was one of acute embarrassment – what a stupid little rich brat this man must think her, she realized. How gullible and naïve not to be aware of what was going on in her own company. Or – worse – maybe he thought she was fully in on Greg's schemes?

The embarrassment was fleeting, however, and was rapidly replaced by anger. At the same time, Julie resolved not to give any one of the three – Goh, Lenny or Cindy – the satisfaction of seeing the turmoil of her emotions. And she knew that this was just a practice run. She had to brace herself for the confrontation with Greg. She decided the best course of action was to play along with the charade till she knew more.

She offered Mr. Goh her hand and, with her most polite finishing-school smile, thanked him.

He brought her hand to his lips and said, "I trust you found your mother in good health?"

There was a glint in his eyes. *The bastard is enjoying himself!*

Julie frowned slightly. "My mother could benefit from a little more fresh air but, other than that, she seems to be in good health."

"Once we set off tomorrow morning and reach the open seas, you and your mother will be most welcome to enjoy the amenities. We have a sun deck, a heated spa pool, even a small gymnasium. You will find the cuisine on board excellent." He smacked his lips.

"Leaving tomorrow?" Julie knew that her face betrayed her panic.

Mr. Goh held up his hand and cut her off. "You will have to excuse me. It is late. Good night." And, with a curt bow, he strode straight past her and was gone.

Lenny had remained slouched in his chair during this exchange. Now, he yawned expansively, pointed at one of the boardroom chairs, and commanded, "Sit!"

He started to work a computer console and a section of wood paneling slid aside to reveal a massive flat-screen monitor. When it flickered into life, Julie saw Greg at his desk, with the Johannesburg skyline clearly visible behind him. Julie was surprised by the picture quality – Greg had his sleeves rolled up and looked so lifelike that she feared he might reach out and grab her arm. She shrank into her seat and watched as he continued to work and ignored her for what seemed like an eternity. Part of her bristled at this calculated insult, but part of her was glad to defer any interaction with him.

Julie noticed that his tie had been loosened and his normally immaculate hair was slightly disheveled. For a moment, she was reminded of the young man she had idolized and fantasized about when she was … what … fifteen or sixteen? Somewhere, in the depths of all her anger, there was still a tiny kernel of disbelief and sadness. The betrayal was monstrous. She closed her eyes; the man in front of her was dangerous, ruthless, and manipulative; a man so greedy he thought nothing of participating in the wholesale slaughter of endangered animals, of collaborating with thugs and criminals, of kidnapping, even of condoning murder. How could she have been so blind? She thought of her mother, and of Chris, and of the dead pilot, and deliberately tried to feed off her anger to steel herself.

Finally, Greg looked up. "Leave us," he said.

Julie heard the door close behind Lenny and Cindy.

Greg ran his fingers through his hair and said, "You gave me quite a runaround."

She did not trust herself to speak – not yet. A silence ensued.

"I wish I could make you understand ..."

"Understand what, Greg? That you have taken the company – *our* company - and turned it into … into a manufacturer of … dreadful, dreadful …" She was lost for the right words. "Dreadful Frankenstein drug- making equipment?" Her voice rose and she fought to control it. "Or that you had my mother kidnapped, and … and myself? What is your plan now … do you even *have* a plan, or do you just make it all up as you go along?" Julie kept her hands firmly clasped to prevent them from shaking.

"Jules, please, let's discuss ..."

"Don't call me Jules; you know I hate it!" Suddenly, she couldn't contain her rage any longer. She slammed her open hand on to the table. Greg appeared momentarily startled; that made the pain in her hand worth it.

He said, "You used to like it when we first met."

"When we first met," she spat, "I used to trust you, Greg. I trusted you like the big brother I never had. I thought you could do no wrong. What happened to you, Greg? *Why?* You had everything!"

"Julie, you must understand. Everything I've done, I've done for you, for us." His voice was low and he had the earnest expression of a preacher entreating his flock. The camera grotesquely enlarged his outstretched hands and Julie inched further back.

"I loved you from the very first moment I saw you," Greg continued. "I knew I would have to wait, because you were so young, but I didn't mind. I knew that you were destined for me."

She looked hard at him; tried to reconcile the face before her with that of the charming, ruffle-haired young man who had made her laugh and who had treated her like an adult when others spoke to her like a child. For a moment, she thought she caught a glimpse, a ghost, of the young Greg. But when she blinked, all she saw was the phony smile, the cold eyes.

"Spare me the rubbish, Greg. All you ever wanted was the company. I've known it for a long time, I just didn't want to admit it to myself - and," she paused, "I didn't want to admit to my mother that she was right about you!"

"Ah! There we have it, the nub of the problem: dear Bridget!" His expression changed and now his voice was laden with loathing. "If only dear Bridget could have confined herself to bridge and booze instead of meddling in the business."

"How dare you speak about my mother like that? *She* built that company with my father; *she* owns it! She has every right to concern herself with the business! You forget that she is your employer, she could fire you at any time!"

His lips curved into an unpleasant smile. "She did." For a moment, his eyes slewed sideways and Julie felt that he was somehow disconnected – processing something that he found hard to assimilate. Then he refocused, went on, "Last Saturday night, when we had our late-night blow-up over the Malaysian contract, she fired me! She actually had the gall to fire me after all that I have sacrificed to build Noble Enterprises!"

He shook his head in disbelief. "She'd tried once before, but Matt stopped her. This time, she put it in an email. That's why I had to act and get her out of the way. You see … she brought this entirely on herself.

With her out of the way, on a nice extended vacation, everything will be fine."

Julie watched him, mesmerized. *How could I have been so mistaken?* She felt a cold fear creep around her heart. This man was delusional; he actually *believed* what he was saying. She realized that she'd have to be very careful, and she forced herself to adopt a more conciliatory tone.

"Greg, I don't want to talk about my mother now. This has gone far enough. You tell Mr. Goh and Lenny to put us ashore and we can just put this whole thing behind us."

"*Ha!* Now who's talking rubbish? Your mother would ..."

"My mother would do exactly what I tell her to do. You know that. She might not like it but, in the end, she always listens to me."

He seemed to contemplate this for a while, but then he shook his head. "There's too much riding on this now. You'll go on a nice cruise, and when everything has quietened down in a few months, I'll come and join you. For our wedding, we will have an exclusive beach ceremony, in Malaysia, or maybe in Bali ... just you and me."

"Greg!" There was panic in her voice. "You can't get away with this. People will notice if my mother and I suddenly disappear ... our friends ... my work ... my ... my mother's charities ..." She was so agitated that she found herself stuttering.

"All taken care of. Noble Enterprises will put out a statement tomorrow to explain that your mother has suffered a nervous breakdown after her kidnapping ordeal. We'll say that company security experts managed to secure her release and you, dutiful daughter that you are, have dropped everything to help her recuperate in an undisclosed location."

"Matt won't stand for it! He'll ..."

"Funny you should mention Matt. As you know, his life hangs by a thread – a thread that you hold in your hands. If you don't play along ..." Slowly, he made a gesture like a pair of scissors snipping an imaginary line.

Julie averted her face and stared blankly at the locked door. She could not bear to see those eyes anymore.

"Julie." He paused, waited until she forced herself to look at him again. "You must know that I would never let anyone harm you. I will protect you like I always have, whether you are right here with me or anywhere else."

She had to resist the urge to stick her fingers in her ears to block out his infuriatingly smug, solicitous voice. Instead, she clamped her teeth together and waited for him to continue.

Greg picked up a golf ball and tossed it from one hand to the other. "*You* will always be safe, but ... but I cannot say the same for your mother and Matt. If *dear* Bridget does not behave and do as she's told, Matt will bear the consequences. And if Matt gets any silly ideas, then your mother will suffer much more than a nervous breakdown." He leaned forward. "So, you see, we are all going to work together very nicely because it is in everyone's best interest."

Coldness had crept into her limbs. She glanced at her hands and noticed that they were white. "You can't get away with this ..."

"Julie, don't be so dim. I already *have* gotten away with it."

She knew she was clutching at straws when she said, "What about the kidnapping? The police ..."

"Ah, the police ..." He looked at his watch. "In another two hours, the police will receive a tip-off that will lead them to the body of one Chris du Toit. They will discover a few thousand rand in marked banknotes in his pockets. That will clearly confirm the fact that he was behind the kidnapping. Unfortunately, as the police will later learn, our security personnel had to shoot him during the rescue operation."

They had shot Chris. Julie heard a muffled ringing in her ears, as though her brain had tried to put up a protective barrier. She continued to stare at the monitor, but she could no longer make out Greg's features – they swam out of focus. All she saw was the golf ball, going from one hand to the other ... to the other ... the other. She could not breathe and clung to the desk for support. *Chris was dead.*

"*Why?*" she whispered. "Why did you pick on him, a complete innocent?"

He stopped playing with the golf ball and leaned forward again. With a half-smile that the close-up lens contorted into a repulsive grimace, and in a voice that was dripping with superiority, he said, "Come on, Julie, don't act like an imbecile."

When she continued to look at him in uncomprehending shock, he sighed. Slowly, deliberately, he said: "Because nobody ... *nobody* ... steals my woman!"

"But that's ridiculous! We were just friends."

"Don't insult my intelligence. I have watched the two of you together."

"But ..."

He looked at her intently. "You crack me up. You really had no idea?"

She stared straight ahead and did not move a muscle.

"I knew there was some risk in giving you a bit of freedom, letting you go to university in Cape Town. But risk is always with us; risk has to be managed. Did you *really* think I would let you out of my sight for even a minute? I've had daily reports on your whereabouts from the first day you went to university!"

It was too much to comprehend, too outrageous, too ... too crazy. He'd had her stalked, watched ...

"So, my little songbird, even when you don't see me, know that I'm always there, watching over you." The right side of his mouth curled up into the faintest of smiles. "We'll talk again soon."

The screen went blank. She sat, unable to move, stunned. And then, slowly, her body folded forwards on to her arms, and she wept. Chris was dead, shot by Greg's thugs. The pilot was dead. Matt's life was hanging by a thread. She and her mother were trapped. Somehow, it felt as if it was all her fault: if she hadn't been so vain, so blind... She felt as cold as the dead. A madman had gained control over her, her family, her company, her entire life. Chris was dead ... dead. Dead like her father. She   started   to   sob   uncontrollably.

##

Chapter 23: Dawn

Thursday morning

Chris ignored the Corolla's groans and pushed the worn-out vehicle as hard as he could on the deserted N1 back to Cape Town.

"Are we going to *Meez* Wendy's to give her the papers?" Thabo asked.

Chris shook his head. "We're going directly to the harbor. The *Moonflower* could sail at any moment; if I go to Wendy and my father, it could take hours for them to persuade the police to mobilize. It's all up to us now."

He did not dare dwell on the thought of Julie and Bridget, helpless in the power of the Dragon Boys, out on the open ocean. An "accident" could happen, an inconvenient passenger might be "swept overboard by a freak wave ..."

Thabo leaned over and looked at the flashing fuel indicator that had been nagging at Chris's consciousness for some time. "Do you have money for petrol?" he asked.

Chris shook his head.

"We can hitch-hike," Thabo offered helpfully.

"We might just get there. There's always a little extra reserve in the tank."

They careered down the road from Constantia to Hout Bay village. Then, just as they reached the familiar sign for the Khanya center, Chris braked hard and pulled off the road.

He turned to Thabo and said, "Listen, partner, you must do me another big favor. I want you to run to the Khanya center and wake Mama Mercy – you know which one is her room?"

Thabo nodded.

"Don't wake anyone else; I don't want them frightened. But Mama Mercy can unlock the office for you and get you Miss Wendy's number. Then you must fax the papers to her and, after that, phone and tell Miss Wendy everything that has happened."

A crease appeared on Thabo's forehead. "But you said it will take too long for her to get help. You said it is all up to *us* now. I want to come help ..."

"Thabo, please. I will go down there and stop that boat long enough for the police to get there; but if we don't get a message to someone very senior in the police ..." He paused. "You *are* helping. This is an extremely important part of the plan."

Thabo looked into Chris's eyes. "Your plans," he said. "They are always changing." Chris was struck by the timeless gravity of the boy's features. He could picture him as an old man, admonishing a wayward grandson about to run off on a headstrong quest.

One foot out of the door, Thabo turned and gave Chris another penetrating look. "Be careful," he said. Then he was gone.

A few minutes later, the old clunker, deprived of fuel, spluttered to a halt. Chris abandoned it and started to jog. The lights of an oncoming vehicle made him duck into the bushes. *Who drives around at two o'clock in the morning?*

He quickened his pace, and the salty sea air seemed to etch itself into every alveolus of his lungs. The burning sensation and physical exertion brought him relief. He kept looking in the direction of where he imagined the yacht to be, but the ocean was hidden by a band of low dunes. He was within site of the harbor's main entrance when he became aware of someone running behind him – whoever it was seemed very light-footed, but Chris could hear breathing. The hairs on his neck rose. He forced himself to keep his pace steady. He mustn't look around, mustn't let on that he knew he was being followed. He continued for another hundred meters and allowed the gap to close; then he jumped to one side and, in a single motion, turned around and kicked hard at the level of his pursuer's stomach.

Chris's kick went into a void. He lost his balance and landed on the sand next to the road. He heard a series of yelps and felt a slobbering tongue on his face.

"What the ..? Get off, get off!" Chris whispered.

He wrestled the furry beast off his chest and sat up to pat the dog that had followed him. "Hey, buddy, what are you doing out so late?" He didn't have to look at the dog's identity tag to know that it was the same one that had "adopted" him and Julie that night on the beach.

"Looks like you're one of those 'self-exercising' dogs, eh? It's time for you to go. *Shoo, go!* Go home!"

The dog turned away and Chris continued down to the harbor. He crouched in the shadows of a boarded-up souvenir kiosk near the harbor entrance and listened to the sound of waves lapping against the pier. Then he heard voices and saw a cigarette glow in the dark. He pressed himself against the wall of the kiosk as he watched two men walk under a streetlight; they had guns tucked into their waistbands and Chris was convinced that they were members of the Dragon Boys. As he watched them swagger through the deserted harbor, he found himself thinking of Desmond, who used to quip, *"And wandereth I through the valley of darkness, I shall fear no evil, because I am the meanest son-of-a-bitch in the valley."*

Where the hell is Desmond, anyway? Bloody convenient for him to be out of town! Chris felt irritated and concerned about his friend, but mainly he wished that Desmond were there, by his side. Desmond knew about gangs.

Chris watched the men as they joined a shadowy group of three or four others clustered around a SUV. Chris recognized it as Lenny's vehicle. Beyond them, far out in the bay, he could see the yacht. Most of its lights were off.

One of the men opened the Pajero's front-passenger door, and the dim interior light cast a glow over the group. Chris caught his breath. In the instant before the door shut, Chris thought he saw Desmond amongst the group – tall, and with his distinctive dancer's posture. Chris blinked and strained to try and see better. He couldn't believe it; his mind must be playing tricks. *That must be it:* he'd been thinking about Desmond a few minutes ago, and now – because he was tired and stressed - his mind had magicked him up. But then he remembered that Julie thought she had seen Desmond in Johannesburg. He'd dismissed it at the time, convinced that Julie was mistaken. But … but what if Desmond really *had* been in Johannesburg, what if he really *had* been near the Noble Enterprises head office? Could it be that his old friend was in some way tied up in this whole conspiracy? It seemed like an incredible coincidence that Desmond had roped Chris into the gala, and then conveniently disappeared. *If he hadn't done that, none of this would have happened.*

The suspicion, having seeded in Chris's mind, began to run riot. He felt deeply ashamed for doubting his friend, but he had to know the truth. Like a moth to a lamp, he inched closer to the group of men, tried to hear what they were saying, tried to make out the one voice that he did not want to discern. He was only meters away when he heard a harsh whisper rise above the low timbre of the rest of the group: *"Shuddup, manne. I heard something."*

Chris did not dare move, or even breathe. The man who had spoken shielded his eyes and peered into the darkness - in Chris's direction.

"Hey," the man said. "Who the *vok* is out there? You's looking for troubles." He drew his gun, hesitated. "You's tangling with the wrong boys," he said into the night, his voice menacing. The others were quiet.

Chris weighed his options. The kiosk could provide some cover. If he ducked and ran, he might escape; but there were five of them, and they were armed. He thought of a full frontal attack – maybe he could surprise the leader, wrestle his gun from him? But he quickly dismissed that idea – it had little chance of success. Besides, gunshots would alert the crew on the *Moonflower*. Perspiration ran into his eyes, but he remained frozen.

A dog growled. The noise came from a few meters to his right. It seemed that his adopted friend hadn't gone home, after all.

"Just a *bleddy* dog. *Voetsek! Voetsek,* you mangy *brak.*"

The release of tension was palpable. The man near the Pajero hesitated before he lowered his gun and Chris could hear the Dragon Boys clearly since they no longer bothered to keep their voices down.

"Jeez, man; how's it that you's now scared of your own shadow?"

"You getting excited by a dog? Are you a bitch or what? I think I can smell your *poes.*"

"Vokof; gaan naai."

Chris listened to the laughter and ribaldry. To his relief, he could not make out Desmond's voice.

One man picked up a handful of gravel and flung it in the direction of the growling. Chris took his cue and faded back behind the kiosk, into the relative safety of a group of sheds. The dog followed as Chris went to retrieve the scuba gear.

Julie couldn't remember how she got back to the cabin. Haltingly, she gave her mother an account of the conversation with Greg. She couldn't believe that the monotone voice she heard was her own. Their situation was hopeless, and a part of Julie didn't care anymore. She welcomed the numbness seeping through her – anything was preferable to the pain she felt when she thought about Chris.

Bridget held Julie's hands. "They will not harm us; I'm sure they won't harm us. That would gain them nothing." She kept repeating these phrases, like a mantra. "They will not harm us; we'll think of something. For the moment, we are safe."

But Julie did not feel safe; she did not feel anything. *Chris - dead, alone. Somewhere. Where? In a field, in an alley? Alone ...* It was too much to bear. Her mind could not comprehend it. She wanted to get up, run to him, hold his head in her lap, and kiss him. *"The magic of true love will wake him out of his slumber..."* If only.

Bridget brought her a glass of water, but Julie's hand shook so badly she could barely hold the glass. Her mother draped a blanket around her shoulders and stroked her hair. "One thing at a time; I'm with you; they will not harm us. They can't get away with this; we'll figure out something."

And then the anger began to well up in Julie, forcing out the welcome numbness. She thought of all the things she should have said to Greg, and all the things she would like to do to him. His image tormented her. She felt humiliated, dirty, violated, and cheated. She started to pace the small cabin and banged her fists against the doors.

A voice from outside shouted, "Shut the fuck up."

The faceless sailor beyond the door suddenly found himself the recipient of all the hatred and loathing Julie felt for Greg. She screamed obscenities at him until Bridget came over and, taking her arm, gently led her back to the bunk. She settled her daughter down like a child, and murmured to her gently until, finally overcome with grief and exhaustion, Julie fell into a fitful sleep.

She woke with a start and looked at her watch – *just past two a.m.* There were voices outside in the corridor. Were they getting ready to leave, to quietly slip out to the open seas in the middle of the night? She sat upright, shook her mother awake, and whispered, *"We have to get off this boat!"*

Bridget was immediately wide awake.

Julie looked around, desperate for any object that could be used as a weapon. She tried lifting a chair but it was too heavy. Then she picked up the brass lamp on the small desk, yanked out the plug, and carefully unscrewed the bulb. The lampshade came off easily enough and the squared base felt solid in her hands.

She said to her mother, "Pretend you have stomach cramps."

Briefly, Julie wondered whether this, the oldest trick in the book, had any chance of succeeding. But they had no other choice.

Bridget started to moan and clutched her stomach. Julie banged her fist on the door. "Open up, my mother's not well! We need help." *Silence.* She hammered her fist against the door again and was about to shout a second time when she heard someone approach. The person hesitated.

"Please, help my mother; she needs a doctor!"

She could hear the key turn in the lock. The door opened a crack and a man's voice said, "What the matter? You no shouting; you go sleeping."

Julie pressed herself against the wall behind the door. The man was about to go away again when Bridget struggled up on one elbow and reached out pathetically. "No, please, water – and my pills. They're in the bathroom." She panted, exhausted, spent, fell back on her pillow, clutched her stomach with a moan. "Please, just get my pills."

Cautiously, the young man stepped into the cabin. Julie never even saw his face – that made it easier. With a sickening thud, she brought the base of the lamp crashing down on his head. He swayed and turned, looked at her without comprehension. Then he staggered back, his fall broken by the side of the bunk. His hair, like a paintbrush, applied a neat, even spread of red on the side of the bedspread.

Julie saw him slide down and shuddered. "Do you think he's dead?"

Bridget said, "I don't know, but let's go."

They hurried down the corridor as far as the staircase. Julie paused. She heard animated voices above them in the lobby – *damn!* Quietly, she led the way past the stairs, further down the passage towards the back of the ship. They went through a door and found themselves in a dimly lit cargo area. Julie picked her way past a number of large crates, a dozen drums, and an area that looked like a workshop, till she found what she was looking for: a fixed ladder leading straight up to a hatch.

"Do you think you can manage the ladder?" she whispered to her mother. Bridget nodded.

"There *must* be a lifeboat at the back of the yacht," Julie said. "Go ahead – I'm right behind you."

She was impressed to see how nimbly her mother clambered up. At the top, Bridget carefully pushed up a cover plate and was about to step on to the deck when she gasped. Cindy blocked her path.

"If you wanted to get some fresh air, you should have just asked," Cindy said, sounding bored. "No need to half-kill a nice young man and sneak around in the dark."

"This has gone on long enough," Bridget said. "You have no idea how much trouble you are in. I suggest you get us ashore immediately."

Cindy's laugh had an animal quality to it. Julie watched apprehensively as her mother slowly climbed the last few steps.

"Well, are you just going to stand there, or are you going to give me a hand?" Bridget asked. Julie was surprised by the authority in her mother's voice. Cindy reached down to take the older woman's hand.

Julie, watching from below, realized what Bridget was planning to do a split second before Cindy did. *God, no!* She wanted to scream, but the sound stifled in her throat. Bridget grabbed Cindy's hand and pulled with all her might, causing the blonde to lose her balance and topple through the hatch. Cindy screamed and clung on to Bridget. Julie watched in horror as the two women plunged from the top of the ladder. Cindy hit the deck first and broke the older woman's fall.

"Mother!"

Bridget sat up slowly, dazed, and brushed sawdust off her sweater. Julie knelt down and looked at her, deeply concerned. "Are you all right? God, you gave me a fright."

"Never mind that, let's go before she comes round," Bridget said, and cast a glance towards Cindy, who lay strangely quiet next to her. "Give me a hand."

But, when Bridget tried to get up, she cried out in pain and sank back into a seated position. "Dammit, my ankle! Oh God, it hurts." She leaned heavily on Julie and tried again to get to her feet. Julie looked up towards the hatch. There was no way Bridget was going to make it up the ladder now. She was about to lead her mother back towards the broad stairs, when the lights in the cargo area blazed alive. The two women squinted and shielded their eyes from the incandescent brightness.

"What the..?" It was Lenny, followed by two sailors. He rushed to Cindy. "What happened?" He looked from one woman to the other. There was menace and confusion in his eyes. Julie instinctively pulled her mother back.

Cindy started to come round. She sat up groggily, clutched her stomach, and gasped for air. "She ... she pulled me down the hatch and made me fall," she moaned, sounding like a petulant child. She lifted her arm to point and gasped with pain. *"Agh*, my shoulder!"

"You old bitch!" Lenny whipped around, gun in hand. "I've had about as much shit from you as I can take." He lifted the gun. Julie leapt in front of her mother, hands outstretched.

"Look, it was an accident! My mother also got hurt." She tried to ignore the barrel of the gun and kept her eyes focused on Lenny's face. Beads of perspiration had formed on Lenny's forehead; his arm twitched with agitation and the gun kept moving. It struck Julie suddenly that he was high on something. She willed him to look into her eyes and tried to placate him. "Let's just stay calm. It was an accident. My mother didn't mean for Cindy to get hurt."

She paused, took a couple of deep breaths. "You know Greg wouldn't want you to hurt us."

"Ha!" he spat. "Greg wouldn't give a shit if I wasted the old bat – he hates her guts; he'd probably give me a bonus."

Cindy clutched her right shoulder and winced as she picked herself up from the floor. She breathed heavily, steadied herself. "Stop the bullshit, Lenny, they're not going anywhere." She ignored his gun, pushed her lips to within six inches of Julie's face, and hissed, *"If you try any escape stunt again, your mother will pay."* Abruptly, she turned and kicked Bridget's injured ankle. The older woman cried out in shock and pain.

Cindy turned to the sailors. "Take them back to their cabin," she commanded.

Thabo tapped on Mama Mercy's window, but got no response. He called repeatedly in a loud whisper, *"Mama Mercy, wake up!"* He wondered how much trouble he would be in if he threw a stone through the window. One more loud *tap-tap-tap*. *"Wake up!"*

A figure emerged from the door to his right and shone a flashlight into his eyes.

"Thabo? What on earth are you doing?"

Thabo was relieved to recognize the caretaker. "*Oom* Hendrik, you have to help me! I have to send a fax and I must speak to *Meez* Wendy."

Just then, the outside area was flooded with light, and Mama Mercy emerged in a floral dressing-gown. *"Hau!* What is the meaning of this? Child, you should be in bed, what are you doing here? It is two o'clock in the morning. It is not safe on the streets at this time of ..."

Oom Hendrik intervened to cut her off, and Thabo managed to convey enough urgency to get the office unlocked.

Minutes later, the fax was dispatched and Thabo was on the phone to Wendy. He explained to her exactly what had happened. Despite his anxiety, he relished the moment. Here he was, sitting behind a desk, discussing important things with the big boss of the Khanya center. Mama Mercy and *Oom* Hendrik listened in silence and Wendy only interrupted once, to tell him she was putting his voice on speaker-phone so that Chris's father could also listen.

Thabo finished his account, and then answered Wendy and Jacques' questions as best he could; they promised to get help immediately.

When he put down the phone, Mama Mercy said, "We need hot chocolate." They followed her shuffling slippers down the passage and into the kitchen.

Thabo was hungry, but when he tried to drink his hot chocolate, he found he was just too worried to do so. They must do something, not just sit here drinking hot chocolate while his partner was in danger! "*Oom* Hendrik, please! We have to go down to the harbor and help Chris!"

Hendrik blew across the top of his mug and then winced as he slurped the hot liquid. He said, "Miss Wendy and Dr. du Toit were very clear. We must wait here in case the police need more information." With awe in his voice he added, "The doctor is going to call the Minister of Security."

"That man owes him," Mama Mercy declared. "He be the one that got the new heart. He will do anything for Dr. Jacques." She folded her hands and said, "That makes me feel much better. All will be fine."

But Thabo could not be reassured. "No! There is no time! Those Dragon Boys …"

"Sheishhh!" Mama Mercy made as if she was going to let him feel the back of her hand, but she had no real intention of doing so. "Don't even say that name! Those *skollies* … and you, just a child." Again, she clucked her tongue.

"I'm sorry, but I have to go. Thank you for the hot chocolate, Mama." Thabo got to his feet, and rushed out of the kitchen. Minutes later, he had reached the main road, and was sprinting toward the harbor.

Mama Mercy and Hendrik looked at each other in shocked surprise.

Thabo had not gone far when he heard a vehicle approaching from behind him. He had no idea whether minibus taxis operated on this stretch of road in the middle of the night but, just in case, he quickened his step and prepared to leap on to the back bumper.

The vehicle pulled up right next to him and *Oom* Hendrik called through the open window, "Hop in!"

Thabo nearly hugged the old man.

They hid under the same porch where Chris had stood a mere twenty minutes earlier. In the far distance, out in the bay, Thabo saw the lights of the big yacht. A thin fog had rolled in from the Atlantic, veiling her in a ghostly shroud. Thabo shivered, but he was relieved. *At least the boat hasn't left yet*, he thought.

Nearby, the Dragon Boys appeared to have grown tired and bored. It looked like two were asleep in the car, and another two lay wrapped in blankets in the rubber dinghy, a few yards away. In the dim light, they looked almost comic, like oversized babies bobbing about in a big Moses basket. One gang member kept watch; he lay on the hood of the car and smoked.

Thabo tugged at *Oom* Hendrik's arm and signaled retreat so that they could confer. Back at the old man's car, Thabo voiced his fears that the Dragon Boys could, at any moment, be summoned out to the yacht. He was gratified that *Oom* Hendrik took him seriously and understood the urgency. They kept looking up the road, hoping to see a police vehicle.

Then *Oom* Hendrik had an idea. "The trick is to sabotage the dinghy," he said suddenly.

"Can we poke a hole in it? Maybe with a knife?"

"*Neh*; too dangerous. They would immediately come after us. And we don't have a knife, anyway." *Oom* Hendrik ran his hand over his wispy hair and said, "You know what *could* work? Rope around the propeller." He rummaged behind the driver's seat and held up an old tow-rope in triumph.

A few minutes later, stripped down to his boxers, Thabo carefully slid down the side of the pier. The water was icy and he had to resist the urge to paddle and splash to warm himself up. Instead, he clamped his teeth down hard on the three-meter-long rope.

"*Be very careful,*" *Oom* Hendrik whispered urgently. "If I hear your loerie call, I will try to distract them." The rope ends, trailing behind, looked like two water snakes following the slender boy as he faded into the darkness. Hendrik's heart was thumping. If something happened to Thabo, Mama Mercy would surely skin him alive.

Chris trod water and surveyed the yacht from up close. Moonlight filtered through the thin fog to illuminate the gleaming whiteness of the hull and the shiny chrome fittings. He could hear waves lapping gently against the side of the boat and briefly thought how stunning it would be to go off on a cruise – with Julie. He gritted his teeth. *When all this is over...*

Silently, he circled the vessel. The main deck was deserted, but light spilled from the bridge on the upper level. A shadow blocked the doorway, and then a figure stepped out from the bridge, lit a cigarette, and leaned against the railing. Chris hardly dared to breathe. He was close enough to make out the man's smooth Asian features.

A voice called from inside, and the man at the railing said something over his shoulder and flicked the cigarette into the water. *At least two on the bridge,* Chris thought, and carefully resumed his recce. He judged there were at least eight cabins on the lower level – two were lit. He swam up close, but the portholes were too high for him to peer in. On the side of the main deck was a set of double doors that looked as though they belonged to a fancy restaurant rather than a ship – clearly the main entrance when the ship was docked. He wondered if these doors were locked.

At the back, he found a diving platform and a convenient stepladder. A rubber dinghy bobbed behind the *Moonflower*. Chris pulled himself up on to the diving platform and sat motionless for a minute. He took off the diving cylinder, flippers, and mask and stowed them out of sight in the dinghy. Next, he located a set of oars and placed them, readily accessible, in the middle of the vessel. *Who knows how much time we'll have to make our escape*, he thought.

Chris crept up a short ladder on to the main deck. Again, he waited, motionless, and surveyed the tidy sun deck with its whirlpool and bar area. Off to the left, there appeared to be hatch of some sort for loading supplies into the hold. Behind the bar, he could make out stairs leading to a portal on the upper level. He reckoned this portal would lead to the bridge. Since this was the only place showing signs of life, he decided to give it a wide berth and concentrate instead on finding a way towards the lower deck. His instinct told him that Julie and Bridget were likely to be locked up in one of the cabins he had noticed earlier.

He crept towards the main entrance doors and peered through the glass panels. The deserted interior reminded him of a hotel lobby, complete with bar and sweeping staircase to the upper level. More importantly, however, there were stairs leading to the lower deck. He tried the doors; they were locked.

Damn!

Slowly, Chris circled the entire main deck, always careful to stay out of sight of the bridge. At one point, he could hear voices from the bridge. He could not understand what was said, but the tone was that of a routine conversation.

No cause for alarm – yet.

When he reached the sun deck again, he stopped to weigh his options, and decided his best chance was to go in via the upper deck, where he knew the door was open. If he could just sneak past the men on the bridge, the central staircase would take him down to the cabins.

Chris was about to step out of the shadows, when a figure emerged from the main entrance. He crouched down, thankful for the darkness of his wetsuit, and watched as a shaft of light illuminated a head of bright blonde hair: *Cindy!* He would have known even without seeing her hair because of her unmistakable perfume. His airwaves constricted and he had to force himself not to cough.

Chris watched as Cindy walked across the deck towards a cargo hatch. The hatch lifted; he heard voices. Cindy appeared to reach down and ... disappeared. Then there was a major commotion: someone screamed out in pain; Chris heard muffled running and shouting. He leapt across to the hatch, lay down on his stomach, and looked over the edge. He had to stifle a shout when he took in the scene below: both Cindy and

Bridget sat on the deck, groaning in pain. Julie stood between her mother and a gun-waving Lenny. Chris pulled himself up on his haunches, ready to jump. Mesmerized, he looked at the gun – was that the same gun he had stared at so many years ago, the gun that had killed his mother? Chris's heart beat so loudly he was sure that Lenny and his henchmen would hear it. *This couldn't be happening, not again.* He gauged the distance down to Lenny; it was an awkward angle, and Chris knew he had to land on the man – had to disarm him immediately. He sized up Lenny's accomplices. At least Cindy seemed to be out of action. He inched forward, his mind completely focused on Lenny's right hand and the gun.

Then he heard Julie's voice, composed and soothing. "Let's just stay calm. It was an accident. My mother didn't mean for Cindy to get hurt ..."

After what seemed like an eternity, Cindy intervened and Chris heaved a silent sigh of relief when Lenny dropped his arm. He was about to surmise that Cindy wasn't an entirely bad human being after all, when she turned around and kicked Bridget on the ankle. Chris was enraged. He knew that if he'd had a gun he would have shot Cindy there and then, and damn the consequences.

He watched as Julie and Bridget were escorted out through the back of the cargo bay. The two sailors half-carried Bridget, who was in obvious pain. When all was clear, Chris climbed down the ladder into the cargo bay and followed them into a wood-paneled passage, where he found cover under the staircase. He watched the sailors emerge from a cabin at the far end. They locked the door, before disappearing up the stairs.

He crept along the corridor and was bemused to see a key hanging on a hook outside one of the cabins. Quietly, he unlocked the door.

Nothing could have prepared Chris for the reception he received. Julie's hand flew to her mouth as she fought to stifle a scream. Both women stared at him in utter shock. Then, in slow motion, he saw Julie's expression change from fear and shock to pure joy. She flung herself against him and he hugged her tightly.

"It's OK, everything's going to be fine," he said, and pushed his back against the door to prevent anyone from entering. He stroked her hair and felt her warm tears against his neck. Her body was convulsed with silent sobs and he held her more tightly.

Bridget eventually said, "We thought you were dead. Greg said you'd been shot."

Through tear-stained eyes, Julie looked at him and he felt his whole being drawn into her; for once, he felt as though he understood her completely. Never in his life had he felt so close to anyone, or so protective. She tried to speak, but he bent down and silenced her with a long kiss. He only pulled away when he felt her grow calmer in his arms.

"I want to see those dimples in your cheeks," he whispered.

"You're wet," she said, but she was smiling now. He touched the dimples, one by one, to reassure himself that she was real, that this was not a dream.

"Ahem." Bridget cleared her throat. *"Excuse me. This isn't exactly a honeymoon cruise, you know,"* she said, in a stage whisper.

They pulled apart and Chris joined Julie to inspect Bridget's ankle, which had swollen to twice its normal size.

"Do you think it's broken?" Julie asked.

"Hard to tell," he said. "Either broken or very badly sprained." Chris soaked a towel in cold water and gently wrapped it round the injured ankle.

"One of these days, we'll have to meet without you having to doctor my legs," Bridget quipped, though Chris could see that her face was gray with pain, the lips almost colorless. She gritted her teeth, closed her eyes, and lay back against the pillows. Julie held her mother's hand and Chris carefully placed a pillow under the leg to raise it.

Julie said, "Fortunately, they left Mother's handbag and she had some painkillers. They should kick in soon."

After a pause, she asked, "Are you alone? What's your plan?"

Chris thought for a while. "I guess the good news is that Greg thinks I'm dead; that still gives me some element of surprise. His henchmen probably haven't had the courage to tell him how they bungled …"

Julie became agitated. "Why? What happened?"

"Later; I'll tell you everything later. The police should arrive soon." He hoped there was more conviction in his voice than he felt.

Chris stole a glance at the door. *God, the moment anyone checks up on the "guests", the game is up.* He had little faith in the police's ability to resolve the situation peacefully. There was a very real chance of the three hostages being used as human shields, and the police shooting indiscriminately. He shook his head and wiped his hand over his eyes. Julie gazed at him. *What now?*

He looked at Bridget, who appeared to have been knocked out by the medication. Her breathing was steady, and some of her color had returned. He held a finger to his lips and gestured for Julie to follow him to the bathroom.

They squeezed into the small space and Chris said, "We have to get off the yacht. There's a dinghy tied to the back …"

"I'm not going without my mother."

He gripped her arms but, noticing her wince, immediately loosened his hold.

"Julie …"

"Don't even try."

Her face was only six inches from his and he was keenly aware of her hip pressing against his thigh in the confined space. He could see the familiar forward thrust of her chin, the determination in her eyes. Her defiance was infuriating, and yet it was this strength that attracted him. He let go of her arms, cupped her face in his hands, and bent down to kiss her.

They were both surprised to hear Bridget say, "Julie, for once in your life, please don't be such a stubborn ass. Lenny and that Goh fellow could decide to take off at any minute."

Her speech was slurred, somnolent. She continued, "Matt's in hospital. Who's … who's going to come looking for us? You have to go." They heard her sigh. "Go get the cavalry …"

He could see the conflict in Julie's face; the earlier determination made way for a moment's hesitation. She squeezed past Chris and went and sat by her mother's side.

"Mother, I just can't. Not with you like this. I really can't just leave you." She implored Chris with her eyes and he knew that she was right. Would he have left his mother under the same circumstances? *Never!*

He stared into the darkness beyond the porthole and said, "OK, we have two choices. We either sit here and wait for the police, or we try to take over the yacht and sail her back to Hout Bay."

Julie looked at him. "How can that work? Cindy and Lenny won't just calmly let us …"

"We only need ten minutes at full speed to reach Hout Bay; and we don't have to dock carefully. We run the boat aground on the beach – that will attract immediate attention and ensure that no one disappears out into the open seas."

"I vote for option two," Bridget murmured, and Julie nodded.

Bridget drifted off to sleep as Chris and Julie discussed the plan in urgent whispers. They shared what little knowledge they had of the yacht and its occupants, and then Chris took the sheets off Julie's bunk and tore them into strips. "To gag and bind whoever is on the bridge," he explained.

"How many do you think there'll be?"

He shrugged. "I saw two, but we might be lucky and there may be only one on duty in the early hours of the morning."

Surprise was the key element of the plan. Chris proposed to leave Bridget locked up in the cabin while he and Julie took over the bridge. They would barricade themselves in there, and race the yacht ashore before any of the sleeping occupants on the boat got a chance to react.

When they had finished tearing the sheet into strips, he took a chair, wedged half of it under the bunk, and proceeded to break it apart. One of the legs splintered with a loud creak. They both froze, waited, but no one seemed to have heard. With some satisfaction, Chris inspected the chair leg. It now resembled a short spear.

In the wardrobe, they found a couple of shirts and shorts left behind by a previous occupant. "Good," said Chris. "Now I can get into something dry."

"Pity; I rather liked my man from Atlantis."

Julie's hands were demurely folded in her lap but, as Chris looked into her eyes, he felt warmth spreading through his entire body. With a glance at the sleeping Bridget, he took Julie's hand and led her into the tiny bathroom. He took her in his arms, kissed the top of her head, her ears, her neck. She tilted her head back and offered her lips with a desire that matched his own. Then she unbuttoned her blouse and he lost himself in the warmth of her skin and the perfume of her hair.

Together, they peeled Chris out of his wetsuit, tugging away at the tight neoprene skin. It was a challenge in the confined space, and, with the wetsuit below his knees, he lost his balance and bumped hard against the thin wooden partition. Julie stifled a laugh, and Chris pulled a face, which made her want to laugh even more. They heard Bridget mutter. Chris held his breath until the breathing from next door was regular again. Then he untangled his feet from the mess of wetsuit.

Julie gripped his naked buttocks and whispered, *"I should spank you for making such a noise."* He pressed against her and smothered her laughter with his lips. Then, hungrily, their hands started to explore each other. Chris knew that this was crazy, reckless. But he didn't care. His heart was full of an intensity of feeling that he would not have believed possible. The constraint of space, and the need for silence, made them cling to each other like survivors in a maelstrom. When he finally entered Julie, he knew that this was what he had been longing for ever since he was a kid, romantically and innocently at first, now with a passion that caused the blood to rush in his ears and his heart rate to accelerate madly. They climaxed together, and, in the short eternity that followed, Chris was totally at peace with the world, his mind as blank and clear as a snow-swept mountaintop. He was at the pinnacle; this moment was all there was, there was nothing else.

She pulled away first. "We came in here for you to get dressed, remember."

##

They left Bridget asleep in the locked cabin and crept along the deserted passage. Chris paused at one of the doors. He had caught a whiff of Cindy's unmistakable perfume. No light shone from underneath the door, so hopefully she had gone to sleep. He assumed Lenny would be with her. His spirits lifted and he gripped the heavy chair leg with its splintered end. Their plan was about as elegant as this weapon: Julie was going to go ahead and distract the crew on the bridge; he was then going to clobber them over the head with his "club".

At the foot of the stairs, Julie signaled for him to wait and give her a head start. He followed at a safe distance and admired the way she pulled herself erect and nonchalantly crossed the lobby as though she were an esteemed guest, rather than an escaped prisoner. She was halfway up the stairs when a disembodied voice spoke: *"And where d'you think you're going?"*

Lenny! He was leaning against the balustrade of the mezzanine, a crystal whisky tumbler in his hand. Judging by the slurred speech, this wasn't his first drink.

From the shadows, Chris watched Julie. Her voice was even when she said, "I was coming up to the communications room to see if I could make contact with Greg."

"*Ha!* You're lying! You lie when you open your mouth! You and your mother both ..."

"I promise, that's all I was trying to do. I just wanted to make peace with Greg."

Furtively, she looked across the room. Her eyes briefly met Chris's. The silent plea for help flew between them like an electric spark. Lenny dropped his whisky tumbler and it crashed to pieces on the bar counter below him. The room was suddenly bathed in bright light and Chris stared straight into the barrel of a gun.

"*You!* Where the hell did you come from? Jesus, you're supposed to be dead!"

The gun swung from Chris to Julie.

She had her back pressed against the wall, arms lifted in surrender. Her lips seemed to be parted in silent prayer as she stared, mesmerized, into the barrel of the gun. Chris blinked repeatedly, for now he wasn't seeing Julie. He saw himself, fourteen years old, standing on a staircase just like this one, staring into the barrel of the self-same gun, staring at the dragon tattoo clearly visible on the arm of the man who would murder his mother.

"Dead?" Chris controlled his voice. "You think I should be dead ... dead like my mother?"

"What? What you talking about?" The gun jerked back and forth. Chris looked Lenny straight in the eyes, and it was as though he had found his way through a time warp back to that fateful day in his own home. His home that was supposed to be a safe haven, his home where Nala lay dead and bleeding on the marble floor. He marveled that he had not recognized Lenny earlier: the eyes, the stance, the tattoo on the outstretched arm. *How could I have missed it?* The images in his mind were in high definition. The film rolled on and he was there again.

Chris's voice was cold and deliberate: "Bastard! You killed her. You killed my mother."

Something like an awakening, a slow dawning, came across Lenny's face. His lower jaw dropped and he gaped through his whisky fog. Wiping perspiration off his forehead with the back of one hand, Lenny looked from Chris to the figure on the staircase, finally making the connection.

"That … that was you that day? The dog, it came at me …"

A loud police siren interrupted. It unnerved Lenny; his eyes darted in all directions, and the gun swung wildly. "Stay! Stay where you are! Don't move!"

Damn the siren, Chris thought. *That's what triggered him to panic last time, that's what...*

Chris took a step forward. Julie stood petrified; only her eyes moved, as they followed the wild gyrations of the gun in Lenny's hand. A part of Chris was right there in her head. He knew that she couldn't do anything but watch - watch like a gazelle caught in headlights. Meanwhile, Lenny's agitation was increasing with every passing second. There was no telling what drugs he might have taken before he started on the whisky. Did he have any shred of rationality left? His whole body spelled "trapped animal". Chris knew how it was going to end; he'd been there before.

"Thy will be done." Instinct kicked in, and his legs moved as if of their own volition. He had to protect Julie; had to get between her and the gun. Suddenly, he felt his mother's presence; he was one with her. In a curiously detached way, he thought: *This is what it was like for her. I've no choice.*

Three swift steps took him to the bottom of the stairs. He had his hand on the railing when the first shot rang out. He saw Julie turn away from the gunman and clasp her ears. At the same time, he heard the glass door shatter behind him. Again, the siren sounded. Chris's eyes remained riveted on Lenny, who licked his upper lip repeatedly, almost, it seemed to Chris, as if in anticipation. *He did that with Mom, too, the bastard.* Chris's blood pounded with raging hot hatred and deep loathing.

The second shot rang out, and Chris felt a scorching pain in his chest and shoulder. It was like nothing he'd ever experienced before, and a part of him observed the defensive shutters of his mind coming down and blocking the pain. Then there was the smell – acrid; hot metal searing into flesh. *How could I have forgotten that?* It seemed that it was his destiny to travel the same road as his mother, the mother who sacrificed herself for the son she loved, as he was now willing to sacrifice himself for the woman he loved.

The scene was surreal, yet familiar: Julie pressed against the wall; Lenny, nervous, flicking his tongue out and licking his upper lip.

Chris was too far to reach him, no matter how fast he ran. This scene had played itself out a thousand times in his mind. It was the subject of his nightmares, nightmares in which he repeatedly asked himself the question: "What could I have done differently?" Not once had he asked, "What could my mother have done differently?" Now he only had split seconds to consider how the outcome could have been different if Danielle had done something other than carry on charging to protect her son.

He realized he was still holding the chair leg. *If only I could get within reach of that bastard!* Then, as if in slow motion, he saw Lenny lift the gun, saw his finger begin to squeeze on the trigger for his third shot. Summoning all his athleticism, Chris hurled the piece of wood towards the gunman. The shot rang out and Julie screamed; Chris lifted his hands to his chest - but there was nothing, no pain. Lenny had managed to dodge the chair leg, but it had upset his aim. The third bullet had missed its target.

Lenny's face was a picture of incredulity. It seemed that he, too, had expected the scene to follow its preordained path. The third bullet was supposed to be the fatal one. Then his expression changed again, and surprise was replaced by pure malice. When he aimed the gun again, it was not at Chris, but at Julie.

"Get down!" Chris threw himself at Julie, rugby-tackling her to the ground. He was not a moment too soon. Lenny's fourth bullet left a hole in the wood paneling in the exact spot where Julie's head had been a split second before.

The police siren sounded again.

Hurry up, Chris thought. *Please God, hurry up!* He stole the briefest of glances behind him, but there was no sign yet of the police. Looking up, he saw that Lenny had moved to the top of the stairs to get a clear shot at the prostrate Julie. His face was a mask. Something had snapped.

"Noooo!" With a superhuman effort, Chris again threw himself at Julie, but this time his intention was to cover her body with his own. *If it has to end, let it end the way it was supposed to.* Time stood still as he waited for the final shot, his eyes tight shut, his face buried in Julie's scented hair.

The shot never came; instead, there was a *click.* In the silence, it sounded to Chris as loud as the bells tolling on Judgment Day. Then realization dawned: *He's out of bullets!* In an instant, Chris was on his feet, charging towards his enemy. His first kick hit Lenny's forearm and sent the gun flying over the banister. The man cried out in pain, clutched his wrist, and tried to escape to the bridge.

"No you don't!" Chris shouted. He grabbed Lenny by the lapels of his shirt, and slammed his head into the wood paneling. The action brought a surge of savage pleasure. In that moment, there was nothing Chris would rather do than spend the rest of the night slamming Lenny's head into the wall, over and over and over again.

But Lenny wasn't done for yet. Ducking low, he broke loose and rammed his head into the younger man's stomach, causing Chris's wounded shoulder to crash into the wall. The pain was so sudden and intense that Chris nearly passed out. Only his blind fury kept him on his feet. Aiming a sharp kick at Lenny's stomach, he used the advantage this gave him to get the man into a headlock with his uninjured arm. Then he started to squeeze. Chris could smell the whisky on Lenny's breath; he wanted that smell to stop, so he tightened his grip and continued to squeeze. Squiggly patterns of red and black wafted through Chris's vision. He was not really aware of the blood pouring from his injured shoulder, but he was conscious of the fact that he was weakening, that he might black out. It was a race against time; he had to finish his mother's killer off before he himself succumbed. Nothing else mattered.

He looked down at Lenny's upturned face: it had turned the brownish-purple color of a fallen plum. With fascination, he observed the bulging eyes, the blue lips. He could not take his eyes off the curious kaleidoscope of hideous colors, but with every second he could feel the veil of black cloud encroaching further. The nothing – the big nothing - was coming to get him, but first there was a job to be completed.

From far away, he heard a voice: *"Chris, no! It's enough."* He blinked to clear the swirling darkness. *Julie?*

But still he squeezed. It seemed that his arm had taken on a life of its own, that it would no longer obey him, even if he wanted it to. The life was draining out of Lenny as fast as the blood was pouring out of Chris. He heard his father's voice: *There is no such thing as a second place; there are only winners and losers.*

And then he heard that other voice again. Someone was calling to him: *"Chris..."* The darkness yielded and in its place he saw blinding light. She drifted out of the light and bent towards him. "Mom?" he said, in wonderment.

"It's enough, Chris; let it go." Her voice was like honey on the wings of a crisp spring morning. *"Let it go."*

"But he killed you!"

"Think of the pigeon, Chris." Her voice surrounded him. It came from nowhere, and it came from everywhere.

The pigeon! How did she know about that? He'd never told a soul about the pigeon he had killed with his slingshot *kettie*. He'd felt so bad that he had dug a grave and buried it; even said prayers. For weeks afterwards, the dead, bloodied pigeon had haunted his dreams.

"Let him go."

Slowly, his arm relaxed and he leaned back against the wall. For a while, it seemed as though Lenny was as dead as that pigeon, but then he started to heave and gasp. And just as Chris registered that the man was still alive, the air was suddenly thick with the sound of people. Bright lights exploded all around them, as the police finally broke in and swarmed through the yacht. But Chris barely noticed. He was only conscious of Julie. *Julie was OK.* His head was on her lap and he could feel her body convulsing with sobs. Her tears streamed down to mingle with the blood from his shoulder, which she was trying to stem with her bare hands.

He wanted to tell her not to cry, and he tried to smile, to squeeze her hand. But his voice was inaudible and his limbs would not obey his commands.

Through the swirling mists, he became aware of another face.

"Dad?" His voice was a croak.

"Just lie still, son. You've lost a lot of blood." He noted the concern in his father's voice and watched as Jacques gently tried to pull Julie away. She refused to budge. Chris suddenly felt very, very tired. His head rolled sideways and he watched the tears and blood seep into the carpet. *So much blood.*

Julie said, "Oh God, Chris. I'm so sorry. I just froze. There was nothing I could do. There was nothing ... nothing I could do."

It took all his strength to move his head and look at her. With a wan smile he said, "I know, Julie, believe me, I know."

A deep sense of peace came over him; a peace like he hadn't known in years. *There was nothing I could have done.* As the guilt that had tormented him ever since that terrible day dissolved away, he blinked into the blinding light. *"Bye, Mom."*

Then the darkness took him.

##

Chapter 24: Chris

Johannesburg, Thursday morning

Greg, refreshed from an early morning jog, was in the office before anyone else. It was a cause of great satisfaction to him to think that here he was, taking control, charting a course for himself - and the company - while everybody was still asleep. *Fools - no wonder I outwitted them all!*

He checked his emails: Matt Baxter's attending physician reported that his patient's condition was unchanged and he was being kept sedated – *good.*   Next, Greg opened a draft press release from the company's chief PR officer. He scanned through it quickly, noting the essentials: *"... Noble Enterprises, working in close cooperation with the police... Mrs. Bridget Noble-Baxter will take an extended break from her duties on various charitable boards ... her daughter, Julie, is to accompany her on a cruise to an undisclosed location ..."*

He printed a batch of documents and scrawled his edits in red. Periodically, he glanced at his watch.

As the first rays of the sun made their way into the office, he put down his pen. The *Moonflower* would be sailing about now. Greg had agreed with Mr. Goh that dawn was an appropriate time for a pleasure craft to set sail; slipping away in the dead of night could attract suspicion.

His thoughts turned to Julie. Greg was not inclined to be poetic but, as he sat looking at the rising sun, he permitted himself the brief luxury of reveling in this new beginning. The company was now his to control, and Julie was fully in his power. She had displayed a strength of character and determination that had impressed him. *Who knows, in time I might even develop some real feelings for her.* Love was too strong a word, but he felt he could respect her – be proud of her. She was finally showing signs of maturity, and that was good. He knew she was upset at the moment, but he felt convinced that she would soon assess the situation and see the merits of aligning herself with his plans and goals. A life of luxury and power by his side compared to - what? Her mother's life on her conscience? Matt's life on her conscience? He smiled to himself as he thought of business associates and others who he had driven into a corner. It usually took them a while to fully grasp that they had been checkmated. But eventually Julie, like everyone else, would see reason.

Greg turned to his computer, looking for any updates from his police contact. He wondered if they had "found" Chris's body yet – the contact was supposed to let him know as soon as the police were ready to make a statement. The Noble Enterprises press release would go out at ten a.m. Ideally, he wanted the news of the kidnapper's death to break at the same time as the story about Bridget stepping down from her duties. The PR team would have to work their contacts at the various newspapers to get the right slant; it was important to have Noble Enterprises and its chairperson, Bridget, cast as the victims of an unscrupulous, opportunistic attempt at extortion. The bad guy got his just desserts.

Again, he checked his watch. There was no reason to expect any contact from the *Moonflower;* they would call in once they were on the open seas.

Muffled noises from the hallway signaled the awakening of the outer office. His secretary brought him a cup of coffee and the morning papers. Two minutes later, she poked her head around the door again.

"Mr. Greg ..."

"What?" he barked. She ought to know by now that he hated being disturbed during the ten minutes it took him to scan the papers and drink his coffee.

"Gerhard from Security is here. He says it's urgent."

"OK, send ..."

The lanky head of security clearly had no intention of waiting to be invited. He stepped past the secretary and closed the door in her face.

Greg looked at the man's sallow complexion and wondered when last he had seen fresh air. He motioned towards a chair. "What is so important that it can tear you away from the surveillance room?"

Gerhard pushed a sealed envelope across the desk. "Thought you might want to see this, boss."

"What is it?"

"I was doing routine scanning of the directors' emails – like you asked me to."

"And?"

"There's been a flurry of emails in the last couple of hours. Looks like the board of directors are planning a secret meeting."

Greg took his time to carefully slit open the envelope.

"Really? Who's instigating it?"

"Dr. Steward. I suppose he's been here the longest; and with Mr. Baxter and Mrs. Noble-Baxter ... away ... he seems to think it is his responsibility to call the board together for an emergency meeting."

Greg quickly scanned the document. "Well, I never. Who would have thought the old goat would have the balls to try a stunt like this? It's a mutiny behind my back!" He carried on reading. "So, they're planning to meet in the Cape Town office to keep me in the dark." He shook his head.

Greg was just about to press the intercom for his secretary to call the pilots and get the plane ready, when he remembered that the plane was to have been ditched. *Good move, the insurance payout will be worth more than the plane itself. I'll get a bigger one.* In the meantime, he would have to put up with a commercial flight.

"Gerhard," he said, "can you try and track down the co-pilot for me? I need to have a word with him."

Cape Town, the same day

Chris drifted in and out of consciousness. He was dimly aware of a nurse taking his blood pressure.

"How's the pain?" He barely heard her. *Why was everything so dark and quiet?*

When he woke the next time, dawn spilled through the window. Chris touched his neck and shoulder and felt a heavy bandage. He became aware of the hospital surroundings. There was no mistaking the smell of antiseptic, the purposeful steps along the corridor. He took in the intravenous drip and the heart-rate monitor. His eyes came to rest on the figure of his father, slumped in a chair, asleep. Chris studied the unshaven face, the graying hair. When had his father aged like that? The doctor looked vulnerable, breathing deeply with his head back and his mouth open.

A nurse came in and saw Chris studying the sleeping figure.

"Best let him sleep," she whispered. *"He must be exhausted."*

Responding to Chris's questioning look, she said, "They've been squeezing blood out of him all night – for you. I've never seen anyone donate that much blood. You lost a lot of it and needed more throughout the operation."

"The operation?"

She nodded and stuck a thermometer under his tongue. "You're lucky – Dr. Menzky came out personally. I don't know when last he responded to a three a.m. call." She read the thermometer and moved on to take his blood pressure. He heard fleeting phrases and wanted to ask her questions but his mind was not yet ready to absorb it all ... *"bullet"* ... *"vein graft"*... *"blood"*. When he opened his eyes, she was gone.

Chris kept looking at his father. The anesthetic tugged at his consciousness and he was not sure if he was dreaming or awake. His fuzzy thoughts circled around blood: *the chalice, blood of our fathers.* When last had he been to church? He used to go with his parents, every Sunday. He realized he hadn't been since his mother's funeral. *"This is my blood, given for you."* He really ought to go to church again; he'd go with Mercy. Her church was a happy place, full of song. He drifted into a dreamless sleep.

Chris woke to broad daylight and a room full of people. Julie sat by his side and held his hand. He looked at her and wanted to let the image of her smiling face infuse every corner of his brain and stay there forever.

"Welcome back." She touched his lips. "We had to promise the nurse to keep you very quiet and resting."

He grasped her hand. "I'm fine. I've been resting all night. Tell me what happened."

Jacques, and a distinguished-looking man with a big paunch, stood at the foot of the bed. The man had a booming voice when he spoke: "Now, you just take it easy, young man, and you'll be good as new." He touched his fingertips together, as if to stretch them. "That bullet made quite a mess of your shoulder but, even if I say so myself, we've done a fine job in repairing it."

"Thanks again for coming out in the middle of the night," his father said. He sounded exhausted.

"Don't mention it, Jacques. You'd have done the same for me. I'll stop by on my evening rounds." He turned at the door and waved an admonishing finger in the direction of Chris and Julie. "Don't overdo it, now."

Chris noticed Wendy for the first time. She had kept in the background. He saw her exchange a quick glance with his father, a silent question about whether she should stay or go. He felt a tremendous pang of guilt - through his blind selfishness, he had forced his father and Wendy to sneak around and hide their love for each other.

"Wendy," he croaked, reaching out for her. His throat was dry and sore and his voice more husky than he had expected. She came to his side and he clasped her hands in his. "Thank you, for everything."

"I haven't really done much." She squeezed his hand. "OK, so maybe I lied to a policeman and pulled a few strings to get the security forces mobilized in the middle of the night. But, really, that was mainly your father's doing. He called the Minister of ..."

"That's not what I meant," Chris interrupted. "I wanted to thank you for taking care of my dad. He needs you."

Jacques stepped up and, careful not to touch the injured shoulder, embraced his son. It was the first time in almost nine years that Chris had allowed himself to feel the unconditionally loving embrace of a parent.

"I was so worried; the thought of losing you ..." Jacques choked up and both father and son had to fight hard to hold back the tears.

"Dad ... I know I can't replace Nala, but I would like to have another dog. Will you get me another dog?"

Jacques pulled away and laughed through his tears. "If that's what you want, I'll gladly buy you a dog." Moving away from the bed, he went over to Wendy, and embraced her. Then they both excused themselves to go and check up on Bridget.

Chris was free to turn all his attention to Julie. She gave him a rundown of the police swoop. It had been a major action, with several boats and a helicopter involved. Realizing they were totally outnumbered, Cindy, Mr. Goh, and everyone else on board surrendered without further incident. Lenny had a crushed larynx, but was expected to recover and stand trial for the murder of Danielle and the pilot, as well as the attempted murder of Julie and Chris. Julie had told the police about the plan to ditch the plane with the pilot's body in it. However, it appeared that the co-pilot had chickened out and taken the plane to Maseru. The police had already apprehended him as well, and he was likely to be a prosecution witness.

There were tears in Julie's eyes when she spoke about the pilot and the way he had tried to protect her. "The police broke the news to his family this morning. As you'd expect, they are devastated. He was such a thoroughly decent man. My mother and I plan to visit the family as soon as possible. Maybe it will help them to hear how brave he was."

Chris let his fingers trace the outline of Julie's face. Gently, he massaged the darkened skin below her eyes. "Did you get any sleep at all last night?" he asked.

She shook her head and, with his good arm, he pulled her on to the bed next to him. She curled up and rested her head on his shoulder. Then she told him about the mad dash by ambulance to the hospital, how scared she'd been, and how the twenty-minute trip had felt like an eternity.

"I sensed that you were with me," he said.

"Really? You were comatose." She touched the tip of his nose. "I can see it growing." Chris tried to laugh, but it was too painful.

She told him about Thabo and Hendrik, and how they had sabotaged the Dragon Boys' dinghy, but Chris could no longer concentrate on the words. He just allowed himself to be lulled by the sound of her voice, the movement of her lips, and the feel of her head on his shoulder. *Julie was safe.*

They must have both fallen asleep, because the next thing they were aware of was Wendy and Jacques bringing Bridget into the room in a wheelchair. Her broken ankle, held up by a support contraption, stuck out like a white plastered battering-ram. Despite the ridiculous hospital gown, Chris thought there was something very resolute, almost regal, about her.

Julie gave her mother a hug. "Glad you're up and about, Mother. I see you've even managed to get your hair washed."

"They are such darlings in this hospital." Bridget winked at Jacques. "Have you been pulling a few strings, or do they treat everyone this well?"

She seemed scarcely aware of any discomfort as she chattered away, reliving the events of the last few days. She did not elaborate on her long running feud with Greg, but gave a blow-by-blow account of her abduction and the time on the *Moonflower.*

"I was never all that concerned," she said, "until they brought in Julie. Then I got seriously worried. Of course, the fireworks truly began when Chris arrived. A real-life hero, Jacques; your son is a real hero. All he's missing is a white stallion – you should buy him a horse."

Chris was beginning to squirm, but Jacques laughed. "I am glad to say he only wants a dog!"

But Bridget was now in full laudatory torrent: "God knows what would have happened to us without him – sold off into the white slave trade, I imagine. I didn't want to alarm Julie, but for a while there, I was getting worried."

"Mother … you over-dramatize."

Bridget tilted her head back and looked at her daughter with a mixture of defiance and amusement. "Remind me to tell you about the dream I had when I was knocked out by those painkillers. It was so real, I swear I could feel the whole yacht rocking."

Both Chris and Julie blushed, but Bridget had already turned her mind to something else. Looking towards Wendy, she said, "I'm going to need your help. Firstly, I must visit the pilot's wife – that poor, poor woman. And then I need to get to the office this afternoon."

"But, Bridget, surely you are not well enough …"

"I have never been better. Never felt so well in my life. I've been working with the chief of police since early this morning. We've engineered a complete news blackout."

"But why?" Julie interjected.

"The police want to see how deep the rot goes; both within Noble and the police force itself. Hence it makes sense not to forewarn them. They also want to bring in the Organized Crime unit to build a case against some of the Dragon Boys. In the meantime they have already rounded up the two who kept me in the Khanya Barn and brought me out to the boat. I still cannot believe that those two – the ginger haired guy and the big African driver - were actually Noble employees, *and* that Greg had managed to procure carte blanche access for them at Silver Pines estates. I'll have to have a word with the Body Corporate."

They were interrupted by the arrival of Thabo and Bruce. Thabo stood silently in the doorway. He seemed awed by the hospital surroundings, the drip, the monitors, and the bandages across Chris's shoulder.

"Hey, partner!" Chris called and lifted his hand. "Come give me a high five."

A grin spread across Thabo's face; he walked past the others to oblige.

Chris said, "You want to talk about heroes. I've never seen a kid with such guts." He launched into an account of how Thabo had helped him every step of the way. The boy stood looking a bit awkward as Chris told of how he spied on the Dragon Boys, fooled the security guard, broke into Bridget's house, felled the driver with a paperweight, and hitched a lift on the back of the panel van all the way to Kontermans Kloof – before then breaking open the back of the van and freeing his partner.

"That's not all he's done," said Bruce, taking over the story. "He and Hendrik then went down to the harbor and sabotaged the Dragons Boys' boat."

"You're quite something else, Thabo," said Jacques, his voice full of admiration. "What do you want to be when you grow up – James Bond?"

Thabo shook his head, shy to be the focus of so much attention. He stood close to Chris and said, "Maybe an architect, like Chris."

"Well, such talent cannot be wasted. Whatever it is you want to be, we'll find a way to help you. Won't we, Wendy?"

"Absolutely." She hugged the boy.

On arrival in Cape Town, Greg instructed the driver to take him directly from the airport to the Noble offices. The clock in the foyer said 3.10 p.m. *Perfect,* he thought. They would have just started, secure in the assumption that they had kept him in the dark. The surprise was going to be so very sweet.

He strode through the lobby and down a corridor towards the boardroom. The receptionist came hurrying after him. "Excuse me! Excuse me, Mr. Louw. You can't go in there."

His hand now firmly on the door handle, he turned and gave her a withering look. With a flourish, he opened the boardroom door and stepped in.

"Well, well, well," Greg said. "What do we have here?"

He was slightly shaken to see that in fact all the directors, other than Matt and Bridget, of course, were present.

"I feel hurt at not having been invited to this little gathering; it seems my invitation was lost in the mail." He circled the room slowly and came to stand in front of a man with a thick white mane of hair. "Or is there some other explanation, Dr. Steward?"

"Greg, please, I strongly suggest that you just leave. It is perfectly within the rights and duties of the board …"

Greg slammed his open hand down on the table and enjoyed the shock on everyone's faces. He said, *"The rights and duties of the board? Give me a break."* Slowly, he circled the table, staring down each of the board members, one by one. "What do you think you would be without me? *Heh...Heh?"* He paused. "I'll tell you. A bunch of impotent windbags!"

A voice behind him said, "Hello, Greg."

He stopped in mid-sentence and spun around to see Bridget, in a wheelchair, emerge from a door at the back of the room. Julie, her face an emotionless mask, was at her mother's side.

Bridget's eyes sparkled. "Surprise!" she said brightly. "We decided to cut short our little … cruise. The whole set-up simply did not agree with us." She turned to Julie. "Did it, darling?"

"What the ..?" Greg began, but he quickly regained his composure. "It's so good to see you, Bridget. We were all so very, very concerned."

"Really?"

Greg pressed on: "I am just relieved to see that paying the ransom did the trick and got you released. We owe thanks to the board here for their swift decision to pay."

There was a murmur around the table.

Bridget said, "I have never doubted the board's commitment and loyalty to the company, and to me personally."

"I was just telling the members here that we need to formulate a vision to take the company to the next level," said Greg smoothly. "I've been working tirelessly in the background to branch out and grow us in a new direction."

Theatrically, he turned and addressed the board: "I probably should have been a little more forthcoming in communicating my vision and plans, but I didn't want to burden you. I wanted to test some of the key concepts first. I know you will all appreciate …"

"Greg," Bridget cut in. "I'm really not interested. You can tell it to the judge. There's only one thing I have to say to you before the members of the board - and boy, I've wanted to do so for a long, long time." She paused. "I repeat what I told you privately on Saturday. You're fired!"

At these words, two policemen entered the boardroom. Swiftly, they walked over to Greg and handcuffed him. The senior officer said, "Gregory Louw, I hereby arrest you on suspicion of illegal trading in endangered wildlife, of kidnapping, and ..." - he paused for effect - "of conspiracy to murder."

There was a gasp around the room. The directors looked at each other in amazement.

"You have the right to remain silent; you have the right ..."

Greg turned and appealed directly to the silent figure standing beside Bridget. "Jules, you know I did it for you, for us. I wanted to make you happy."

"No, Greg. You wanted to own me – that's not the same thing. The only person you ever wanted to make happy was yourself."

She turned and left through the back door. The members of the board watched as Greg was led out, past a line of gaping employees. Nobody spoke for a while. Then Dr. Steward jumped up and wheeled Bridget to the head of the table.

Bridget addressed the board: "Ladies and gentlemen, our company has been dealt a number of severe body blows. The media will be in a frenzy, and it's going to be ugly. With immediate effect, I intend to take over the role of MD and the day-to-day operations of Noble Enterprises. Will you support me?"

There was unanimous assent around the table.

##

Epilogue

Three months later

It was a Saturday afternoon, and Chris had stopped by the Khanya center to pick up Julie. As he passed the kitchen, Mama Mercy invited him to join her for a cup of tea – that peaceful ritual she indulged in when the last of the lunch dishes had been washed and cleared away. The weather had grown cooler and Mercy clasped her mug in both hands, feet outstretched to catch the autumn sun creeping through the window.

She looked at Chris across the table until, disconcerted, he asked, "What?"

Mercy just shook her head.

"Come on. There's something on you mind."

"I can't explain it. And I don't want you to laugh at me."

It took a little more prodding, but eventually Mercy gave a big sigh and began slowly: "In the week before that horrible night, when you were shot, I was constantly besieged by spirits from the other world." Now, her words started to gain pace, as if she needed to get whatever she had to say out as quickly as possible. "I was convinced that they were going to call home to them someone I loved, or maybe even myself. Those spirit voices got so insistent that I thought I heard them in the day, not just at night." She wiped her brow. "But, since that night – nothing. It is as though all the spirits have gone to rest."

Chris paled. He hadn't told anyone about the vision he'd had when he was just about to strangle Lenny; he'd put it down to the blood loss, the bright lights of the approaching police boat, his subconscious.

Mama Mercy narrowed her eyes. "Something happened that night, didn't it?"

How well she could read him! He told her then, and as he did so, it was as if a burden fell from his shoulders. What a relief it was to tell the incredible story to someone who was receptive to it.

Mama Mercy broke into a broad smile. "Now I understand. The spirits were not getting ready to call someone home. No, no, no." She wagged a finger. "Your mother must have stirred up all the angels in heaven to protect you. That's why they were all active. They were trying to warn us."

Later that afternoon, Chris and Julie were wandering along the beach. Chris had his good arm protectively around her shoulders, and his new golden retriever bounded along besides them, chasing seagulls.

They stopped and looked at the ochre reflection of the sun against the cliffs and invariably their eyes were drawn to the spot where the *Moonflower* had been anchored in the middle of the bay. Chris felt a spasm in his injured right shoulder.

Julie asked, "Is it sore today?"

"The physio really cranked it hard. But she says I should start swimming next week. So that's good."

"What do you hear from your father and Wendy?"

"Dad's always wanted to go diving on the Great Barrier Reef. They must be enjoying their honeymoon; don't seem to have much time for emails."

"I'm glad," Julie said.

"Three weeks!" Chris shook his head. "I can't believe my father actually took off a full three weeks. I don't know how his ego will cope with the fact that the hospital will still be there and functioning when he gets back."

She laughed and he kissed her forehead. It was good to take a breather from all the media attention. The sensational trial of Greg Louw, Lenny, and Cindy had started two weeks earlier. The lesser players like Ginger, Lucas the driver, and the co-pilot, had all clamored to cut deals with the prosecution and to testify against the ringleaders. An internal police commission had been set up to assess the conduct of various policemen. In a controversial twist, Mr. Goh was released and allowed to leave the country. His lawyers made a convincing argument that he had, in good faith, purchased equipment to make artificial rhino horn, and that he had offered hospitality on his yacht to a business associate. It looked as if Greg, Cindy, and Lenny were going to carry the can.

As a consequence of the media frenzy, Chris found himself inundated with requests for interviews from newspapers and magazines. He learned that the editors had a way of blowing things completely out of proportion. A week ago, he had been embarrassed at Pick 'n Pay when he saw two magazines with his picture on the front page. One showed him with the auctioneer at the AIDS gala. The heading splashed across the page read: "Simply Priceless". The second showed him and Thabo in wetsuits (it must have been taken with a long lens when he took Thabo surfing), under a banner proclaiming: "Hout Bay Heroes." A group of teenage girls had mobbed him right there at the check-out counter and it turned into an impromptu autograph-signing session.

"Speaking of parents," Chris went on, "how's your mother?"

"Totally in her element. She's a different person - working twelve-hour days and looking ten years younger. I never really understood how much the business was a part of her. Over and above the police investigations, she's launched a major internal probe and fired nearly everyone in the security department. She's promoted Charlie to a formal role on the Management Committee. He fortunately had the sense to 'disappear' right after he spoke to me. Other than that, she's hired a PR consultant to help restore the company image. It's going to be tough, but I'm convinced she's up to it. " After a pause, she added, "I still feel a bit sorry for Matt. He's retired from all his posts and is taking it hard … Greg was his protégé – and, of course, he is also his nephew - so he feels responsible, as well as deeply betrayed."

"What's he doing with himself?"

"He's recuperating. Mother says he's been out on the golf course once or twice and talks about remodeling the house. Maybe you should help him with some ideas."

"Did I tell you I got another job offer today?"

"No, you didn't. Gosh, the benefits of being a famous hero," she teased. "How many does that make – seven?"

"Nine; and that's only the offers from architectural firms. I'm not even counting the approaches I've had to act as spokesman for everything from wetsuits to body lotion."

"Are you going to accept any of them?"

"Don't know yet. For the moment, I'm concentrating on getting the first cottage built at the Khanya center. Since Thabo and his family are to be amongst the occupants, he's there every day, driving the workmen crazy with his quality control – every brick has to be perfectly aligned."

They reached the end of the beach and stopped. The dog had settled down to chew on a piece of driftwood. Chris looked at Julie intently - he studied her dimples, the few freckles on either side of her nose. The wind played with her hair and accentuated her perfectly formed neck.

"What?"

"Nothing, I just want to look at you." He wrapped his arms around her, kissed both of her ears, then sought out her mouth.

"Let's go back to my place," he said huskily.

The security guard at Chris's apartment complex hurried out from behind his desk. It seemed to Chris that the man had grown three inches ever since the police and media had interviewed him. He insisted on personally pressing the elevator call button for the most famous tenant in the building. Chris thanked him and both he and Julie managed to contain their laughter until the elevator door shut.

Ever since their encounter in the bathroom on the *Moonflower,* Chris found himself getting aroused whenever he and Julie found themselves together in a confined space. He wanted to stop the elevator and have sex right there and then. But she knew him too well by now, and promised that patience would be rewarded. They reached his apartment and she got in close behind him, squeezing his buttocks as he fumbled with the key.

When Chris finally managed to open the door, he was hit by an aromatic cocktail of beer, wine, pizza, and burning candles.

Then, all of a sudden, a group of people jumped up and shouted "Surprise!" in unison.

It was the Toreros, all of them, including Desmond.

"Jeez, guys. Don't do this. Man, I hate surprise parties."

"Yes, we know," Cedric said. "That makes it all the more fun for us. Don't just stand there, come inside, come inside!"

"Have you got any more beer?" Bruce's voice came from the kitchen. "We seem to have finished what was in your fridge."

The surprise party was soon in full swing. Copies of newspaper and magazine articles were strewn all over the coffee table, and it seemed that all the Toreros had a story of their newfound fame as a result of Chris's adventures, and everybody wanted to talk at once. At one point, however, Julie managed to have a few words with Desmond in the kitchen.

"Have you and Cedric made up yet?" she asked.

He sighed. "He's still going to make me pay, but yes, at least we have a truce."

"I still don't understand why you lied to all of us. We thought you were with your sick sister, and meanwhile you were up in Johannesburg."

"I'd been invited to audition for the National Ballet. I didn't want anyone to know, because I didn't want to deal with Cedric and everyone else's expectations - and their disappointment if I didn't get in." He smiled wryly. "And, of course, I didn't make. Got to the final round, but it was not quite good enough."

"You're such a fool," Julie said, but she said it affectionately. "Next time, you let us all know. Win or lose, we'll come and cheer you on."

He kissed her cheek. "Thanks, Julie. Chris is one lucky guy to have found you."

Meanwhile, in the living room, Cedric had risen to his feet. Clinking a couple of glasses together, he proclaimed, "A toast ... no, two toasts!"

He nearly tripped and had to steady himself.

"The first toast is to my prodigal partner." He raised his glass. "You're a silly ass; you hurt my feelings, but I'm very glad you're back." Desmond bowed low and Cedric blew him a dramatic kiss.

"The second toast is to us, and our tour!"

"What?" Chris and Julie asked in unison.

The Toreros all started to talk at once, but it was Bull who finally prevailed. "With all the publicity we've had recently – because of you, man - we've become hot property. The Toreros have been made an offer to go on a tour around the country and – wait for it – even to Sun City! What do you think of that?"

"I'm speechless," Chris said.

"You've got to come!" they all chorused.

Chris put his arm around Julie's shoulder and pulled her towards him. He shook his head. "No, I don't need to dance anymore." He kissed the top of her head. "All I want is right here."